KAA

THE GIRL BELOW STAIRS

Edie Cooper has grown up at Fairley Terrace. Now twenty, she spends her days working as lady's maid to Christina, the beautiful adopted daughter of the powerful Fairley family, and her nights dreaming of a life with handsome local lad Charlie Oglethorpe. Although broken-hearted when Charlie leaves for London, Edie finds consolation in her friendship with Christina, who asks for help in uncovering the mystery of her true parentage. But their search for answers puts Edie and Christina in grave danger. Someone at Fairley Hall wants to keep long-buried secrets hidden. Will Edie be able to protect Christina? And will she find her own path to happiness with Charlie?

THE GIRL BELOW STAIRS

THE GIRL BELOW STAIRS

by

Jennie Felton

Magna Large Print Books
Long Preston, North Yorkshire,
BD23 4ND, England.

British Library Cataloguing in Publication Data.

A catalogue record of this book is
available from the British Library

ISBN   978-0-7505-4555-6

First published in Great Britain in 2016 by
Headline Publishing Group

Cover illustration © Steve Peet by arrangement with
Arcangel Images Ltd.

The right of Janet Tanner to be identified as the author of this work
has been asserted by her in accordance with the Copyright, Designs
and Patents Act, 1988

Published in Large Print 2018 by arrangement with
Headline Publishing Group Ltd.

Magna Large Print is an imprint of Library Magna Books Ltd.

Printed and bound in Great Britain by
T.J. (International) Ltd., Cornwall, PL28 8RW

For my grandchildren, Tabitha, Barnaby, Daniel and Amelia, with all my love.

Acknowledgements

As always, there are so many wonderful people without whom my books would never make it to the shelves.

At Curtis Brown, my agents, Sheila Crowley and Rebecca Ritchie are always there for me. At Headline, Kate Byrne is the most wonderful editor I could wish for, often coming up with suggestions as well as improvements and helping me keep tabs on the network of characters who make up The Families of Fairley Terrace. Jane Selley is one of the best copy editors I have ever worked with. Huge thanks to Katie Bradburn and the publicity team, who also provide updates for my Facebook page which are far more beautiful than anything I could post myself! A special thank you to the Creative team for the lovely cover designs. And not forgetting Beth Eynon who, as editorial assistant, helps to keep the wheels running smoothly.

As always I must thank my lovely family from the bottom of my heart for their love and support – my daughters Terri and Suzanne, their husbands Andy and Dominic, and my wonderful grandchildren Tabitha, Barnaby, Daniel and Amelia (who, of course, loaned me her name for my alter ego, Amelia Carr!)

Last but not least, thank you to you, my dear

readers, for taking The Families of Fairley Terrace to your hearts. Thank you too for your e-mails, comments on my blog and messages. Being a writer can be a lonely occupation – it is so lovely to hear from you! And I do hope you continue to enjoy my stories.

Prologue

Christmas Eve, 1895

'Father – oh Father! Come quick!'

Hetty Jones came bursting into the sacristy where Father O'Brien was preparing for Midnight Mass. Flakes of sleety snow clung to grey-streaked hair where it was not covered by her shawl and to her eyelashes; her puffy face was red and anxious. She was also breathless. Plump as she was, with swollen ankles that bulged over her stout boots, the slightest exertion made her heart race and her breath come hard and shallow.

Father O'Brien turned, his hands, which were beginning to stiffen with the onset of arthritis, still gripping the stole he was arranging around his neck. It was unheard of for Hetty to rush into the sacristy without knocking, even though she often helped with setting out prayer books and lighting candles, and even laying a clean cloth on the altar – the soiled one she would take home for laundering. Clearly something was very wrong.

'Mrs Jones! Whatever...?'

'Oh Father, there's a baby...'

'A baby?' he repeated, bewildered.

'Yes! In the porch!' Hetty pressed her hand to her throat, struggling to catch her breath. 'You've got to come! It'll catch its death, poor little thing!'

Struggling to comprehend, Father O'Brien

13

followed her out of the sacristy. As yet the church was still almost deserted, with just a handful of the most devout worshippers kneeling in their pews to recite a rosary before the service began, or lighting a candle on the votive rack at the feet of the statue of the Blessed Virgin to the right of the high altar. The majority of the congregation would arrive at the last minute, having been busy with their preparations for tomorrow, and possibly a little inebriated. But Hetty had left the heavy wooden door open in her haste, and through it he could see a little knot of people gathered in the porch, all staring down at the same spot, where a woman crouched beside a shadowy object.

As Father O'Brien emerged, they all turned towards him, with the exception of the crouching woman.

'Father … the most awful thing!'

'Oh Father, thank goodness you're here!'

The crouching woman looked up, though one hand still rested on a white mound inside what appeared to be a drawer from a dressing chest.

'It's a baby, Father. Somebody's been and gone and left a newborn baby!'

In his thirty-odd years as a parish priest, Father O'Brien had encountered almost every imaginable situation. He had comforted the bereaved, given advice to troubled souls, heard confessions that had shocked and saddened him. But this … it was entirely outside his experience, and for a moment he could do nothing but stare at the tiny puckered face half hidden by a lacy shawl and the little body tightly wrapped in white swaddling

14

here in the deep shadow of the porch. It might have been the Christ child himself, reborn here in a church that had once been, not a stable, but a barn. Then, as his shocked sensibilities registered the several pairs of eyes trained on him and looking for guidance, he pulled himself together and tried to summon the calm common sense he knew they were expecting.

'Let's get the mite inside where it's warm.'

The woman crouching beside the makeshift crib was May Cooper. She carefully lifted the tiny scrap from the wooden drawer, rose to her feet and cradled it tenderly against her bosom, one hand supporting the little head. With two children of her own, seven-year-old Ted and five-year-old Edie, the handling of a newborn came naturally to her.

Father O'Brien held the heavy oak door open, motioning to her to take the baby into the sacristy. Hetty Jones followed, and the others stood watching from the doorway as May carefully lowered herself on to a chair and eased the baby's face free of the shawl. The blue eyes of a newborn stared unblinking; fine hair, dark and slick, covered a head that bore a deep indentation from ear to little flattened ear. Then the puckered lips opened and the baby began to wail, a persistent mewling that tore at the heartstrings.

'He's hungry as well as cold, poor mite.' Hetty was still out of breath; the excitement was having the same effect on her as exertion. But her eyes were dark with pity – and anger – in her pouchy face. 'Whoever would do such a thing, Father?'

'I can't imagine, Hetty. Some poor desperate

15

woman, I suppose. And she knew he'd be found without delay tonight. At least we can say that much for her. There was certainly no baby in the porch when I opened the church – she slipped in and left him when she knew the congregation would soon be arriving for Mass.'

'But what are we going to do, Father?'

'Go and fetch one of the altar boys. Ask him to go for Sergeant Love.' Father O'Brien was beginning to regain his usual authoritative demeanour. 'This is a matter for the police. Can you look after him, Mrs Cooper, until someone comes to take him away?'

May was carefully unwrapping the swaddling, allowing the baby to stuff a tiny fist into that hungry mouth.

'Course I can, Father. You get on with whatever you've got to do. But you're wrong to call it "him". This baby's not more than a day old, I'd say, but one thing I am sure of: it's not a boy – it's a lovely little girl.'

'Is that so.' Father O'Brien smiled wryly. He knew very well why he'd made the assumption – the parallel he'd drawn between a newborn babe on Christmas Eve and the Christ Child himself. What foolishness, he chided himself.

But whatever the sex of the child, here was a new little soul abandoned in a cruel world, and somewhere not far away would be a mother in deep distress and possibly requiring medical attention. Caring for their physical needs did not fall within his remit, but their spiritual ones most certainly did. Whatever he could do to help, he would do it. He hoped and prayed the mother

16

could be found and reunited with her child, and that he could somehow persuade a judgemental society to forgive her for whatever sins she had committed. And if she could not be found, or was unwilling to take responsibility for the baby, then he personally would see to it that the child was placed in a good and loving home, not removed to an institute or orphanage.

Perhaps the mother was some young and foolish girl, perhaps the father was one of the twelve men and boys killed back in the summer in the terrible accident at Shepton Fields pit that, it was said, had not been an accident at all but a deliberate and wicked act when someone had severed the rope so that the hudge carrying them to the bowels of the earth had gone crashing down. Or perhaps she was some poor woman who already had more children than she could afford to raise. He didn't know, but he meant to try to find out and offer what assistance he could.

For the moment, however, he had a Midnight Mass to say in celebration of the birth of the Lord Jesus Christ.

It was, Father O'Brien knew, a Christmas Eve he would never forget.

Chapter One

September 1910

'Edith Cooper! There you are! Lady Elizabeth wants to see you.'

Edie looked up from the silverware she was polishing to see Quilla Brimble, lady's maid to the mistress of Fairley Hall, standing in the doorway of the servants' hall. She was startled by the summons, and her heart came into her mouth.

Had she done something wrong? Nothing came immediately to mind, and in any case it wasn't usual for Lady Elizabeth to mete out a tongue-lashing for some omission or misdemeanour. It was up to Mr Stevens, the butler, or Mrs Parker, the housekeeper, to take care of that sort of thing. But Quilla Brimble's tone was sharp with disapproval, and her face set in stern lines.

Not that that meant anything in itself, of course. In the six years she had worked for the Fairley family, Edie couldn't ever remember seeing Quilla smile, unless it was a smirk of satisfaction at besting one of the other servants, to whom she considered herself vastly superior. And her tone of voice when speaking to them was invariably the same. Short. Haughty. As if having to communicate with them was beneath her.

'Make haste, girl,' she said now. 'Don't keep her

ladyship waiting. You'll find her in her sitting room.'

And with that she swept off, her black silk skirts rustling. Reg Deacon, the footman, who had been polishing a pair of Sir Montague's boots, stared at Edie goggle-eyed.

'What's all that about then?'

Edie simply shrugged and pulled a face.

'You're not going to get the sack, are you?' He sounded worried. It was no secret that Reg was sweet on Edie, though she gave him no encouragement. He wasn't the sharpest knife in the box, but Edie was quite fond of him in a pitying sort of way, and she was careful not to do anything to lead him to think he stood a chance with her. He didn't. Edie's affections lay elsewhere, though much good had it done her.

'I'm sure it's not that, Reg,' she said with more confidence than she was feeling.

'But what if...?'

'Oh don't be so silly.' She replaced the spoon she had been working on in the cutlery box and dumped her polishing cloth on the table beside it. 'You can finish the silverware when you've done with the boots,' she instructed him. Six years of service to his four gave her seniority, and exerting it sometimes helped to keep him in his place. Though even when she gave him orders, he still stared at her with those adoring puppy-dog eyes.

As she climbed the stairs, Edie hastily checked that her hair was neat under her small white cap and straightened her apron. Then she hurried along to Lady Elizabeth's sitting room, a sunny bower at the rear of the house that overlooked manicured lawns and a honeysuckle arch leading to her pride and joy, the rose garden. Edie tapped on the door, which stood ajar, and waited a moment, then, with some trepidation, went inside.

'Milady,' she said respectfully.

'Edith.' Lady Elizabeth always called Edie by her given name. She rose from the brocaded chair beside the big bay window, and to Edie's relief she was smiling. 'Do come in, my dear.'

The warmth of her greeting came as a surprise to Edie. Though Lady Elizabeth, sister of Sir Montague Fairley and the mistress of the house since his wife died many years ago, was invariably pleasant, Edie could never before recall being addressed as 'my dear'.

'Milady,' she said again, bobbing automatically, though her mind was racing.

'Don't look so worried.' Again Lady Elizabeth smiled, and the smile lent a beauty that had long since faded to a face that otherwise reflected the passage of the years, though they had been much kinder to her than to her brother, with his paunchy cheeks and swollen purple nose, the result of his fondness for too much brandy. 'You're wondering what I want to talk to you about, I expect.'

'Milady,' Edie repeated yet again, as if the cat had got her tongue.

'The thing is this, Edith.' Lady Elizabeth clasped her hands together in the folds of her skirt, heavy rose-coloured damask. 'Miss Christina is growing up, and I think it's high time she had a maid of her own. I'd like to offer you the position.'

'Oh!' Edie couldn't stop the involuntary gasp of surprise. Of all the possible reasons for Lady

20

Elizabeth wanting to speak to her that had flitted through her mind since Quilla Brimble had summoned her, this one had not occurred to her for a moment. Lady's maid to Miss Christina, Lady Elizabeth's adopted daughter! The prospect was a dizzying one, and Edie couldn't imagine why she should have been singled out for such an honour. She had no experience in the position – she wasn't even entirely sure what the duties entailed, beyond helping the lady with her dressing and her hair and keeping her wardrobe in good order. As Lady Elizabeth's maid, Quilla Brimble was forever commandeering the ironing table and flat irons, officiously warning the other servants to keep their distance in case they soiled the fine silks and linens, and her sewing box, for any minor repairs, was strictly off limits to them. Beyond that...

'But Nellie Saunders has been here much longer than me,' Edie protested, knowing very well that the senior housemaid's nose would be well and truly put out of joint if she found she'd been passed over.

Lady Elizabeth's mouth twitched as if she was amused by the prospect of the furore the appointment would cause below stairs, but she was far too kind to be malicious about it.

'That's true, I know, and I hope Nellie won't take it as a personal slight. But Miss Christina is quite insistent: she wants nobody but you. She's fond of you, I know, and I'm confident you will suit her admirably. If you're agreeable, I'll have Quilla give you instruction as to what will be expected of you, and perhaps arrange for you to have some lessons in hairdressing. For the rest, all you have to do is whatever Christina wants or needs, and...' her lips twitched again, 'keep an eye on her. You know as well as I do, I'm sure, that sometimes she thinks or behaves in ways that are not quite ... suitable. I'm sure I can rely on you to talk her out of her wilder notions, or to let me know if you are unable to persuade her to a more decorous course. Now.' She lifted her chin, cocking her head to one side so that the ear bobs she wore swung and tinkled faintly. 'What do you say? Would you like to take up the position? Or do you need time to consider?'

'Oh no, milady... I mean, no, I don't need time to think about it.' Startled though she was by the offer, apprehensive as to how the rest of the staff below stairs would react to the news, Edie was in no doubt at all. 'Thank you for thinking of me, milady. And thanks to Miss Christina, too. I'd love to be her lady's maid. I can't think of anything I'd like better.'

'I'm glad.' The lovely smile lit Lady Elizabeth's face once more. 'That's settled then. I'll tell Miss Christina you have agreed. You can begin your new duties just as soon as we can find a replacement parlourmaid, and that shouldn't take long. There are always plenty of local girls looking to go into service. I'll gather the staff and tell them myself what is happening, so perhaps you would keep this to yourself for the time being. Can I ask you to do that?'

'Of course, milady.'

It wouldn't be easy; there would be plenty of questions as to the reason why Lady Elizabeth had sent for her, and Edie felt sure she'd turn scarlet when they tried to get it out of her – she always did if she had something to hide.

But she wouldn't tell. She wouldn't do anything that might jeopardise this wonderful opportunity.

Lady's maid to Miss Christina! Who'd have thought it? She might not be a famous singer on the halls like her old friend Lucy Day, or Lucy Dorne as she was now known. But for a girl from a little tied house in a terrace of miners' cottages she certainly hadn't done badly. And who knew what this new position might lead to? From the day she'd started in service as a lowly housemaid, she'd been determined to work her way up the pecking order, but she'd never expected the opportunity to come so soon. To become a lady's maid at the age of just twenty was almost unheard of.

Perhaps now she'd taken a step up in the world, Charlie Oglethorpe would take her more seriously – Charlie, ten years her senior; Charlie, whom she'd adored for as long as she could remember, and who had eventually become her young man, in a manner of speaking, but who'd treated her so casually and gone off to London to make a new life for himself; Charlie, who'd broken her heart. Next time he came home to South Compton, perhaps he would see her through different eyes. For years she'd cherished the hope that one day she and Charlie would be together, marry and raise a family, but her dreams had turned to dust. Now, excited by this surprising new development, it seemed to Edie that anything was possible.

With a spring in her step, she went back downstairs to finish polishing the silver.

Christina Fairley pirouetted like an excited child, arms outstretched, skirts fanning out all around her.

'Oh Mama, I'm so happy! She agreed! Edith agreed to be my very own maid!'

She came to a stop, cheeks flushed, turquoise eyes sparkling, a little out of breath, then twirled again.

Lady Elizabeth gave a slight shake of her head, smiling. Nothing gave her more pleasure than to see her daughter happy, but as always the pleasure was tempered with a tinge of anxiety. Christina might be almost fifteen, but she still behaved as if she was much younger. Her exuberance and naivety worried Elizabeth a little, coupled as they were with her sweet and trusting nature. Growing up as the only child in a household of much older people, Christina might have been expected to be serious and a little staid, but in fact exactly the opposite was true. In many ways she hardly seemed to be growing up at all, and Elizabeth fretted that if it didn't happen soon, she might well be taken advantage of, and badly hurt, if not worse.

Something of the sort had almost happened already. Sam, the gardener's boy, had behaved towards her in a totally unsuitable way while helping her to train Beauty, her King Charles spaniel puppy, and she had been putty in his hands. It had been Edith who had consoled her when Sir Montague had discovered what was going on and sacked the impertinent boy, Edith who had explained to her that such a friendship was just not right, and even downright dangerous. Somehow the young parlour-maid had connected with Christina where Elizabeth had been unable to, and from that moment on, Christina had transferred her affections to Edith. Although it was in its way just as unacceptable a relationship, at least Edith was a sensible girl, not an adventure-seeking young man. She was much closer to Christina in age, too, than anyone else in the household, with the exception of that foolish kitchen maid Flo Doughty, and Elizabeth was hoping that having her company would be good for Christina. She'd have someone to talk to and confide in, someone who would keep an eye on her and ensure that nothing like the episode with the gardener's boy happened again.

What Sir Montague would have to say about it, of course, was a different matter entirely, Elizabeth thought. He was a hard man, who resented spending a penny he didn't have to, either on the coal mines he owned, the estate or the household. When it came to charity, he was cold and ruthless, as witness the way he had behaved towards the families of the men who had been killed in the terrible incident with the hudge at Shepton Fields pit fifteen years ago – an incident that would never have occurred if he'd been willing to spend the money needed to replace the hemp rope that lowered the hudge with a chain, as he should have done. Elizabeth had done her best to make amends, taking gifts to the bereaved and showing them sympathy, but nothing she could do or say had dissuaded her brother from raising the rents on the tied cottages, thus forcing the widows out of the houses they could no longer afford to live in.

That rankled with Elizabeth, and always had. She didn't much like her brother, but if she wanted to continue to live at Fairley Hall, she had to accept him for what he was – a pompous, overbearing bully who trampled on anyone who got in his way.

That had included his poor wife Laura, and Elizabeth thought it was no wonder that she had come to such a tragic end. But Elizabeth herself was a very different proposition. She had long ago learned how to get her own way with her brother if needs be.

The adoption of Christina was a case in point. When the poor wee mite had been abandoned in the porch of the Roman Catholic church on Christmas Eve, almost fifteen years ago, Elizabeth had been determined to take her in, though Montague had been totally opposed to the idea. The very suggestion had made him apoplectic, but Elizabeth had refused to bow to his wishes.

'Really, after what happened back in the summer, it would be to your advantage to show some compassion,' she had argued, referring to the terrible incident at the pit, and when he still prevaricated, she played her trump card.

'Well, Montague, I intend to offer a home to that poor little baby whether you agree or not. If you refuse to have her here, then I will move to the cottage and live there with her. It's up to you, but if you don't want people to think even more badly of you than they already do, you'll allow us to remain here, under your roof.'

The cottage, set deep in the woods that

bordered the grounds of Fairley Hall, had once been the assistant gamekeeper's house, but with a much smaller estate staff these days, it was no longer needed. It was beginning to fall into disrepair, and Elizabeth would have been hard put to afford the necessary work out of the tiny allowance she had been left under the terms of their father's will. But she was confident that the last thing Sir Montague would want would be for her to move in there with the baby.

She was right: the threat worked, and with a bad grace, Sir Montague had eventually given in. The baby – they called her Christina because she had been found on Christmas Eve – was brought to Fairley Hall, a wet nurse, and later a nanny, engaged, and one of the bedrooms converted to a nursery. Elizabeth herself had taken responsibility for Christina's education – no easy task, since the little girl had no interest whatever in learning her letters and numbers, though she loved looking at the pictures in the books Elizabeth bought for her, and weaving stories round them.

'That child has the most vivid imagination!' Elizabeth told anyone who would listen. 'I'm not sure it's good for her. Fairies and handsome princes and beautiful golden-haired maidens are all very well, but sometimes she frightens herself so much with the goblins and monsters that she wakes screaming in the night, and Nanny has the most terrible time trying to get her back to sleep. She's convinced they are hiding under her bed, or in the cupboard. They're all so real to her, you see.'

Also very real to Christina was her imaginary friend Ursula. She insisted a place be set for her at the nursery table, and little portions of food put on her plate. Throughout the meal, she would chatter in a made-up language that no one but she – and Ursula – understood, even pausing for Ursula to reply.

'It fair makes the hair on the back of my neck stand on end,' Nanny said to Lady Elizabeth.

Elizabeth wasn't unduly worried, though. It seemed to her only natural that without other children of her own age to keep her company, Christina should invent a friend.

'She'll grow out of it,' she'd predicted, and of course, she was right. There had been no mention of Ursula for years now.

Then, of course, there were Christina's fantasies as to who she really was. Elizabeth had never tried to hide from her the way she had come into the family; she didn't want her to hear it from anyone else, and Christina seemed quite excited at the thought that she could be whoever she chose. Perhaps her father was one of her fairy-tale princes, and her mother one of the fair maidens! Or she had been left in the church porch by the fairies! Her wild imaginings knew no bounds.

Although these days her speculation as to who she really was was more realistic, in many ways the years had done little to change her. She was just as she had always been, sweet-natured, sunny-tempered (most of the time), gentle, loving and almost fey. The down-to-earth Edith could only be good for her, Elizabeth thought. She'd be far less lonely with a lady's maid to talk to and confide in, and hopefully some of Edith's good sense would rub off on her. If it didn't, she wasn't at all sure how Christina would survive in the harsh world that awaited her when she became a woman.

'Now, you are not to breathe a word of this to anyone until I've had the chance to tell the staff myself,' she said sternly. 'If you do, I may have to think again.'

'Oh I won't! I won't!' Christina promised, her eyes big and earnest in her elfin face.

But Elizabeth was not certain she'd be able to keep it to herself for long, no matter how good her intentions.

It would be wise, she thought, to gather the servants together at the earliest opportunity and tell them she had asked Edith to take up the duties of lady's maid.

The news, of course, caused quite a stir below stairs.

Nellie Saunders was every bit as put out as Edie had known she would be, and Quilla Brimble tight-lipped and disapproving, as if her standing in the household had been diminished somehow by Edie becoming a lady's maid too, even if her charge was only Christina.

'You'll find her a handful,' she sniffed, as the staff, having finished serving the family's dinner, sat down around the long scrubbed-wood table in the servants' hall for their own evening meal.

'I'm sure we'll get along fine,' Edie said. 'Miss Christina is as sweet as a nut.'

Quilla sniffed again, helping herself to the juiciest piece of meat on the serving dish. In her opinion, Miss Christina was 'not all there', as she put it when she talked to Jeremiah Dando, Sir

Montague's valet, the only member of staff she considered her equal, apart from Percy Stevens, the butler, and Lilian Parker, the housekeeper. But those two were as thick as thieves, and utterly loyal to their employers. Quilla knew better than to breathe a derogatory word about Miss Christina to them.

'I don't know why you were asked and not me, Edie,' Nellie said. Her cheeks were flushed with indignation as well as the heat in the kitchen. 'I've been here a lot longer than you. It should have been me.'

'The trouble with you, Nellie, is that you chatter too much,' said Martha Davey, the plump and motherly cook. 'You can't keep a secret to save your life, and Lady Elizabeth must know that as well as we do.'

'That's not true!' Nellie protested, but of course it was. Nellie liked nothing better than listening at doors and gathering titbits of information that she could gossip about. 'No, it's favouritism, that's what it is, and it's not fair. Why should Edie get a raise up and not me? I think I shall start looking out for a better position, one where I'm appreciated.'

'You'll be lucky to find anything better than this,' Mrs Davey said tartly. 'Working for Sir Montague and Lady Elizabeth, that's a real feather in your cap.'

'All the more reason why anyone would be glad to take me on,' Nellie retorted. 'And in any case, me and Teddy will be getting married soon as we've got enough saved up, and then they can stick their stupid job.'

Mrs Davey snorted at that, shaking her head. Nellie had been engaged to Teddy Vranch, who worked for the council as a road sweeper, almost as long as she had been in service at Fairley House. Teddy was known for a wastrel, and spent most of his hard-earned wages on beer and betting on the horses. He didn't seem in any hurry to take on the responsibility of a wife.

'And how am I supposed to manage all the extra work when Edie's lording it upstairs?' Nellie demanded.

'You'll just have to work harder, and not spend so much time gossiping,' Quilla snapped. 'In any case, Lady Elizabeth made it quite plain she'll be employing another maid – or weren't you listening, for once?'

'I know just the girl for the job,' Mrs Davey said with satisfaction. 'My brother's daughter Alice. Will you put in a good word for her, Mrs Parker?'

The housekeeper nodded. 'That I will, Mrs Davey.'

Reg Deacon's face brightened. He'd been down all day, thinking that her new duties would mean he'd see less of Edie – though of course that was far better than if she'd lost her job, as he'd been afraid she was going to. But a new maid ... well, she might prove a lot easier a nut to crack.

'Is she pretty, Mrs Davey?' he asked eagerly.

'She is. And she's much too good for the likes of you, Reggie,' Mrs Davey retorted.

Edie smiled to herself. It would be a load off her mind if Reg found a new object for his affections.

A bell jangled on the board to one side of the

door. Sir Montague, ringing from the drawing room – Lady Elizabeth and Miss Christina would almost certainly have retired to Lady Elizabeth's sitting room as they did every evening after dinner.

'What does he want now?' Mrs Davey said irritably. 'Can't he let us have our dinner in peace?'

Reg made no move, but Percy Stevens pushed his chair back and stood, as attentive and uncomplaining as ever. He had been at Fairley House since he was just a boy, rising through the ranks from footman to butler. Light from the overhead gas lamp gleamed on his pink and shiny bald spot, which was amply compensated for by thick pepper-and-salt sideburns. Sir Montague's wish was his command.

'His brandy decanter's empty again, I shouldn't wonder,' Mrs Davey said archly, and he threw her a disapproving look before disappearing out of the door.

Truth to tell, he was not sorry to escape the endless chatter of the women, and he wondered, as he so often did, how it was that any of the goings-on in this house over the years had remained secret. There wasn't much the servants missed, nothing much they didn't know. But Quilla Brimble was always tight-lipped when it suited her own ends, and Mrs Parker – Lilian, the housekeeper – shared his unquestioning loyalty, and between them they'd managed to keep things from the others.

He only hoped they could continue to do so.

Chapter Two

Friday was Edie's afternoon off, and as usual when luncheon had been cleared away she put on her best bonnet and set out for home, bursting with the news of her advancement, and hoping against hope that Charlie Oglethorpe might be home from London. He visited his mother, Dolly, regularly, and she felt certain he was about due for a visit.

For as long as she could remember, Edie had had eyes for no one but Charlie.

When she was a little girl, he'd been close to a grown man, a big hulking lad already working as a carting boy at Shepton Fields, and with a reputation for being able to handle himself. In fact, though she didn't like to admit it, it had been worse than that – she had vivid memories of him and his gang setting on Billy Donovan – the 'Didiky', as they used to call him – who lived further along the rank of the Ten Houses. But after the terrible accident at Shepton Fields, Charlie had changed. He'd been lucky not to be in the hudge when it went down – his pal Frank Rogers had been one of those killed, along with Jack Withers, Paddy Donovan, Billy's father, and John Day, all close neighbours. And it had been Charlie who had run home that dreadful morning to deliver the awful news.

'From that day on he were like a different boy,'

May Cooper, Edie's mother, always maintained. 'Grew up all of a sudden, he did. That's what staring death in the face does for you, I suppose.'

The immature loutishness had been outgrown almost overnight, it was true, but the wild streak remained. Charlie was still not above using his big fists when the occasion arose, though now it was not about tormenting lads who couldn't fight back, but rather in their defence, or if he perceived something as downright wrong. He still had a fiery temper that he got from his father, Ollie, but he also had the big heart that he'd inherited from his mother, who had been delivering babies and laying out the dead in the Ten Houses and beyond ever since she'd lived there.

Something about him had attracted Edie long before she'd understood the meaning of love between a man and a woman. After the pit tragedy, he'd always had time for her, and for Kitty and Lucy Day, who'd lost their father that terrible morning. If a wheel came off the trucks they used for a doll's pram, he'd fix it; if he happened to catch them up on the long road home from the town of High Compton and saw that they were looking tired, he'd give one or the other of them in turn a piggyback. Once, when they'd lost their ball in the weeds and long grass that had gone wild in the Days' garden with nobody to tend it any more, he'd fetched his father's scythe and hacked it all down. And even after the Days had moved away to live with Algernon Pierce, he'd continued to be nice to Edie.

'When I grow up, I'm going to marry Charlie,' she had confided to Lucy Day, her best friend, and her five-year-old heart had warmed at the thought of it.

Through the years, the childish adoration had subtly changed, little by little, and by the time she was fourteen, she realised she was in love with Charlie. He had by now grown into a strongly built young man with hard muscles that rippled in his arms and across his back – visible when he went shirtless in warm weather across the track that led along the back of the houses on his way to the privy. It was scarred now with black coal dust from years of crawling in the narrow faulted seams where he still worked as a carting boy far beneath the green fields, but in Edie's adoring eyes those scars only lent him an aura of romance, as did the wildness that had brought Sergeant Love to his door more than once, much to Dolly's dismay.

He was also known to be a bit of a one with the girls – Edie sometimes saw him walking out with one pretty young woman or another, and once she caught a glimpse of him kissing one of them in the deep shadows at the corner of the terrace. She'd wanted to cry then, and felt sick with a jealousy that burned as fiercely as the fires that sometimes started in summer on the railway embankment when a spark from a steam engine caught the undergrowth alight. They continued to smoulder for weeks, those fires, creeping along underground in the compacted coal dust that formed the embankment before bursting into flames once more, and so it was with Edie. She'd try to bury her feelings for Charlie deep, but they always erupted again, though she knew it was hopeless. Charlie would never look at her the way she wanted him to. He'd never kiss her the way she wanted to be kissed. To him, she was still a little girl, with none of the charms of the young women he walked out with. And even if by some miracle he did notice her, her mother would never allow it. She could just imagine the fuss it would cause. 'You're far too young to be seeing a boy at all,' May would say, 'and certainly not one Charlie Oglethorpe's age.'

Everything changed, though, in the year that Edie was seventeen. She'd been working at Fairley Hall for three years by then, and no longer looked like a child. She'd lost what May had called her puppy fat, and her breasts had developed, firm and full above a small waist and curvy hips. Her features had become more defined in her heart-shaped face, a tip-tilted nose that was more cute than beautiful, a well-shaped mouth that she dared to stain with just a touch of rouge on her days off, and long, thick lashes that framed her hazel eyes. She brushed her hair religiously every night before going to bed so that it fell in lustrous waves to her shoulders and still gleamed even when it was pinned up beneath her maid's cap. Young men were beginning to notice her; she'd seen the admiring glances and been gratified, but still she gave a fig for no one but Charlie, and still she dreamed about him, though she believed it could never be more than that – an impossible dream.

And then came the day of the Foresters' Fete, which was held every year in the field that was also the home ground of Hillsbridge football club.

Fairley Hall was more or less equidistant from the twin towns of South Compton and Hillsbridge. It was Edie's afternoon off, and she arranged with Polly Britten, a friend who was also in service, and also had an afternoon off, to meet there. By the time she arrived, however, Polly had met up with a young man, Thomas Yarlett, who had been in their class at school, and was too busy flirting with him to have any interest in Edie.

After a while, tired of feeling like a gooseberry, Edie wandered off alone. She was standing near the swing boats, feeling a little fed up, when she saw Charlie heading in her direction with a couple of pals. As they passed, the two lads with Charlie began whistling and calling out to her, and the colour rose in her cheeks, already pink from the unexpected encounter.

'Leave her alone!' Charlie admonished them.

They laughed and ignored him.

'Hey – you all on yer own, darlin'?'

'You can have a swing with me any time!'

'Leave her alone, I said.' Charlie's tone was belligerent now. All too often this was a precursor to one of his violent flare-ups, warning anyone within earshot that he meant business.

'Keep your hair on, Charlie,' one of the lads responded, and the other asked: 'What's she to you, then? Never seen you with her, though if I had, I'd have called you a lucky bugger all right.'

'She's a neighbour, and a good kid. Just lay off her, OK?'

They laughed and went on their way, but Charlie came over to her.

'Don't take any notice of them, Edie. They're just playing silly buggers.'

'I know that!' she replied pertly, though her

37

cheeks still felt hot.

'So what are you doing here all on your own?'

'I'm not. Or at least I'm not supposed to be. I was meeting Polly Britten, but it seems she's got better fish to fry.'

'So you are on your own. You didn't oughta be. Things might get rowdy later.'

'I can take care of myself,' Edie retorted. 'I'm not a little girl any more.'

'No, I can see that.' Charlie grinned. 'When did you go and get all grown up, Edie?'

Her cheeks flamed again, but she lifted her chin. 'When you weren't looking, Charlie Oglethorpe.'

He laughed outright now. 'You've got the cheek of the devil, too.'

'And what if I have?' Edie was determined not to let him get the better of her.

'Well,' Charlie said. 'How do you fancy a go on the swing boats?'

Edie's heart gave a gigantic leap, but she hesitated for what she judged to be just about the right length of time. Then she said, as if it couldn't matter less to her: 'I suppose there's no harm. If you're offering.'

A small queue had formed. Edie and Charlie joined it, and Edie swelled with pride that people should see her standing there beside Charlie, for all the world as if they were sweethearts.

At last it was their turn. Charlie paid the boy in attendance and they climbed into one of the gaily painted boats. Edie wished they could sit side by side, but of course they couldn't; the boat needed to be balanced. But at least sitting opposite

38

Charlie she could look at him, at his roguishly handsome face and the muscles flexing in his arms as he pulled on the rope to get them going.

Harder and harder he pulled, higher and higher they went, until they seemed to be flying through the air in great swooping arcs, way above the heads of the people passing by, and the field and the football grandstand away on the far side seemed to be on the point of turning upside down.

'Charlie, stop! That's enough!' Edie cried, as he yanked on the rope, taking the swing boat so high she thought it would go clean over the top of its wooden frame.

Charlie only laughed. Beads of sweat, from both the exertion and the hot sun, rolled down his face and inside the open collar of his shirt, and the more Edie screamed, the higher he swung the boat.

'Hey – that'll do!'

The man who owned the attraction had returned and was shouting up at them, and Edie half expected Charlie to ignore him. But to her surprise he eased off, and eventually the arcs became smaller and lower until the swing boat came to a stop, held firm by the showman's brawny hands, big as Charlie's own.

'You trying to wreck my ride?' he asked gruffly.

'No, just having a bit of fun.'

'Not on my ride you don't.'

'I thought that's what they were for – fun.'

'There's fun and fun. And don't be so bloody cheeky,' the man grunted. 'Now get out of it and don't come back.'

Charlie climbed out easily on to the wooden

platform and reached back to help Edie. She clutched his hand, dizzy now, and feeling a little sick, as if her stomach was still describing crazy arcs, and the ground felt unsteady beneath her feet. She held tight to his hand – how wonderful it felt! – and as she went down the wooden steps clutching the handrail with her free hand, his arm went round her waist, supporting her as she wavered.

'I reckon that calls for a drink,' he said. 'What about it?'

Edie did not need asking twice. She nodded wordlessly, and together they walked towards the refreshment tent.

'You're wicked, Charlie Oglethorpe,' she said when she got her breath back.

He grinned. 'So they say.'

'You could have got us both killed.'

'In a swing boat? I don't think so.'

'Well I do! You frightened the life out of me.'

'Go on with you. You loved every minute.'

'I did not!'

'Yeah, you did. You can't fool me.'

It was hot and crowded in the refreshment tent. Charlie bought a lemonade for Edie and a beer, foaming in the glass, for himself, and they took the drinks outside, where chairs and tables had been set out on the grass.

'So,' he said when they were sitting down, 'how are you getting on these days? What's it like working for Sir Montague?'

Edie pulled a face. 'He's a bit of a one. Will have everything just so. But Lady Elizabeth's nice. It's all right really.'

'The rank's not the same without you. You're missed, Edie.'

Her heart gave a little fillip of pleasure. He missed her!

'What about you?' she asked to cover the moment. 'You're still down the pit, I suppose?'

'Where else would I be? Marston's a lot better than Shepton Fields, but one seam is much like another.'

'Still carting?'

'Still carting.' His tone was grim. 'They've got more than enough colliers and not enough carting boys. But I won't be doing it for ever. I've got plans.'

'What sort of plans? There's nothing much round here but the pits. Or farm work.'

Charlie sipped his beer, which left a rim of foam round his mouth, and stared into the middle distance.

'Me and some of the lads are talking about trying our luck in London if you really want to know.'

'London!' Edie felt her stomach fall away all over again.

'One of these days,' he added, and she breathed again. He wouldn't really go. It was all talk.

'The dancing's started,' Charlie said as music floated towards them from the other side of the field. 'That's early! D'you fancy a turn?'

'Oh – I can't dance! I never learned how...'

'Come on. There's nothing to it. I'll show you.'

He took Edie's hand, leading her across the grass to where a makeshift dance floor had been laid out and a man with a piano accordion and another with a set of drums were playing jolly music. Then he put his other arm around her waist, turning her to face him.

'You're s'posed to hold on to me like this.'

He placed one of her hands in the small of his muscular back and lifted the other so it stuck out at an angle. Edie felt as if she'd died and gone to heaven, and her first self-consciousness quickly ebbed away as Charlie propelled her around the dance floor. When her feet went in the wrong direction or got in the way of his, she giggled.

'Charlie – I'm useless! I'll never get it right!'

But he only laughed.

'Practice makes perfect. You're doing fine for a first go.'

Sure enough, after a while she thought she might be getting the hang of it, but in any case, she didn't much care. Being in Charlie's arms was all she could have wished for.

Too soon, though, it was over, and Edie realised it was time she was getting back to Fairley Hall.

'I'll walk you,' Charlie offered.

'Oh, you don't want to do that!' she objected, though of course she was very much hoping that he would.

'I want to make sure you get back safe,' he said. 'Don't want louts like those so-called pals of mine bothering you. Did you ought to look for that friend of yours, tell her you're going?'

Edie shook her head. She'd seen no more of Polly all afternoon, and suspected she and Thomas Yarlett might well have snuck off somewhere they could be alone.

Charlie walked with her all the way back to Fairley Hall as soft dusk fell, holding her hand

and only letting it go when the house came into sight at the end of the long tree-lined drive.

'We ought to do this again sometime,' he said. 'Get your dancing up to scratch.'

Edie couldn't believe it. She'd spent the whole afternoon with her idol, and now he was asking her out! She felt as if all her Christmases had come at once.

'If you're prepared to risk it,' she said, a little cheekily.

'When's your next day off?'

'Not until next Sunday. And Mam will expect me home.'

'Oh well, at least that'll give my toes a chance to recover,' he said lightly. 'I'll see you then.'

And so it was arranged. They'd meet and go for a walk if the weather was fine. It would be – it had to be! Edie thought.

That had been the start of it. Except that in reality, nothing had really started at all; things had just gone on in much the same way.

At first Edie was perfectly satisfied with the affectionate, casual relationship. She looked forward to the times when she saw him and they went for a walk, or sometimes, if she had a Saturday evening off, to the dances that had been started in a local hall, run by a mysterious and glamorous woman who went by the name of Madame Caroletta. She arrived each week from Bath, or maybe it was Bristol, Edie was never sure, wearing extravagant gowns and dancing shoes and with flowers or feathers in her hair, to run what amounted to classes. Edie learned the old-time waltz and the quickstep, the veleta and the St Bernard's waltz, which involved a lot of stamping of the feet but was a pattern of simple steps and twirls that weren't difficult to memorise. She was quite light on her feet, Madame Caroletta said.

The part Edie liked best was having the chance to be in Charlie's arms, but it was about the only chance she got. Though he always saw her safely home and gave her a cuddle and a goodnight kiss or two, he never seemed to want more, which, very soon, Edie certainly did. She longed to see him more often, longed for him to take her somewhere where they could be really, truly alone, and kiss her and kiss her until her cup was full instead of half empty and leaving her aching for more. And she began to hanker after some sort of commitment from him too.

'I see you've got a young man, Edie,' Mrs Parker, the housekeeper, said one night when she'd spied Charlie walking Edie down the drive after an evening out.

Edie had flushed with pride to hear Charlie described as her young man. It made the relationship sound a lot more serious than it really was.

'Just you be careful,' Mrs Parker warned her, her tone stern. 'It looked to me as if he's a good bit older than you. You don't want to end up in trouble, do you.'

'Oh, he's not like that!' Edie said quickly. 'And I've known him ever since I was a little girl. We lived next-door-but-one to one another.'

'All young men are like that, given half a chance,' Mrs Parker retorted. 'Just you mind yourself, and don't let him take advantage.'

'I won't, Mrs Parker,' Edie said meekly, but she was thinking she'd given Charlie plenty of chances and he'd never taken one of them.

It wasn't, of course, that she wanted to do what Mrs Parker was suggesting she might. Although little thrills ran through her when Charlie held her hand, and especially when they were dancing or having a bit of a cuddle, she knew the dangers of going too far. She didn't want to end up in disgrace as some girls did, and the shame of it would kill her mother. But oh, she did so want the sort of kissing session that Charlie always stopped short of!

She had a horrible suspicion too that she wasn't the only girl he was romancing. She saw him only once a week at the most, and sometimes not even then. She fretted that he was seeing someone else in the days when he wasn't with her – after all, he'd always had quite a reputation that way. And perhaps he was getting all the kisses he wanted, and more, from that other girl, whoever she might be.

She didn't dare ask him, though. She didn't want to risk upsetting the pattern of their relationship, and she was too afraid of what she might learn. Better not to rock the boat, she decided. As things were, she was at least partway to what she wanted most in the world. If she scared him off and he stopped seeing her altogether, Edie didn't think she could bear it.

Chapter Three

And so it went on, with Edie clinging to the hope that Charlie would come to realise she meant as much to him as he did to her and take their relationship a stage further. Until the awful day when he told her that he and a couple of pals were off to London.

He'd never mentioned it again since that first day at the Foresters' Fete, and Edie had decided nothing was going to come of it. Then one day Charlie told her, quite casually, that they intended to leave the very next week.

'Oh Charlie, you can't go to London!' she gasped, horrified.

'Why not?' He seemed quite oblivious to her distress. 'I've had enough of pulling putts of bloody coal day after day. There's all kinds of work to be had in London.'

'But ... it's such a long way!'

'Couldn't be far enough for me. There's a whole world out there, and I'm going to see some of it while I've got the chance.'

'But what about me?' The words were out before she could stop them.

Charlie looked puzzled and a little dismayed.

'You don't want to go to London, do you?'

'No, of course not!' *Though I would if you asked me.* The words were on the tip of her tongue.

'I don't suppose it's any place for a girl. It's

different for us. We can doss around until we get settled. I'm quite looking forward to it.'

Tears were pricking Edie's eyes. 'But how will I get to see you? Oh Charlie, don't go! Please don't go!'

'Hey, Edie...' Charlie was nonplussed and lost for words. Edie clung on to his arm, all pride forgotten. 'Please, Charlie! If you go to London, I'll die!'

'For goodness' sake!' he spluttered.

'I love you!' she burst out before she could stop herself.

Charlie stiffened. 'Don't be so soft, Edie!'

'But it's true! I do! I've always loved you! Don't you feel anything for me? Anything at all?' she wailed.

'Well – of course I do. I really like you. We've had some good times. But I'm not ready to get serious about anyone...' He was clearly embarrassed and shocked. 'You're a good kid, Edie. We've always been friends, haven't we? Nothing's going to change that. But hey ... I'm ten years older than you.'

'What does that matter?'

'Look, I'm sorry – I never realised that you...' He huffed breath over his upper lip. 'We can still be friends, can't we?'

Friends. Tears stung the back of her throat, burned in her eyes. Was that really all she was to him – a friend? Someone to share good times with? But it was better than nothing. Anything – anything at all – was better than nothing. It left her something to cling to.

Somehow she swallowed all the things she

wanted to say and knew she must not. Unless she wanted it to be over, really and truly over. Already she'd said far too much and was beginning to feel ashamed.

'Course we can,' she managed. And then: 'You will come home sometimes, won't you?'

'Ma would kill me if I didn't.'

'And I'll see you then?'

'Well ... yes, I expect so. But don't go getting ideas, Edie. I'm not making any promises.'

'I know. It's all right. Just as long as we can still be friends.' Somehow she had to placate him, undo some of the harm she'd done.

'That's OK then.' He sounded relieved. 'Wish me luck, Edie.'

'Good luck.' The words caught in her throat.

For a long time after he'd gone, she stood outside Fairley Hall, hidden in the shadows as she cried. She felt so mixed up, hurt, disappointed, despairing, and yet still she couldn't let go of the hope that someday, somehow, things would work out. He had been all she had wanted for so long, it was a part of her being.

'One day, Charlie, you'll want me too,' she whispered. 'You will. I know you will.'

Then she dried her tears and went inside.

It was two years now since Charlie had packed his bags and left for London as if he were Dick Whittington hoping to find the streets paved with gold. He hadn't, of course. He'd tried different jobs, everything from working for the borough as a road sweeper to cleaning windows at the Houses of Parliament, an endless task. He'd gone to Margate for a summer and earned a living as a beach attendant. And he'd seen some of the seedier side of life with a bookmaker who'd become a friend, accompanying him to the races and learning the skill of tic-tac as well as watching his friend's back in the dives and alleys of the East End of London.

Until recently he'd written to Edie fairly regularly, recounting his exploits – though not the ones he didn't want her to know about – and her heart always missed a beat when she saw an envelope addressed to her in his surprisingly neat slanting hand. The letters always began 'Dear Edie' and ended with an abrupt 'Love, Charlie', but not a word between to indicate he was missing her, or that his feelings towards her had changed in any way. However much she tried to read more into it – he was writing to her, after all – she really couldn't. As he had said, they were nothing more than friends.

It was the same on the rare occasions she saw him – rare because her days off had to coincide with his visits home to see his mother or she missed him altogether. The first time they met after that night when Edie had bared her soul to him was horribly awkward, both of them painfully aware of the things she had said, but later, when he realised she wasn't going to mention it again, their old easy relationship resumed, and it was as if that cringe-making scene had never happened.

And still Edie clung to her dream that one day Charlie would come back to her and they would make a life together; still the yearning for him was an ache deep inside her that refused to go away; still she took out her memories of the times they had shared, polished them lovingly and stored them away again in her heart. Perhaps if she'd had the opportunity to meet more boys she might at least have tried to forget him with one of them. But really the only young and unattached men she met were the staff at Fairley Hall, and she'd never fancied any of them. Compared with Charlie, they were pathetic specimens, gawky, sometimes spotty, sometimes not very bright, and the fact that they invariably fancied her and made advances made them even less attractive to her. She could only be interested in a real man, she thought, and a real man was like Charlie. Strong. Rugged. A little bit dangerous. Unobtainable. If she couldn't have him, she didn't want a pale substitute.

One day ... one day... Surely that day must be coming? Edie thought as she walked home that September afternoon.

Charlie was thirty years old now. He was bound to outgrow his wandering ways and look to settle down some time soon. And then he'd see what had been under his nose all the time. A young woman who was no longer a child or even a girl, but a lady's maid, with responsibilities and respect, who was trusted with the secrets of the gentry. A young woman who adored him and always had.

Just one thing niggled at her – she hadn't had a letter from him lately. She told herself he had probably been too busy to write. And she was hoping very much that she might find him at home on one of his regular visits to his mother. She'd worked out that he was just about due. What would he say when she told him her news?

What would her mother say? Edie couldn't wait to share it with them.

It was a warm, bright afternoon, the trees, beginning to turn colour for autumn, russet and gold against an intensely blue sky. Edie walked with a spring in her step, but her heart sank as she turned into the lane leading to the Ten Houses. Heading in the opposite direction, a shopping bag over her arm, was Hester Dallimore, the gossip of the rank, and there was no way Edie could avoid her.

'Another day off, then?' Hester greeted her.

'The weeks seem to fly by, don't they, Mrs Dallimore?' Edie tried to walk on – she had no wish to stop and chat with Hester, and certainly not to tell her about her promotion. Telling Hester anything was like hiring a town crier, and proud of herself as she was, Edie didn't want the news spread abroad before she'd had the chance to tell her family and close friends.

But Hester wasn't about to let her go so easily. Whenever she met Edie she fished for titbits of gossip about the Fairley family – the gentry – and besides, today she had some news of her own she was eager to share. After an enquiry after Sir Montague and Lady Elizabeth, which met with short shrift, she puffed up with importance.

'You'll be sorry to have missed Charlie Oglethorpe,' she said, watching Edie closely – her prying eyes had long ago seen them together, and the way Edie looked at him. 'He was home yesterday, but he's gone again now.'

Edie's heart fell like a stone.

'Oh that's a shame,' she managed in an effort to conceal her disappointment, and again went to

51

walk on. But Hester had no intention of letting her go until she'd finished what she had to say.

'Had a woman with him, too. A woman – and a little boy. A toddler. Brought her home to meet his mother, I shouldn't wonder. Looks to me as if he's going to settle down at last. If he hasn't already,' she added smugly.

'Lady's maid to Miss Christina!' May Cooper exclaimed. 'Well I never!'

'Yes, as soon as they can get someone to do my work,' Edie said, her tone flat. All the joy had gone out of her, sucked away by Hester's news.

They were sitting at the kitchen table over a pot of tea, but a slice of May's home-made fruit cake – Edie's favourite – lay untouched on her plate. Usually she could hardly wait to tuck into it, looking forward to the treat just as she looked forward to spending time alone with her mother when her father was out at work, and enjoying the fact that they could talk and share the sort of mother-and-daughter conversation that had been all too rare in the days before Ted, her brother, had married and left home to live on the other side of High Compton in a tied cottage closer to Marston Colliery where he worked. But today she was holding back, unable to bring herself to mention what Hester had told her for fear of making it more real than it already was.

'Well, it's a funny old world and no mistake.' May shook her head wonderingly, so excited by Edie's news that she quite failed to notice her daughter's preoccupation. 'I can't believe that babe's grown up enough to need a lady's maid!'

She broke off, a strange expression momentarily crossing her face. Then she gave herself a small shake and went on. 'And just fancy that it should be you of all people that's going to be looking after her.'

'Nellie Saunders is up in arms about it,' Edie said, feeling obliged to make some contribution to the conversation.

'I'll bet she is!' May got up and fetched the teapot from the trivet over the fire where she'd left it to keep warm. 'Are you ready for a top-up, our Edie?'

'Thanks.' Edie pushed her cup and saucer across the table, and May poured in a drop of creamy milk before adding the strong tea.

'You haven't touched your cake,' she scolded. 'Eat up now. You're getting so thin a puff of wind could blow you over.'

'Oh Mam, don't talk so silly.' But she broke off a small piece anyway and popped it into her mouth, not wanting to upset her mother, who had likely baked the cake freshly in anticipation of her visit. Though light and moist as always, it tasted like sawdust in her dry mouth.

'And what's that Quilla Brimble got to say about it?' May asked.

'Not a lot. But she did look a bit peeved not to be the only lady's maid in the house any more.'

'That's her usual expression, isn't it?' May had replaced the teapot on the trivet and was sitting with her own fresh cup held between both hands. 'She's got a face to turn the milk sour, that one. And likes to think of herself as a cut above.'

Edie nodded, struggling to swallow the crumbs

53

of cake, which seemed to stick in her throat. She didn't like Quilla Brimble any more than her mother did, with her sharp tongue and scheming ways, and she knew for a fact that she often snitched on her colleagues below stairs, passing on reports of any misdemeanour to Lady Elizabeth, but always in a way that made it seem she only had the good order and smooth running of the household at heart. She was sly and nasty, Edie thought. But she really couldn't care less about Quilla Brimble, or anyone else, just now. The only thing of any importance was that Charlie had brought a woman home to meet his mother. And not just a woman, but a little boy too. Her heart felt like a lump of lead in her chest and her head was reeling with questions, but at the same time she wasn't sure she wanted to hear the answers.

She couldn't avoid the subject for ever, though, even if May was doing her best to do so.

'I ran into Mrs Dallimore on my way here,' she said, crumbling another morsel of cake between her fingers. 'She said Charlie had been home, and he didn't come on his own.'

'Oh that one!' May huffed. 'She just can't stop that mouth of hers running away with itself.'

'It's right, though, is it?' Edie asked. 'That he had someone with him?'

May blew on her tea, giving herself a moment to answer. She knew what Charlie meant to Edie.

'There was a woman with him, yes, and a little lad. It don't necessarily mean anything, of course. You know what Charlie's like.'

'Hester seemed to think differently,' Edie said. Now she'd started, she needed to find out all she

54

could. 'Bringing a woman home to meet his mother, she said. Has Mrs Oglethorpe mentioned anything about it to you?'

May shifted uncomfortably in her chair.

'Well … in passing.'

'So what did she say?'

'Just that this woman was the wife of Charlie's bookmaker friend, and the little boy was their son.'

Edie frowned, puzzled. From Charlie's letters, she knew that the bookmaker was called Victor something and that Charlie lodged with him when he was in London. But he had never mentioned anything about him having a wife, let alone a baby.

And in any case…

'Why would Charlie bring a friend's wife and little boy with him when he came to visit his mother?' she asked.

May's lips tightened. 'Exactly what I said myself. Dolly had some tale ready that this woman – Gracie, her name was – has got relatives down this way, and she took the opportunity to come and see them when she knew she'd have company on the journey. She's not used to travelling on her own, Dolly said, and what with the little one… But they were only here the one day, didn't even stop the night, and as you know, Charlie always comes for two or three days, to make it worthwhile. So why they didn't stay longer I don't know.'

'I don't suppose there would be room for them all,' Edie said, grasping at straws. Since Charlie had left home Dolly had taken a lodger, a lad who'd come to High Compton to work for Saville Stone, the gents' outfitter, when Reuben Hillman, the previous assistant, had left to 'better himself in Bath', so the story went, though no one seemed to know quite what that meant. With his old room occupied, Charlie had to make do with the box room, and if that was given to his friend's wife and little boy, then he'd be reduced to spending the night on the living room settee – far from ideal given his size.

'That's true enough,' May agreed. 'But if she'd come all the way from London to see her relatives, why didn't she stay with them? They could have met her at the station, taken her home with them and brought her back again, and Charlie could have stayed at number three just like he always does. No, there's something fishy about it if you ask me.'

Edie read her mother's mind, and it was much the same as she was thinking herself, though she was trying not to. Charlie was having a fling with his friend's wife, and they'd used the excuse of visiting family to spend a couple of nights together, perhaps in some hotel or lodging house in Bath or Bristol.

The thought of Charlie in bed with another woman was a horrible one. But she'd always known what he was like, and she couldn't imagine he lived the life of a monk in London. It was an unwelcome truth she'd somehow managed to come to terms with. Just as long as none of those other women meant anything more to him than a good time and a bit of fun. Just as long as he didn't get serious about any of them. Just as long as in the end he realised that Edie was the one for him, and when he was ready to settle down, it was with her.

That he had actually brought someone home with him, though, had shaken her to the core. But maybe it was not so different. Maybe they had just stolen a few nights together. If she was married to his friend, that was all it could be, surely. Edie didn't like it, and she wasn't proud of herself for hoping that was what was behind it. Where was her pride and self-respect? But almost anything was preferable to the awful thought that she might have lost Charlie for good.

In an effort to get off the subject she knew was upsetting her daughter, May went on chattering about anything and everything, but Edie was barely listening. She was still wondering why Charlie had never mentioned a woman in Victor's life, and why he should have brought her and a child home with him unless there was something going on between them. Now that she came to think of it, she didn't think Charlie had mentioned Victor much in his letters recently, except for saying he had accompanied him to the races, and on the rare occasions when he was home and they'd met up, the subject had never arisen.

Another unwelcome thought occurred to her. The last time she'd seen him, Charlie hadn't said much at all. He'd been very quiet, not at all his usual self. At the time she'd thought perhaps he was feeling a bit under the weather, but now she wondered. Had he been hiding something?

All her misgivings came flooding back, and suddenly the little kitchen felt airless and claustrophobic. She didn't want to be here, listening to her mother's small talk as she tried to take Edie's mind off the very real possibility that Charlie had got involved with somebody else, somebody totally unsuitable. And she didn't want her pity, especially when she knew all too well how pathetic she was, with her obsessive love and her silly dreams.

It didn't really matter at all who this woman was, and whether she and Charlie were having an illicit affair. If it wasn't her, it would be someone else, but never Edie. Suddenly it was as if the scales had been ripped from her eyes and the truth was crystal clear. If Charlie had ever been going to fall in love with her, it would have happened a long time ago. She'd been fooling herself for years. It was time she forgot him once and for all and looked elsewhere for love, unless she was going to finish up an embittered old maid like Quilla Brimble.

But in spite of her sudden resolve, emptiness yawned in Edie like a vast barren desert. She'd loved Charlie too much for too long to be able to forget him, no matter how she tried, no matter if she accepted it was hopeless. Even if she recognised that he was never going to feel about her the way she felt about him, she couldn't imagine that anyone else could ever take his place in her heart.

'I think I ought to be going, Mam,' she said.

'So soon?' May sounded sad. She still missed Edie, even though it was six years since she'd lived at home.

'The nights are drawing in,' Edie, said. 'You know you don't like me out on my own in the dark.'

'No, you're right, I don't,' May agreed. 'Not along the lanes and that blooming long drive down to Fairley Hall. Anybody could be hiding in

58

the bushes.'

'Only poachers.'

'Well, you never know,' May said darkly. 'And poachers could turn nasty if they thought they were going to get caught. No, best you get back in the daylight, our Edie.'

Edie reached for her bonnet, thinking sadly how excited and happy she'd been when she'd put it on earlier to come home. How a few hours had changed everything.

'Get off with you then.' May kissed her. 'And no fretting about Charlie Oglethorpe. He's not worth it. Just you enjoy being a lady's maid to Christina.'

Edie nodded.

'And be sure you do a good job of looking after her,' May added.

Chapter Four

Christina Fairley wriggled impatiently on the brocaded stool in front of the dressing table and raised her wide turquoise eyes imploringly to the small, beady dark ones of Quilla Brimble, reflected in the mirror as she brushed Christina's long nut-brown hair. Unmoved, Quilla continued, her hand keeping time with the ticking of the mantel clock.

'A hundred strokes, Miss Christina, if you want your hair to shine. I hope you'll make sure Edith does it properly when she's the one responsible.'

'But it seems to take for ever! It is such a bore!'

'Some things in life are,' Quilla said tartly. 'That's the way of things. We can't always be running around having fun. You are a young lady now, and you have to act like one and do what young ladies do, I'm afraid. But we're nearly finished now. Ninety-nine ... a hundred.'

She put down the tortoiseshell-backed brush and picked up the comb, tugging it through the unruly little curls that clustered under Christina's hairline at the nape of her neck.

'Perhaps it won't be so boring when Edith does it,' Christina said ingenuously. 'We shall have interesting things to talk about, I expect.'

She didn't notice the tightening of Quilla's lips or the puckers of displeasure that pinched her cheeks, and it never occurred to her that she might have caused offence – like a child, she simply said whatever came into her head without giving any thought to the effect it might have. But she felt the sudden tug of the comb at those persistent little curls all right, sharp enough to make her cry out.

'I'm sorry, Miss Christina. Did I hurt you? There was a knot that I didn't see.' Quilla didn't sound in the least sorry, but as always, Christina took her words at face value.

'It's my own fault, I expect. I was down by the lake this afternoon, and I got caught in the brambles. They're hanging down all over the path at this time of year. And the hedges are thick with blackberries! If I'd had my basket with me, I'd have brought some home so that Mrs Davey could make jelly – or perhaps a pie.'

'It's not your place to pick blackberries, Miss Christina,' Quilla reprimanded.

'I don't suppose it is, but I don't see why I shouldn't.'

'Because it's not proper.' Then, in an altogether gentler tone, she added: 'What are we going to do with you, I should like to know.'

In the mirror she had seen Lady Elizabeth appear in the doorway, Beauty, Christina's King Charles spaniel at her heels, and Quilla knew better than to speak sharply or disrespectfully to Christina in her mother's presence. In all the years she had been Lady Elizabeth's lady's maid she'd always watched her tongue. Though she had good reason to bear the Fairley family a grudge, and though she knew enough of their secrets to cause trouble if she had a mind to, it was an ingrained habit to be deferential, and never do or say anything that might make Lady Elizabeth feel she was overstepping the invisible line that separated the classes.

Lady Elizabeth was her better – or thought she was – and it suited Quilla to go along with that – for the moment, at least.

'Now, here's your mother come to say goodnight,' she went on in the same falsely affectionate tone. 'And Beauty too.' She even managed to say the dog's name without revealing her dislike for it – silly, yapping little beast. Sir Montague's Labradors, Nero and Noble, were bad enough, leaving wiry hairs everywhere, especially on the hems of Lady Elizabeth's skirts, but at least they were well trained and didn't get under your feet. Beauty – well, Quilla took the greatest satisfaction in giving the little dog a sly kick when no one was looking.

'To say goodnight, yes, but we have some news,

61

too!' Elizabeth came into the room, preceded by Beauty, who ran to Christina to be petted. 'Cousin Beatrice and Julia and Raymond are going to pay us a visit. They have been holidaying in Devon, and will call on us and stay a night or two on their way home to Wiltshire. They arrive tomorrow.'

'Oh how lovely!' Christina cried.

She wasn't overly enamoured of Beatrice, a rather doleful woman who seemed to have been in mourning for her late husband, Horatio, for as long as Christina could remember; and Julia, at twenty-five, ten years older than her, was serious and intense, though Christina did rather admire her – there was something almost magnetic about Julia.

Raymond, however, was a different matter entirely. At nineteen, he was much closer to her in age and, Christina thought, very handsome, with fair hair that flopped over a narrow face with high cheekbones and an aquiline nose. He was always nice to her, too, listening to her chatter and spending time with her, even winking at her when Sir Montague embarked on one of his long, boring discourses. Yes, a visit from Raymond was certainly something to look forward to.

Her spirits lifted even more when Elizabeth gave her a conspiratorial smile.

'It's pleased you, I see. And there's every chance that Raymond will be here for much longer.'

'Why?' Christina demanded, wide-eyed.

'I'm afraid you are going to have to wait and find out when everyone else does,' Elizabeth teased.

'Mama! That's not fair!'

'Maybe not, but you know very well you can't

be trusted with secrets, and your uncle would be very cross if word of this got out before he has had the chance to speak to Raymond.'

'Oh!' Christina pouted.

'Perhaps I'll tell you later if you promise not to breathe a word of it. But in the meantime, I've some other news that will put a smile on your face.' Elizabeth touched the corner of her adopted daughter's mouth fondly. 'I think we may well have found a replacement maid for Edith. Mrs Davey has a niece who is looking to go into service, and I would imagine she might be very suitable.'

'Oh that's wonderful!' Her peevishness forgotten Christina jumped up from the stool, clapping her hands, and her freshly brushed hair fanned out over the neckline of her white cambric nightgown. 'I can hardly wait!'

'It's not very kind to Quilla to let her think you'd rather have Edith attending to your needs than her, my dear,' Elizabeth said, with an apologetic glance at her lady's maid.

Quilla's thin lips twisted into a parody of a smile.

'Don't worry, milady, I'm quite used to it,' was all she said.

The imminent – and unexpected – arrival of guests had caused a flurry of activity below stairs. The guest rooms had to be aired and the beds made up with fresh linen, and fires laid in the grates in case the evenings turned cold.

'We don't want them catching a chill while they're in this house,' Mrs Parker said as she headed upstairs with an armful of clean towels to be stacked on the washstands, and Edie found herself running up and down with bundles of kindling and buckets of coal that she piled in little pyramids in the fire baskets, and giving the fire irons a good polish so that the brass shone. 'You can see your face in the shovels now,' she said with satisfaction when she went back below stairs.

The kitchen was a hive of activity too as Mrs Davey returned with the new menus she had drawn up with Lady Elizabeth.

'I don't know where her ladyship thinks we're going to get all the extra supplies at this short notice,' she huffed. 'I shall need at least two dozen more eggs and a quart of milk, and her ladyship wants partridge for dinner tonight if we can get hold of any, which I doubt – the season's only just started. Failing that, it's to be roast beef, and I haven't a joint big enough to feed three extra mouths and still have cold for tomorrow.'

'Don't worry, Mrs Davey, I'll see if Simon can be spared to run into town in the motor, if Sir Montague doesn't need it, that is,' Percy Stevens suggested.

'Oh – and how will *he* know what to get?' Martha Davey scoffed. 'All he knows or cares about is what goes on under the bonnet of that great monstrosity.'

Simon Ford was the chauffeur Sir Montague had employed when he'd bought the Rolls, a young man with far too high an opinion of himself, Martha thought.

'I'm sure if you make out a list, Mr Price at the butcher's will do you proud,' Percy soothed. 'Goodness knows, you've trusted him for long enough, and he's never let you down yet, has he?'

'There's always a first time,' Martha returned darkly.

In the event all was well, and Simon returned not with the hoped-for partridge, but with a nice baron of beef and all the other things Martha had asked for.

Soon after eleven, Percy summoned the staff. The guests had arrived, he said.

'You need a clean apron, my girl. That one's a disgrace!' Martha huffed at Flo Doughty, the kitchen maid, and the girl scurried to change it before hurrying out after the others to line up and greet the guests.

The motor that had drawn up at the main entrance to Fairley Hall was a bright yellow Vauxhall – a 1908 A-type, Raymond told them proudly later – and it was not only newer but also far sportier than Sir Montague's stately Rolls. Raymond, wearing a shirt that was open at the neck, and a red and white checked cap, was in the driving seat with Julia, his sister, beside him. Beatrice, their mother, in her usual black coat – though silk for summer – and a black-straw hat trimmed with silk flowers, was installed in the rear.

'Thanks be to God we're here!' she said as Simon opened the car door and made to help her out. 'Without His good grace we would all be dead in a ditch.'

'Don't you trust me, Ma?' Raymond drawled, climbing down from the driver's seat and stretching.

Beatrice's only answer was a small, impatient shake of the head.

'You have to live a little before you die,

Mother.' Julia hopped down on to the gravelled driveway without waiting for assistance.

She was a tall, striking-looking young woman, with her brother's fair hair, fastened in a knot at the nape of her neck, and the same narrow features. But there was a steely set to her jaw, and curiously, when she smiled, her mouth appeared to curve not upwards, but down. There was something of her mother in her bearing, too – Beatrice had always been proud of her erect posture until a widow's hump had rounded her shoulders.

'How lovely to see you all!' Elizabeth greeted them. 'It hardly seems possible that it's a year since you were last here. Julia, my dear, you are looking so well – and Raymond, too. And dearest Beatrice...' She kissed her cousin on the cheek, trying not to wrinkle her nose at the overpowering scent of violets. Beatrice had long since grown so used to the smell, she never now knew that she was overdoing it.

'Julia! Raymond!' Christina came dancing up to them, as childlike as ever in her excitement. 'Oh, what a beautiful motor! I adore the colour! Will you take me for a drive?'

'Christina!' Sir Montague cautioned. 'Don't begin pestering poor Raymond before he has even set foot in the house.'

'He's probably had quite enough of driving, in any case,' Elizabeth added with an apologetic smile at her cousin's son.

'But if he's going to be staying here, there will be lots of opportunity, won't there?' Christina continued, unabashed.

'Christina!' Sir Montague snapped.

66

'But Mama said–'

'That will do!' Sir Montague glared at her, and Elizabeth took her arm firmly, pinching it through the thin fabric of her sleeve.

'Take no notice. She's overexcited,' she said to the guests with a conciliatory smile and a quick glance over her shoulder at the welcoming party of servants lined up well within earshot. 'Do come inside. You must be hungry and thirsty after your journey. And longing for a chance to wash away the dust of travel, too.'

'I just need to sit down in a chair that doesn't feel as though it is running away with me,' Beatrice replied with feeling.

'What was all that about Mr Raymond staying for longer?' Nellie Saunders asked as the servants went back downstairs. Her sharp little features were eager with curiosity.

'Mind your own business, Nellie,' Quilla Brimble said in her customary bossy tone, but her lips were set in an even tighter line than usual, as if something had seriously displeased her.

'Sorry, I'm sure,' Nellie replied, but it sounded more like cheek than an apology.

'You're too nosy for your own good,' Quilla snapped.

'What's eating her?' Nellie asked of no one in particular when Quilla had gone back upstairs. 'She looks as if she's lost a pound and found a penny.'

'She thinks she'll have extra work to do looking after the guests as well as Lady Elizabeth, I expect,' Mrs Davey said. 'But then so have we all.'

But it wasn't like Quilla to baulk at any duty that meant her mingling with the upper classes, Nellie thought, and continued to wonder just what had put Quilla in such a bad temper.

'Did I hear right? Mr Raymond is going to stay on longer? Nothing's been mentioned to me about it,' Lilian Parker said to Percy Stevens, following him into the butler's pantry where they were out of earshot of the other servants.

Lilian and Percy were friends and allies. Over the years they'd grown as close as two kindred souls in their positions ever could while still maintaining a respectable distance. There were secrets they shared that were never mentioned; there were memories of happy times, and sad, and a mutual devotion to the family they served, in particular to Lady Elizabeth and, of course, Christina. Though they respected Sir Montague and never spoke ill of him, he was not an easy man to like. They could read one another's moods as a shepherd or sea-man could read the weather, and they talked more freely together than to anyone else in the house-hold. Though neither had ever been wed – 'Mrs' was a courtesy title only for Lilian – they were in some ways very like an old married couple in the years when the passion has long since gone.

Percy looked out into the corridor, checking that none of the other servants was nearby, and closed the door.

'From what I gather, Sir Montague is hoping to persuade Mr Raymond to move here and begin to learn about running the estate and, of course, the mines,' he said in a low voice. 'He's not getting any younger, and as you know, he has no direct heirs. As things stand, everything will pass to Mr Raymond in due course, and Sir Montague would like to feel he will be well prepared to take over when the time comes.'

'Well I never! But it makes good sense, I suppose.' Lilian removed the spectacles she had taken to wearing lately, and which Lady Elizabeth had paid for, and polished them with her handkerchief. 'Is it all arranged? Is that why they're here now?'

'I don't think Sir Montague has put it to him yet, so he won't be best pleased at Miss Christina blurting it out like that. And not to mention in front of all the staff.'

'Oh, there's no telling what that one will do next, bless her.' Satisfied that her spectacles were now clean, Lilian returned them to her nose. 'Well, we'll get to hear the rights of it before long, I dare say.'

'No doubt. Now, I'd best see about getting the cold meats for luncheon upstairs. Do you think Flo can be trusted to carry a tray, or is she going to drop it as she did the other day?'

'Safer to get Nellie to do it, with guests here,' Lilian advised. 'How much wit it takes to do a simple thing like that I don't know, but she goes sillier than ever when there's a good-looking young man like Mr Raymond on the scene. And he'll be turning Miss Christina's head too, I wouldn't wonder.'

'Let us hope not,' the butler said fervently.

He turned to leave, but Lilian laid a hand on his arm.

'And another thing. Did you notice that brooch Miss Julia was wearing?'

'I can't say I did, Mrs Parker. I'm not much given to looking at ladies' jewellery,' Percy said drily. 'What of it?'

'Well, it was one of those brooches the Women's Social and Political Union have been selling to raise funds for their cause. It's got a portrait of Mrs Pankhurst on it,' Lilian informed him. 'And she had ribbons tied round her bun, too, purple, green and white. That's their colours – purple for dignity, white for purity and green for hope.'

'You seem to know a lot about it, Mrs Parker,' Percy observed, a little stiffly. He was not at all sure that he agreed with what the Women's Social and Political Union stood for, and certainly not with the ways they were going about trying to achieve their objectives.

'Well I read the papers, don't I?' Lilian said, a little defensively. 'I like to keep up with the news. And if you ask me, it can only mean one thing. Miss Julia must be one of them. She's only gone and joined the suffragettes.' She emphasised each word of her last sentence with a corresponding tap of her finger on the butler's cuff.

Percy bristled.

'Miss Julia – a suffragette? Never!' He dashed at his cuff as if to brush away her words. 'Don't let anyone else hear you say such a thing, Mrs Parker.'

'I wouldn't! It's just between ourselves. But I'm sure I'm right – you see if I'm not.' Lilian's glasses seemed to have steamed up again; once more she took them off. Without them her face looked curiously naked and defenceless, and when Percy

70

spoke, the crossness had gone out of his voice and he just sounded concerned.

'Well let's hope you're wrong, Mrs Parker. That way lies nothing but trouble.'

He opened the pantry door, and the time for confidences was over.

Lilian Parker was not the only one to have noticed Julia's ribbons and brooch. Elizabeth, too, had seen them, and also knew what they meant, and her heart too had sunk.

It wasn't that she disagreed with what the suffragettes were fighting for. In many ways she agreed with them wholeheartedly. As an independent-spirited woman herself, she often resented the way her sex were treated as second-class citizens, while men had all the power as well as holding the purse strings. But she couldn't agree with the way they were going about trying to change things. Committing acts that got them sent to prison, and then refusing food so that they ended up being force-fed – it wasn't ladylike, and would do no good. It only strengthened the arguments of the ruling elite and made the protesters look like hysterical females who were in no way responsible enough to be trusted with the vote. The thought that Julia might be mixed up in such goings-on was a disturbing one. Her poor mother must be worried out of her mind if it were true. And what Montague would have to say about it, Elizabeth couldn't imagine. She could only hope he wouldn't notice the brooch, and that Julia wouldn't get on a soapbox over luncheon or dinner. She did so want everything to go smoothly,

71

especially with the proposition Montague was intending to put to Raymond. If Montague got himself worked up about women's suffrage and Raymond took his sister's part, there might well be a falling-out that would put the proposed arrangements at risk.

Although maybe that would not be such a bad thing under the circumstances. If Raymond came to live at Fairley Hall to be initiated into the running of the estate and the coal mines that belonged to it, then that would mean Julia would visit a good deal more frequently. Christina admired Julia, Elizabeth knew; supposing she swayed the impressionable girl into joining the movement herself? The thought was a horrifying one.

With a tremendous effort, she turned on her brightest smile.

'Shall we have luncheon, then?' she suggested, and her normal light and charming tone belied the anxiety she was feeling.

The telephone call came during dinner, just as the family were enjoying one of Mrs Davey's delicious syllabubs.

'I'm very sorry to interrupt your meal, Sir Montague, but the caller did say it was a matter of the utmost importance,' Percy said, standing discreetly at his employer's elbow.

'The caller? Who is it, dammit?'

Percy glanced at Beatrice, who was chatting to Elizabeth. He didn't want to alert her to the fact that it was her gardener and odd-job man who was telephoning. The man, Blacker, had especially asked to speak to Sir Montague, and made it clear that it would be best he should take the call and decide how to break some very distressing news to his mistress.

'I really think you should come to the telephone, sir,' Percy said quietly, raising his eyebrow in the direction of Beatrice.

'Oh ... very well, very well.'

Sir Montague laid his napkin on the table in front of him, rose, and strode out of the dining room.

The telephone was on an ornate occasional table in the entrance hall; he picked it up.

'Yes?' he barked. Then his frown deepened. 'What? Good God, man, how could such a thing happen? Yes ... yes ... of course I will break the news to Mrs Fairley. This is appalling – appalling...'

When he'd replaced the receiver, he turned to Percy, who was hovering discreetly in the doorway.

'Oh Stevens ... such a thing. Will you fetch me a brandy? I think I am in sore need before I speak to poor Mrs Fairley.'

'...and their house is burned to the ground!' Nellie announced, going back below stairs with a tray loaded with used crockery.

As was her habit, she had managed to listen at the dining room door, and had heard every word Sir Montague had said when, fortified with a large brandy, he had broken the shocking news to Beatrice.

Earlier in the evening, it seemed, a fire had broken out at their manor house in Wiltshire.

73

How it had started, no one seemed to know. But it had taken hold before the alarm was raised, and for all the efforts of the local fire brigade, it seemed much of the house was gutted.

'Of course you must all stay here for as long as you need to,' Elizabeth said to a distraught Beatrice.

And thought that all her anxieties about the bad influence Julia might be on the naive and impressionable Christina had just been exacerbated a thousandfold.

Chapter Five

'Oh, this is so wonderful!' Christina trilled. Her words were almost drowned out by the spluttering of the Vauxhall's engine and blown away on the stiff breeze, but the expression on her face as she sat bolt upright in the front seat said it all. She glanced over her shoulder at Edie, who was sitting in the back behind Raymond. 'Aren't you glad I persuaded Mama to let you come with us?'

'Of course I am!' Edie smiled back at her. She could still scarcely believe she was riding in a motor car; she only hoped it wouldn't break down and leave them stranded up here on the Mendips, miles from home. She was already feeling a little chilly – her coat was not nearly as warm as Christina's thick woollen one – and the sun was sinking into a band of thick cloud on the horizon. 'Don't you think we've gone far enough, though, Mr Raymond?'

Raymond, struggling to change gear, inclined his head.

'Sorry – I can't hear you.'

'I said...' Edie repeated herself, shouting against the wind in her face.

'Not much further,' he shouted back. 'Got to make the most of a dry day at last!'

Edie lapsed into silence. It really wasn't her place to tell Raymond what to do, and she knew she was lucky to have been included in the outing, something she knew had vexed Quilla and outraged Percy Stevens, with his strict views about what was and was not proper. But she was also very aware that the most likely reason Lady Elizabeth had agreed was so that she could not only act as a chaperone to Christina, but look after her too, and she had every intention of doing just that. If Raymond didn't turn around soon, she'd have to insist, but it wouldn't be easy. Over the past few weeks, since he'd been staying at Fairley Hall, she'd come to realise he could be stubborn as well as having a wild streak, and Christina ... well, Christina would be certain to back him up. Easily influenced as she always was, she seemed enchanted by her cousin.

Edie couldn't argue with what Raymond had said about the weather, though. Autumn had come in with a vengeance, high winds that had started bringing down the first deluge of leaves from the trees, and almost incessant rain.

'If it had been like this when the fire started, and they'd had it in Wiltshire too, that house would never have burned down,' Mrs Davey had said as she huffed and puffed over all the extra work that had come from three extra mouths to feed.

Now Edie couldn't help smiling to herself as she remembered the altercation that had followed the remark.

'I don't think you're right there, Mrs Davey.' Simon Ford, the chauffeur, had been warming his backside in front of the kitchen range. 'It was a proper inferno, so they say.'

'But it would never have turned into an inferno, as you call it, if it had been raining cats and dogs.' Martha had been determined to stand her ground. 'And there'd have been no shortage of water to fight it, either.'

'Oh, you're talking out of your hat,' Simon had said, cheeky as ever.

'Am I indeed! And you'll be nursing a sore ear if you don't get out of my way!' And with that, Martha had approached the range, waving her basting spoon threateningly.

Both of them had been spoiling for a fight, Edie knew, Mrs Davey because all her usual catering arrangements had been turned upside down, and Simon Ford because he was jealous of the yellow monstrosity that could outperform the Rolls he drove by a mile, and angered by the dismissive manner in which its young upstart of an owner spoke about the motor that was Simon's pride and joy.

'He's heading for a fall, that one,' he'd prophesied darkly. 'I wouldn't be surprised if he doesn't end up in a ditch, or halfway up a tree.'

I hope he doesn't do it with Miss Christina and me in the car, Edie thought nervously.

At that very moment the car jolted alarmingly, causing Christina to squeal and Edie to cling on to her seat, her heart thumping with fright. Then, with a loud clonk, Raymond pulled on the brake and the car juddered to an abrupt halt on a patch of uneven grass.

'This is the place,' he declared. 'I found it the other day when I drove out alone. Now – what do you think of the view, Christina? Isn't it splendid?'

'It's wonderful!' Christina exclaimed, but Edie thought her enthusiasm was more for Raymond's benefit than for her appreciation of the vista that spread out before them.

Little minx! Edie thought fondly. But there was no denying it: even in the fading light, the view was superb. From their vantage point the land sloped steeply away, vast expanses of still green grass divided here and there by low dry-stone walls. In the distance, on the other side of the broad valley floor, more hills rose, shades of purple and grey against the pink-streaked clouds.

'I'm going to explore!' Christina was already fumbling with the door handle.

Raymond climbed out and, ever the gallant gentleman, went around to help her down. She skipped off towards a makeshift stile – two large and more or less flat stones on top of one another at a place where the wall was slightly lower.

'Christina!' Edie called. 'Be careful!'

'I will!' She was already clambering on to the stone step.

'And don't go too far! We ought to be setting out for home!'

Christina ignored her, lifting her skirts to climb over the stile, then jumping down the other side and turning to wave before running off along the ridge of the escarpment.

'Oh!' Edie huffed. Fond as she was of Christina, she sometimes despaired of her.

'Let her be.' Raymond lolled casually against the chassis of the Vauxhall.

'I'm supposed to be looking after her,' Edie retorted. 'She'll come back all muddy like as not. And what if she gets lost?'

'She won't. You worry too much.' He gave her a sideways grin.

'I've got my position to think of.' She was craning her neck, trying to catch sight of Christina, who had disappeared from view.

'Forget Christina. Think of yourself for a change, Edith.' He reached out a lazy hand, curling it around her waist.

Edie froze in momentary panic. She'd heard of servants being molested by members of the families they worked for, but she'd never experienced anything of the sort. Sir Montague scarcely acknowledged her, or any of the other maids, and until now there had never been any other men in the household. But Raymond, young, good-looking in a slightly foppish way, clearly fancied his chances. She couldn't help but notice the way he looked at her, with narrowed eyes and a knowing half-smile, but she'd thought it was just his way – he looked at the other maids too. And, it had to be said, Christina. There was no doubt that in spite of her young age and the fact that he was four years older than her, he was playing up to her, and it worried Edie. Christina was so easily flattered by any attention, and very naive, and she would be seeing a good deal of Raymond now that he was living at Fairley Hall.

'Sir ... please...' Her voice was thready, uncertain, but instead of releasing her, he slid his hand downwards, caressing her hip and then, to her horror and disbelief, squeezing her bottom.

Afterwards, Edie could scarcely believe how quickly and instinctively she reacted. Before she had time to think about what she was doing, she had swung around and slapped him full in the face.

At least it had the desired effect, and Raymond released his hold on her. But in that same moment Edie realised the possible repercussions of what she had done. Above his hand, which had flown to his stinging cheek, his eyes were first shocked, then outraged.

'Well!' he exclaimed 'You're a fiery filly and no mistake!'

'I ... I'm sorry, sir,' Edie said. 'But you shouldn't have done that.'

His lip curled. 'Don't tell me no one has ever squeezed your arse before? A pretty girl like you.'

'I'm not like that,' Edie said defiantly. 'I'm sure there are plenty who would be flattered by a gentleman's attentions, but I'm not one of them.'

'We'll see about that.'

As he removed his hand from his cheek, Edie could see the red imprint her fingers had left, and she felt a twist of anxiety. The family were bound to notice. How was he going to explain it away without letting everyone know that she had actually dared to slap him?

As if reading her thoughts, Raymond looked at her with a hint of challenge in his eyes.

'You like working at Fairley Hall and being Miss Christina's maid, I take it? You wouldn't want to be sent back below stairs, or even dismissed?'

A pulse in Edie's throat jumped uncomfortably. So that was it. Raymond would find some way of explaining away the mark on his face without telling anyone what she had done, but there would be a price to pay for his silence, and she could guess what it would be. Well, if he thought she was going to let him paw her and maybe worse because he was threatening her with what amounted to blackmail, he couldn't be more wrong. In fact, two could play at that game!

'If you should complain about me slapping you, then I would have to tell the reason for it,' she said, surprising herself with her own daring. 'I can't imagine Sir Montague would approve of such behaviour.'

Cold anger flashed in Raymond's eyes, but before he could respond, Christina was calling to them from the other side of the wall.

'Come and see! It's the most wonderful view! It's like being a bird with the whole world spread out beneath your wings!'

For just a moment Raymond held Edie's defiant gaze, then he shrugged.

'It's time we were going home,' he called back.

Reluctantly Christina rejoined them. Raymond handed her into the front passenger seat of the car and Edie climbed unaided into the rear.

At least Christina, excited as she was, didn't

seem to have noticed Raymond's bruised face, but Edie was in no doubt that through no real fault of her own she had made an enemy. She wished with all her heart that it was not so, but there was no undoing what had happened. She would just have to live with it and hope that Raymond didn't try to stir up trouble for her and put her new, and much-prized, position in jeopardy.

Julia was alone in the drawing room when Raymond returned. The other ladies had gone to their rooms to change for dinner, but Julia had no patience with primping and preening. She would slip up with minutes to spare to put on something a little grander than her plain brown day dress, but only out of respect for Elizabeth and Montague. Fashion was of no interest to her whatever; besides, she had wanted to take the opportunity of being alone for an hour or so to read through the latest pamphlets the Women's Social and Political Union was preparing for publication, and come up with some ideas of her own.

The WSPU was the greatest passion in Julia's life, and had been for the last year, since she'd been introduced to it by her good friend Lettice Winterton, who had become an activist for the cause. It had chimed with her at once. Why should women be treated as second-class citizens, chattels almost, unable to inherit, not allowed to manage their own affairs, and denied the vote? It struck her as horribly unfair that every penny piece of the family's assets would go to Raymond, two years younger than her and not nearly as capable, and that women could have no say whatever in electing the Members of Parliament who were the only ones who could bring about a change in such a state of affairs. Julia had enthusiastically thrown herself into the cause, even though she knew it horrified her mother. She had begun selling rosettes, badges and jewellery to help raise funds, and distributing tracts she had written herself to raise awareness and garner support wherever and whenever she could. But buried in the heart of rural Wiltshire, she had been cut off from the main pockets of action she longed to be a part of.

She had managed to take a trip to London back in June to join a deputation to the House of Commons along with Letty, as Lettice was known to her friends, and had been lucky to escape arrest when things had turned nasty – several women, Lettice included, had served time in Holloway as a result, and after their release, at a ceremony when Mrs Pankhurst herself was awarding the medals for their part in the protest, two of them had been rearrested for assaults on wardresses during their time in prison. But it had only served to make her more eager to be a part of the real action; prison, hunger strikes and the enforced feeding that went with it, awful though the prospect was, didn't deter her at all. She hoped it wouldn't happen to her, but if it did, well, she would just have to put up with it. It would be worth it, just as long as it furthered the cause and spread the word, and Julia had wished with all her heart that she could do more.

Now, however, the fire that destroyed their home had given her the chance she had longed for. Letty was back in Bristol, helping Annie Kenney, the

WSPU organiser for the west of England, and Bristol, a hotbed of activity, was within reach of Fairley Hall. She could easily catch a train there from either High Compton or Hillsbridge without having to plead with Raymond to take her in his motor, as she did when she was at home in Wiltshire and which he all too often refused to do. That had happened on the night when Winston Churchill, a Liberal MP and President of the Board of Trade, had spoken at the Colston Hall the previous November. Windows had been broken all over town, and one suffragette had even been arrested on a tram, from the top of which she had been hurling stones at the glass entrance to the Colston Hall. Julia bitterly regretted missing all the excitement. But now Churchill's crony, Mr Augustine Birrell, every bit as staunch an opponent of women's rights as Churchill, and a fellow member of Mr Asquith's cabinet, was coming to the self-same hall, and there was sure to be fun and games on that night too. Julia had arranged to go and stay with Letty so as to be there, and in fact was due to leave tomorrow. The thought of being part of the action was an exciting one, and she was really looking forward to spending time with Letty too.

As Raymond came into the room, Julia looked up from her paperwork, a little annoyed by the interruption. But she could see from the clock on the mantelshelf that she would have to make a move soon anyway, and she was only surprised that Raymond had been out until this hour.

'Where on earth have you been?' she asked.

'You know very well – I took Christina and her

83

maid for a spin in my motor.'

He sounded testy; in one of his sour moods, Julia thought.

'But why until this time?' Julia asked. 'It's almost dark. And what has happened to your face?'

Raymond's hand flew protectively to his cheek.

'I was lifting the bonnet to check the water and banged it on the blinking thing.'

'Hmm. It looks to me more as if someone has slapped you.' Julia fixed him with a straight stare. She had few illusions, about her brother, and sometimes despaired of him. 'I hope it's not the result of inappropriate behaviour on your part. I need hardly remind you that Uncle Montague would take a very dim view of such a thing.'

Raymond huffed crossly and threw himself down in the brocaded armchair opposite her.

Julia set down the pamphlets she had been reading on the occasional table, capped her pen and pushed it into the pocket of her dress.

'You do know that I'm going to Bristol tomorrow, to stay with Letty for a few days, don't you?' she said, changing the subject.

'Lettice Winterton?' Raymond chuckled sarcastically. 'You have a nerve lecturing me when you're associating with women like her! Wasn't she in prison the last I heard?'

It was Julia's turn to refuse to rise to the bait.

'Only for a few days. She has her freedom again, and she's back in Bristol.' She stood up, determined not to give Raymond any ammunition with which he could worry her mother or cause trouble with Sir Montague. He was fiercely opposed to women's suffrage, she knew. 'Please don't stir things up, Raymond. And in return I'll keep quiet about how you came by that bruised cheek. In fact ... perhaps it would be a good idea if you came to my room with me and I'll put some powder on it – that should calm it down and make it less obvious.'

'Powder? Whatever next?' Raymond scoffed. But he really didn't want the others remarking on it, and in the dim light of the dining room, a flick of powder might well disguise it entirely.

How dare that little upstart of a maid do something like that to him! But he had to admit, it made her all the more attractive.

A servant with spirit and a pretty girl who hung on his every word... He was spoiled for choice. Perhaps being here at Fairley Hall wouldn't be so bad after all.

His bad humour lifting a little, Raymond followed his sister upstairs.

Chapter Six

May was just crossing the track with her washing basket clutched to her chest when Dolly Oglethorpe came by, on her way back from the shops judging by the look of the laden bag on her arm.

'Is it going to dry, do you think?' She sounded doubtful.

'I don't know, but at least it'll harden a bit. There's quite a breeze going and I'm fed up of the sight of the clothes horse in front of the fire.'

'You can say that again. It seems to be raining all the time lately.' Dolly shifted the shopping bag from one arm to the other, sighing.

'You look a bit done up,' May said.

Dolly huffed resignedly.

'It's that walk back from town. It seems to get longer every year. But then I suppose that's what we must expect now, May. We're not getting any younger, either of us.'

'Why don't you come in and have a cup of tea?' May suggested, not very hopeful that Dolly would agree. They used to be in and out of one another's houses all the time, but since Charlie had brought that woman home with him, it was almost as if Dolly was avoiding her, and she missed the company. Besides, she was bursting with curiosity, not least because she was all too well aware of Edie's feelings for Charlie, even if she did think they were rather misplaced, and she was eager to boast about Edie's promotion to lady's maid, too.

To her surprise, Dolly nodded. 'Do you know, I think I will.'

'Come on then. The kettle's on the hob. You know me.'

'I should do!'

They went into the kitchen. Dolly put down her bag of groceries and sat herself at the table, undoing the buttons of her coat.

'Take it off, why don't you?' May suggested, busying herself with the teapot.

'I didn't ought to stop long.' But she slipped out of the coat anyway, draping it over the back of the chair.

'I haven't told you about the good lift-up our

Edie's had, have I?' May said as she set out the cups.

'No – what's that then?'

May told her.

'Well, I'm pleased for her,' Dolly said when she'd finished. 'She's a good girl, your Edie. She deserves it.'

'I think so, but then I would – I'm her mother.' May fetched the biscuit tin and put it on the table – no cake today; she hadn't yet got around to baking.

'No, she is,' Dolly said. 'She's settled herself down nicely. I only wish I could say the same about our Charlie.'

She sounded regretful, but May snatched at the chance.

'I bet you wish he'd stayed around here, Dolly. It would break my heart if Edie or our Ted was to go off to London. I miss them bad enough as it is even though they're both still within walking distance. Still there, is he? Only he did go to Margate for a bit, didn't he?'

Dolly shook her head despairingly.

'It's a job keeping up with him, May. But at least he does make sure to come home regular like, though whether he'll keep that up now, I couldn't say. You know the old saying – "A son's a son till he takes a wife, a daughter's a daughter all of her life."'

May very nearly dropped the teapot in her surprise.

'Your Charlie's got married?'

'No, worse luck. He worries the life out of me the way he carries on. I wish he'd made a go of it

87

with your Edie, and that's the truth. No, he's not married, but...' She broke off, staring down at her teacup and seeming to almost sag for a moment, not just her shoulders, but also her triple chins concertinaing on to her chest and the pouches of her plump cheeks sinking in the same direction.

Then, with an effort, she pulled herself together, wiping her mouth and nose with the back of her hand and sitting up straight Once more. 'You don't want to hear my troubles.'

'Dolly, you know anything you say won't go any further...'

'I know that, but I'd rather try and forget about them for five minutes. Let's change the subject. I heard a bit of news in town today that will interest you.'

'What's that, then?' May asked, trying to hide her disappointment.

'Father O'Brien is retiring, or so they say. But perhaps you already know that. You're Catholic, aren't you?'

'Yes, but I don't often go to church,' May confessed. 'And no, I hadn't heard, but I can't say I'm surprised. He's getting on now, and he's riddled with arthritis. You should see his hands! He had a dickens of a job to hold a wafer, let alone the cup, the last time I did go. I thought he was going to drop it when he was giving me the wine. I was all ready to try to get out of the way. I didn't want it all over my Sunday best.'

'I should think not!'

'Who's taking over from him, I wonder?'

'I couldn't really say. I wasn't taking that much notice seeing as I'm not a Catholic. Some young monk from the abbey, I think. Father O'Brien will be missed, I expect. He's been the priest here for donkey's years, hasn't he?'

'That's true enough. He married me and Wesley, and that'll be twenty-five years ago come next April. Where does the time go?'

They chatted for a while about inconsequential things until at last Dolly got up, slipping her coat on again but not bothering to button it. 'Well, it's time I was going. Thanks for the tea, May. You must come in to me next time.'

'I'll do that.'

May saw her to the door. The rain had started again, a thick drizzle blown on the wind.

'Oh darn it! I'll have to get that washing in...' She dashed back inside for the clothes basket. The pillowcases and underwear that she'd hung out not half an hour earlier, had hardly dried at all – hardly surprising in such a short time with no sun to warm them. May wished she hadn't bothered. But if she hadn't hung the washing out she wouldn't have met Dolly, and the awkwardness between them might have gone on for weeks, since with winter coming neighbours no longer sat outside their back doors of an evening, or at any other time, come to that. She'd missed their easy-going friendship; the days could drag without somebody to chat to now that the children were grown up and flown the nest.

She wished she could have found out a bit more about what was going on with Charlie. Whatever it was was clearly upsetting Dolly, and May guessed that was the reason she had been avoiding her. But now that the ice had been broken, perhaps Dolly would be a bit more forthcoming next time they had a cup of tea together.

The news about Father O'Brien had been worth hearing, though. May knew that her reluctance to go to church was because she felt awkward with the old priest. He was a good man, gentle, kind, non-judgemental. But he knew too much about her, far too much, for her comfort, and there had been plenty of times when May had wished she'd never made that confession to him. He'd never betray the confidence, of course; the sanctity of the confessional was absolute. But he knew, and that was enough. She could never forget the shame of what she'd done, never had, never would, and she couldn't imagine he'd forgotten either, no matter how many confessions he'd heard. She'd missed going to Mass, it was true, but she'd come to the point where she just couldn't face him.

If he was retiring, though... A fresh start with a clean slate and a priest who knew none of her secrets would be just the ticket. She had nothing more shameful to confess now than her pride in her children and perhaps a few unworthy thoughts about people like Hester Dallimore, she thought, smiling to herself. Yes, when the new priest took over, she might well start going to church again. Her faith had always meant a lot to her, and the thought was a comforting one.

Father Michael Connolly crossed himself for a final time and rose from his knees to stand for a moment, head bowed, before the altar in the lady chapel. Morning sunshine slanted in through the stained-glass window, throwing a warm golden path all the way to the top of the two stone steps where he had knelt, though the statue of the Blessed Virgin was still in the shadow of the thick stone walls.

Father Connolly loved the lady chapel, so much lighter and brighter than the main body of the abbey – vast and echoing and dark, with the high altar set in its centre and only the glow of a few votive candles here and there to lighten the gloom. It was to the lady chapel that he invariably came to pray when something was bothering him, and usually he left feeling as if a burden had been lifted from his shoulders.

But not today. The weight of his new appointment still rested heavy on his heart... 'Lord Jesus Christ, grant me the wisdom, understanding and humility to minister to my flock as you would have me,' he had prayed. But no warmth had spread through his veins, no enlightenment filled his heart. He felt no more ready to take on the duties of a parish priest than he had when the abbot had summoned him and told him that he had been chosen to replace Father O'Brien, who was too infirm now to carry out the role, riddled as he was with arthritis. He was showing signs of senility, too, his memory failing him, and he could become quite confused at times. A priest who forgot an appointment with a parishioner, who sometimes stumbled over the order of a service he'd been taking for so many years that it should have come automatically, clearly had to be relieved of his duties.

But why me? Father Connolly had asked himself over and over again, just as he had asked the abbot.

'Young blood will be good for the parish,' the abbot had replied. 'You will bring a vigour and freshness to the task that has been sadly lacking of late. You are a good man, Michael, and you've learned a great deal since you first joined the order. You are still young, I grant you, but I am confident you will make a good parish priest.'

Michael wished he shared the abbot's confidence. Wasn't this what he'd aspired to for almost as long as he could remember? He'd attended a boarding school run by the Church for the training of future priests, and then entered holy orders. He was twenty-eight years old now; he should be eager to take this step, flattered to have been chosen. Yet he was daunted by the enormity of what the job entailed, and his doubts refused to go away.

Lost in thought, Michael didn't hear the great oak door at the rear of the abbey open, nor the soft sandalled footsteps on the flagged floor until they almost reached him.

'Michael! I thought I'd find you here.' It was Father O'Brien. He touched the younger man's sleeve. 'You're troubled, I know. Would it help to talk?' His creased old face was kindly, his faded eyes concerned. Goodness shone out of them, but it only served to make Michael feel more unworthy.

'I can't do it, Francis,' he said.

Father O'Brien shook his head sadly. 'Oh Michael, I thought there was something like that going on in that head of yours. It's only natural, so it is. But you'll be fine, just see if you're not.'

'There's no way I'm fit to replace you.'

Father O'Brien sighed. 'You're wrong there, Michael. Shall we sit down? Standing for too long doesn't suit me these days. My poor old knees...' Even as he spoke, he tottered a little, and Michael took his arm, helping him towards a pew.

'Ah, that's better, so it is.' But he was massaging his legs through the thick cloth of his soutane, his gnarled fingers making a soft scratching sound. 'Now tell me, why is it you think you're not up to the job?'

Michael rubbed his angular jaw. 'I don't think I'm ready.'

'In what way?'

'In any way! I can take a service, of course, but what can I say week after week in my address?'

Father O'Brien smiled slightly. 'Believe me, you'll think of something.'

'Maybe. But the thing that really concerns me is ministering to the parishioners on a day-to-day basis. How qualified am I to advise young couples about to marry? I only know a celibate life. How will I cope with offering sympathy and encouragement to the sick, and comfort to the bereaved? All I have to give them is prayer and quotations from the Holy Bible. I suppose I'd find the words to try to restore faith to folk who are wavering, but what of the rest of it? When they come to me with their problems and ask for help, what advice will I be able to give them? I know nothing of the world beyond these walls. I have no experience to draw on.'

Father O'Brien patted Michael's hand.

'There's nothing unusual in that. But as you so

rightly say, the scriptures are there to guide you, and prayer will point you in the right direction. Listen humbly, Michael, and the answer will be there – a voice speaking in your head, an urge in your heart. For the most part, they won't let you down.'

'My instinct at this moment is to ask the abbot to appoint someone else.'

'Then this is one of the instances where your instincts are wrong. You will make a fine parish priest.'

Michael shook his head. 'It's easy for you to say that.'

'It's what was said to me forty years ago.' The old priest smiled faintly. 'Oh yes, when I was given my first ministry I felt just as you are feeling now. Unworthy ... and frightened.'

Michael's eyes, the colour of ripe chestnuts, narrowed in disbelief.

'You?'

'Me. It's a daunting prospect, isn't it? And I won't deny there have been difficult situations over the years that have tested me sorely, but in the end all you can do is your best. There are burdens to bear alone, too. You will become privy to secrets you'd prefer not to know, and can never share. But strength and guidance will come to you through the power of prayer. Never doubt that and your faith will carry you through. God has chosen you for this task, Michael. He will not forsake you.'

Michael was silent, rasping a hand over his chiselled jaw.

'And you know I am always here if there's anything you need to talk over,' Father O'Brien added. 'At least, as long as the good Lord spares me.'

'You think I should take the appointment, then?' Michael said at last.

'I have no doubt about that. And now perhaps we should be getting back to our quarters. We'll be missed, and questions will be asked. We don't want that, do we?'

Michael smiled faintly. 'No, we don't. But thank you, Francis. I came here to pray for help, and you've answered my prayer.'

'I'm glad.'

The two men rose, the one young, fit and strong, the other old and frail. Michael took Father O'Brien's arm, supporting him over the flagged stone floor, past the shrines that stood in alcoves the length of the aisle, and out through the porch. As they emerged from the gloom of the abbey, the sun shone warm on the path through the broad expanse of grass before them, and for the first time in days Michael felt that the load on his heart had lightened.

His prayers had indeed been answered. He only hoped they would be answered again and again as he sought to be a good parish priest in the ministry he now knew he must accept.

'Do you think you could help me with something, Edith?' For once in her life, Christina sounded serious.

Edie had been helping her get ready for bed. Her underwear was stacked neatly, her dress, which needed a stitch or two in the hem, hung on the back of the door ready for Edie to take downstairs and do the necessary repairs, and her hair had been brushed and twisted into a fat plait that fell over the shoulder of her nightgown. This was usually a time of day when she chattered animatedly, but tonight she had been uncharacteristically solemn, and now she was looking at Edie through the thick fringe of lashes that might almost have belonged to a china doll, lip caught between small pearly teeth.

Edie's heart sank a little. She hoped that whatever Christina was going to ask her had nothing to do with Raymond. Since that day on the Mendips he had made no further advances towards her, thank goodness, but she'd noticed that he seemed to be turning on the charm with Christina. And she, predictably, was lapping it up. If he should try to become overfamiliar with her, Edie didn't think Christina would rebuff him. She idolised the smarmy creature; to her he was a romantic and exciting hero, and Edie was afraid she would be far too naive to recognise improper advances until it was too late. But what could she do about it beyond slipping in a few tactful words of advice and keeping an eye on Christina when she could?

'What's that, miss?' she asked, hoping very much that the worst hadn't already happened, or that Christina wasn't going to ask her to help her meet Raymond in secret. She wouldn't do anything of the sort, of course, but a refusal was bound to upset Christina.

She was relieved then, as well as surprised, to discover that the subject Christina wanted to raise had nothing whatever to do with Raymond.

'You know that Mama is not really my mama,

don't you? That I was found in the porch of the Catholic church when I was just a few hours old?'

'I had heard, yes,' Edie said, relieved that the request didn't have anything to do with Raymond, but uncomfortable with the subject all the same.

She'd only learned of Christina's past history since coming to work at Fairley Hall. She had known she was Lady Elizabeth's adopted daughter, but that was all. It had occurred to her to wonder if that was a subterfuge and Christina was really Lady Elizabeth's illegitimate child. It would explain why Lady Elizabeth had never married – no gentleman would want what he would think of as soiled goods – but as far as Edie was concerned, it added a dark romance to her employer. Perhaps there was a tragedy in Lady Elizabeth's past, a fiancé who had died, or maybe she had been seduced and abandoned by a faithless lover.

Her fantasies hadn't lasted long, though, and predictably it was Nellie Saunders who had set her straight. Miss Christina was a foundling. She'd been left in the porch of the church one Christmas Eve. That, however, was about all she had been able to learn before Mrs Parker intervened, telling them that if they wanted to keep their jobs, they'd refrain from discussing the Fairley family's private business. Edie had never forgotten how stern she had looked when she said it. Later she had taken Edie aside and explained more kindly that it wouldn't do for Lady Elizabeth to overhear them talking about such sensitive matters and Edie would do well to forget all about it. If anything, that had done even more to arouse Edie's curiosity, and she had asked her mother about it when

97

she next went home, thinking that since it was their church where Christina had been found, May must have heard about it at the time. But to her disappointment, May had brushed her questions aside.

'Why in the world are you asking about that?' she'd said, quite snappily. 'It's ancient history.'

'I'm curious, that's all. It must have caused an awful upset.'

'I suppose so, but it was nothing to do with me. You and Ted were small. I had quite enough to be getting on with without worrying my head about that.'

'But–'

'Oh for goodness' sake, our Edie, can't we change the subject?' May had bustled away, busying herself with laying the table for dinner, and Edie could get no more out of her.

For a while, Edie had puzzled as to why May seemed not to want to talk about something that must have caused a tremendous stir at the time, especially amongst the congregation of the Catholic church. Though she seldom went to Mass now, Edie thought May had once been quite devout; certainly she had ensured the children attended church regularly when they were young, and Edie would have expected that she would have been at Midnight Mass the night the baby had been found. But then May had never been one to engage in gossip, and it did occur to Edie to wonder if perhaps she knew more than she was saying; maybe even knew the identity of the poor desperate woman who had abandoned her baby and was trying to protect her.

As time went by, however, Edie had more or less forgotten about the mystery surrounding Christina, but now it all came flooding back, along with a clear memory of Mrs Parker's warning of instant dismissal for any servant caught speculating about the girl's origins. But how could she avoid the subject when it was Christina herself who had raised it, and was now regarding her with a serious expression so unlike her usual demeanour?

'I thought you'd know about it,' Christina said solemnly. 'Mama told me long ago that I was a foundling – isn't that a romantic word? – but that I was very special because she had chosen me to be her very own daughter. But of course I'm not. Not her daughter, not really. And I do so very much want to know who I am and where I came from. And I thought you were just the person to help me find out.'

'Oh miss...' Edie really didn't know what to say. This was dangerous ground. 'It's your mama you should be talking to about this.'

'Don't you think I've tried?' Christina pouted. 'If I ask her about it she just says it doesn't matter who I was. That I'm a Fairley now, and her daughter, and that is all there is to it. If she does know anything, she won't share it with me. That's why I'm asking you to help me.'

'I wouldn't know where to begin!' Edie said.

'You know lots of people and you can ask questions. I would have thought you of all people might be able to help me find out the truth. If you don't know it already.'

'Why would you think I knew anything?' Edie asked, puzzled.

99

'Well, because it was your mother who found me, of course,' Christina said impatiently.

'What?' Edie stared at her, flabbergasted.

'Don't pretend you didn't know.'

'But I didn't... I had no idea...' Edie was lost for words. 'Are you sure?'

'It's what Mama told me. "Edith's mother was very kind to you." That's what she said.'

'Really, Miss Christina, this is the first I've heard of it. I think you must have got it wrong.'

'I haven't got it wrong,' Christina insisted. 'If you don't believe me, ask her.'

'Don't worry, I will!' But Edie still thought Christina must have got hold of the wrong end of the stick somehow. Surely if May had been the one to find the baby in the church porch, the story would have become family lore, repeated many times over the years. And if it were true, why hadn't her mother mentioned it when she'd asked about Christina rather than just fobbing her off?

'And while you're about it, ask her if she has any idea who I might really be,' Christina went on. 'She may have seen the person who left me there, or even if she didn't, she might have a good idea who it was. And what about the priest who was taking the service that night? He might know something.'

'I don't often go to church,' Edie said, stalling.

'But you could, couldn't you? Oh Edith, please say you'll help me. I've no way of learning anything myself. I'm never allowed to go anywhere without a chaperone. I never even went to school. Mama taught me herself. But you know lots of people. Oh please at least say you'll try...'

100

She broke off at the sound of footsteps on the landing, pressing her fingers to her lips in a conspiratorial gesture.

The door opened and Beauty came dashing in, followed by Lady Elizabeth. Edie's face flamed scarlet, terrified that her employer might have heard something of the conversation. But Lady Elizabeth was her usual serene self, though she did look a little tired.

'What a day! I've spent most of it consoling dear Beatrice – I think the reality of what has happened has just caught up with her.'

'Poor Mrs Fairley,' Edie said, trying to put the conversation with Christina out of her mind. 'It must be awful for her.'

'She's worried that Horatio's things may have been destroyed. They should have been disposed of years ago, of course. Keeping them after all this time is quite morbid. But I couldn't tell Beatrice that, of course.'

Edie did not feel it was her place to comment, though privately she agreed with her employer. She knew that Mrs Rogers, a neighbour in the Ten Houses, had kept her son Frank's room untouched after he had been killed in the tragedy at Shepton Fields, a shrine to a boy who would never come home, and she'd always thought it quite creepy.

Christina, however, took the opposite view.

'Wouldn't you keep my things, Mama, if I were to die?' she asked, pouting. 'I wouldn't like to think you'd want to forget all about me.'

'Oh Christina, of course you wouldn't be forgotten!' Lady Elizabeth assured her. 'But you are

101

not going to die, so put such nonsense right out of your head.'

She turned to Edie.

'Will you take Beauty downstairs, Edith? She can be put to bed too. Beatrice has retired now, and I intend to do the same. Sir Montague and Mr Raymond are still talking in the drawing room, but they won't want Beauty running in and exciting Nero and Noble.'

'Yes, milady,' Edie said, but she was thinking that if Sir Montague and Raymond were talking business, it was likely to be a long session, which would mean a late night for the servants. They were expected to stay up until the last member of the household had retired, regardless of the early hour they had to be up again, and she was glad this no longer applied to her. Like Mrs Davey, Mrs Parker and Quilla Brimble, she could now go to bed when she had finished her duties. Though with her mind racing with what Christina had said, she thought it would be a very long time before she was able to go to sleep.

She picked up Beauty, feeling the little dog's heartbeat beneath her silky coat, said goodnight to Lady Elizabeth and Christina, and went downstairs.

Chapter Seven

Julia was relishing her few days' stay in Bristol with her good friend Lettice Winterton. For the first time she felt close to the heart of the action, one of the sisters of the WSPU, rather than just a bit player.

Lettice rented rooms on the top floor of a grand house in the Clifton district that was owned by a well-to-do supporter of women's suffrage. Her home was a hive of activity, with her fellow activists forever coming and going, and Julia met several prominent suffragettes who had been only names to her until now – Vera Holme, Emily Young and Florence Hill. Plans were made around the kitchen table, which was piled high with propaganda pamphlets, and the women often talked long into the night. There were meetings on the Downs, overlooking the deep gorge of the River Avon and Brunel's magnificent suspension bridge, though at this time of year there were none of the picnics that the members of the WSPU enjoyed during the balmy days of summer. Julia had even been to number 3, The Mall, where the Bristol branch of the society had been founded forty years earlier.

It was invigorating stuff, for here the members lived up to their motto, 'Deeds not words', and Julia wished she could stay for ever. The prospect of having to return to the frustrating loneliness of life as her mother's companion, with only brief periods of escape, almost suffocated her.

Today promised to be especially exciting as it was this evening that Augustine Birrell, Chief Secretary for Ireland, would be addressing a meeting of the League for the Taxation of Land Values at the Colston Hall. The sisterhood knew it wouldn't be possible for too many of them to get into the hall, so they had decided to hold a demonstration on the street outside, but one or two, whose faces were less well known, would actually attempt to infiltrate the meeting. One of these would be Sylvia Frost, a well-respected doctor's daughter who had only recently joined the movement; Julia, not being local, was the obvious choice for the second.

'Do nothing to draw attention to yourself,' Lettice instructed her.

'You mean we are not to interrupt the speaker?' Julia asked.

'Absolutely not. It's useful to have a couple of faces that aren't instantly recognised,' Lettice told her.

'But what's the point of us getting in if we can't make a protest?' Julia was a little disappointed. She'd seen herself leaping up and causing a disturbance when Mr Birrell was in full flow.

'There's something already planned.' Lettice touched a finger to her lips, then held it upright with a conspiratorial smile. 'We don't want anything to spoil the moment. Your role is to observe and report back.'

'What's going to happen?' Julia asked, thrilling with excitement, but Lettice would say no more.

'You'll find out,' she replied, with a Cheshire cat grin.

Julia could hardly wait. When at last the evening of the meeting arrived, she and Sylvia Frost, a tall, elegant and well-dressed woman in her late twenties, made their way into the centre of Bristol and approached the main entrance to the Colston Hall, which stood on a steeply inclined side street. The protesters were already gathered with their placards, but Sylvia and Julia ignored them as they had been told to do, and they in their turn ignored their two fellow conspirators.

Most of the crowd pouring in were men, and distinguished-looking men at that, and Julia's heart beat a tattoo, so afraid was she that they would be refused entry. But miraculously they were not challenged, and one of the doorkeepers actually tipped his hat to Sylvia, whom he had apparently recognised as being his physician's daughter.

Once inside, they took their places in a row of seats as close to the platform as they dared, but also on an aisle in case they needed to beat a hasty retreat. Neither woman knew what had been planned, but they guessed it was to be quite spectacular, and trouble might well follow.

To begin with, the meeting was nothing if not deadly dull. The taxation of land values was hardly a stimulating subject, and Julia gave up trying to follow the drift of what was being said. She even wondered if perhaps the WSPU were simply testing her and Sylvia's loyalty by having them attend a meeting guaranteed to send them to sleep. But when Mr Birrell himself rose and began to speak, a disembodied voice suddenly

105

rang out loud and clear.

'Votes for women!'

Mr Birrell paused, a look of puzzlement cross-ing his square-jawed face, then gathered himself and continued as if nothing had happened. But barely had he managed a full sentence when the cry came again.

'Votes for women!'

This time Birrell looked around him, from one side of the platform to the other, but the woman's voice seemed to be coming out of thin air.

A third time he tried to continue; a third time the voice rang out.

'Votes for women!'

A chuckle from someone in the audience was infectious, and within moments, a wave of hilarity was sweeping through the hall, along with boos and catcalls. Julia and Sylvia exchanged glances that were both delighted and amazed, their gloved hands pressed to their mouths to suppress their own laughter. The secret plan was seemingly working wonderfully well. Mr Birrell was now un-able to make himself heard above the uproar, and was looking furious as well as puzzled – where on earth were the cries coming from?

Several burly stewards were making for the front of the hall now, and moments later the puzzle was solved.

There was a pipe organ at the rear of the plat-form, which was used to accompany the singers at various choral events. Now from deep inside it emerged a slight figure, dishevelled but triumph-ant.

'It's Vera Holme!' gasped Sylvia.

'But how...?'

'She's a violinist and a singer. She'd know the organ would provide her with a hiding place. But she must have slipped in hours ago, when there was no one about, or she'd never have been able to get away with it. Oh, she's a live wire and no mistake!'

The stewards had reached Vera now and were bundling her off stage. She was struggling violently, but still shouting her slogan at the top of her voice.

'Come on!' Sylvia gripped Julia's hand.

Julia thought she was suggesting they make a hasty exit, but that wasn't what Sylvia meant at all. Instead she was scrambling up on to her seat, punching the air and shouting herself. 'Votes for women!'

For just a moment Julia remained where she was, as if paralysed by the shock of it, and mindful of Lettice's instruction that they should do nothing to draw attention to themselves. But now Sylvia had well and truly given the game away. Without a doubt they would both be thrown out of the hall, if not arrested, and Julia thought she might as well be hung for a sheep as a lamb. Her heart racing, she too clambered up on to her seat.

'Votes for women!' she cried, exultant.

Their voices were almost lost in the general hubbub, but there was no mistaking them for what they were: two more suffragettes stirring up trouble. Several more stewards emerged from nowhere, called in perhaps from outside, where they had been policing the main group of protesters with their placards and banners. As they reached the two women, lunging angrily at them, Julia lost her balance and came crashing down in an ignominious heap. Almost immediately she was hauled to her feet and half dragged into the aisle.

Her ankle throbbed painfully – she had twisted it when she fell – and she felt as if her arms were being wrenched out of their sockets, but she didn't care. She was high on a mixture of adrenalin and triumph. Even when she was bundled, along with Sylvia and Vera Holme, into a Black Maria and taken to the nearby Bridewell police station, she had no regret for what she had done. She'd earned her stripes now, she thought, and really was an activist for the cause.

She was undeniably relieved, however, to find herself let off with a caution – simply shouting slogans apparently didn't warrant her occupying a cell on a busy night – and she and Sylvia were able to meet up with their fellow members at the home of Emily Young to review the evening's work.

'A roaring success!' Emily declared with satisfaction. 'It worked like a dream.'

'You should have seen Birrell's face!' Sylvia laughed. 'I think he thought he'd met with divine judgement.'

Lettice, however, was more critical. 'You weren't supposed to reveal yourselves. Now that the police know you belong to us, you won't be able to go undercover again.'

'We just couldn't resist it,' Julia said, hoping her action hadn't jeopardised a friendship that was very precious to her.

'You need to learn to obey orders,' Lettice said tartly. Then her voice softened, and she squeezed

Julia's hand. 'I'm proud of you, though. It took courage to do what you did, just the two of you, surrounded by that baying crowd. You are one of us now.'

Julia felt her cheeks growing hot, and the whole of her body was suffused by a rosy glow. She smiled at Lettice, noticed for the first time how fiery her hair was with the gas light gleaming on it, how blue her eyes.

'I'm so glad,' she whispered. And thought that in the whole of her sheltered life, she had never felt happier.

Whilst Julia was enjoying herself enormously, Raymond certainly was not. Though at first he'd been quite taken by the idea that one day he would inherit the Fairley estate, and rather enjoyed visiting the pit heads and the estate farms, where he was treated with due respect, he soon developed a hearty resentment of the hours he was forced to spend in the company of curmudgeonly Sir Montague, and was frustrated by the sheer volume of knowledge he was supposed to be acquiring, courtesy of Clement Firkin, the agent, and Edward Johnson, the estate manager. They were responsible for the day-to-day running of the estate and the mines, but Sir Montague had always liked to keep his finger on the pulse, and he intended that Raymond should carry on the tradition.

Personally, Raymond could not see the point of this. If you kept a dog, why bother barking yourself? He could think of many more pleasant ways to spend his days than poring over leather-bound diaries and ledgers. The dust that flew when the pages were opened made him sneeze, and the columns of figures in the account books numbed his brain.

Not, he sometimes thought, that he had much of a brain to numb. He'd never been good with academic subjects, careless with spelling and grammar in English classes, and as for maths ... he could never be bothered learning geometric theorems, puzzling out algebra, or even double-checking his answers in straightforward arithmetic, and the masters at the public school he'd attended had despaired of him. But their lectures had been water off a duck's back. Raymond had excelled at sport: he still held the record for the hundred- and two-hundred-yard races, and had been a valued member of both the cricket and rugby teams, and that had been enough, along with his easy-going personality and devilish streak, to make him popular, all he had really cared about.

This, though, was worse than being back at school, especially since he knew he needed to impress Sir Montague. He didn't suppose he could actually be disinherited – since Sir Montague had no sons of his own, he was the closest male in line for the estate and the title. But he wasn't sure whether things could be tied up in trusts if he was deemed to be incapable of running the estate, and he was anxious not to appear thick in front of the professional managers who might one day be working for him.

Another annoyance was that Sir Montague expected him to take an active role in politics. The general election at the beginning of the year had been a close-run thing, and backed up by the Irish parliamentary party, the Liberal leader, Mr Asquith, had formed a government. But Sir Montague was convinced it couldn't last and there would be another election before the year was out, and was doing all he could to support the Conservative Party. Raymond had not the slightest interest in who was governing the country, and hated being dragged into long and tedious meetings where the local party members waffled on for hours about their strategies and decried both the Liberals and the new and emerging party known as Labour, which was being backed, as far as he could make out, by most of the workforce of Sir Montague's pits.

Perhaps worst of all as far as Raymond was concerned was the lack of female company. There were plenty of pretty girls in his circle at home in Wiltshire who fell over one another in competing for his attentions – he was, after all, good-looking and athletic, and his beloved Vauxhall had made him even more attractive to them. But here in High Compton he met none. Only men worked in the pits and on the farms – though their wives and daughters laboured in the dairies and might help out with the milking or even the lambing when the spring came, they were never out and about on the land when Raymond and Edward Johnson came to call, and even if they had been, it would have been a brief flirtation only, for Raymond considered such women far beneath him.

A maid, of course, was a different matter. What were maids for if not the pleasure of their masters? But the only one amongst them he had

111

given a second glance to – Edith – had put him firmly in his place, and of the others, one was too old, one too fat, and the other too thin and a bit simple as well. That left only his cousin Christina.

Christina was rather childish, he thought, but she was very pretty, and she had a habit of hanging on his every word, which flattered his ego. Yes, perhaps there was some fun to be had with Christina. If he didn't find a distraction soon, he thought he would go quite mad with boredom.

'I suppose there's nothing for it, I must be brave.' Beatrice mustered a tiny smile, gazing at her reflection in the dressing table mirror as Quilla fastened her necklace, but her chin was wobbling and her china-blue eyes filling with tears.

'You *are* brave, madam,' Quilla said, the apparent sympathy in her tone belying the resentment and scorn she felt for the woman. At home in Wiltshire, Beatrice didn't have a lady's maid; why did Lady Elizabeth think she needed help with dressing here at Fairley Hall? She was nothing but a pathetic parasite, and that son of hers was an arrogant upstart, swanning around as if he already owned the place when he had no right ... no right at all. It made her blood boil.

'Do you really think so?' Those tear-filled eyes met Quilla's in the mirror. 'I suppose I must be to survive all my misfortunes. Losing my dear husband at such a young age, and now my home ... really, it's more than one woman should have to endure.'

'I'm sure it won't be long before your house is put to rights and you'll be able to go home again,'

Quilla said, adjusting the necklace so that it sat straight. 'And you still have your son and daughter. They must be a comfort to you.'

'Oh, they are. Of course. Much as I would love to see Julia settled in a happy marriage, I'd miss her company dreadfully. Why, now, with her away in Bristol, I feel quite like a lost soul.'

'I'm sure you do, madam.'

'And Raymond ... the thought of going home without him when my house is eventually habitable again is quite unbearable. He's been everything to me since his poor dear father left us in such tragic circumstances, and I don't know what I would have done without him. I should be grateful, I know, that his future is now assured, and I dare say when he inherits he will bring me here to live with him. But that day is a long way off. Montague is in rude health...' She broke off. 'Please don't think I am wishing him dead. Of course that is not the case. It's just that I can't stand to think of the long years with Raymond missing from my home and my life.'

'That's quite understandable, madam.' Though she was burning with the all-too-familiar fury at the unfairness of the laws of inheritance, Quilla managed to sound sympathetic.

'It is, isn't it? If you had a son, Quilla, you would know exactly how I feel.' Her eyes misted again.

She adored Raymond, and always had. She loved Julia too, of course, but that was quite different. Julia was a woman, and there was no mystery to another woman. But Raymond ... from the moment she had given birth to him she had

113

felt an overwhelming adoration. She had been able to refuse him nothing. Horatio had complained that she was spoiling the boy, but she'd been unrepentant, and if Horatio disciplined him, Raymond had known exactly where to come for comfort and support. She'd cradle him in her arms and tell him that everything would be all right, Mama would ensure it.

Raymond was only just fourteen when Horatio died in the riding accident, and overnight their relationship had taken on a new dimension.

'You are the man of the house now, my dearest,' Beatrice had said, holding him in her arms and weeping into his mop of silky fair hair. 'It's a terrible burden for one so young, but you will look after us, I know. You are your father's son through and through.'

It was true that in many ways Raymond did take after Horatio, and not only in looks. He had the same fearless, devil-may-care attitude to life, a love of fast horses and fast women. But he was also petulant, spoilt and lazy, and though these traits had probably been exacerbated by Beatrice's over-indulgence of his every whim, she refused to acknowledge them, giving him the same unquestioning adoration she always had whilst worrying a little that one day his recklessness would bring about an accident of the kind that had claimed his father.

Now she dabbed delicately at her eyes with a lace-edged handkerchief, then applied a generous quantity of the violet perfume she favoured behind her ears, on her neck and on her wrists.

'Would you very much mind tidying up for me,

114

Quilla?' she said, changing the subject. 'Dinner will be served shortly and I would like the chance to speak to Raymond and find out how his day has been before we all gather.'

'Of course, madam.'

Once again Quilla hid her true feelings beneath a tone of deference. But as she hung Beatrice's day dress in the wardrobe and rolled discarded stockings into a ball to be put in the drawer, she was still seething with indignation and helpless rage.

She crossed to the dressing table, tidying hairpins into a pot and wiping up a dusting of face powder. Amidst the clutter was a small silver box that she recognised immediately as the snuff box that had belonged to Beatrice's late husband. Raymond and Julia had brought it back from their house along with a few other valuables when they had gone to assess the damage, and ever since, Beatrice had carried it around with her, cradled between her hands as if she couldn't bear to let it go. 'It reminds me so of dear Horatio,' Quilla had heard her say to Lady Elizabeth. 'I used to complain to him about using snuff, such an unpleasant habit, I thought. But now ... oh, I wish I had been less judgemental. It was him, you see. If this snuff box had been lost in the fire, or looted by scavengers, it would have broken my heart.'

Beatrice didn't take the box to dinner with her, though – it would not have been polite to put it on the table and upset the carefully laid place settings. Quilla's mouth twisted scornfully as she moved it to one side, then a spiteful thought occurred to her. If she couldn't find the box, Beatrice would be distraught. Quilla wouldn't leave

115

herself vulnerable to a charge of theft by taking it, but she could hide it somewhere Beatrice was unlikely to find it easily. She opened Beatrice's underwear drawer and stuffed the box between some of the violet-scented garments. Since she now had the services of a lady's maid, Beatrice was unlikely to come across it by accident, but when she did eventually find it, she would assume she'd absent-mindedly put it there herself. Or Quilla could pretend to find it and earn Beatrice's undying gratitude.

A glow of malicious satisfaction went some way to mitigating Quilla's burning anger and resentment as she finished tidying the room and went back downstairs.

The plan worked perfectly. When Beatrice was unable to find her precious keepsake, she was beside herself, and the entire household was charged with searching for it. But of course it was nowhere to be found, and eventually Sir Montague lost patience.

'Go to bed and forget about it, Beatrice,' he said grumpily. 'The wretched thing will turn up, it's bound to.'

'I couldn't sleep while it's lost,' Beatrice wailed.

'Darling, you must try.' Lady Elizabeth was more sympathetic, but even she was growing tired of the house being turned upside down. 'Montague is right. It'll turn up tomorrow, you'll see. Let Quilla help you get ready for bed and I'll have a nice cup of warm milk sent up for you. Warm milk is wonderful for helping one to sleep.'

Beatrice could hardly argue with her hosts, but

she wept quietly as Quilla braided her hair and helped her into her nightgown. The warm milk arrived and was set on the bedside table, then Quilla set about hanging Beatrice's dress in the wardrobe and folding her underthings. It was then perfectly natural that she should open the drawer where she had concealed the snuff box, and a moment later she held it triumphantly aloft.

'Look what I've found, madam!'

'Oh! Oh!' Beatrice actually ran across the room, taking the box from Quilla and cradling it against her heart. 'Thanks be to God!'

'You see, madam? You needn't have got yourself in such a state. It was here all the time.'

'But how did it come to be in the drawer?' Beatrice puzzled.

'It must have fallen in, madam.'

'I don't understand...'

'Don't worry your head about it any more,' Quilla said. 'You've got it back, that's all that matters, isn't it?'

'Yes. Yes, it is. I shall be more careful in future. If I'd lost it ... oh...' Her voice trailed off, then she looked up at the maid, her eyes brimming with tears of relief and gratitude.

'Thank you, Quilla. I see now why my cousin thinks you such a treasure.'

'Oh, I don't know about that, madam,' Quilla said. But as she left the room, a satisfied smirk replaced the look of modesty she had put on for Beatrice's benefit.

She'd enjoyed every moment of the stupid woman's distress. It had gone some way to assuaging her anger and resentment. But not far

117

enough. Not nearly far enough. The beginnings of a plan were beginning to take shape in her shrewd head. If Sir Montague thought he could treat her and hers as if they were unimportant, he had another think coming. Quilla was going to do her best to ensure that things worked out the way she felt so passionately they should.

'Why don't you stay a few days longer?' Lettice suggested, and Julia did not need asking twice.

'I'd love to!' she replied. 'But are you sure I'm not in the way?'

'Not a bit of it! You're an asset to the cause, and we can do with all the help we can get.'

It'd been another busy day preparing and distributing pamphlets, and not without its excitement. One of their number had thrown a stone through a window and been arrested, and some of the sisterhood, Julia included, had gathered outside the police station in Bridewell with their banners, clamouring unsuccessfully for her release. Now she and Letty lay side by side in Letty's narrow bed, tired out but too tightly wired for sleep.

'And you don't mind having to share your bed with me?'

'My dear, of course not! It's a pleasure to have you here.'

Letty fumbled for Julia's hand, and held it between hers on the slight mound of her stomach. Julia curled herself around the curve of her friend's hip, revelling in the warmth and happiness and unfamiliar sensations that suffused her.

Given the chance, she thought, she would stay here for ever.

Chapter Eight

'Have you been able to find out anything about my real mother?' Christina asked as Edie plaited her hair ready for bed.

'How could I have?' Edie tied a ribbon neatly around the fat braid and patted it into place. 'You know I haven't had a day off since you asked me to.'

'I thought perhaps you might have asked around below stairs.'

'I don't think that would be very wise,' Edie said firmly. 'You mustn't be so impatient, Miss Christina. Put it out of your mind now or you'll never sleep, and it's already long past your bedtime.'

'But I'm not in the least tired.'

She'd been saying that for the last hour, each time Elizabeth had urged her to go to bed, and Edie knew the reason why she had wanted to stay up later than usual. Raymond had gone to a meeting of the local Conservative Party with Sir Montague. It was the chauffeur's day off and Sir Montague had asked the younger man to take him in the Vauxhall – though what he'd think of Raymond's driving, Edie dreaded to think. They'd been expected back by ten at the latest, but the meeting must have dragged on – either that or Raymond had run the car off the road on the way home, which wouldn't surprise Edie. But that wasn't her concern. It was the interest Christina was taking in Raymond that worried her. And he, of course, was encouraging it.

'You might not feel tired now, but you certainly will in the morning,' she said sternly. 'And so will I. Even your mama has retired for the night.'

Christina sighed theatrically, but she did as she was bid, slipping down under the covers. Beauty, who had remained in the bedroom after Lady Elizabeth had come in to say goodnight, took the opportunity to hop up beside her mistress, and Edie huffed in exasperation.

'You know you're not allowed on the bed, Beauty!' she scolded.

'She just wants me to stroke her and give her a cuddle,' Christina pouted. 'I wish she could stay with me and not have to go downstairs at night.'

'Well she does,' Edie said firmly. She blew out the candles, leaving just a small night light burning on the dressing table, and scooped up Beauty. 'I should think she must need to go out to relieve herself, too. It was raining earlier, and you know what a dickens of a job it is to get her to go out in the rain. Now, goodnight, miss. And go straight to sleep,' she added, as if Christina were a child.

'Goodnight, Edith. Goodnight, Beauty,' Christina said dutifully, but she sounded regretful.

Edie pulled the door closed behind her and went along the landing to the servants' staircase. It led down to a passageway that skirted the kitchen and ended at the tradesman's entrance. On the other side of a cobbled yard were the outbuildings that had once been stabling for the horses but had now been converted into garaging for Sir Montague's Rolls, and a little further on a strip of grass bordered the shrubbery. At this time of night it was an ideal place to give Beauty the chance to do her business.

As she stepped outside, Edie shivered. The earlier persistent rain had stopped now and the moon was shining, bright and full, but there was the unmistakable smell of autumn in the chill night air, and drifts of wet leaves on the path squelched beneath her feet. A feeling of sadness overcame her. She didn't like autumn, though she knew that for many people it was their favourite season. She found it depressing – the end of the warm summer days, the death of the flowers and plants she loved, and nothing to look forward to but the bitter cold of winter, which would seem to last for ever, even after the first snowdrops had poked up their heads, drifts of purest white against the drab mud browns and faded greens that were all the end of the year and the beginning of the next had to offer. They stretched ahead now, those miserable months, dark and cheerless. Not even Christmas would provide much respite; it was just a day like any other, spent here at Fairley Hall, as likely as not, and busy with the same tasks she had to perform day in, day out.

Oh Charlie ... she thought. If only ... if only...

For a brief moment she allowed herself to imagine what might have been. She wouldn't mind the coming of winter if she and Charlie were together, kicking up the fallen leaves as they walked hand in hand, snuggling up in front of a roaring fire. If snow came, perhaps they would pelt one another with snowballs just for the fun of it, until Charlie caught her hands in his, pulled her to him

121

and kissed her so that her frosty lips were as warm as the glowing heart of her. And as for Christmas ... that would be wonderful. Once, Edie had dreamed of the family she and Charlie would have, and Christmas had always figured in those dreams. She longed to lose herself in preparations – baking mince pies and roasting a chicken, buying treats, decorating the house with holly and mistletoe, filling stockings with an orange, an apple and a nut as well as some small toys and creeping into the children's room when they were asleep to hang them at the foot of the bed. And next morning, of course, the children would wake her and Charlie early, piling into bed with them to unpack those same stockings, and there would be love and laughter and...

She brought herself up short, thrusting the imaginings to the back of her mind. It was no use pining for something that was never going to happen. Charlie was in London, with a woman. She had to put him out of her head.

As she crossed the path leading to the shrubbery, Beauty running ahead of her, something made Edie turn her head, and she was surprised to see two figures, no more than shadows, in the shelter of the jut between the outbuildings. Two red dots glowed in the dark, and Edie guessed that one of them belonged to Quilla, who often stopped outside to smoke a cigarette before going to bed. But who was she talking to? It couldn't be Simon the chauffeur, her usual smoking companion – it was his day off. Unless of course he had returned early, but that would be very unlike him. And Edie had the distinct impression that as she emerged from the doorway the two of them had moved further back into the shadows, as if trying to avoid being seen.

When she reached the strip of lawn, her curiosity got the better of her and she glanced back again. The two figures had moved back to their original positions now, as if they thought that the danger of being seen had passed. Edie's eyes were becoming more used to the dark, and she was sure the man sharing a cigarette with Quilla was not Simon, who was tall and lanky. This man was shorter and stockier, more like Percy Stevens in build. But it certainly wouldn't be Percy, who thoroughly disapproved of smoking, even Sir Montague's cigars.

Edie couldn't imagine he would approve of Quilla meeting a man in the grounds of Fairley Hall either, especially after dark. He could be quite strait-laced. But Quilla was one to do as she pleased, answering to no one but her mistress.

She shrugged her shoulders and turned her attention to what she was doing. Staring at Quilla and her mysterious companion, she'd lost sight of Beauty. She stood for a moment listening for the sound of rustling in the shrubbery that would alert her to the dog's whereabouts, but could hear nothing, and when she called her name, there was no response.

'Beauty!' she called again, beginning to feel a little anxious. Supposing the little dog had picked up the scent of some animal – a cat, or even a fox – and was following it? It could be ages before she came back, and Edie didn't fancy searching the vast grounds of Fairley Hall in the dark.

A faint chuntering sound in the distance broke

the silence of the night, and a pale tunnel of light sliced through the trees that lined the drive. Raymond and Sir Montague, home at last from their meeting. Edie's heart sank. She really didn't want to have to admit she had lost Miss Christina's dog. But she couldn't see how she would be able to avoid them. Raymond was driving at top speed along the long drive; in no time at all he'd be rounding the curve at the end of it, and that would be that.

'Beauty!' Edie called again desperately. 'Beauty – come here, you bad dog! Where are you?'

To her enormous relief, the spaniel appeared from the deep shadow of the shrubbery some way away, and Edie hurried towards her, intent on catching her by the collar and preventing her from running off again. But each time she reached her, Beauty danced away playfully, as if she thought this was some new and fun game.

And then, just as the Vauxhall was rounding the bend, she darted straight out on to the drive, staring as if transfixed at the approaching headlamps.

Edie's heart leaped into her mouth. Surely Raymond must have seen her there! But the motor didn't seem to be slowing at all.

'Beauty!' she screamed.

And then it seemed everything happened at once. Without so much as a single thought for what she was doing, Edie ran into the drive and scooped up the little dog. Raymond hastily jammed on the brakes, but heavy as the car was and fast as it had been travelling, it still kept coming. With Beauty in her arms, Edie threw herself towards the grass verge, and at the same moment Raymond swerved violently, but a glancing blow from one of the protruding head-lamps sent her sprawling. The Vauxhall came to a halt then, and Raymond ran back to where she lay at the side of the drive, momentarily too shocked to move.

'Edith – for the love of God! Are you all right?'

Edie struggled into a sitting position. The palms of her hands and her cheek stung horribly, and a sharp pain in her ribs where the headlamp had caught her was making it difficult to catch her breath.

'I'm fine,' she tried to say, but somehow the words wouldn't come.

'What the devil do you think you were doing?' he demanded, clearly as shocked as she was.

She did find her voice then; it came out jerky and breathless.

'What were *you* doing? Didn't you see Beauty?'

She looked around now anxiously. Had the little dog run off again? But to her relief, she was sitting on the lawn just a foot or so away, none the worse for her brush with death and regarding them curiously.

'Who is that?' Sir Montague had climbed down now from the motor and was approaching them. He sounded irritable and indignant.

'It's Edith.' Raymond offered her his hand. 'Can you get up?'

'Yes, get up and be quick about it!' Sir Montague instructed her.

For some reason Edie felt guilty and ashamed, as if the whole incident had been her fault.

'I'm sorry, sir. I was just taking Beauty out

before putting her to bed and she ran off...'

'Damned dog! She needs to be taught obedience. Don't you know she nearly caused us to have an accident?'

'If Mr Raymond didn't drive so fast, he would have seen her,' Edie retorted before she could stop herself.

She went to take a step to grab Beauty before she could make another dash for freedom, but as the weight went on to her right ankle, it almost gave way beneath her, and pain shot up her leg, making her cry out. As she staggered, Raymond caught her.

'Steady on, Edith!'

'My ankle...' she gasped, leaning heavily on his arm.

'I think we'd better get her inside, sir.' Raymond actually sounded a little abashed now.

Sir Montague merely snorted, but Raymond picked her up bodily, carrying her to the car, where he deposited her in the front seat recently vacated by Edie's tetchy employer.

'I'll drive her round to the tradesman's entrance,' he said. 'She shouldn't be trying to walk.'

Without further ado, he climbed into the driver's seat and started off at what was for him quite a pedestrian pace, leaving a furious Sir Montague and a chastened Beauty to follow. When they reached the house, he carried her into the servants' hall, where the staff had been awaiting Sir Montague's return so that they could at last retire to bed themselves.

The unexpected spectacle of Raymond with Edie in his arms caused quite a stir, of course, but the young man had no intention of hanging around to be asked questions. He set Edie down on a chair, mentioned that Beauty was still outside unless Sir Montague had brought her in himself, and beat a hasty retreat, and it was left to Edie to explain what had happened.

'That boy and his car!' Lilian Parker shook her head disapprovingly. 'He'll be the death of some poor soul – if he doesn't kill himself first!'

'Perhaps Sir Montague will see sense now and realise he's not fit to be his heir.' That was Quilla, sour as always. It was unusual for her to still be in the servants' hall at this time of night. When she'd seen Lady Elizabeth to bed she usually retired herself. But then of course it was only a short time ago that she'd been outside talking to the mysterious stranger, Edie thought, and wondered again who it could have been.

'Has she broke her leg?' Reg asked, keeping his distance as if a broken leg was infectious.

'We'll soon see. But it's just sprained, I expect.' Mrs Parker was taking charge. She knelt down beside the chair where Edie sat, embarrassed now by all the fuss she was causing, eased off her boot and examined the ankle, which was already beginning to swell. 'Yes, that's what it is – a bad sprain, by the look of it. Fetch a bandage, Nellie, and run it under the tap. The sooner we can get a cold compress on it the better.'

For once Nellie did as she was told without complaint, and Lilian wound the wet bandage tightly round Edie's ankle and fastened it with a couple of large safety pins.

'There, that's the best I can do. But you're

127

going to be laid up for a bit if I know anything about it.'

The drawing room bell jangled and Percy rose from his chair.

'That'll be Sir Montague wanting his brandy.'

'It would be nice if it was to ask if Edith is all right, seeing as she nearly got killed stopping Beauty from being run over,' Mrs Parker said tartly. 'And talking of brandy, I expect you could do with a drop yourself, Edie. Flo – you must know where Mrs Davey keeps it.'

Flo, who had been almost falling asleep before all the excitement, but was now wide awake again, fetched the bottle and a glass, and Mrs Parker poured a generous measure and handed it to Edie.

'It's only the stuff she uses in cooking, not the best, like Sir Montague drinks, so go steady with it.'

Edie sipped and almost gagged as the rough spirit rasped on her throat and burned her stomach.

'I don't think I can drink this, Mrs Parker.'

'Just have a little drop. It'll help you to sleep,' the housekeeper urged.

'No – I can't, really. It's going to make me sick.'

'Let's get you to bed then. That's the best place for you.'

Reg was detailed to help Edie up the stairs, but the only way she could manage them was on her bottom, bumping up step by step, and then he supported her along the landing to the room she shared with Nellie. Mrs Parker drew the curtains and turned back the covers on Edie's bed, then folded her clothes neatly while she got into her nightgown.

As she left, she turned back, holding the door ajar.

'That was a brave thing you did, Edie.'

'Anyone would have done the same. I couldn't let Beauty get knocked down, could I?'

'It would have broken Miss Christina's heart if anything had happened to her,' the housekeeper agreed. 'She worships that dog. Now just try to get some rest, and we'll hope you're better in the morning. But I wouldn't bank on it,' she added.

Mrs Parker was right. Edie's ankle was no better in the morning; in fact, if anything, she thought it was worse. Clearly there was no way she could carry out her duties, and Lady Elizabeth decided that the best thing for her was to go home for a few days' rest.

'I'll have Simon drive you,' she said.

That was a relief to Edie, who had been afraid that Raymond might be the one to take her. She had no wish to see him or his wretched Vauxhall.

'I shall miss you so much, Edith!' Christina said, looking as if she was about to burst into tears. Then she brightened. 'But at least you'll be able to ask your mother about you-know-what.'

Edie sighed. 'I'll ask her, but like I said before, Miss Christina, I don't think she'll be able to tell me anything more than you know already.'

'You will ask, though, won't you? It means so much to me, Edith!' Her turquoise eyes were haunted suddenly, the sparkle replaced by shadows.

'I know it does. And I will try. I just don't want you to be disappointed if I can't help you, that's all.'

But of course Christina *would* be disappointed.

It must be very odd, Edie thought, not to know who you were. She knew that she wouldn't like it at all. Her home might not have any of the luxuries that were taken for granted here at Fairley Hall, but at least she knew she belonged there. Her mother and father might not have the breeding or the education of the Fairleys, life might be a hard daily struggle for them, but they were her own flesh and blood and she loved them dearly.

She thought of her father, who had been a hero to her for as long as she could remember. He was a quiet man, slow to anger but strong and solid, always there for her when she needed him. Thank goodness he hadn't been on the hudge that terrible day when it had gone crashing down. Thank goodness she hadn't lost him, as her friend Lucy Day had lost her father. If she had, Edie didn't think she could have borne it.

She thought of her mother, loving, hard-working, wise. They clashed sometimes, because May was far more outspoken than Wesley and, as she herself put it, 'two women in one kitchen is one too many'. But the bond was strong none the less, and Edie couldn't imagine how it would feel if she knew that May had not given birth to her. Surely it was those unremembered days in the womb and at the breast that had forged the silken chain between them?

She thought of Ted, her brother, and what a very

special relationship they shared. Oh, they'd quarrelled often enough when they were growing up, of course, but they were always fierce in one another's defence if the attack came from anyone else. She didn't see a great deal of Ted now that he was married and lived on the other side of town, but she was fond of Sally, his wife, and adored their two little children, Georgie and Freda, enjoying playing with them when the opportunity arose and even spoiling them a little with treats of sweets or toys.

Lady Elizabeth seemed to be a good mother to Christina, it was true, and she had never wanted for anything. But she would never be part of a tight-knit family unit like Edie's.

No, Edie wouldn't change places with Miss Christina for all the tea in China.

And even if her efforts proved fruitless, she would do her very best to try and help her mistress discover who she really was, and where she belonged.

The arrival of the Rolls caused quite a stir in Fairley Terrace. Hester Dallimore was washing her doorstep when it rounded the corner and stopped outside number 1; she wasted no time in rushing indoors to get her shopping bag so as to have an excuse to walk down the alley and take a closer look, almost kicking over her bucket in her haste.

Outside number 6, Ewart and Cathy Donovan's two youngest sons, who had been looking for chalky stones to mark out a hopscotch grid on the cobbles, stopped what they were doing and gazed in awe at the big black motor with a uniformed chauffeur no less sitting behind the wheel, and the roar of the engine brought Queenie Rogers at number 2 to the kitchen door.

The racket even made Dolly Oglethorpe at number 3 look up from the letter she was reading and go to the window, and when she saw May Cooper come hurrying out of the house and the uniformed chauffeur helping Edie out of the back of the car, she dropped the letter on to the linoleum-covered scullery counter and ran out to see what was wrong, and if there was anything she could do to help.

'I'm all right, really!' Edie was reassuring her mother.

'But whatever has happened?' May's voice was shaking with concern. It must be something serious, she thought, for Sir Montague to send Edie home in his motor car.

'I've just sprained my ankle, that's all, and Lady Elizabeth thought I'd be better off at home.' Edie was horribly embarrassed by all the commotion she was causing. Being the centre of attention wasn't her style at all.

'Oh, our Edie, whatever next!'

The chauffeur was scooping Edie up in his arms and carrying her into the house as easily as if she was just a child, May following.

'May!' called Dolly. May looked over her shoulder, and she went on: 'Just let me know if you need anything, all right?'

'Thanks, Dolly.'

The little procession disappeared inside and Dolly went back to her own house and retrieved the letter that had arrived that morning.

The letter was from Charlie, and Dolly didn't quite know what to make of it. He'd written to say he wouldn't be able to come home this weekend as he'd planned because Victor, the bookmaker friend he lived with, was in hospital, and he wanted to be on hand for Victor's wife, Gracie.

I don't like her travelling across London on her own with Alfie, he had written, and all Dolly's misgivings had returned as she read the words.

There was something not right about that setup; in fact, in her opinion it was downright peculiar. To the outside world, she supposed it would seem logical enough for Victor and his wife to offer lodgings to a friend who was a single man when it would benefit all of them. But Dolly suspected there was a great deal more to it than that, and the thought that Charlie might be carrying on with his friend's wife disturbed her, though it didn't altogether surprise her.

Charlie was a good-looking young man and he had a way with him, while Victor ... well, she didn't care for Victor at all, though she'd only met him the once, when he'd driven down with Charlie and the two of them had taken her to Weston-super-Mare for the day. He was some years older than Charlie – in his late thirties, she'd guess – a big man whose youthful muscle was fast turning to flab. He'd lost most of his hair and he had the purplish-red nose of a habitual drinker. He was also a sight too full of himself, a boastful fast-talker, and Dolly had quickly decided she wouldn't trust him any further than she could throw him.

His young wife, on the other hand, was small and pretty, and when Charlie had brought her home with him that day back in September, Dolly could hardly have failed to notice the adoration in her eyes when she looked at him.

But they couldn't be having an affair, Dolly had told herself. What man would put up with something like that going on under his own roof? Surely he'd be bound to see what was happening and tell Charlie to find somewhere else to live pretty sharpish – if he didn't punch him on the nose first.

Now, however, all her niggling anxieties resurfaced. Charlie didn't say what was wrong with his friend, or whether it was serious, but he was clearly concerned about this Gracie. With Victor off the scene in hospital, things might well escalate, and it could only lead to trouble.

Oh why in the world didn't he find himself a nice girl and settle down rather than messing about with a married woman who had a little boy. A nice girl like Edie, for instance. Nothing would have pleased her more than if they'd made a go of it, and she knew that Ollie, Charlie's father, felt the same way. He'd been less than pleased when Charlie had brought Gracie to see them, and if he got to know about this latest development, she dreaded to think what he'd have to say about it. She wouldn't show him the letter, she decided; she'd just tell him Charlie had called off his planned visit, and Ollie wasn't likely to ask to see it. He was usually happy just to have any news relayed to him.

Shaking her head, Dolly folded the letter, replaced it in the envelope and put it in the kitchen drawer.

Sometimes, much as she loved him, she despaired of her son.

When Edie was settled in an easy chair with her injured foot propped up on a footstool, May made a cup of tea for both of them and sat down on the sofa opposite her.

'I'm sorry you've hurt yourself, but it will be nice to have you home for a bit,' she said, stirring sugar into Edie's cup as if she was a proper invalid. 'It'll give you a chance to see more of your dad, too. He's generally at work when you get time off, but now you'll be here in the evenings when he gets home from work.'

'He won't be able to have his bath in front of the fire with me stuck in this chair,' Edie said, smiling.

'True enough. But don't you worry, he won't mind having it over in the wash house. He'll be too made up that you're here. It sounds daft after all this time, I know, but we do still miss you about the place.'

'I miss you both too.'

May clicked her tongue against her teeth. 'Get away with you! You've got plenty of company at the Hall.'

'It's not the same, though.' Edie felt a pang of nostalgia for the old days, but they seemed so long ago now. Just as Charlie seemed to belong to another life even though she knew she would always love him.

'How are you getting on with Christina?' May asked.

'Fine.' It occurred to Edie that this was an opportunity to raise the subject of her mistress's curiosity about who she really was, and to ask May about the night that she had been found in the church porch. But for some reason she shied away from it. There would be plenty of time for that in the coming days. 'I do feel dreadfully responsible for her, though,' she said instead. 'She's quite young for her age, more like a ten-year-old than a young woman of almost fifteen. Certainly I know I was a lot wiser to the ways of the world at her age.'

'She's led a very sheltered life,' May said. 'She'll grow up overnight, I wouldn't wonder.'

'You're probably right,' Edie conceded. But the feeling that Christina would never quite grow up persisted. There was a part of her that would always be innocent and childlike. It was a winning trait, but a dangerous one, and it might well lead her into situations she was ill equipped to handle and relationships where she might end up badly hurt.

'Now,' May said. 'When I've had my cup of tea, I think I'll make one of my fruit cakes. I expect you'd like a slice hot from the oven later on.'

'That sounds too good to turn down,' Edie said, and thought that perhaps getting a badly sprained ankle once in a while was not such a bad thing.

Chapter Nine

Edie was still putting off asking May about what had happened the night Christina had been found in the church porch. Though she had promised Christina that she would find out as much as she could, and was admittedly curious herself, she also clearly remembered how impatient May had been that time when she'd first asked her about Christina's mysterious origins, and she was still puzzled as to why her mother hadn't told her it was she who found the baby. For some reason, it seemed, she didn't want to talk about it and Edie couldn't understand why. Was it possible she knew something, had seen someone hurrying away from the church perhaps, and kept quiet about it so as to protect them? If so, it was all the more reason why Edie should ask a few pertinent questions. But at the same time she shrank from raising the subject.

Persuading her mother to talk about things she thought were best forgotten, and trying to get her to reveal long-kept secrets, would be awkward to say the least, and Edie wasn't looking forward to it one little bit. But there was nothing for it, it had to be done, and the following afternoon Edie decided to take the bull by the horns.

May was getting ready to do the ironing, a day late this week as Monday – wash day – had been too wet to get the washing dry. It had had a good blow now, though, and was sitting in a neat heap

137

in the laundry basket, small items on top, sheets and towels underneath. The kitchen table was covered with a rough grey blanket topped with an old flannelette sheet, and the flat irons were stacked one on top of the other on the hob to heat.

As May began on the handkerchiefs, Edie took her chance.

'Mam, can I talk to you about Christina?' she asked, shifting her leg into a more comfortable position on the footstool. 'I know you said once before that you didn't know anything about how she came to be left in the porch, but she's desperate to find out who she really is, and she's asked me to help her get to the truth.'

'You're not going to start asking me a lot of questions again, I hope.' There was an edge in May's voice. 'I don't know what you think I can tell you. Like I said before, it was nothing to do with me.'

Edie took a deep breath. 'That's not the whole story, though, is it? According to what Christina has been told, you were there the night she was abandoned. In fact, she said it was you who found her.'

May froze, her iron stopping short on one of Wesley's handkerchiefs.

'Where in the world did she get that from?'

'Mam, you're going to burn that,' Edie warned, as a smell of scorched cotton filled the kitchen.

'Oh darn it...' May banged the iron down on to its metal ring stand.

'The thing is, she thinks you might have some clue as to who it was that left her there,' Edie went on, thinking it best not to ask May why she had never mentioned being the one to find the abandoned baby.

'Well I haven't,' May said shortly. 'And even if I had, it would be of no consequence to anybody. She's a Fairley now and that's an end of it.'

'But it isn't,' Edie argued. 'Can't you see how she must feel, not knowing who she really is, or where she belongs?'

'She's got a darned good life, a whole lot better than many, and she should be grateful. That's what you should be telling her, rather than encouraging her in such nonsense.' May folded the handkerchief and reached for another, smoothing it out on her ironing blanket.

'It's not nonsense to her,' Edie persisted. 'Please think, Mam, if you saw anything that night that might provide a clue. I take it you were on your way to Midnight Mass when you found her? Did you see anyone outside the church?'

'Of course I did! There's always folk out on a Christmas Eve, rolling out of the pubs and into services, a lot of them.'

'I don't suppose it was a drunkard rolling out of a pub who left her there.' Edie was beginning to feel exasperated. 'You didn't pass anyone who seemed to be in a hurry, or upset? Someone you wouldn't expect to see there?'

'I've told you – no! I was going to Mass, I went into the porch, and there she was, and that's all I know.'

This was getting her nowhere. Edie decided to try a different tack.

'Who else was there?'

'What d'you mean?'

139

'There must have been others arriving for Mass – and I don't mean the blokes who roll in late from the pub. Parishioners. Regular worshippers that you'd know.'

'For goodness' sake, our Edie, it's years ago – how do you expect me to remember?'

'I'd have thought,' Edie said, 'that something like that, you'd remember every detail.'

May huffed impatiently. She was a little red in the face, whether from the heat of the irons or from annoyance, Edie didn't know. But she wasn't going to give up.

'Think, Mam, please,' she urged.

'Well, Hetty Jones was there, of course. She was always there. She used to help set out the prayer books, that sort of thing. But she's been dead and gone for years now. Had a stroke, poor soul, not that long afterwards. She ran in and fetched Father O'Brien, and he sent for Sergeant Love. I don't remember who else was there, I was too taken up with the baby. I took her into the sacristy and stayed there until they came and took her away. Now, please, can we change the subject?'

Edie, though, with the bit now between her teeth, was not ready to let it drop.

'Father O'Brien,' she said thoughtfully. 'I wonder if he knows anything.'

'Oh don't be so soft! He'd have no more idea than I have who could have left her there – less. He was in the church, getting ready for Mass.'

'Priests have a way of knowing things, though, don't they? I think I might have a word with him.'

May, in the act of changing the cooling iron for the hot one, jerked violently, and it came crash-

ing down from the hob on to the tiled fire sur-
round.

'Now look what you've made me go and do! It's
cracked the tile – look! One of those lovely pink
tiles!' She sounded as if she was about to burst
into tears.

'Oh Mam, I'm sorry... I didn't mean for you to
get so upset...'

'You just couldn't shut up about it, could you?
Well I hope you're satisfied!'

'I'm sorry,' Edie said again. 'But I'm sure the
crack won't show if we put some polish on it.'

'It blooming well will.' May was rubbing at it
with her iron holder. She looked up, fixing Edie
with a hard stare. 'And you're not to even think
of bothering Father O'Brien, either.'

'Why not?' Edie was beginning to feel annoyed
as well as puzzled by May's attitude. It seemed
utterly ridiculous that a few simple questions
about something that had happened almost fifteen
years ago should have caused such a rumpus.

'Because he's an old man, that's why. He's
riddled with arthritis, and they say his memory is
going too. He's not even going to be our parish
priest any more, so you wouldn't be able to go
and see him anyway.'

Edie's heart sank. 'Oh well, I suppose that's
that then.'

'And just as well too. There's some things, our
Edie, that are best left alone.'

Edie laid her head against the back of the chair
and closed her eyes. Perhaps her mother was right.
But the conversation, if it could be called that, had
raised more questions than it had provided

141

answers, and her curiosity was thoroughly aroused now. There was definitely something about that night that May wanted to forget, and it might well be that she knew – or suspected – the identity of Christina's real mother. Trying to elicit answers from her was probably futile, but Edie made up her mind that she'd continue asking questions of anyone else who might be able to lead her to the truth, as much to satisfy herself as to honour her promise to Christina.

Since she had been unable to return to her own home because of the fire, Beatrice had been corresponding with her dear friend Myrtle Adams. Myrtle was the long-suffering wife of their village rector, and almost as doleful as Beatrice herself, since although her husband was still very much alive, she often felt she was a widow to his parish duties. It would be nice, she sometimes said, if he could only spare her half as much time and compassion as he did his flock. Beatrice and Myrtle often took tea together, sharing their woes, and the regular exchange of letters had been a great comfort to Beatrice in her enforced exile.

In the last letter she had written to Myrtle – or Mrs Adams as she still called her despite their close friendship – she had mentioned what a marvellous luxury it was to have the services of a lady's maid.

I only wish I could afford to employ someone to look after me in my declining years. Quilla Brimble is the most wonderful help to me, and though I long to be back in my own home, close to my good friends such as

142

yourself, I cannot help but think how I will miss her assistance. To have a button sewn on for me or a hem stitched now that my eyesight is failing too much for me to be able to thread a needle is practically a necessity. To have my clothes laid out ready for me to put on, and put away for me when I take them off, is pure heaven.

If only dear Montague's father had been the second son, and my beloved Horatio's father the elder, how different things would be! But no, as things stand, the admirable Quilla is Elizabeth's maid, and I must count myself lucky to have the use of her services for the duration of my enforced stay here at Fairley Hall.

Myrtle's reply had arrived in the morning mail, and what she had to say had come as a great surprise to Beatrice.

What a very small world it is! I believe I am acquainted with your lady's maid. Some years ago a young woman by that very name stayed for a short while at the vicarage in Laversham – as you know, the Reverend Healey was a good friend of my dear husband until he sadly passed away last winter. This poor young woman had disgraced herself, and was anxious to hide her predicament from her family and friends, and the Reverend Healey and his good wife had taken her in out of Christian charity.

For some reason known only to her, however, she ran away before her due date, and the Healeys never heard from her again. They often wondered, as did I, what had become of her. I am so glad to hear that she is alive and well and has made a good life for herself. It was always our greatest fear that, unable to bear the shame, she had done away with herself.

It may be, of course, that your lady's maid is a different young woman entirely, but Quilla is not the most common of names, and I am quite minded that her surname was Brimble.

Beatrice read and reread the letter, a sort of prurient excitement bringing a flush to her pale face.

'Well!' she exclaimed aloud. 'Who would have thought it!' and the phrase kept repeating itself over and over in her head.

It was almost impossible to visualise the highly efficient and rather dour woman who helped her with her toilet as a young and frightened girl hiding her shame in a Wiltshire village. Neither did she seem to be the kind of person who might disgrace herself, nor, indeed, have the attributes to attract the attentions of a man. But Quilla Brimble was certainly a distinctive name; it was unlikely there was another one in the whole of England, much less here in the West Country. And she could well have been handsome in her younger days before a harsh fate had turned her sour. Perhaps it was even the very fact that she was not feminine and pretty in the accepted way that had persuaded her to let some man have his wicked way.

Try as she might, Beatrice could scarcely think of anything else. Though she sat in the drawing room, a copy of *Northanger Abbey*, borrowed from Sir Montague's library, open in her lap, she was not able to concentrate on a single word. Usually when her mind wandered it was to fret over her fire-damaged home, or mourn for her

144

dear dead Horatio, but this ... this was quite different, a sort of fascination that tingled in her veins even though she found it quite repulsive. Could it be that she really was in such close contact with a fallen woman? To her knowledge Beatrice had never met such a creature, let alone been in her bedroom with one when she was wearing no more than her petticoats.

Should she mention Wiltshire to Quilla, ask if she knew it at all? Perhaps she would admit that she did, and the thought that she might hear the details of the whole sordid business was a darkly thrilling one. But if she was indeed the girl Myrtle had known, she would only want to put the past behind her.

Elizabeth might be more forthcoming, though. Quilla had been in her employ for a very long time, and if there was any truth in this, surely she would know about it? Indeed – a thought struck Beatrice – perhaps Elizabeth or Montague themselves had made the arrangements for Quilla to hide away, through their cousin, her own dear Horatio. Although she could scarcely believe her husband would have been party to such goings-on, it seemed too much of a coincidence that the servant – if it was indeed her – had been staying just a few miles from their home, and with a friend of the rector of their own parish.

She'd speak to Elizabeth, she decided. But that would have to wait for the moment. Elizabeth was out visiting tenants on the estate. She had asked Beatrice if she would like to go with her, but Beatrice had declined. She didn't fancy being offered cups of tea in poky kitchens by working-class

145

women – why, the cups might not even be clean!

Now, she almost wished she had accepted the invitation. At least she and Elizabeth would have had some time alone together in the back of the Rolls – though of course Elizabeth might not have wanted to talk of such things in the hearing of the chauffeur. It was quite usual to discuss almost anything in front of the staff as if they weren't there, but everyone knew they didn't miss much, especially if the conversation concerned one of their own number.

In any case, that was hardly here nor there. She hadn't gone with Elizabeth and would have to contain her curiosity until she could find a suitable moment to raise the subject.

She could hardly wait.

It was time for luncheon before Elizabeth returned, and the middle of the afternoon before Beatrice got her chance. Montague had taken Raymond with him to meet Clement Firkin, the agent, at one of the pits, and Christina had gone out for a walk, to collect some pretty fallen leaves for pressing, she had said.

Elizabeth was in the parlour, working on a petit point that would be framed when it was finished, and Beatrice joined her, novel in hand, pretending that she intended to read a few chapters. But after what she considered a respectable length of time, she slid her tasseled bookmark between the pages and rested the book in her lap.

'The most curious thing,' she said, striving, and failing, to keep the prurient excitement out of her voice. 'I received a letter this morning from Mrs

Adams, the wife of our rector, and a good friend of mine. I had mentioned how wonderfully well Quilla Brimble is looking after me – thanks to you, my dear Elizabeth – and she replied that she believed she was acquainted with her.'

'Really?' Elizabeth glanced up from her needlework. 'Surely that is highly unlikely?'

Beatrice's lips twitched into a small, satisfied smile that she was quite unable to suppress.

'You would think so, wouldn't you? But Mrs Adams was in no doubt that Quilla Brimble was the name of a young woman who was staying at the vicarage in the next village to ours. A young woman who was – not to put too fine a point on it – taking refuge there from the scandal that her condition would have caused had she remained amongst people who knew her. Naturally, my first thought was for you, Elizabeth, and whether you were aware of the kind of person who is employed by you in the most ... well ... intimate capacity.'

For just a moment, though to Beatrice it felt like an eternity, Elizabeth remained perfectly still, her eyes fixed on her petit point, the needle threaded with a length of pink silk poised above it. Then she looked up, her cool green eyes meeting Beatrice's muddy grey-brown ones.

'I'm sure your friend must be mistaken, Beatrice,' she said. 'But in any case, why should it matter to me if my lady's maid was unfortunate enough to have made the same mistake all too many young women do? She may have been foolish in her youth, but that's of little consequence. It doesn't mean she would be any less able to do a wonderful job of taking care of my every need.

And it wouldn't make her a bad person.'

Beatrice was dumbfounded.

'But ... a fallen woman in such a position? Surely that's not seemly? And a creature such as that around a young and impressionable girl like Christina? In my opinion that is far from wise, Elizabeth ... if you will forgive me for saying so.'

'Christina is in absolutely no moral danger from Quilla,' Elizabeth said firmly. 'Even if what you say is true–'

'And how can you be sure it is not?' Beatrice interrupted before she could stop herself.

'Whether it is or not, such things should be left in the past where they belong,' Elizabeth said tartly. 'No one should have to pay for a foolish mistake for the rest of their lives.'

'Not even murderers?' Beatrice was so shocked by her cousin's laissez-faire attitude, she hardly knew what she was saying.

'Now you are being ridiculous, Beatrice.' Determinedly, Elizabeth bent over her needlework again. 'Murder and serious crimes are quite a different matter. We are not talking about acts of wickedness here, simply weakness in the face of temptation. Have you never been tempted?' Her lips curved briefly and unconsciously at the ludicrousness of the idea. 'No, I don't suppose you have. But believe me, it's a very human frailty, and not one a woman should be condemned for.'

'I must say you surprise me, Elizabeth.' This conversation had not gone in the least as Beatrice had expected, and she was still none the wiser with regard to Quilla's past. 'I would never have thought you'd have taken the part of a fallen woman. I'm sorry, but I couldn't bring myself to condone such wanton behaviour. Once a harlot, always a harlot, in my opinion.'

'Then in that case I assume you'll no longer require Quilla's services?' Elizabeth said smoothly.

That took the wind out of Beatrice's sails. Quilla's ministrations were such a luxury, and besides, despite her very real disgust, Beatrice was at the same time experiencing the same feeling of fascination as when she had first read the letter this morning – dark and strangely thrilling.

'I'm sorry if I appeared to be criticising you or your judgement, my dear Elizabeth,' she said, summoning a false tone of regret. 'I'd hate us to quarrel over something that is really none of my concern. You are quite right, of course. This may well be a case of mistaken identity, and even if it is not, it would be only Christian to put my own narrow opinions to the back of my mind and give the poor woman the benefit of the doubt. I'm quite prepared to allow her to continue to look after me.'

'Are you quite sure?' Elizabeth glanced up again.

'Quite sure, dear cousin.' Beatrice smiled sweetly.

But she couldn't help thinking that those green eyes that held hers so directly were full of secrets, and neither could she help wondering what they were.

Outside the parlour, Quilla stood for just a moment, her hand still on the doorknob, as the conversation came to an end. She had heard every word and it was all she could do to contain the fury that consumed her.

How dare that prissy Mrs Fairley talk about her in such a way? How dare she judge her? What did she know about anything, cocooned in her sterile little world where, for all Quilla knew, she might still hide the legs of the piano in drapes to keep them from exciting the animal urges of men, as had been done not so long ago in Victorian times.

She was every bit as bad as those other two old biddies, Mrs Adams and Mrs Healey, with their ramrod backs and faces that would turn milk sour. They were jealous, that was all, jealous and hypocritical. She'd told herself that when they had condemned and shamed her, but she'd hated them then and she hated them now with a ferocity that had only grown over the years as it smouldered deep inside her. She'd been young then, frightened and vulnerable, and in the end she'd been unable to stand their sanctimonious nastiness any longer and had run away.

But she wasn't young and frightened any more. She'd grown hard and bitter with the years, but also more and more determined. Her life might have been ruined by one stupid mistake – it was too late by far to change that – but things would be different for her child. If she achieved nothing else, she would make sure of that.

Being careful to make not a sound, she gently released the doorknob and held her skirts tight to her legs to keep them from rustling. Then, like a shadow, she moved away down the hallway and down the servants' staircase. She didn't want Beatrice or Lady Elizabeth to know that she'd overheard their conversation, but it was fortunate

150

that she had. It had alerted her to the danger Beatrice might pose to the plans that were beginning to take shape in her head. That she had talked to Lady Elizabeth, who of course knew all the facts of the matter, was one thing. But there was no telling who else Beatrice would take her tittle-tattle to. It couldn't be allowed to happen, and Quilla was determined to stop at nothing to make sure it did not.

Chapter Ten

Edie was alone in the house when a knock came on the back door. May had gone into town to buy sausages for dinner. Ted's wife, Sally, and the children, Georgie and little Freda, came regularly once a week, and when they did, May cooked in the middle of the day and dished up a plate of the same food for Wesley – which she would heat up on a saucepan of water over the fire – when he got home from work in the evening.

Edie's first thought that it was them arriving, but of course it was too early; they wouldn't arrive until close on midday, and in any case Sal wouldn't knock. A neighbour might, out of courtesy, but then they'd almost invariably open the door without waiting for it to be answered and pop their head round with a 'Coo-ee!'

That didn't happen today, though. Instead the knock came again. Edie called, 'I'm coming!' then struggled to her feet and made her way gingerly across the kitchen, taking care not to put weight on her ankle, which, though improved, was still painful and not entirely to be trusted.

When she opened the door, she was startled to see a young man she did not know on the doorstep, and even more surprised to see he was wearing a dog collar.

A priest! In all her life Edie could remember only one occasion when a priest had come to the house, and though she'd been only a very small girl at the time, it was still clearly etched in her memory because she had been so frightened by him. In his heavy black cloak and black soutane he had seemed to her a figure from a nightmare – the bogeyman May sometimes threatened her with when she was naughty, or the dead and decomposing crow she'd almost stepped on when she'd been running ahead on a walk with her father across the fields behind the terrace. She'd scuttled, terrified, into the kitchen, then, when she'd heard May inviting him in, retreated further, to the bottom of the stairs, pulling the door closed behind her and peeping, round-eyed, through the crack at the apparition that seemed to dominate the room.

She hadn't been able to hear what was being said, but she could tell from the tone of her mother's voice that she was distressed, and her childish imagination had run riot.

When at last he had gone, she had darted out of her hiding place and buried her face in her mother's skirts.

'Whatever is the matter, my love?' May had asked.

'That man ... I didn't like him ... I didn't like

him!' she'd sobbed.

'For goodness' sake, our Edie, it was only Father O'Brien! You know Father O'Brien.'

Edie had looked up, tear-filled eyes full of doubt. On the few occasions May had taken her to church, she'd seen the priest, of course; he'd even placed his hand on her head to bless her when she went to the altar rail with May when she took communion. But that Father O'Brien wore a sort of white cotton frock and a pretty silky scarf; he wasn't dressed head to foot in black. And her mother didn't get all upset when he talked to her.

May had dried her tears and calmed her down and gradually her world had righted itself. But for a long time afterwards she'd had nightmares, just as she had over the crow, and for years she trembled when she caught a glimpse of a man dressed all in flowing black – stupid, she knew, but she just couldn't help it.

Now, in that first fleeting second when she opened the door, the memories came flooding back. But she wasn't a child any more and there was nothing even faintly demonical about the face above the dog collar, fresh and clean-shaven, with a chiselled jaw and smiling brown eyes.

'Do I have the right house?' he asked, and his voice was low and pleasant with just the hint of a West Country burr. 'I'm looking for Mrs Cooper.'

'Oh, yes.' Edie recovered herself. 'But she's not in at the moment.'

'That's a shame. I wanted to introduce myself. I'm Father Michael Connolly. I've just taken over from Father O'Brien as parish priest. Is she likely to be home soon, would you know?'

'She shouldn't be too long,' Edie said.

'Then would it be possible for me to wait? It's quite a step out here.'

'Well ... yes ... I should think so...' For some reason Edie felt quite flustered – because of the childhood memories, perhaps. 'You'd better come in.'

She held the door open and stepped aside. As he passed, she caught the pungent smell of incense clinging to his cloak and was transported back to the days when May had taken her to Mass. She'd quite liked that smell until her fright with Father O'Brien.

'Would you like a cup of tea?' she asked as they went into the kitchen. 'I'm her daughter, by the way. Edie.'

'It's good to meet you, Edie.' He smiled – it was a nice smile, she thought, broad and genuine, crinkling the corners of those brown eyes. 'I didn't expect to find you at home, though. I was given to understand by Father O'Brien that you were in service.'

'I am, but I've sprained my ankle and am no use to anyone at the moment,' Edie said.

'I'm sorry to hear that. Is it very painful?'

'It's much better than it was, thank you. I dare say I'll be back at work in a couple of days.'

'I'm glad I caught you, then. Perhaps I can kill two birds with one stone.' He smiled apologetically. 'Not the most Christian of metaphors, but it sums things up quite nicely. I know your mother doesn't often attend church now, but I was hoping to persuade her back into the fold. Perhaps I can talk you into coming along too –

when your duties allow, of course.'

'I'm not sure about that,' Edie said. 'Now, what about that cup of tea?'

The priest hesitated. 'Would you be dreadfully offended if I declined? Yours is the fifth family I've called on this morning, and each one has, with the best of intentions, given me tea. I'm not sure I could face another just yet.'

'I understand, and of course I wouldn't be offended.' In fact Edie was quite relieved; her ankle was throbbing again, and making tea would involve several trips to the pantry to fetch cups, saucers, sugar and milk, besides filling the kettle. 'Do please sit down, though.'

'Thank you.' He took a seat on the sofa and Edie gratefully returned to the chair she had been occupying before he had knocked at the door.

'So where is it that you're in service?' he asked, settling himself comfortably and crossing his legs beneath his soutane.

'At Fairley Hall. I'm lady's maid to Miss Christina.' Compared to the exotic life her old friend Lucy Day now led – a star on the music hall stage in London – it was hardly the most exciting of occupations, Edie thought, but she was proud of it nevertheless.

'Christina. Ah yes.' His brow furrowed a little. 'Correct me if I am wrong, but I believe Lady Elizabeth Fairley adopted her, didn't she? Wasn't she the baby who was left in our church porch one Christmas Eve?'

'Yes, that's right.' Edie was surprised that this young priest, who couldn't be much more than thirty, and probably not even that, knew Chris-

155

tina's story. 'But that must have been long before your time. It was almost fifteen years ago.'

'Before my time, yes,' Father Connolly agreed. 'But a startling enough event to never have been forgotten. It's become part of our lore at the abbey and is talked about still. Father O'Brien tells the story of how his first thought was of our Lord Jesus, born in a stable. I think for a moment he imagined that His coming again had occurred here in High Compton, before realising that the truth was far more ordinary. Some poor desperate woman had simply left her newborn child here, confident that she would be found and praying, no doubt, that someone would give her a good home. Which of course they did. The baby was fortunate indeed to be adopted by Lady Elizabeth when she could so easily have ended up in the workhouse. As things turned out, she has a far better life than some poor struggling girl could ever have given her, even though it's a matter of regret that she is not being raised as a Catholic. The Fairleys are Anglicans, I believe.'

'Yes, they are.' The family had a pew reserved for them at the parish church, though to Edie's knowledge they didn't worship regularly. But she said it mechanically, without giving it any thought. Her mind was elsewhere.

May had been adamant that Father O'Brien could know nothing about the circumstances surrounding Christina's appearance in the church porch, but her violent reaction when Edie had suggested approaching him made her think that in fact the very opposite was true. Father O'Brien did know something – and so did May. And while

Edie didn't like going against her mother's wishes, not only had she promised Christina that she would try and discover the truth, but her own curiosity had been thoroughly aroused. Perhaps this was her chance.

'You think it was a Catholic who left Christina there then, do you?' she asked.

'Undoubtedly. All churches have services at midnight on Christmas Eve. If the poor mother had been a member of one of those rather than a Catholic, she would surely have chosen to leave her baby there.'

'Unless that was exactly what she wanted people to think,' Edie said. 'If she was trying to conceal her identity, she might have thought it would help throw people off the scent.'

'That's possible, I suppose,' Father Connolly conceded. 'Unlikely, though. No, I think it's safe to assume she was a good Catholic girl fallen on hard times.'

'That's what Father O'Brien believes, is it?' Edie pressed him.

'He does, yes.'

Edie drew a deep breath.

'Do you think he knows who she was – the mother? Has he ever said?'

Father Connolly's nut-brown eyes narrowed slightly as they met Edie's directly.

'No. Certainly that night he had no idea where the baby had come from.'

'But later...?'

'Are you suggesting someone may have made a confession to him? It's possible, of course, but that would be between him, the person on the

157

other side of the confessional, and God. What is said under those circumstances is sacrosanct. You must know that.' There was reproach in his tone and it made Edie squirm uncomfortably.

'I'm sorry, Father. Of course I do know. It's just that ... well, Miss Christina is desperately anxious to find out who she really is and she has asked me to help her. I've promised I will – I can see how much it's troubling her, and I can understand that. It must be awful, not knowing where you belong. I want to help her, but I really don't know where to start and I thought perhaps Father O'Brien could tell me something that would set me on the right track. But I see now... I'm sorry,' she finished lamely.

The priest was silent for a few moments, deep in thought.

'I do understand,' he said at last, 'but it's a difficult situation. Whoever that poor mother was, she isn't likely to want her past to raise its head now. She may have made a new life for herself, or continued with her old one, and no one knows her secret. It could cause terrible trouble for her if it all came out now.'

'I suppose so. And I do realise that of course Father O'Brien couldn't reveal anything that was said to him in the confessional. But if there was just something I could tell Miss Christina, something that would help her come to terms with things as they stand... I would be discreet, I promise. I'd never mention a word of it to anyone else and I'd see to it that Miss Christina didn't pursue it either. If her real mother wants the past to remain her secret, I'd make sure of that. But you never know, it could be that she would very much like to have contact with her child again.'

The priest nodded slowly.

'I can see your intentions are entirely honourable, Edie, and I'll certainly talk to Father O'Brien. If there's anything I can tell you, I will. But you must understand I can't promise anything. The confidentiality of the confessional aside, Father O'Brien's memory is failing him. If ever he did know anything that he would be morally able to pass on, it's quite possible he won't remember it.'

Faint hope flared in Edie.

'Oh thank you...' She had been about to say 'Father', but somehow it didn't seem quite right. Michael Connolly might now be the parish priest, but in a strange way he felt more like a friend.

'Well, we have strayed a long way from my reason for calling today,' he said with a smile. 'I hope, though, that perhaps I shall see you in church soon, when your duties permit? And your mother, too. She is the one I really came to see, but–'

'I'm here now, Father.' The door between kitchen and scullery, which had been ajar, was pushed open and May came in carrying a bag of shopping. She deposited it on the table, where it promptly fell over, and a couple of apples and oranges she'd bought for Georgie and Freda rolled out and on to the floor.

The priest seemed unconcerned, but Edie felt a hot flush rising in her cheeks. She hadn't heard the back door open – perhaps it too had been ajar – and now she found herself wondering guiltily how long May had been standing there listening. Her face, too, was flushed, perhaps from hurrying on the long walk back from town, but Edie thought it was more likely because she had overheard at least part of the conversation, and her flustered manner seemed to bear that out. She had expressly warned Edie not to ask Father O'Brien about the night when the baby was found, and she'd come home to find her doing just that with his successor.

'Mrs Cooper.' He rose now, holding out his hand. 'We haven't met, but I'm Michael Connolly, your new parish priest. Your daughter kindly agreed that I could wait here for you, and so I've had the pleasure of meeting her too.'

'Yes. Well.' May gave Edie a sharp, angry look that left Edie in no doubt – she had heard enough to know what they had been talking about and was far from pleased about it.

'I suppose you're here to ask me why I don't come to church much any more,' she went on, her tone a little aggressive.

'I'm sure you have your reasons, and I wouldn't dream of asking you what they are,' the priest said easily. 'But I must confess I'd like nothing better than if you were to return to the fold. Father O'Brien has been a wonderful parish priest, but his health has been declining for some years now, and maybe things haven't been quite as you would wish, or expect. But I hope to be able to breathe new life into our little community. For one thing – and I know it's breaking with tradition – I would like to be known as Father Michael, rather than Father Connolly. It feels less formal to me.'

'Oh really?' May's tone was faintly disapproving, but the priest seemed not to notice.

'I have plans for study groups, and for social activity too – a club for wives and mothers, for instance, and social evenings when the whole parish can come together and enjoy themselves,' he went on.

'I don't know that I'd have time for that sort of thing, Father, even if I wanted to. By the time I've finished my day's work, all I want is a bit of a sit-down, not to be gallivanting about,' May said, unbuttoning her coat. 'It's very good of you to have taken the trouble to come and see me, but I think you've had a wasted journey.'

'I very much hope that's not so,' Michael said evenly. 'Just remember – should you ever need me, you have only to ask and I will do my best to help, whatever the problem might be.'

'That's kind, Father.' But her tone was short. *I'm not likely to be bringing my problems to you any time soon,* it said.

'Well, I don't want to take up any more of your time, Mrs Cooper,' the priest said, picking up on it. 'But you know there will always be a warm welcome for you at St Christopher's.' He turned to Edie. 'I'm very glad to have met you too, Miss Cooper.'

'Edie!' Edie interjected. Hadn't he called her that a few moments ago? He must have decided to be more formal in her mother's presence.

'Edie.' He smiled at her, that lovely smile that brought warmth and even a sparkle to his eyes. 'And remember, what I said to your mother goes for you too. I'd love to see you at Mass, but equally my door is always open if there's anything you want to talk over – what we've been discussing

161

today, perhaps.'

He held out his hand, and she took it, aware suddenly of nothing but those brown eyes smiling into hers, and his firm clasp.

'I'll see you out, Father.' May's tone said she couldn't wait to get rid of him.

They went out into the scullery, and a moment later the back door slammed shut. If May had closed it like that when she'd come in from the shops, Edie thought, she couldn't have failed to hear it.

'It didn't take you long to get acquainted with the new priest,' May said acidly as she came back into the kitchen.

'He seems very nice...'

'And it didn't take you long to start asking him questions, either.'

'Mam, don't be like this!' Edie pleaded 'I'm only trying to help Christina with something that's really important to her. I can't understand why you are so against it.'

'I thought I made myself clear the other day. It's best to let the past lie. No!' She raised a warning hand to prevent further discussion. 'I don't want to hear any more about it.'

'But–'

'I'm not going to talk about it, and that's my final word. And if you go poking about asking that priest or Father O'Brien a lot of questions now that you know how I feel about it, I shall be most upset.'

Edie sighed, shaking her head. She was more certain than ever that her mother was hiding something. But what?

She went cold suddenly as the most awful explanation flashed into her head.

May had been the one to find the baby, yet Edie would never have known that if Christina hadn't told her. Could it be – was it possible – that it was May herself who had brought the baby to the church, and she had only *pretended* to find her? Was that the reason she became so agitated and refused point blank to talk about it? And if that were the case, had she done it for a friend or neighbour? Or could it even have been her own baby?

Oh, you're letting your imagination run away with you, Edie told herself. Of course Christina couldn't be May's baby. Though Edie herself would have been far too young to know what was going on, May couldn't possibly have hidden her pregnancy and a birth from Wesley, and he would never have been party to abandoning a child. Unless...

Another unwelcome thought occurred to Edie. Hadn't her father once gone to South Wales to try his luck in the coal mines there, where the seams were thicker and conditions far better than here in Somerset? It hadn't worked out because Mam hadn't wanted to leave her home, and he'd come back again.

Supposing Mam had had an affair and fallen pregnant whilst he was away? Supposing she'd somehow managed to conceal her pregnancy, given birth in secret, taken the baby to the church and then pretended to find her?

Her thoughts churning, Edie desperately tried to remember if there had been anything out of the ordinary that long-ago Christmas, such as Dad being absent, but she couldn't. In her memory, all the Christmases of her childhood seemed to blend into one. Puddings boiling in the copper in the lead-up – she'd always hated the smell of the cloth that was tied over the top of the basins, hot and sodden – and then, on Christmas Day, the mouthwatering aroma of roasting cockerel. The anticipation building on Christmas Eve, the trying to stay awake so as to see Father Christmas and his sleigh and reindeer in the night sky. The falling asleep and waking in the middle of the night to find that miraculously he had actually been, and the old pillowcase she'd hung at the foot of the bed was now bulging with interesting shapes – a book, a jigsaw puzzle, an orange, an apple and some nuts... Even though that particular Christmas had been the first one after the terrible tragedy at Shepton Fields, nothing about it stood out to Edie, who had been too young to appreciate what the families who had lost loved ones were going through. The childish excitement surrounding Christmas left no room for other memories.

But now that she came to think logically about it, the timings didn't add up. Edie was pretty sure it was after the disaster that Dad had gone to Wales – they'd never have been allowed to remain in their tied cottage otherwise, but in the aftermath of the tragedy, Sir Montague had shown more leniency to his tenants, for a while at least. But since Christina had been born in December, she must have been conceived in the spring, several months before the tragedy, and Edie simply couldn't imagine that May would have

164

had the opportunity for an affair at that time.

She felt a huge rush of relief. The thought of her mother being unfaithful to her father, let alone abandoning her own baby, had horrified her.

But somehow, now that the possibility had occurred to her, she couldn't quite forget it. It hovered at the back of her mind, a shadow that wouldn't completely go away.

For her own peace of mind, she decided, she must make every effort to discover the truth, whatever that might be.

Father Michael stood for a moment in the track between the rank of houses and the privies and outhouses on the other side, drawing his cloak more tightly around him against the cold October wind and thinking that being a parish priest was even more difficult than he had feared it would be. Life had been a good deal more comfortable when he'd had only his duties at the abbey to worry about. Now not only was he responsible for the moral welfare of his flock, he felt as if all the cares of the world had fallen on to his shoulders. Already this morning he had visited an old man suffering so badly from silicosis that he was scarcely able to draw breath and his wife who had developed dropsy. They were childless so had no one to help care for them, and he wondered how they would manage. At least he had been able to give them the communion they could no longer attend church to receive, but beyond that he was helpless to do anything for them, and the platitudes he had uttered had sounded empty even to his ears.

Then there had been a family struggling to survive because the breadwinner was unable to work following an industrial accident. Their faith had been badly dented. 'How can I believe in a God who lets this happen to us?' The woman, already a mother of four and not far off giving birth again from the look of her, had spoken bitterly. 'That's a joke! A cruel one, too. I've been a good Catholic all my life, gone to church regularly, always tried to do the right thing by others, and this is what I get. I'm sorry, Father, but I'm giving up on God, because sure as light He's given up on me.'

Now he faced yet another dilemma. Should he try to find out what Father O'Brien knew about the circumstances that had led to Christina Fairley being abandoned in the church porch, and if he learned anything, what should he do about it? None of his training had prepared him for this. How could it, when there were as many problematic situations as there were living human beings?

Well, there was nothing he could do but pray for guidance. Just at the moment, though, his faith seemed to be on rocky ground, and he wasn't quite sure why, though perhaps it had something to do with Edie Cooper.

Something about her had unsettled him, and he found himself remembering one summer when he was on holiday from the seminary. He had met a girl of about his own age, a very pretty girl with long auburn curls and blue eyes who had a laugh that sounded to him like a stream tinkling over stones. Nothing untoward had ever happened – they had only talked – but he hadn't been able to stop thinking about her and wishing he dared ask her to go for a walk with him. When he had gone back to the seminary she had still been on his mind, and the thoughts he'd had about her had tormented him. It was wrong, surely, that he should feel this way when he was preparing to commit himself, and his whole life, to God. Eventually he had summoned up the courage to talk to one of his mentors about it, but to his dismay the older man had questioned whether perhaps Michael was not suited after all to become a priest.

'If you think you will be unable to resist temptation, then I suggest this is not the way for you,' he had said. 'Better that you acknowledge that now than go forward and discover your frailty too late.'

Michael had assured him that the priesthood was all he wanted from life, and he had worked hard to banish the girl from his mind. Since that day there had been no temptation – until now, when suddenly it seemed as if the Devil was sitting on his shoulder.

His head had told him he should advise Edie against pursuing her search for Christina's true identity, yet he'd felt a powerful urge to agree to her request for help. He admitted to himself now that he wanted her gratitude and admiration, and it made him wonder if perhaps his desire to help all his parishioners came in part at least from his ego. Could it be that there was an element of self-aggrandisement – the desire not just to be a good priest, but to be seen as one – and it had taken Edie to hold up a mirror to him?

167

God forgive me, Michael whispered to himself. Then, with a sigh, he turned and began to walk along the track, checking the numbers on the doors as he went. He had one more call to make while he was here. He didn't suppose the husband, Ewart Donovan, would be at home – almost certainly he would be at work. But with any luck Cathy, his wife, would be there. Though not from a Catholic family, she had been baptised into the Church when she'd married Ewart and, according to Father O'Brien, taken a first communion. But now they were on the list of parishioners who no longer attended church regularly, and Michael intended to try and persuade them too back into the fold.

Trying to put his doubts – and the haunting image of Edie Cooper's pretty, pleading face – out of his mind, he knocked on the door of number 6.

Chapter Eleven

Julia, Lettice, and a few other members of the WSPU, including Sylvia Frost, were sitting around the kitchen table discussing tactics for their next move when there was a tap at the door and Prissy, maid to the lady who owned the house, popped her head in.

'There's a telephone call for you, Miss Fairley.'

'For me?' Julia was startled. She'd thought she'd heard the faint ringing of the telephone bell echoing up the stairwell from the hall below, but had not for a moment thought it might concern her.

'Yes, ma'am.'

'It's probably that young police inspector we met the night we were arrested,' Sylvia Frost teased. 'I saw the looks he was giving you. In fact I think it was down to him and the fact that he fancied you that we got let off with a caution.'

'Oh what rubbish!' Julia pushed back her chair and stood up, all too aware that such a suggestion would not go down well with Lettice. The two of them were growing closer with every passing day, and Julia did not want Lettice to think that she had secured their release by flirting with a policeman.

Curious as to know who could be telephoning her, she hurried down the stairs and lifted the receiver from where it lay on the polished occasional table in the hall.

'Hello? Julia Fairley speaking.'

'Julia. Thank God I've got you!' It was Raymond, and he sounded flustered.

'Raymond?' Julia felt the first prickle of alarm. 'Is something wrong?'

'It's Mother. She's had a bad fall. You really need to come home.'

'A fall?' Julia's head was spinning, but Raymond allowed her no time to ask questions.

'I'm coming to get you. If you could give me directions and be ready for me, I should be with you in a little over an hour.'

'But ... this is such a shock, Raymond. What–'

'Just tell me how I can find you,' Raymond interrupted. 'I'll give you all the details when I see you.'

169

'I'm in Clifton, as you know...' Julia explained as best she could the way Raymond should take through the city to reach the house, then placed the telephone receiver into its elaborately decorated brass holder and went back upstairs.

'I'm sorry, but I'm going to have to go back to High Compton,' she said. 'That was my brother Raymond on the telephone. It seems our mother has had some kind of an accident.'

'Good heavens! How dreadful!' Sylvia exclaimed, and Lettice rose from her chair, crossing quickly to Julia and taking her hand.

'Of course you must go, darling. Would you like me to come with you?'

'Oh ... no... It's a lovely thought, but... Well, it isn't as if we're in our own home.'

'I understand. At least let me help you pack your things.'

Julia nodded. 'Thank you. I'm all of a dither.'

It was not an understatement. She felt quite stunned by the news, and from the urgency Raymond had exhibited, she feared that Beatrice must be seriously hurt, perhaps in danger of her life.

In the bedroom they shared, she took dresses from hangers and underwear from drawers while Lettice folded the things and packed them in Julia's suitcase.

'Do you need to take everything, or do you think you'll be back?' she asked.

'I certainly hope I'll be back – if you'll have me. But I can't say when...'

'Of course I'll have you back, you goose! And soon, I hope. I shall miss you dreadfully.'

'Letty ... dear Letty...' Julia caught her bottom

lip between her teeth to keep it from trembling. 'I shall miss you too! But if Mama is badly hurt... Oh, I'm so frightened!'

Lettice straightened, putting her arms round Julia.

'You will be equal to whatever you have to do, darling. And remember, I'm always here for you.'

For a moment Julia rested her head against Lettice's shoulder, eyes tight shut, breathing in the now-familiar rose-scented perfume that her friend favoured. Then she looked up into the deep blue eyes she had grown to love, nodding and trying to smile.

'I know that. And I am so, so grateful.'

'I'm the one who should be grateful to you, my darling. You've made my life complete.'

Lettice ran her finger lightly over Julia's cheek, brushing away the suggestion of a tear, then pressed her lips lightly to Julia's for a fleeting moment.

'Now, we'd better finish this packing or your brother will be here and you won't be ready for him.'

Julia nodded, wanting nothing more than to remain here with Lettice and never have to return to the constraints of her former life. But that wasn't possible for the present, and perhaps never. She had other responsibilities – those of a dutiful daughter. They must take precedence over her own selfish desires.

The packing finished, Letty carried Julia's suitcase down to the hall and left it beside the front door. Then they went back to the kitchen and, disregarding the glances of the other women, sat

171

holding hands as they waited for the knock at the door that would tell them Raymond had arrived.

The moment the Vauxhall came to a juddering halt in front of Fairley Hall, Julia jumped down and ran inside, fearing the worst. From what Raymond had told her on the way home, their mother was in a bad way – unconscious, he'd said, and had been ever since they'd heard a scream and a clatter and found her lying in a heap at the foot of the staircase. Beyond that, he knew nothing – he'd telephoned Julia immediately after the doctor had been called and left for Bristol before he arrived. In any case, it had been hard to hear what he was saying over the roar of the engine, and Julia was muffled up to her ears with her fur tippet in an effort to escape the worst of the biting wind. In the end she had shouted at him to just concentrate on what he was doing – though she was usually a far from nervous passenger, she couldn't help feeling that today his driving was bordering on the reckless, and it would help no one if they ended up having an accident of their own.

Nellie Saunders was in the entrance hall, polishing the silver salver that had once been used for visiting cards, though hardly anyone observed that convention any more.

'My mother!' Julia cried, breathless with anxiety. 'Where is she?'

'She's in the drawing room, miss. Sir Montague wanted to get her upstairs, but the doctor said it was best not to move her.'

Julia scooted along the hallway, not stopping to reply.

172

Beatrice was lying on the big brocaded sofa, covered in a blanket, with pillows piled beneath her head. Elizabeth knelt beside her, applying a cold compress to her forehead, and Christina hovered, looking frightened.

'Julia! Thank goodness you're here,' Elizabeth said, looking up. 'Your poor mama has taken a very bad fall, I'm afraid, but she will be so pleased to see you.'

'Raymond said she was unconscious.' Julia drew off her gloves and approached the sofa.

'She's come around now, but she's still very dazed. Dr Mackay says we must keep a close eye on her for the moment at least.'

'Julia?' Beatrice's voice was faint and weak. 'Is that you?'

'Yes, Mother.' Elizabeth vacated her place at Beatrice's side and Julia dropped to her knees, taking her mother's hand, which lay limply across the blanket.

She looked ghastly, Julia thought, deathly pale and with a dark swelling the size of a duck's egg on her temple and a livid graze to her cheek. Julia brushed it lightly with the tip of her finger and Beatrice winced.

'Oh Mother, whatever have you been up to?' she asked in the sort of tone she might have used to a child.

Beatrice's mouth worked for a moment or two before she answered.

'I don't know. But my head hurts. Why does it hurt so, Julia? And where am I?'

'You're in the drawing room,' Julia said gently.

'*Our* drawing room? No – it doesn't look right.

173

My lampshades are tasselled. Those are glass. They don't look at all like mine.'

'That's because they're not yours. We're at Fairley Hall with Cousin Montague and Elizabeth. Don't you remember?'

Beatrice closed her eyes.

'No... I can't... My head hurts too much... What's wrong with me, Julia?'

Elizabeth had drawn up a small spindle-legged chair.

'You had a nasty fall, Beatrice dear. You tumbled down the stairs.'

Beatrice was silent for a moment, her mouth working, her brow furrowed. Then her eyes shot open, wide and staring.

'Someone pushed me!' Her voice was stronger and full of bewildered accusation.

'I'm sure that's not so,' Elizabeth soothed. 'You caught your foot, I expect. I'll have Nellie check the carpet to make sure it's not come loose.'

'Someone pushed me!' Beatrice repeated.

Julia glanced around at Elizabeth, who gave a small shake of her head. *Humour her*, it seemed to say.

'Let's not worry about that now, dear,' she said gently to Beatrice. 'Save your strength for getting well. Ah – here's Raymond come to see you,' she added as he came bursting into the room, then hung back as if suddenly afraid. 'Raymond, come and sit with your mama for a while so that I can speak with Julia. And hold this compress to her forehead while you're about it. She's complaining of a bad headache, which is hardly surprising.'

Reluctantly Raymond took the gauze pad from

her and she led Julia out of the room.

'I am so sorry, my dear, that this should have happened under our roof. Poor Beatrice... But at least she does not appear to have broken any bones, and she has regained consciousness – we can take comfort from that. When I first saw her lying there, not moving and senseless, I feared...' She broke off, not wanting to voice her first awful thought, that Beatrice was dead. It was too dreadful to contemplate. 'If she fell through any fault of ours, I shall never forgive myself,' she said instead.

'How could it be your fault?' Anxious as she was, Julia felt obliged to reassure Elizabeth. 'Mother does suffer dizzy spells from time to time – perhaps she had one at the top of the stairs. Perhaps she fainted. That could be the reason she hasn't broken any bones – because she was quite relaxed when she fell. What did the doctor say?'

'He didn't offer any explanation. How could he?'

'No, of course he couldn't,' Julia agreed. 'What I meant was what did he say about her condition now?'

'He was very worried, I could see that, though he did his best to be reassuring. And he did say she was fortunate not to have broken her neck with such a fall. He's coming back later – he had another urgent visit to make, or I believe he would have stayed – so you will be able to ask him any questions then. But he did say there was little more he could do until she recovered full consciousness and that it was best not to move her any more than was necessary until he'd had the chance to examine her thoroughly. And also that it was likely that when she did come round, she would be confused.'

'She's certainly that,' Julia agreed. 'Not knowing where she is, for instance. And this notion that someone pushed her. Why on earth would she think that?'

Elizabeth shook her head helplessly.

'Who knows what any one of us might imagine when we've had such a bad blow to the head? It's ridiculous, of course. But the mind can play strange tricks. I remember once when I had a fever being convinced I was in terrible danger from a faceless man in my room whom no one else could see.'

'A sort of dreaming while you're awake. Yes. But she did sound very sure of it. It was the one thing that came out loud and clear.'

'That's no doubt how it seemed to her. But of course it's quite ridiculous. She was alone when we found her, and in any case, who would do such a thing? No, it's a hallucination, you can be sure of that. And the very fact that her mind is functioning again, albeit imperfectly, must be a good sign, don't you think?'

'Julia! For goodness' sake! Can you come and sit with Mother? She's mumbling like a madwoman and I can't stand it a moment longer.'

Raymond was in the doorway, looking dreadfully harassed.

'That's only to be expected, Raymond.' Julia exchanged a glance with Elizabeth– *Men!* that look said. 'It's all right, though. I'll sit with her and you can go and hide away somewhere and

176

pretend this isn't happening.'

'Thanks, sis,' Raymond said gratefully, without the slightest hint of offence taken at her derogatory remark. 'Come on, Christina. You don't like it either, do you?'

Christina, who had withdrawn to the window seat, looked at Elizabeth with wide, pleading eyes.

'Can I go too, Mama?'

'Of course you can, my darling. Julia and I will stay with poor Beatrice.'

Christina and Raymond left and Julia and Elizabeth took up the vigil. Until Beatrice had completely recovered her senses, there was nothing else they could do.

Dr Mackay returned within the hour, and was plainly relieved to find that Beatrice had recovered consciousness, even if she was still confused. After he had examined her again, he pronounced that it was now safe to move her, and that she would be a great deal more comfortable in bed rather than on the drawing room sofa. Reg Deacon and Simon Ford were summoned, and between them they carried her upstairs, where Julia settled her against the pillows and the doctor administered something to ease the headache that Beatrice was complaining of.

'You could easily have broken your neck, Mrs Fairley.' His soft Scottish burr took the sting out of his words. 'A painful head is better than that, don't you think?'

'Is she going to be all right then, Doctor?' Julia asked him when they were back on the landing and out of Beatrice's earshot.

'She's been lucky, I'd say. But we're not out of the woods yet. When a patient has been knocked unconscious, it's possible there might be damage to the brain,' he said with due seriousness.

'You mean she'll go on being confused – or worse?' Julia asked anxiously.

'I think that's unlikely.' He bent to fasten the clasp of his medical bag. 'But I think someone should stay with her, at least for the next twenty-four hours or so. Would you like me to arrange for a nurse?'

'That won't be necessary,' Julia said quickly. 'One of us will sit with her. I'm sure she would be more comfortable with someone she knows rather than a stranger.'

'Very well, if that's what you prefer. I'll call back this evening to take another look at her, but in the meantime don't hesitate to call me if there's any change, or if you are at all worried.'

'We will. Thank you, Doctor,' Julia said.

'Do you fancy going for a drive?' Raymond asked Christina.

They'd had luncheon, a fractured meal, since Elizabeth and Julia were taking it in turns to sit with Beatrice, and one that no one apart from him had felt like eating. Now that both Elizabeth and Julia had gone back upstairs and Sir Montague was taking an afternoon nap in his study, something he did more and more frequently these days, he and Christina were alone.

Christina's face brightened at the suggestion, then she frowned, biting her lip as a child might.

'I'm not sure Mama would allow me.'

'She won't even know you've gone. She's too caught up with nursing my mother.' Raymond stuck his hands in his trouser pockets and cocked his head to one side, giving her a challenging look. 'Come on, Christina! Live a little!'

Christina giggled. 'You are naughty!'

'That's half the fun! Do what you want to, and the hell with it. You do want to come, don't you?'

'Oh yes!' Christina said emphatically. 'Of course I do!'

'Then let's go. You'd better wrap up, though. It's a bit cold, and I can't keep you warm if I'm driving.'

Christina giggled again.

'You mustn't be cross, though, if I try to steal a kiss,' he added.

Christina pressed her fingers to her lips, blushing. 'Raymond!'

'Don't tell me you wouldn't like me to?'

'You wouldn't! Would you?'

'You'll just have to wait and find out. Go on, get your coat.'

All of a dither, Christina ran upstairs, skipping nimbly past the half-open door of Beatrice's room before either Elizabeth or Julia could see her. This was so exciting! A ride in Raymond's car was tempting enough, and as for the thought that he might actually kiss her...

She'd been kissed just once, by Sam, the gardener's boy, and she'd quite liked it. But he'd been dismissed, and she'd never seen him again. Mama had been angry with her – well, as close to anger as serene Mama ever came – and talked about Sam not being of her class, as well as the fact that

179

she was far too young for that sort of thing. But she was older now, no one could say Raymond wasn't a gentleman – wouldn't he one day inherit Sir Montague's title, along with the estate? – and she was eager to repeat the experience.

All things considered, Christina felt it was worth taking the risk of incurring Mama's displeasure if only Raymond really would kiss her.

And kiss her he did. After an exhilarating drive, when she'd hung on tightly to her seat and squealed as the Vauxhall bounced over rough bits of road and cornered at speed, he'd pulled in to the side of a deserted lane and reached for her.

'Raymond – no!' Now that the moment had come, she was panicking.

'Christina – yes!'

His mouth found hers, tightly pursed up, and a little thrill ran through her. Tentatively she raised a hand, curling it around his back, enjoying the warm pressure of his lips on hers, the feel of his shoulder beneath the thick cloth of his coat, the slight smell of tobacco that tickled her nose.

He raised his head a fraction, looking down at her and smiling. 'That wasn't so bad, was it?'

'No. It was nice,' she whispered.

'You want me to do it again?' She nodded. 'All right, but don't pucker your lips so.'

His mouth covered hers once more, and this time Christina made an effort to relax her mouth, though that didn't feel to her like a proper kiss at all, and when she felt his tongue gently prising her lips apart, she drew back.

'Don't be frightened,' he said softly, his breath

180

warm on her cheek. 'This is how grown-up people kiss. You want to be grown up, don't you?'

'Yes... I'm sorry...'

'No need to be sorry. You'll soon learn – I'll teach you.'

He kissed her again, not too deeply, just tickling the inside of her lips with his tongue and touching it teasingly against hers. Then he released her, sitting back in the driver's seat.

'That's enough for your first lesson.'

Christina pouted. She wanted this exciting new experience to go on for ever. But Raymond was a skilful operator; he knew the trick was to leave her longing for more. As he climbed out of the car to crank the engine back to life, a satisfied smile played about his lips.

Just as he'd thought – Christina was putty in his hands. Perhaps his enforced stay at Fairley Hall wouldn't be so bad after all.

It was early evening and the family was at dinner. For once the ladies had not bothered to change from their day dresses. They toyed with their food, anxious and subdued. Sir Montague was in a bad humour – his agent had told him earlier that the men at one of his pits were agitating for a pay rise – whilst Raymond kept catching Christina's eye and even giving her a sly wink, making her blush and look down coyly at her plate.

Beatrice had seemed to rally a little during the afternoon. She had slept a good deal, but she seemed less distressed during her periods of wakefulness, though she was still insisting that her fall had been as a result of someone pushing her. Otherwise, however, Dr Mackay's potions seemed to be doing their work, and he had pronounced himself reasonably satisfied when he had called by yet again after his evening surgery.

'I'm hoping that by tomorrow we shall see a marked improvement,' he had said.

After he left, Quilla had offered to sit with her so that both Elizabeth and Julia could go down to dinner.

'You need to take a break, milady. You and Miss Julia both. You'll be exhausted. I'll call you if there's any cause to, don't worry.'

Julia, though, was reluctant to leave the sickroom and it took Elizabeth's assurance that Quilla was more than reliable to persuade her.

Even so: 'I won't be long,' she had promised her mother. 'Just rest.'

Beatrice hadn't replied; her eyelids were drooping again. Julia dropped a kiss on her forehead, looked back anxiously from the doorway, then followed Elizabeth downstairs.

The first two courses were over and dessert – an apple Charlotte – was being served when Quilla came bursting in, almost colliding with Nellie, who had just entered the dining room with a jug of creamy custard.

'What the devil...?' Sir Montague exploded.

Quilla ignored him. 'Milady... Miss Fairley...' There was no mistaking the distress in her tone.

Julia was out of her seat in a trice, almost overturning her chair in her haste.

'Mother?'

'Yes, miss.' Quilla was twisting her hands together in a tight knot at her bosom. 'I think she's

182

stopped breathing.'

As Julia rushed from the room, Elizabeth turned to Nellie, who was still standing, a little shocked, in the doorway.

'Call for the doctor. Ask him to come immediately.' Then she followed Julia upstairs.

Julia had dropped to her knees beside the bed, where Beatrice lay motionless against a heap of rumpled pillows, calling her mother's name and shaking her gently.

'Oh my dear...' Elizabeth's racing heart seemed to miss a beat. Beatrice's eyes were open but staring; her hands, slightly clawed, seemed to be clutching at thin air. With just that first glance Elizabeth was almost certain that she was beyond help.

'Is there a pulse?' she asked.

'I don't know...' Frantically Julia took one of those clawed hands, turning it over to expose the underside of the wrist and pressing against it with her fingertips. 'I don't think so. I can't find one.'

'A looking glass.' Elizabeth crossed to the dressing table and fetched the tortoiseshell-backed mirror, holding it in front of Beatrice's face. For a long moment she waited, then she checked the glass. It was quite clear, not a single spot of the condensation that would indicate that in spite of all appearances to the contrary Beatrice was still breathing. Reluctant even now to accept the seemingly inevitable, she tried again. The result was the same.

'Oh Beatrice!' she murmured, then looked up into Julia's anguished face.

'I'm so sorry, my dear,' she said quietly. 'I'm

afraid... I think she's gone.'

In the commotion that followed, a wary Quilla was able to slip unnoticed out of the house. In a dark corner between the outhouses a cigarette glowed, and Quilla made her way towards it. The bulky figure of a man stood there in the shadows. Her brother, Dick Brimble, the town blacksmith.

'What's going on?' His voice was rough, uncultured.

'Give me a drag of your cigarette and I'll tell you.' She held out her hand to take it from him. It was trembling.

'Haven't you got one of your own?' he asked.

'No. And I can't stop out here long enough to smoke a whole one either, though goodness knows I need it after what I've had to do. Just let me...' She took the cigarette from him, inhaled deeply, blew out smoke and took another puff, making no attempt to return it.

'What have you had to do?' he asked gruffly.

'Never you mind. You don't want to know. Let's just say there's been a death in the family.'

'Not Sir Montague?' He sounded shocked.

'No, that stupid cow Beatrice, Raymond's mother. Now look, there's something I need you to do. I'd do it myself but I don't know if I'll get the chance...'

She quickly outlined what it was she wanted.

'Just make sure you don't get caught,' she finished.

'D'you think I'm stupid?'

She didn't answer that.

'I've got to get back.' She took one last drag of

the cigarette and handed it to her brother. Then, after quickly checking that the coast was clear, she hurried back into the house.

Chapter Twelve

'I think Charlie's home,' May said. 'I'm sure it was him I saw going into number three when I went over to the coalhouse.'

Edie, sitting at the kitchen table peeling potatoes for dinner, felt her heart miss a beat. Stupid how the mention of his name could still have this effect on her, let alone the thought that he could be just the next house but one away at this very moment.

'Was he on his own?' she asked before she could stop herself.

'I couldn't say. I only caught sight of the back of him.' May plonked the full coal scuttle down beside the grate and picked out a few lumps with the tongs to stoke up the fire. 'I know what you're thinking, our Edie, but don't go getting your hopes up or you'll only be disappointed again.'

'I'm not thinking anything,' Edie lied, denying that imp of hope that had surged through her. Common sense told her she'd lost Charlie. If ever anything was going to happen between them, it would have happened long ago. He'd never have gone off to London if he'd thought anything of her, and it was a long time now since he'd even written to her. He'd made a new life for himself and she wasn't a part of it.

So why did she still get this hollow feeling in the pit of her stomach whenever she thought about him? Why didn't she feel the slightest interest in any other man? An image flashed into her mind of nut-brown eyes and a chiselled jaw above a clerical collar. Now Father Michael was a man she could have fancied. There was something about him that attracted her in a way no one but Charlie ever had. But Father Michael was a priest. He was as far out of her reach as Charlie – even more so. It would be almost laughable if it weren't so depressing. Perhaps it was her fate that she would only ever fall for men she couldn't have.

Thinking of Michael reminded her of the other matter that was weighing heavily on her mind – the mystery of the identity of Christina's real mother. Though she'd told herself over and over again that it was a ridiculous notion, still the unanswered questions haunted her. Why did May refuse even to talk about it? Why had she become so upset when Edie had suggested asking Father O'Brien what, if anything, he knew, and similarly, when she'd caught her discussing it with Father Michael? Why did she no longer go to church when once she'd been so devout? There were other things too, little things that taken alone meant nothing but when added together only seemed to support her awful suspicion.

She seemed to remember that her mother had been less than enthusiastic when she had first been offered the position at Fairley Hall; then, when she had taken it anyway, May had always asked after Christina when Edie came home for a day off. And what was it she had said when Edie had been appointed lady's maid to Christina? 'Fancy you of all people!' or words to that effect. And 'Be sure to take good care of her.' Surely that was a strange thing to say?

It could be of course that May felt responsible for Christina, since she had been the one to find her. But then again, why had she never mentioned that? Even if the subject hadn't arisen over the years, wouldn't it have been natural for her to say something when Edie told her about her new appointment?

Around and around inside Edie's head the arguments went until she really didn't know what to think. She wondered about asking May straight out, but somehow couldn't bring herself to do that. It was almost certain to cause another upset. Even if May denied there was any truth in her suspicions, Edie wouldn't know whether she was telling the truth. And given her reaction to any mention of the subject, Edie couldn't imagine for a moment that she would admit it.

No, if she wanted to learn the truth she would just have to continue to investigate without May's knowledge. And for the moment her only hope of that lay with Father Michael.

Edie cut the potato she'd been peeling in half and dropped it into the saucepan of water.

Why oh why did everything have to be so complicated?

Two doors away, at number 3, Dolly was fussing happily over Charlie.

'This is a treat and no mistake!' she said, pour-

187

ing a cup of tea for her son and stirring in two heaped spoonfuls of sugar as she always did. 'Everything's all right, is it? You haven't got the sack from that window-cleaning job, have you?'

'No, I haven't got the sack,' Charlie said. 'I do have some news, though. I'm going to get married.'

'Married!' Dolly stopped stirring the tea, leaving the spoon motionless in the cup.'

Charlie laughed a little self-consciously. 'Yes, that's right. I thought I ought to let you know.'

'I should think so too! But ... it's a bit sudden, isn't it?'

A red flush ran up Charlie's neck. 'Not really, no,' he said awkwardly. 'You've met her. Gracie.'

'I thought there was something going on there. I knew it! But you said she was your bookmaker friend's wife.'

'She was. But he's gone and passed away. He's been a sick man for a long time and he died last week. So Gracie and I are getting married.'

Dolly pushed the cup of tea across the table to her son and sat down abruptly. She couldn't make head nor tail of this.

'He only died last week and you're going to marry his widow? That doesn't seem right and proper to me. What's the rush?'

The flush crept further up Charlie's neck and over his chin where a dark shadow of stubble was already showing though he'd shaved before he left London this morning.

'There's a baby on the way.'

Dolly huffed breath over her top lip, giving Charlie a hard stare.

'Ah, we're getting, to it now. If you're going to take on a woman with two children, I'm guessing there's more to it than some promise you might have made to your pal. Is it yours, then, this baby?'

Charlie cradled the cup in his hands, looking down at it.

'Yes, it's mine.'

'You stupid boy!' Dolly exclaimed. 'I'd have thought you'd have more sense. And more decency too. Carrying on with your friend's wife behind his back, and him on his sickbed. I thought I'd brought you up better than that.'

'It's not what you think,' Charlie said wretchedly.

'Oh, and how's that then? I'll tell you what I think. You're going to saddle yourself with a wife who's no better than she should be and two children. But how do you know for sure that this baby is yours? Why couldn't it be her husband's, or anybody else's for that matter?'

'The baby's mine,' Charlie said flatly. He hesitated for a moment and then added shame-facedly. 'And so is little Alfie.'

'What!'

'He's mine too.' Charlie still couldn't look at his mother. 'So I'm only doing what I should have done a long time ago. Facing up to my responsibilities.'

Dolly shook her head in bewilderment.

'Goodness only knows what your father is going to have to say about it. It's a tidy kettle of fish and no mistake.'

Charlie took a sip of his tea, hot enough to burn the roof of his mouth, grateful for once that his mother hadn't stinted on the sugar.

'You could say that,' he agreed gruffly.

He didn't blame his mother for her disgust. He was ashamed enough himself for the profligate way he'd behaved and he knew he had no one but himself to blame for his situation.

He should never have gone to London in the first place, he sometimes thought. He should have stayed in High Compton, worked his way up to being a collier instead of a carting boy, married Edie, and settled down. But he'd been restless and dissatisfied, sure that somewhere in the world a better way of life was waiting for him. And in the beginning, he'd thought he'd found it.

He'd enjoyed the feeling of freedom that came from not having to drag putts of coal from the coalface to the main roadway day after day, with his back aching and his knees bleeding beneath his rushyduck trousers. He'd enjoyed being able to pick and choose where he worked, changing occupation with the season and relishing the fact that even in winter he still saw daylight, unlike his days down the pits when he went to work and came home again in the dark. He'd enjoyed escaping his father's disapproval of his wild ways, which Ollie never troubled to hide, and he'd enjoyed being out from under Dolly's thumb. He loved her dearly but he'd come to feel guilty for resenting the fact that she ruled her household with a rod of iron. Many miners' wives were like that, strong, independent women, matriarchs used to being in control while the menfolk, more often than not, were content to let things be. 'Anything for a quiet life' was the motto of many of them, along with a host of platitudes that covered every situation, such as 'Worse things happen at sea'.

In contrast, London – and the freedom to do as he chose, when he chose – was a dream come true. He'd made new friends, Victor, the bookmaker, among them, learned new skills, such as the tic-tac method of communication used at the race courses they went to, and enjoyed the company of women to whom the fast track was a way of life.

And then he had met Gracie.

She was a waitress in a corner teashop; when he and Victor had called in for a hot buttered teacake and a good strong brew, she had served them and Charlie had been taken with her instantly.

She was small and dainty and very pretty, with a Cupid's bow mouth and blue eyes fringed with thick dark lashes, and her uniform – black skirt, high-necked white blouse and frilly apron – flattered her instead of making her look frumpy as it did some of the other waitresses. When she brought the bill on a little silvered saucer he'd asked her out – Charlie didn't believe in wasting time – and she'd agreed.

They began going out together, and things moved quickly – too quickly. For the first time in his life Charlie found he wasn't looking around and playing the field. He was entranced by her. She came, he discovered, from Cheddar, only fifteen miles or so from his own home. But she was unlike any of the girls he'd ever met. She'd come to London with a friend in search of a new and exciting life just as he had done – something he'd never known a girl to do – and like him she was enjoying the freedom and experiences it offered.

It wasn't long, though, before Charlie began getting restless again. 'Footloose and fancy-free' might have been an expression coined just for him. Summer was coming, when London would be dusty and unbearably hot, and he fancied being beside the sea. He'd heard there were jobs going in the coastal resorts where people flocked to sit on the beach, paddle in the sea or stroll on the pier. He took a train to Margate, asked around, and was offered a job as a beach attendant.

When he told Gracie of his plans, she'd become quite excited.

'A summer by the sea!' she exclaimed, her blue eyes shining. 'I can't think of anything nicer! And I'll be able to find a, job there without any trouble at all. They're bound to want waitresses in the cafés and tea shops.'

Fond as he was of her, taking Gracie with him hadn't been in Charlie's plans at all. He wanted to be free to enjoy the company of a succession of young lady holidaymakers, not have to go home each night to the same girl, even if that girl was Gracie. He'd feel responsible for her since she wouldn't know anyone but him, and that would put a damper on new adventures. He might just as well be married, he thought, and he wasn't anywhere near ready for that yet.

He didn't want to tell Gracie outright though, that he had no intention of taking her with him. He remembered all too clearly how Edie had begged him not to go when he'd told her he was off to London, and he didn't want a repeat of that.

'Yes, you could get a job all right, I expect. But where would you live?' he asked, managing a

192

dubious look.

Her eyes clouded. 'Couldn't I stay with you?'

'I haven't got any lodgings for myself yet,' Charlie said. 'I can sleep rough until I find somewhere, but you couldn't do that.'

'I don't mind, really I don't!'

Charlie shook his head. 'I can't have you doing that, so don't even think about it. It wouldn't be right. It's different for a man. No, the best thing is for me to go first, find out the lie of the land, see what places there are. When I've settled in myself, I can look around and find something suitable for you. Then you can come down at least knowing you'll have a roof over your head.'

Gracie's face fell. 'But what if all the summer waitressing jobs have been taken by then?'

'They won't be,' he assured her. 'There's cafés all along the seafront and back into the town. There'll always be something going.'

'I suppose.'

Much as she wanted to go with Charlie right away, Gracie could see the sense in his argument. She couldn't doss down for the night under the pier or on a park bench as he could. Especially not if, as she was beginning to suspect, she might be pregnant.

She wasn't ready to tell Charlie that yet, though, and she was worried he might be less than pleased when she did.

And so it was agreed. Charlie would go alone to Margate, and when he'd sorted something out, Gracie would join him. At least that was the arrangement as far as Gracie was concerned. Charlie, of course, had other ideas.

Looking back now, he wasn't proud of the way he'd behaved; in fact he was downright ashamed. He'd gone to Margate and was soon enjoying himself too much to spare a thought for Gracie, waiting vainly to hear from him. Working on the beach wearing only a vest and with his trousers rolled up to his knees, he quickly acquired a deep tan, and when he was promoted to lifeguard it made him even more of a magnet for the giggling girls in search of a holiday romance. More than one pretended to get into difficulties so that he was called on to go to the rescue. He'd learned to swim in the pool built into a broad curve of the river that ran through High Compton and Hillsbridge, and in a disused water-filled quarry a few miles from his home, and that was paying off now as he took to the water, all sun-bronzed muscle, under the admiring gaze of those eager girls.

The summer seemed to fly by, the days grew shorter and cooler, the swallows that nested under the eaves of the house where he had lodgings headed off to warmer climes and the beach grew ever more deserted, until the day came when the tea stall put up its shutters and the deckchairs were stored away in a beach hut. Charlie's services were no longer required as a lifeguard and it was time to head back to London.

Ever the cheerful optimist, he had no doubt but that he could pick up with Gracie where he had left off. So it came as a total shock to him to find her heavily pregnant and with a ring on her finger. Unable to contact him, frightened and increasingly desperate, she had married Victor in a brief civil ceremony and was now living with him in the house he had shared with Charlie.

It was not, however, a conventional marriage. In his wild younger years Victor had contracted syphilis, which flared up again from time to time after lying dormant, and there was no way on earth he would risk giving Gracie the dreadful disease. But he had always had a little more than a soft spot for her, and when he had learned of her situation he had offered to marry her and give her some respectability, though he had explained there could be no question of them living as man and wife. A desperate Gracie had eventually agreed to the arrangement. In all honesty she had never expected to see Charlie again, and she couldn't imagine she would be tied for long to Victor, who, in his own words, wouldn't be long for this world if the disease progressed as he seemed fatalistically sure it would. Now, however, when Charlie turned up again out of the blue, Gracie castigated herself for not waiting, though she wasn't convinced he wouldn't disappear again when he found he was going to be a father.

Charlie, for his part, was totally confused by his own feelings. His head told him that things had worked out for the best; to be forced into a marriage he wasn't ready for, and on top of that to find himself responsible for a child, was the stuff of his worst nightmares. But he still felt a strong attraction to Gracie and it was clear she felt the same way.

'Why didn't you write and let me know how I could get in touch with you?' she asked, her eyes full of tears.

'I'm sorry,' Charlie said helplessly. 'I never for a

minute thought–'

'Well you should have done, shouldn't you?' she flashed. 'You know as well as I do what can happen when people do what we did.'

Charlie had been counting months in his head.

'You must have known when I went to Margate there was a chance... Why didn't you say anything?'

'I was afraid to. I thought if I did I wouldn't see you for dust.'

'A fine opinion you have of me!'

'I'm right, though, aren't I?'

Charlie couldn't answer. Truth to tell, he really didn't know what he would have done. Perhaps he would have fled and never come back. He hoped not, but he couldn't be sure. His fear of being tied down might well have won the day.

'Oh, come here,' he said.

He put his arms round her and she laid her head against his shoulder, the swell in her belly that was his baby trapped safely between them. He buried his face in her hair and felt for the first time the stirring of a love that was not lust but tenderness, a primeval urge to protect her and their unborn child. It startled him, even frightened him a little, but so did the thought that he might lose them both.

'The way I see it, you'd better move back into your old room, Charlie.' Victor was in the doorway. The red veins were prominent in his waxy cheeks, his nose purplish, his eyes bloodshot, and angry-looking pustules had begun to appear in clusters around his mouth. 'Then you can take care of her the way you should.'

Startled, Charlie looked at him over the top of Gracie's head.

'What are you saying, Victor?'

'You know damn well what I'm saying. I married Gracie to give her some respectability – and a bit of security. I've made good money over the years. What do they say? The bookie always wins.' His scarred lips twisted into a wry smile. 'Except of course when it comes to this bloody plague. But I've only got myself to blame for that, and if I had my time over again I don't suppose I'd do any different. Anyway, when I kick the bucket, Gracie will have a bit of money to keep her going. But I don't want her having to look after me all on her own when things get bad – and they will. Move back into your old room. And if Gracie wants to move in with you, that's fine by me.'

Until this had happened, Charlie had never thought of Victor as an altruistic man. He'd seen only the hard-nosed, hard-drinking, fast-living bookmaker. But now he was seeing another Victor, a soft underside that had been buried beneath the boozing, the womanising and the wheeler-dealing.

'All right then, I'll take it,' he said. 'Thanks, Victor.'

And so the *ménage à trois* had begun. He must love Gracie, Charlie thought, or he would have run for the hills, knowing Victor would leave her well provided for. And when little Alfie was born, he'd come to love him too, though it was Victor he called Da-da when he began to talk. To the outside world they were a family, Victor, Gracie and Alfie, and Charlie was their lodger. But it was to his bed that Gracie came, and Charlie found to

197

his surprise that he was more settled than he had ever been before. Sometimes, as he sat Alfie on his knee, jiggling him up and down and singing to him – 'The Galloping Major' was his favourite because of the jaunty chorus, 'Bumpety, bumpety, bumpety, bump; here comes the Galloping Major', and he was far too young to be aware of the saucy double entendre in the words – Charlie found himself wishing he could tell him that he, not Victor, was Da-da, but he never would. Better for him to have the stability of a mother and father who were to all outward appearances a respectable married couple, and Charlie was content to let things go on as they were.

It wasn't long before Gracie was pregnant again and the neighbours were congratulating her and Victor, though there was a bit of whispering and rumour as to who the father might really be. And then quite suddenly the disease that Victor had fought for so long had taken hold and his condition worsened rapidly. In the end there was nothing for it but for him to be taken into hospital, where he had died.

Gracie had cried for him, the man who had been there for her in her hour of need, and left her well provided for. But when the worst of her grief was spent, she saw there was no longer anything standing in the way of her and Charlie being together properly.

'Do you think we could get married now?' she asked, her eyes still shining with tears. 'It's what I want more than anything. For you, me, Alfie and the baby to be a proper family.'

And surprising himself, Charlie had replied:

198

'Yes. Of course we can.'

There was no question in his mind but that it was the right thing to do, and he found he really didn't mind at all. He'd like it if the new baby learned to call him Da-da, and perhaps in time so would Alfie. The thought of it warmed his heart in a way he'd never imagined it could.

Now, however, sitting in his mother's kitchen and admitting the lie he'd been living, he felt deeply ashamed as he realised how it must look to her, and would look to his father. So when Dolly said: 'Edie's at home; she sprained her ankle and wasn't fit for work. I reckon you ought to go and tell her while you're about it,' he was horrified.

'Oh, I don't know as I want to do that.'

'You used to be such good friends, I reckon you owe it to her,' Dolly said.

She was so cross with Charlie that seeing him discomfited gave her some small satisfaction. But for all her efforts to persuade him, Charlie refused to be talked into doing any such thing, though he cursed himself for a coward. In spite of everything, he still thought a lot of Edie and was almost as ashamed of the way he'd treated her as he was of the way he'd treated Gracie. At least he hadn't left her pregnant when he'd taken off on his wild adventuring, and he'd never made her any promises he couldn't keep, but he shouldn't have just stopped writing to her. He knew he owed her an explanation, but he found he couldn't bring himself to go round and tell her the story he'd just told Dolly.

'I don't want to talk about it any more,' he said. 'You can tell her mam, can't you?'

'I suppose I shall have to,' Dolly sniffed.

She didn't like the situation one little bit, and was dreading Ollie's reaction when he found out. But as far as the neighbours were concerned, she supposed it would be a nine days' wonder, like all gossip and scandal. This Gracie had seemed a nice enough girl the day she'd visited with Charlie, and Alfie was a lovely little boy. Her grandson! she thought with the first swelling of pride. Perhaps if Charlie and Gracie got married, she'd see a bit more of him, and the new baby too.

In Dolly's world, every cloud had a silver lining, and this was no exception. Just get the awkwardness over with, and things might not be so bad.

But she couldn't help feeling sorry for Edie. She still carried a candle for Charlie, Dolly felt sure, and to carry a candle all these years must mean she thought an awful lot of him.

She glanced at Charlie. He'd looked shamefaced, even regretful, when she'd mentioned Edie's name. Did he still carry a candle for her too, even if it had burned a bit dim over the past few years? Well, he'd made his bed and he must lie on it. She only hoped he wouldn't live to regret the choice he'd made.

When she heard that Charlie was to be married, Edie felt her heart drop like a stone. Dolly had waited until Charlie had left to go back to London before sharing the news with May, and May, of course, had relayed it to Edie.

Well that was that, Edie thought wretchedly. It was no more than she had expected, but still the finality of it was gut-wrenching, and the dark shadow it cast enveloped her like the dusk that fell earlier and earlier each day now that winter was fast approaching, and which was almost as depressing.

Her ankle was almost healed now, and she couldn't wait to get back to Fairley Hall. At least there she didn't have so many reminders of Charlie as she did at home, where she could hardly step outside the back door without glancing towards his house and thinking of what might have been, and hard at work she would have less time for brooding over her broken dreams. Besides this, her curiosity about Christina's origins and her mother's refusal to talk about it had made for an awkwardness between her and May that was really quite uncomfortable.

All in all, Edie thought, it would be a great relief to be away from Fairley Terrace. And that, too, made her sad.

Chapter Thirteen

Winter came in with a rush, the murky days of early November giving way to a bitterly cold snap when milk froze in the churns and the servants at Fairley Hall shivered as they went about their early morning duties, their fingers numb, their noses red and dripping.

Beatrice's death had cast a dark cloud over the whole household. Elizabeth was mortified that her cousin had met her demise whilst under her

201

roof, and Julia and Raymond were each mourning her in their own way. Raymond, in particular, felt her loss keenly. He had always been a mother's boy, and though she had frequently bemoaned his wild ways, Beatrice had also indulged him and defended him fiercely when others castigated him. Without her, he felt like a rudderless ship adrift on a stormy sea. As for Julia, though she longed to go back to Bristol, to Lettice and the suffragette movement that was so close to her heart, she didn't feel able to leave him.

For the moment, his preparations for the day when he would inherit the estate and all that went with it had been put on hold, as Sir Montague was busy with political matters. Another election was to be held at the beginning of December, and the Conservative Party, of which he was a staunch member, was working hard to ensure their candidate's success and, hopefully, the overthrow of the Liberal government that had come to power by the skin of their teeth back in January. The House of Lords had refused to back the reforms Asquith had tried to push through Parliament, and he had had no option but to call another election in an attempt to win a working majority. At something of a loose end, Raymond had continued dallying with Christina, taking her for rides in his motor when the weather allowed and indulging in the kissing sessions she enjoyed so much and which he was hoping to take a stage further some day soon. But he was taking care not to rush things; little as he was enjoying his introduction to the dry-as-dust minutiae of managing an estate, he didn't want to risk upsetting his uncle and throwing his future into jeopardy.

He and Julia had also driven up to Wiltshire to check on the progress of repairs to their fire-damaged home, but they had discovered it was still far from being fit for habitation. The bad weather had impeded the work and the local builder and craftsmen, perhaps concerned about the family's ability to pay, seemed not to be treating it with the urgency he and Julia felt it warranted. They drove back a second time, taking Elizabeth with them and, charmed and impressed by her demeanour and obvious breeding, and her promise to ensure he was reimbursed for his work, the builder had promised to do his best to expedite the repairs.

Elizabeth had also called on Myrtle Adams, who was understandably distressed at her friend's sudden death, and they had spent some time closeted together in the stuffy rectory parlour. What passed between them neither Julia nor Raymond knew, but as they left, Myrtle had pressed Elizabeth's hand and whispered cryptically: 'Don't worry about it any more, my dear. And I'm very sorry I was less than discreet.'

Raymond and Julia had exchanged puzzled glances but hadn't pressed their aunt to explain, and clearly she had no intention of enlightening them as to what Myrtle had meant by her remark.

The wintry weather, when some days the sky seemed hardly to lighten from dawn till dusk, had done nothing to help Edie's depressed mood. It wasn't that she thought constantly of Charlie – she didn't. In fact, whenever he edged his way into her thoughts, she made a determined effort to shut him out again. But still the knowledge that he was in all likelihood married by now and lost to her for ever hung over her, a dark cloud on the periphery of her consciousness, a bad taste in her mouth that refused to go away.

She had made no more progress in the mission she had set herself either. She hadn't seen Father Michael again, and she didn't know how she could possibly discover who it was who had left the newborn Christina in the church porch that long-ago Christmas Eve.

The suspicion that it might have been May still haunted her, but she couldn't see any way of finding out the truth. It was just another frustration, adding to the feelings of helplessness that were dragging her down.

Perhaps I'll feel differently when spring comes, she thought. But spring seemed a lifetime away, and she couldn't truly believe that it would make things any better.

There was one single bright spot in the dark days of December to look forward to though – the grand Christmas social held each year for the Hillsbridge Church of England parishioners. It had become a tradition that Lady Elizabeth would lend one or two of her servants to help with the catering, and this year Edie and Nellie had been assigned to the task. Simon was to drive them to the church hall during the afternoon, taking with him two large trifles Cook had prepared, and then help with decorating the hall with holly, mistletoe and paper chains whilst Edie and Nellie joined some of the ladies of the parish in the kitchen to cut sandwiches, pork pies and slab cake, set out cups and saucers, and scour and fill the tea urn ready to be put on the heat. They would also be expected to help serve the refreshments and of course stay to clear up afterwards. By way of reward they would be allowed to join in the games and dancing if and when their duties permitted.

Nellie was delighted she'd been chosen – it would give her an opportunity to see Teddy Vranch, her long-term fiancé, and perhaps have a dance with him. Teddy wasn't a regular church-goer, but he had bought a ticket for the social when Nellie had told him she'd be 'doing the teas', as the duty was euphemistically referred to. Edie, though, was finding it hard to summon up much enthusiasm. Seeing young couples enjoying themselves together would only make her feel her own loneliness and heartache more keenly.

When the band – a piano and drums – struck up and people began arriving, Edie and Nellie went out into the main hall, separated from the tiny kitchen by a window that would remain shuttered until it was time for refreshments to be served. Everything was ready, cups and saucers laid out and platters of food covered by clean tea cloths, and they were free to enjoy themselves for a couple of hours. Chairs lined the hall on all four sides, but Edie and Nellie were not allowed to sit on them, so they stood in the kitchen doorway, from where they had a good view of everything that was going on, and Edie waved to a few people she recognised. None of her former close neighbours were here, though; they were all either Catholic or Methodist. The congregation of the Church of

England was mainly made up of middle-class folk – or those who considered themselves middle class.

Stanley Bristow, who ran the local concert party that Edie's friend Lucy Day had sung with before running off to go on the professional stage, had agreed to act as MC for the evening, and seeing him there made Edie feel quite nostalgic for the old days and the times she and Lucy had shared. She smiled to herself as she recalled one occasion in particular, after Lucy and her mother and sister had moved away from the terrace, when she had been invited to Lucy's new home to celebrate her birthday. There had been a very grand lady there, Lucy's aunt Molly, who was on the halls, and Lucy's stuffed shirt of a stepfather had caught her prancing about wearing his best hat and swinging his cane as she sang 'The Man Who Broke the Bank at Monte Carlo'. Mr Pierce had been furious and thrown her out, and at the time Edie had been very frightened, but now it was something she remembered with amusement.

Stanley announced a veleta, the blind pianist struck up a tune, and as couples took to the floor, Nellie and Edie joined in, Nellie taking the part of the man, and both of them giggling as they tripped over one another's feet, any ill feeling between them, generated by Edie's promotion, forgotten for the moment. Then Teddy arrived, looking a little uncomfortable in a smart shirt and tie; he was much more used to the baggy trousers and jumper patched at the elbows that he wore for his work as a council road sweeper. He whisked Nellie off for a St Bernard's waltz, and Edie was left leaning against the door to the kitchen, watching them enviously and remembering how she and Charlie had danced at the Foresters' Fete.

More people were streaming in now, and Edie was taken by surprise to see that one of them was Father Michael. He was the last person she would have expected to encounter at a Church of England event. With his thick black cloak over his soutane, he stood out like the proverbial sore thumb, and he was smiling a little uncertainly, but almost at once the rector spotted him, made his way between the dancers and shook him by the hand before guiding him to a quiet spot on the far side of the hall from where Edie was standing.

'Hmm. He came, then.' Mrs Evans, the parish stalwart who was overseeing refreshments, emerged from the kitchen doorway – controlling busybody that she was, she hadn't been able to resist checking several times over that everything was in order and that none of her assistants had sneaked in to steal a sandwich or a slice of pork pie. 'I don't know why in the world Rector Holley invited *him*. We don't have anything to do with the Catholics.'

'I'm a Catholic,' Edie said, a little affronted.

Mrs Evans's nose wrinkled as if she'd come across a bad smell.

'That's neither here nor there, is it?' she said, still sounding indignant. 'You're here to help. That old father is a guest.'

'He's not old,' Edie objected.

'I don't trust any of them. Always creeping

207

around. It's not natural. And goodness knows what goes on up at the abbey behind closed doors.'

Edie gave a small shake of her head and put a little distance between herself and Mrs Evans. It was all she could do not to argue, say that Father Michael was not some sort of demon and neither were any of the other priests she knew, and defend the church she'd been raised in even if she didn't often attend services. But what was the point? You couldn't change the mind of a bigot, and that was what Mrs Evans was.

There were plenty of others like her, Edie knew, mistrustful of what they didn't understand. She only hoped Father Michael wasn't made aware of their hostility, though his nervous smile as he'd come into the hall suggested he might have been expecting something of the sort. But at least the rector was welcoming his guest and doing his best to put him at his ease – Edie could see he was introducing the priest to one or two of his parishioners, and they, at least, were nodding and smiling.

Would she have a chance to speak to him? Edie wondered. Ask him if he'd been able to learn any more about Christina's origins? A little knot of nervousness constricted her throat as she thought of it. Very soon it would be Christina's birthday, fifteen years after she had been found in the porch. How wonderful it would be to be able to give her some news as to who she really was as a birthday present! But supposing that news was that May was her real mother? What then? Edie wanted to know the truth almost as much as Christina herself did, and yet at the same time she shrank from it. Bad enough to have this awful suspicion hanging over her; she wasn't at all sure how she would feel if it was confirmed, or what she'd do about it. The repercussions were more than she dared think about, and she was beginning to wish Christina had never raised the subject.

'May I have the pleasure of this dance?'

Jolted out of her reverie, Edie turned to see a slightly built young man looking at her expectantly.

'You are allowed to dance, are you?' he added.

'Oh ... yes...' Edie hesitated, surprised to have been asked and a little unsure. The dance was a foxtrot, one she had never really mastered. Then, as she saw the young man's smile falter, she took pity on him. 'Thank you,' she said, and allowed him to lead her on to the floor.

Apart from her jig earlier with Nellie, Edie hadn't danced with anyone since Charlie had gone away, and she had to concentrate hard not to make a mistake. But at least it took her mind off her dilemma for a little while, and the young man danced well, making it easy for her to follow his lead.

'I haven't seen you in church, have I?' he asked as they twirled around the floor.

'No, I'm a Catholic,' Edie said for the second time that evening.

'That explains it, then,' he said, without any of the disapproval Mrs Evans had displayed. 'I'm Walter Thomas. My father is the tower captain.'

'Tower captain?' For a moment, Edie was baffled.

'In charge of the bell ringers.'

'Ah.' Edie liked to hear the bells on a Sunday morning, and on Friday evenings too, when the ringers did their practice. 'What's your name, then?'

'Edie Cooper. I work at Fairley Hall.'

'Yes, I know.'

For some reason, that made her uncomfortable again. She glanced up at her partner from beneath lowered lashes – he was several inches taller than her. He really wasn't bad looking, except for a snaggle tooth that protruded over his lower lip, and he seemed pleasant and well mannered, but suddenly she was anxious for the dance to end, and she couldn't quite understand why.

Then, as she caught herself looking for Father Michael amongst the revellers gathered around the perimeter of the hall, light dawned. She wanted to talk to the priest, and not just to ask him if he'd managed to find out anything of interest about Christina.

The realisation came as something of a shock. What in the world was the matter with her? Fool that she was, she found him attractive; the first man, apart from Charlie, that she'd ever felt that way about. But why? Was it the aura of mystery that surrounded a priest? The sense of the forbidden? Whatever, it was senseless, and a waste of time and energy. He was as far out of her reach as Charlie was, and she'd do well to remember it and concentrate instead on trying to find herself a young man before she turned into a dried-up old spinster like Quilla Brimble. A young man like Walter Thomas. She didn't fancy him the way she fancied Charlie and Father Michael, but perhaps she was just being too choosy.

The dance was coming to an end, the music slowing to a final flourish, and Walter walked her back to her place by the kitchen door.

'Can I have the next dance too?' he asked.

'I need a bit of a breather,' Edie said, and then, almost flirtatiously: 'You can come and ask me again a bit later, though, if you like.'

'I might just do that,' he said, smiling so that the tooth jutted alarmingly.

As he left her and walked away across the floor, Edie sighed to herself. All very well to make up her mind she must give other boys a chance, but it wasn't going to be easy and she had a horrible feeling she was going to have to force herself every step of the way.

'Who was that you were dancing with, then?'

Nellie and Teddy joined her. They were holding hands and a bit breathless. Edie hadn't seen them on the dance floor and wondered if they'd stepped outside for a bit of a kiss and a cuddle.

'Oh, just a boy who asked me. Where have you two been?'

Nellie tapped the side of her nose. 'That's for us to know and you to find out.'

'Come on, Nellie.' The music had begun again and Teddy was pulling Nellie towards the floor.

'All right ... all right...' She cast a look of pretend exasperation at Edie over her shoulder and Edie looked away, overcome once again by envy that Nellie had something that seemed destined to be denied to her. No matter that they had been engaged so long that it had become something of

211

a joke. They were happy with the way things were, happy with each other. Edie would have given anything to be in the same position.

'Edie. It is Edie, isn't it?'

Father Michael was approaching her, smiling. Edie's heart gave an uncomfortable lurch.

'Father!'

'How good to see you enjoying yourself! Your ankle is quite healed now, is it?'

'Yes thank you, Father. I'm back at work, and helping tonight with the refreshments.'

'Yes, Rector Holley told me.'

So they had been talking about her. Edie felt the colour rushing to her cheeks.

'It's quite warm in here, isn't it? And I've just been dancing,' she said, hoping to explain her blush.

'So I saw. Perhaps you'll have a dance with me later on.'

The very idea of it pleased her, unlike the thought of dancing with Walter Thomas again. She laughed a little self-consciously.

'I didn't know priests danced.'

'Not often, I admit. But why shouldn't we?'

'I never saw Father O'Brien dancing.'

'I expect he did in his younger days. He wouldn't be up to it now, though, and probably hasn't been for many years.'

'How is he?' Edie asked.

'Not so good, I'm afraid. He's in quite a lot of pain from the arthritis in his joints, I believe. But that's just from my observation. He never complains. His faith sustains him, I'm glad to say.'

Now that the subject of Father O'Brien had

arisen, Edie saw her chance. 'And his memory?' she asked tentatively.

'It comes and goes. Strangely, he seems quite clear about things that happened years ago, but he can't recall where he left his spectacles, or what he had for dinner yesterday. It's very sad.'

'Yes.' Edie hesitated for a moment, then launched into the question that was at the forefront of her mind. 'Have you had a chance to find out if he knows anything about Miss Christina's real mother?'

'Well, I have talked to him. But...' He looked around. 'Is there anywhere a bit quieter? I can hardly hear myself think in the midst of all this merrymaking.'

Hope flared, and with it a dart of apprehension at what she might be about to find out.

'We could go in the kitchen,' she suggested.

She opened the door, hoping she wouldn't find Mrs Evans checking on arrangements there yet again. But the kitchen was deserted, though the urn was singing noisily.

'So was he able to tell you anything?' she asked, holding her breath.

To her disappointment, Father Michael shook his head.

'Very little, I'm afraid, though I did get the impression there was something he knew but was unwilling to share. As I told you before, anything revealed to him in the confessional has to remain confidential, but I'm sure you already knew that.'

'Yes, of course.' But the need to know was greater now than her fear of learning an un-palatable truth. 'He didn't mention my mother, I suppose?' she ventured, watching his face closely.

Even if he was unable to tell her because of the strict rules of the confessional, perhaps his reaction would give her an answer. And for a moment Edie thought she saw a guarded expression in his eyes.

'He mentioned her, of course,' he said.

Edie hardly dared to breathe. 'And?'

'He remembered her looking after the baby until the authorities took her away. He remarked on her kindness and concern. She even missed Mass so as to remain with her in the sanctuary – he gave her communion later, privately, because she was very upset and asked especially for it.'

'She was upset?'

'Everyone was. It was a terrible thing. That poor little mite... Quite understandably, there were tears when she was handed over.'

'My mother cried?'

'She's a good soul, Edie. She was afraid the little one would be taken to an orphanage, I expect.'

'She cried,' Edie repeated. Her own eyes were misting, then filling with tears.

How dreadful it must have been for May if it was her own baby she had been handing over! She must have been quite desperate to be able to bring herself to do it, especially as she wouldn't have known then what would become of the child. Though she may have told herself it would find a loving home, there was no way she could be sure of that, and the alternatives didn't bear thinking about.

'Father ... you don't think...?' Her throat ached as she managed the words.

'I don't think what, Edie?' His expression was puzzled.

'That...' She could hardly bring herself to say it. 'That the baby was hers?'

'Good Lord, no! Whatever makes you say such a thing?' He looked startled, then his eyes narrowed. 'Is that what all this is about? Is that the reason you asked me to help you discover the truth?'

Edie shook her head. 'Not in the beginning. It was Miss Christina who started it, just as I told you. But since then ... I've begun to wonder. Mam gets in an awful state every time it's so much as mentioned, and she more or less forbade me to ask anybody else about it either. She'd be furious if she knew I was talking to you about it now. And I can't understand why she never said she was the one who found the baby. I'd have thought a story like that would have got told and retold over the years. But she never mentioned it, not even when I was given the job of being Miss Christina's lady's maid. Doesn't that seem odd to you, Father? And if she had something to hide, wouldn't it explain why she stopped going to church when she used to be so devout?'

Her tear-filled eyes, fixed on his face, tore at his heart.

'People stop going to church for all manner of reasons,' he said evasively. 'We all lose our faith from time to time, and find it again when the time is right.'

'But Father...'

He laid a hand on her arm. 'Edie, no good will come of you thinking like this. You are letting

215

your imagination run away with you.'

They were interrupted by the sudden opening of the kitchen door. Mrs Evans came bustling in but stopped in her tracks when she saw them.

'Oh! What are you doing in here?' Her tone was indignant, her small eyes behind her wire-rimmed spectacles suspicious.

'I'm sorry if we are intruding,' Father Michael apologised. 'We just wanted a quiet place to talk.'

Mrs Evans puffed out her thin chest. 'There are plenty of places for that without coming into my kitchen.'

'I'm sorry,' Michael said again. 'We'll leave, of course.'

He slipped an arm around Edie, ushering her towards the door.

'I shall need her in a minute!' Mrs Evans called after them. 'It's nearly time for the refreshment break.'

'And you shall have her, I promise.' Michael continued propelling Edie out of the door. Back in the hall, he turned her to face him.

'I expect you have got hold of the wrong end of the stick,' he said, continuing their interrupted conversation where they had left off. 'But you mustn't let this come between you and your mother. Perhaps she finds it too painful to talk about for some reason that has nothing whatever to do with what you suspect. Leave it, and she may come to feel differently, and answer your questions in her own good time.'

Edie was chewing her lip. 'You would tell me if you found anything out, wouldn't you, Father?'

Stanley Bristow had been entertaining the

revellers with one of his music hall songs, and now a sudden burst of applause as he finished saved Michael from replying directly. How could he promise anything of the sort when it might well be a question of confidentiality? Not to mention the Pandora's box of mischiefs the truth might release.

'Look, Edie, if you continue to be troubled about this, why don't you come to see me and we will talk some more?' he said as the applause died down. 'My door is always open, and if I can help you with this, or anything else, then of course I will.'

'Thank you, Father.'

'Edith!' Mrs Evans was calling from the doorway. 'Fetch that other girl from wherever it is she's hiding and tell her you are both needed here.'

Her lips were tight, and Edie couldn't help remembering the disparaging remarks she had made earlier about Father Michael.

In her book he was probably 'creeping around' now, a danger to the moral welfare of anyone who crossed his path. For a reckless moment, Edie wished that were true. She could think of no one she'd rather be led astray by. And it wasn't just the strong physical attraction she felt for him. He was kind and good, too, and upset as she had been, for the space of those few moments when his arm had been around her waist, she'd felt comforted and safe. When she was with Father Michael, she felt that she could somehow cope with whatever she might discover, take whatever blows life might throw at her. But that was just wishful thinking.

From the other side of the room she could see

Walter Thomas looking at her, and she curled up inside with something close to revulsion. But she wouldn't have to pretend to like him any more; there would be no more time for dancing tonight. For the next half-hour or more she'd be busy pouring tea, and after that there would be stacks of washing-up to be done, which they would be lucky to finish before midnight.

'I have to go,' she said to Michael.

'Of course. Don't forget, though, what I said. Any time you want to talk...'

She nodded and went in search of Nellie, thinking she might well take him up on his offer.

The thought cheered her a little as Mrs Evans opened the serving hatch and the first hungry and thirsty revellers began queuing for their refreshments.

Father Michael drank an obligatory cup of tea with his host, Rector Holley, then left the warmth of the church hall for the long walk back to the abbey.

It was a bitterly cold night, a smattering of sleet that might yet turn to snow blowing on an icy wind that even Michael's thick cloak wasn't able to keep out for long.

Usually he relished walking, even in bad weather. Alone with nothing but God's creatures in the world that He had created, he often felt more at one with his faith than he did even in the sanctity of the abbey. The rustle of a bird in the hedgerows, a fox or badger in the undergrowth, the song of a blackbird or the hoot of an owl called to his spirituality even more than the sonorous murmur of the voices of priests joined in prayer; the scent of a shower of rain on parched grass, the pungent odour of wild garlic, the heady aroma of new-mown hay stirred his senses more acutely than the perfume of incense. Walking until his legs ached and his feet throbbed was balm to his soul and brought him a more profound peace than any period of meditation in the dusty cloisters.

Tonight, however, he barely noticed the smells and sounds of the night, and he felt not peace but troubling confusion. He couldn't get the image of Edie's face out of his mind; her tear-filled eyes seemed to follow him in the darkness, the sound of her voice, anxious and pleading, echoed in his ears. Worse, he could still feel her narrow waist beneath his arm, the little tremble of the taut muscles in her back, the jut of her hip.

More than anything he had wanted to take her in his arms and comfort her. Not so wrong in itself – offering comfort was not beyond the remit of a priest, and sometimes the caring touch of a hand offered more solace to the suffering than even the Mass itself. It was the feelings it had aroused in him that were wrong, so wrong. Feelings he had not experienced since he had renounced the girl with auburn curls and a tinkling laugh all those years ago, when he was just a boy.

But he was not a boy now. He was a priest. He had taken the solemn vows of poverty, chastity and obedience. Until now he had believed it was obedience he would struggle with the most, as he had a stubborn and independent streak that he sometimes found it hard to curb. Poverty he didn't mind at all – everything he needed was provided for him, and he had no desire for anything that money could buy. To be filled with the love of God was all he asked, and that, he had felt sure, would also keep him from carnal desire, for it far surpassed the love of a woman.

Now, however, as he thought of Edie, he realised to his utter dismay that it was not so simple, and he was horrified at how nearly he had given in to unexpected temptation. That moment when he had wanted to take her in his arms – had it only been a desire to comfort her, or had he wanted to feel her body soft against his, her head on his shoulder, her arms, perhaps, around him? It had been a mistake to invite her to come and see him, another moment of weakness that he had excused as nothing more than concern for one of his flock. But he knew now that if she did, the temptation would be there before him again, perhaps even stronger and more difficult to resist.

Besides which, there was the matter of what he should and should not tell her of what he had learned from Father O'Brien. Already he had gone too far in mentioning how upset her mother had been on giving the baby up, in an effort to explain to Edie why perhaps May was so reluctant to remember the events of that long-ago night.

But there was something else he had not told her, and never would. When he had asked Father O'Brien why he thought it was that May didn't want to attend church any more, Father O'Brien had shaken his head, sad and resigned.

'I think it may have to do with a confession she made to me,' he had said. 'I gave her penance and absolution, of course, but sometimes it's not enough. The poor lost soul is so ashamed of sharing the secret of their guilt that they can't face their confessor again. It brings it all back, you see, every time. I don't know, of course, but I feel in my bones it might well be that with May.'

He had not, of course, told Michael what it was May had confessed, but given what Edie had said, he could not help but wonder. Had it been her mother who had left Christina in the church porch that Christmas Eve? Was that the confession she had made to Father O'Brien, and did it haunt her still so that she couldn't bring herself to return to the scene of her last parting with her baby? Perhaps he should visit her again, talk with her and try to assure her of God's love, whatever it was she had done; even try, very gently, to draw the truth out of her. But that was establishing yet another link to Edie, and the temptation he felt every time he thought of her was every bit as bad as the temptations the Devil had laid before Christ in the wilderness.

Michael raised his chin from the collar of his cloak and bared his teeth into the wet and bitter wind.

'Get thee behind me, Satan!' He ground out the words with every ounce of determination he could muster, and for a few minutes he truly believed he could beat the Devil.

Chapter Fourteen

Sir Montague was in a foul mood. For all their efforts, the Conservative Party he supported so fervently had failed to break the deadlock of the January election. Although they had gained the most votes, it was the Liberals who had taken the most seats, and with the support of John Redmond and his Irish parliamentary party, Mr Asquith was once again prime minister.

As if that were not bad enough, he was beginning to despair of Raymond. The young man seemed to have no enthusiasm for anything but his motor car, and was given to making vacuous remarks that set Montague's teeth on edge. His sister had a good deal more sense than he did, Montague thought; she'd be far quicker to grasp the niceties of running the estate, and had the sort of steely determination Raymond was sadly lacking. But of course there was no question of him making her his heir. It wasn't for a woman to inherit, so all he could hope was that Raymond would develop more stability as he grew older. Though he would never be the sharpest knife in the box, he would with any luck gain enough sense to employ a manager who could run the place for him. But it was far from ideal, and not at all the way Montague would wish things to be. He should have had a son of his own to carry on the line; he'd have made sure any boy of his was grounded in his heritage from the moment he was put into trousers, and perhaps even before. But it hadn't happened; in fact nothing had turned out the way he had imagined it would when he had married.

Laura, his wife, had given every appearance of being the perfect mother for the children who would carry on the family name – an heir and a spare, as the saying went. She was twenty-three years old when he began courting her, with passably good looks and fine wide hips perfect, so he had heard, for childbearing. She was gay and amusing, but with a way of hanging on his every word that boosted his ego. And she was the only child of a self-made man who had settled a small fortune to come to her on her marriage – both he and Laura's mother had recently died. All in all she had seemed a perfect prospect.

It wasn't long, however, before Montague realised he had made a bad mistake. For all his efforts, Laura seemed unable to conceive; the months and years went by with no sign of her falling pregnant. He discovered, too, that there was another side to her that wasn't at all to his liking. She could be flirtatious, not only with friends and acquaintances of a similar social standing to their own, but also with employees – the estate and colliery managers, his agent, the engineers and sometimes even the household staff, in particular a young footman who had very soon received his marching orders. It was far from seemly, and infuriated Montague. But even worse was the dark, fragile side that lay beneath the superficial gaiety. Sometimes, when something had upset her, she would retire to her room and remain there for days on end with the drapes pulled so no daylight could get in, refusing food and shaking uncontrollably if he tried to order her to come downstairs and behave in a normal fashion.

'What in God's name is wrong with you?' he had demanded on more than one occasion, but she couldn't, or wouldn't, answer him, and he was left to stomp off and abandon her to her misery, until the mood lifted and she returned gradually to her sunny, if increasingly brittle, self.

Yes, truth to tell, Laura had been a terrible disappointment to him and an increasing embarrassment. He had felt no grief when she had died; only relief, and a determination never to marry again.

Now, with a glass of brandy in his hand, and feeling morose, he wondered as he sometimes did how things might have been different if he had married any one of the other girls he had known as a young man rather than Laura. What did it matter in the long run that he had found them unappealing? One of them might have given him a son and heir, and he would not have ended up like this with no one but that nincompoop to inherit the estate. Damn Laura!

Montague drained the brandy glass in one glug and refilled it from the crystal decanter that stood on a side table. Dammit, that was almost empty too. He rang the bell, and when Reg Deacon answered it, he instructed him to refill the decanter and take it to his room.

'You're retiring, then, are you, Sir Montague?' Reg asked hopefully.

'Not yet,' he barked. 'I simply want the comfort

of my own room. I'll let you know when I am ready for bed.'

'Very good, sir.'

By the time he had climbed the stairs, gritting his teeth against the pain in his foot caused by an attack of gout, which he suffered from at regular intervals, the refilled decanter was standing on the dressing table. He poured himself another large measure and took a few sips. Then he eased his painful foot out of his shoe, took off his coat and tossed it on to the bed ready to be hung up by Jeremiah Dando, his valet, and shrugged into a silk dressing gown. He turned the wicker chair to face the window and sat down, resting his foot on a matching footstool so that he could look out as he drank his brandy.

The rain that had come down with depressing persistence all day had stopped now, and the moon was shining between fitful clouds so that the lawns and the woods beyond were alternately dappled silver, then dark. But the brandy was doing nothing to ease the pain in his foot nor to lighten his mood. If anything, it was stoking the fires of frustration.

What was wrong with the whole blasted world? Why did everything seem to conspire against him? What the hell damage would the bally Liberals do to the country before he and his chums could have another crack at getting them out? Why did he have to put up with this throbbing pain in his toe every few weeks? And what was he going to do about that stupid boy Raymond?

Suddenly a light moving in the darkness beyond the lawns caught his attention. What the devil...?

He blinked, then rubbed his eyes with the back of his hand. He did occasionally see flashing lights just out of his line of vision, which concerned him a little, though he'd refrained from mentioning them to his doctor for fear of giving the physician more ammunition for nagging him about his drinking. But he was fairly certain this light was no trick of the eyes, and as he squinted into the darkness he saw it again, bobbing against the backdrop of trees at the edge of the copse.

Poachers! It had to be poachers! The bare-faced cheek of them, coming so close to the house! And where the devil was Hill, the gamekeeper?

Fury coursed through Montague's veins along with the alcohol. He slammed down his glass and hobbled to the bell-pull, almost oblivious to the pain in his toe. Not waiting for one of the servants to answer, he made for the top of the stairs, and was halfway down when Reg Deacon appeared.

'There's poachers in the copse!' he bellowed. 'Get out there and catch the buggers! Go on, what are you waiting for?'

Fuming, he started back to the window. Though he was wearing no shoe on the offending foot, his toe felt as if it were on fire, and a pulse throbbed in his temple. In his haste, he blundered into a small table, sending a bowl of Christmas roses crashing to the ground. Before he could stop himself, his bare foot squelched into spilled water and snow-white blooms, and he swore again.

By the time he reached the window, figures were emerging from the rear of the house, no more than dark running shadows, but he recognised Reg and Simon Ford, and behind them, Percy Stevens.

226

Good God, surely the man was too old to be chasing about in the dark? If it was left to Stevens, the intruders would be long gone. Nevertheless, Montague had to acknowledge he was making a fair effort at keeping up with the younger men.

Well good for him. Montague just hoped he didn't give himself a heart attack. It would be a huge inconvenience to have to train up a new butler.

At the edge of the copse, Percy Stevens slowed and came to a stop, pressing a hand to his heaving chest. There was no way he could keep up with the youngsters, and he supposed it had been foolish of him to try. But like Sir Montague himself, he was outraged at the thought of poachers on Fairley land. There had been a spate of them last year until Hill had caught a couple of them red-handed – literally – their fingers stained with rabbit blood, and with a couple of cock pheasants in a sack. He'd had them up before the magistrates and they'd both been sent to prison for a spell of hard labour. That had sent out a clear message to anyone tempted to follow suit, and things had been quiet for a while. But now, it seemed, they, or some other thieving toads, were ready to chance their luck again. Percy fervently hoped that Reg and Simon could get their hands on them so they could be taught a lesson they wouldn't forget in a hurry, and he'd like to be there to see it.

As he got his breath back, he set off again, at a walking pace this time, following the line of the copse in the direction Reg and Simon had taken.

He wasn't going to risk venturing into the wood itself; there were too many tree roots to trip him up, and he didn't want to snag his smart butler's coat on jutting branches or dead hanging brambles, so he stayed on the grass until he came to a well-worn pathway, where he stopped again, listening.

All was quiet but for the hoot of an owl somewhere over the park, and there was no sign of the lights that had attracted Sir Montague's attention. Percy sighed deeply, mopping his damp brow with a large white handkerchief. The poachers could be anywhere by now.

Then, quite unexpectedly, he heard a shout deep in the woods – he recognised the voice as Simon's – and a moment later the rustle of branches and the cracking of twigs underfoot, louder with every passing second.

They were coming this way, making perhaps for the very path close to where he was standing! Percy felt a thrust of alarm. For all he knew the villains were armed with shotguns or cudgels, and even if they weren't, they'd be young and fit, thugs who could fell him with a single blow. But it was a momentary aberration only. Though the thought of coming face to face with a desperate man was a daunting one, Percy was no coward.

If he took them by surprise, he might be able to trip up at least one of them, he thought. The loud crashing in the undergrowth suggested that Simon and Reg were hot on their heels; if he could impede their progress, there was a good chance they could be collared yet.

He ducked behind the trunk of the nearest tree

and waited, his heart beating so hard it reverberated in his throat. Any minute ... any minute...

Just as two running figures came into view and he prepared to step out from his hiding place, the fitful moon emerged from behind a cloud, illuminating the faces of the trespassers, and Percy froze in shock, his resolve wavering as he recognised the man pounding towards him and the lad a step or two behind.

All very well to aid in the arrest of unknown poachers, young ruffians or maybe didicoys – he'd heard some had set up camp on some common land nearby. But someone he knew...

Percy took a step backwards. As they ran past, the man's eyes flicked up, looking directly at him. Percy remained motionless and silent. The pair headed off across the grass to the drive, and were almost out of sight before Simon and Reg came panting out of the woods.

Simon swore, a word he'd never dare use in the presence of Mrs Parker or even Cook, Percy thought, and doubled over, breathing heavily. Reg too stopped.

'We'll never catch them now.'

'I know that, you bloody fool.' Simon straightened up, still breathing hard. 'They had the edge on us. If I'd got my hands on them, I'd have wrung their ruddy necks. But they must have run straight past you, Mr Stevens. Couldn't you have tried to stop them?'

Percy didn't know what to say.

'Did you get a look at them?' Simon continued. 'Was it anybody you recognised?'

Again Percy hesitated. Of course he'd recognised them, but he needed time to think this through before he said anything.

'It was dark,' he said. 'I couldn't be sure.'

'Were they young? Older? Big? Small? You must have seen that at least.'

'Didn't you?' Percy countered.

'Nah. It was pitch black in them woods. All we saw was their light, and when I shouted, they legged it. I couldn't see 'em at all – could you, Reg?'

Reg shook his head. 'You know I couldn't. I caught my foot in that tree root and fell over.'

'You're bloody good for nothing!' Simon exploded. 'I don't know why they keep you on.'

'I don't suppose there's any more we can do then,' Percy said, relieved to have the attention diverted from his own less than truthful account. 'We might as well get back in the warm.'

'Yes, you're right.' Simon swore again, looking regretfully along the drive. 'They'll be long gone now. The only good thing is I think we disturbed them before they could get any of Sir Montague's game.'

'It did look as if they were empty-handed,' Percy said, and immediately regretted it as Simon jumped on his words.

'I thought you didn't see anything.'

'It just didn't look to me as if they were carrying anything. They were going like the clappers.'

'Sir Montague's not going to be best pleased we lost them,' Reg said, rubbing at his chin where a bramble had caught him and scraped the skin.

'He hasn't been best pleased all day!' Simon retorted. 'I've had the length of his tongue more than once, miserable old bugger.'

'Mind your language,' Percy said, glad to be able to change the subject. 'And don't let me hear you talking about Sir Montague like that again.'

'Well it's what he is.' Simon was not going to be dictated to by the butler. Strictly speaking he wasn't responsible to him.

'He's taken it very hard that the Liberals have got back in,' Percy said. 'Now let's get back in the warm before we all catch pneumonia.'

And with that he turned and led the way back to the house.

Lilian Parker was very concerned about Percy. She'd already gone to bed when Sir Montague had spotted the lights in the copse; disturbed by all the commotion, she'd come downstairs wrapped in her green wool dressing gown, and with curling rags in her hair, to find out what was going on. Now, after Simon and Reg had reported to a furious Sir Montague their failure to apprehend the supposed poachers, the servants had been given leave to retire, and had done so gratefully. Percy, however, who had not seemed at all himself since he'd returned to the house, had remained in his chair by the dying fire, and Lilian was reluctant to leave him there alone.

'Whatever were you thinking, going out in the middle of the night chasing poachers?' she demanded when the two of them were alone. 'You should have left it to Reg and Simon.'

Percy rubbed his hands together in the fading warmth of the fire and said nothing.

'You seem to forget you're not as young as you

231

used to be,' Lilian scolded. 'They could have turned nasty for all you knew. Anything could have happened.'

'Well it didn't,' Percy said shortly.

'But it's upset you. And don't try to make out any different – I know you too well. Shall I make you another cup of cocoa? That might do you good.'

'No – no, I don't want anything else to drink,' Percy said hastily. Cocoa might help him to fall asleep, but if he had any more he'd be up and down half a dozen times during the night needing to use the chamber pot, though he'd never admit as much to Mrs Parker.

'What *do* you want, then?' She was fussing like an old mother hen.

Percy turned in his chair, looking at her with a worried expression.

'I've got things on my mind, Mrs Parker.'

'And what things are those?' she asked, exasperated. 'You were right as rain earlier on. If it's just that you couldn't keep up with the young 'uns, that's only to be expected. You weren't to blame for not managing to catch those dratted poachers. You're getting older. We both are. It's something that comes to us all.'

'That's true enough.' Percy rubbed his legs, which were aching. 'But I wish that's all it was. The truth of the matter is...' He stopped, looking towards the door. 'The others have all gone to bed, haven't they?'

'They have. And that's where you should be. You'll be good for nothing in the morning.'

'The truth of the matter is, just between

ourselves, Mrs Parker, that I could have stopped them. I was all ready to stick out my foot and trip them up.'

'And then you thought better of it, I suppose. That's nothing to be ashamed of.'

'No, I'd have done it all right. I let them go because I recognised them.'

'What!' Lilian was agog now. 'Who was it?'

Percy hesitated for a moment, then made up his mind. He and Lilian didn't keep secrets from one another, and besides, she might help him decide what he should do.

'It was Quilla's brother and that boy of his.'

'Dick Brimble?' Lilian was astonished. Brimble was the local blacksmith, and though he was surly and uncouth, he didn't, to her knowledge, have any criminal tendencies. 'Are you sure?'

'Positive. The moon came out and I saw them clear as day.'

'Good gracious me!' Lilian folded her arms around herself. 'I'd never have thought that of him. I don't like the man, never have. But *poaching*... I wouldn't have thought he'd have any need for that. There's always enough horses in need of shoeing to keep food on his table. Why ever would he risk *poaching?*'

'I don't know, Mrs Parker. I only know what I saw. Him and that boy of his making a dash for it when they thought they were going to get caught. And so they deserve to be if they were poaching. But I didn't want to be the one to put him up before the magistrates, perhaps get him sent to prison. Not seeing we have to work with Quilla. Only now I'm wondering if I did the wrong thing. Whether I ought to tell Sir Montague who it was trespassing on his land.'

'I suppose by rights you should,' Lilian said.

'They didn't seem to have caught anything, though. Didn't even have any bags with them.'

'I expect they dumped 'em when they had to make a run for it.' Lilian shook her head. 'Gamekeeper'll find 'em in the morning, I shouldn't wonder.'

'Maybe so. And what else would they have been doing, creeping around the estate in the dark?'

'Did the others see him?' Lilian asked.

'I don't think so. They just rooted him out, so to speak.'

'And you didn't tell them you recognised him?'

'I didn't want to admit I'd let them go on purpose.' Percy looked a little shamefaced.

'No, I don't suppose you did,' Lilian said. 'You can't just ignore it, though, Mr Stevens. I reckon you ought to go to Sir Montague and own up.'

'And have him set the police on Quilla's brother?'

'If that's what he decides to do. It ought to be his decision, not yours.'

'What I'm hoping is that Dick will have learned his lesson,' Percy said. 'He knows I saw him, knows I recognised him. I should think he'd have more sense than to come out here again.'

'It's up to you, of course.' Lilian was not at all happy about this. 'But I reckon at least you ought to have a word with Quilla, tell her straight that you know it was her brother out there tonight, and hopefully she'll warn him he'd better not do it again. That would probably be best all round. I

234

can see that if you started accusing Dick without any proper evidence, things might get a bit awkward.'

'That's what I'll do, then.' Percy was beginning to feel a little more like his usual decisive self. 'I'll speak to Quilla in the morning. Now...' He hesitated, then threw caution to the winds. 'Perhaps I will have that cup of cocoa after all, Mrs Parker,' he said.

'Do you think you could spare me to go into town for an hour, milady?' Quilla asked. 'The hem of your purple dress needs a stitch and I seem to have run out of the right colour cotton.'

'Yes, of course, Quilla. I'll ask Sir Montague if Simon can drive you.'

'Oh, there's no need for that, milady,' Quilla said hastily. 'It's a nice dry day and the walk will do me good.'

'Are you sure? I'm confident Sir Montague would be agreeable, and there's no telling if it might start raining again.'

'Quite sure, milady. I'll be there and back before there's any chance of that.'

Before Lady Elizabeth could press her further, she hurried up to her room, put on her hat and coat, then slipped down the servants' staircase and out of the back door. The last thing she wanted was for Simon to drive her. He'd probably stop the car right outside the haberdashery and wait while she went in – and needing purple cotton was just an excuse Quilla had come up with to give her the chance to go into town. She had to go to the forge and talk to her brother, and she couldn't do that with Simon taking notice of her every move.

As she set out down the long drive at a brisk pace, Quilla's mouth was dry, and her stomach was still churning from the encounter she had just had with Percy Stevens. He'd taken her to one side and told her what had happened last night, and how for her sake he had decided to keep quiet about it, but that if such a thing occurred again he would be forced to go to Sir Montague and tell him he knew the identity of the poachers.

'Dick should be ashamed of himself, and introducing that boy of his to a life of crime into the bargain is nothing short of a disgrace,' he had said. 'I know there are some folk who think poaching is fair game, but it's theft by any other name. I could understand it if your brother was some poor starving wretch, but he's far from that, and I can think of no good reason for such behaviour.'

'No, Mr Stevens, and neither can I,' Quilla said. Her legs had turned to jelly and her stomach to water.

She knew very well why Dick had been on the estate last night, and it had nothing to do with shooting pheasants or rabbits. He'd only been doing what she'd asked him to do the last time she'd seen him – looking for evidence to back up her plan. How could he have been so stupid as to get himself spotted? And as for taking Richard with him ... what had he been thinking of? Bad enough that Percy had recognised them – at least it seemed he was keeping that to himself – but if Simon and Reg had caught them, it would have meant the end of all her hopes and plans for the boy. As it was, she'd have to delay what she intended until this poaching business was forgotten. If he got wind of it, Percy might change his mind and decide Sir Montague should be told the truth after all.

Well, she was going to give Dick a piece of her mind all right, and tell him to stay well away from Fairley Hall from now on. She'd manage without his help. All brawn and no brains, that was her brother.

Still simmering with barely controlled rage, Quilla quickened her pace and headed for town.

Chapter Fifteen

The days leading up to Christmas were always busy ones at Fairley Hall, since preparations had to be made not only for Christmas Day itself, but also for Christina's birthday, which was celebrated the day before. Mrs Davey, flushed and flustered but efficient as ever, had become used to making two fruit cakes, one large and one small, both topped with almond paste and royal icing; and the Christmas tree, which in the old days had always been cut on Christmas Eve, was now put up in the hall a day earlier. Christina loved to help decorate it, carefully unwrapping the fragile glass baubles and crystal icicles from their tissue paper, inserting new miniature candles into their holders, and hanging ornaments on the branches within her reach. Since the tree was at least ten feet tall, one of the servants was usually summoned to assist,

237

but this year Raymond had done the honours – apart from the angel who sat on the topmost branch. Christina had named her Joy, and always maintained she was her very special birthday angel.

'I don't trust you with her,' she declared. 'If you drop her, she might be smashed to pieces. Let Edie do it.'

So, in spite of Raymond's protestations, it was Edie who climbed the stepladder and perched Joy in her usual place, all too conscious of having to hitch up her skirt while Raymond held the ladder steady. He hadn't made any more advances to her since the day they had driven up on to the Mendips but it flustered her all the same to know he would have a fine view of her ankles and, if she wasn't careful, a great deal more besides.

Christina's birthday itself had always been celebrated with a party, with guests of her own age invited to tea. When she was little, they had often been the children of the estate workers, who came scrubbed and squeezed into their Sunday best, some shy and so overawed by the grand surroundings that they barely joined in at all, others who became raucous and silly, galloping round the house in search of the treasure hunt clues that Elizabeth had laid out and fighting for places round the table so as to be closest to the trifle or the plate of cakes and biscuits they most fancied. But those days were over now, and instead the guests were to be a few young people from suitable families, and the party was to be held in the evening. Edward and Alexandra Grattan, whose father was a peer of the realm, no less, and owned a large estate on the far outskirts of Hillsbridge, had been invited, along with Rachel Holley, daughter of the rector, Peter and Paul Osborne, twin sons of another coal owner with a group of collieries in the locality, and Selena and Ruth Johnson, daughters of Sir Montague's estate manager. Raymond, too, was going to join the celebrations – he was much of an age with Edward Grattan and Selena – but Julia had decided to make herself scarce. She had nothing in common with these very young people, and in any case Lettice, whom Elizabeth had suggested she invite for Christmas, had arrived that morning, and she was looking forward to catching up with her dear friend in private.

Below stairs things were even more frenetic than usual, since in addition to the family's dinner, refreshments had to be prepared for Christina's guests. As soon as the roasted pheasant had been sent up, Mrs Davey supervised her small working party of Edie, Nellie and her niece, Alice – the new maid – as they piled pâté on to the little biscuits she had made earlier and filled tartlet cases with jellied fruit – Flo Doughty could not be trusted with such a finicky task; she was sweating over a sink full of hot water as she washed soup bowls and tureens. Things were progressing more or less to Mrs Davey's satisfaction, but when Percy Stevens and Reg Deacon returned from serving the pheasant, it was to disrupt her careful plan of campaign.

'Edie's to go up and keep an eye on the young people,' Percy announced.

'But I need her here!' Mrs Davey protested,

wiping her damp forehead with her sleeve. 'We're up to our eyes, as you can see.'

'Sir Montague's orders, I'm afraid,' Percy told her. 'He believes things are becoming a little wild and he's afraid damage may be done.' He turned to Edie. 'In particular, he's concerned for his gramophone, so perhaps you could station yourself beside it to make sure no harm comes to it, or to his collection of recordings.'

'I don't know how I'm supposed to do that,' Edie said, worried.

She'd heard the music carrying loudly down the stairwell – they all had – and while it simply sounded to her as if they were having a good time, she knew as well as any of them how protective Sir Montague was of his gramophone and the records he had purchased to listen to. They were mostly classical pieces performed by symphony orchestras, and what seemed to be operatic arias, though Edie had no idea what they were or who was singing them, as well as a few lighter offerings, such as 'Annie Laurie', sung by a male quartet. The music this evening, though, was much jollier; Edie thought she'd recognised Florrie Forde's powerful voice belting out 'The Old Bull and Bush' and guessed that one of Christina's guests must have brought some records with them.

'Perhaps you could offer to be in charge of the gramophone,' Percy suggested.

Edie looked horrified. 'But I've never ... never so much as touched it, except to polish the case,' she protested. 'I'm more likely to damage it than any of them are.'

'You'll be careful, I'm sure,' Percy said. 'Now

make haste – and you'd better take that apron off before you go.'

'Oh ... yes.' Since she had become Christina's lady's maid, Edie had seldom had to wear an apron, and now she had quite forgotten that Mrs Davey had given her one to cover her dress. She wiped her hands on it, took it off and hung it on a peg on the wall, then, feeling a little daunted, headed upstairs.

She tapped before opening the drawing room door but no one answered. No doubt they hadn't heard her over the loud and raucous music – Harry Champion, now, giving his all to 'Boiled Beef and Carrots'. But as she entered the room a little tentatively, Christina saw her and ran across to take her arm.

'Edith! I'm so glad you're here! You must listen to this – isn't it a scream? Have you ever heard anything like it?'

'It's Harry, isn't it?' Edie said.

'You know him? How marvellous!' The recording was coming to an end. 'Look, everyone, this is Edith, my very own maid,' Christina announced. 'She is such fun! I know you'll all love her as much as I do.'

'Oh, Miss Christina...' Edie was blushing, and uncomfortably aware of Raymond's amused eyes on her.

One of the young men – Edie thought it was one of the Osborne boys – was crossing to Sir Montague's precious gramophone. Edie took a wary step forward, then thought better of it. The young man appeared to know exactly what he was doing, which was more than she could say for herself. She

241

watched closely as he lifted the disc carefully from the turntable, wound up the machine with the handle she had always been afraid to touch when she was dusting and polishing, slipped another record on to the spindle, and expertly set the needle in a groove at its outer edge. At once another jolly tune came blasting out of the big fluted horn. Edie made up her mind to leave him to it. For all the noise, the young people didn't seem to be doing any harm.

She remained beside the gramophone, though, feeling a little out of place but enjoying the party atmosphere.

The tune now was 'By the Light of the Silvery Moon', and Raymond, a glass of wine in hand, was singing along to it. He tipped a wink at Christina, beckoning to her, and she left Edie's side and skipped across the room. Raymond slipped his free arm around her shoulders and smiled into her face as he sang.

Place park, scene dark, silvery moon is shining
  through the trees;
Cast two, me, you, sound of kisses floating on the
  breeze.
Act One, begun. Dialogue, 'Where would you like to
  spoon?'
My cue, with you, underneath the silvery moon...

Edie shifted from one foot to the other, a little uncomfortable now. She didn't like the way Raymond was looking at Christina, nor the besotted expression on the girl's face. And she certainly didn't like the squeeze he gave her as the song

242

came to an end. She almost wished he would begin bothering her again, as he had that afternoon up on the Mendips; at least she knew how to deal with his advances. Christina was so naive, she might even be flattered by them. Edie resolved to keep an eye on things. She might have been sent up here to make sure Sir Montague's precious gramophone came to no harm, but she couldn't help thinking it was Christina who was in the most danger.

The refreshments arrived, brought on silver salvers by Reg and Alice – Edie smiled to herself as it occurred to her that Percy didn't think the party important enough to bring the food himself. The guests were soon tucking in to the delicious canapés she had been helping to prepare when she had been called away, but Edie didn't think she should eat any of them. Being almost a part of the celebrations of her betters was one thing; eating food that was meant for them was quite another.

When the platters had been cleared of the last morsel and taken away, someone suggested it was time for a game. The first they settled on was Blind Man's Buff, and Edie squeezed into a corner while they blundered about, making much of the excuse to snatch a quick squeeze when the blindfold was over their eyes. It was harmless fun, though, and Edie saw that like her, Raymond was sitting this one out. Then someone suggested Sardines. It would involve spreading into the rest of the house, of course, but Christina declared that no one would mind that, just as long as they didn't go upstairs and into the bedrooms, and

243

though she was a little dubious about it, Edie didn't see that she could object.

'You must play too, Edie,' Christina insisted. 'In fact, I think you should be the first one to hide. You must know far more good places than anyone else.'

'Oh I don't think I should, Miss Christina,' Edie protested, but the others took up the cry, the young men, Edie couldn't help but notice, rather more eagerly than the girls, which made her a little nervous about being squashed into some hidey-hole with one of them until they were discovered by the others of the party. But there was nothing for it, Christina was insistent, and reluctantly Edie went off to conceal herself while they counted – very loudly – to a hundred.

Anxious about invading the family's private quarters, Edie decided upon the hall. Not even Sir Montague could complain about her being there, she thought, and it was unlikely the party-goers would search somewhere so obvious, to begin with at least. A giant wardrobe with intricately carved doors stood in one corner; Edie had never quite worked out why, since it was unused except for a few shooting sticks and an ebony-topped cane. It might be a bit of a squash when one by one the others discovered her, but then that was half the fun of the game.

She scuttled across the tiled floor and had just slipped inside the wardrobe when she heard the shouts of 'Coming!' She pulled the door closed, wrinkling her nose at the musty smell and thinking she must ask Mrs Parker to get one of the maids to give it a good airing. Though dim inside, it wasn't completely dark, as light from the hall crept in through the cracks around the door, and through a knothole in the oak she could just see a bit of the giant Christmas tree, the glass baubles shimmering in the light of the dozens of miniature candles on almost every one of its branches.

For all that she had thought the hall might be the last place any of the players would look, it wasn't long before she heard footsteps on the tiled floor. She remained perfectly still, scarcely daring to breathe, and struggling to control a sneeze from the dust that had flown up as she closed the door. But to no avail. Though she covered her nose and mouth with both hands, it erupted all the more violently from being suppressed, and a moment later the door was opened.

Silhouetted as he was against the light, Edie couldn't see which of the boys it was who had found her, but as he exclaimed, 'Got ya!' and climbed in beside her, she recognised him as Edward Grattan, who had been in charge of the gramophone earlier.

'Well this is jolly!' he said, closing the door behind him.

'Ssh! You'll give the game away!' Edie warned.

'Mm ... and that would be a pity so soon,' he agreed.

Edie could only giggle nervously, hoping against hope that he wasn't going to take advantage of the situation. But Edward was no Raymond, and he merely exchanged whispered pleasantries.

One by one the other members of the party discovered the hiding place and crammed into the wardrobe, giggling. Edie found herself trapped against the back board with Paul Osborne's bony elbow jutting into her ribs and the rather plump Rachel Holley's bosom squashed against her so that she could scarcely breathe – besides being well-endowed, Rachel was a good six inches taller than she was. Now the only two who had not found them were Raymond and Christina herself.

'Where the devil *are* they?' Peter Osborne asked in a voice loud enough to have given the game away if Raymond and Christina had been within earshot, but still nobody came.

'How much longer?' Ruth Johnson asked plaintively. 'My whole arm has gone to sleep.'

'Let's move around a bit,' Peter suggested.

'Better still, let's just get out of here!' Ruth rejoined.

'Yes. I think it's agreed – we've beaten them.' That was Edward, a little fed up not to have been squashed in next to Selena Johnson, if the truth were to be known. 'I think we've all had enough of this game. I suggest we play charades, or put on some more music and have a bit of a dance.'

No one objected, and they all piled out of the wardrobe and made their way back to the drawing room. There was still no sign of Raymond and Christina.

'Where the devil have they got to?' Peter asked.

Edie was beginning to have misgivings.

'I'll go and look for them,' she said.

The murmur of female voices came from behind the closed door of Lady Elizabeth's sitting room – she, Julia and Lettice had retired there after dinner, Edie supposed – and the door to Sir

246

Montague's study was closed too. He'd probably taken refuge there with a brandy and a cigar.

She looked into the dining room, empty now, with the table cleared and the lamps extinguished. Then she went along to the library. The door was ajar; through the crack came the unmistakable sound of Christina's breathy giggle. Edie paused with her hand on the handle – should she knock? But one didn't when playing Sardines, and it would only announce the fact that she thought she might be interrupting something. She couldn't just burst in, though. It would be too embarrassing. She decided on a discreet cough, then, after a moment, pushed the door open and went in.

The room was in semi-darkness; only a wash of moonlight slanting in through the unshuttered windows bathed it in soft light, and by it Edie could see Raymond and Christina in the far corner. Raymond's back was towards her, while Christina was squashed between him and the bookshelves. Just as she had feared.

'We've finished the game, Miss Christina,' she said.

'Spoilsports!' Raymond moved languidly away, but Christina remained where she was, head thrown back against the dusty volumes so that her throat was exposed as if for the kiss of the vampire, thought Edie, who had seen illustrations of victims of Dracula. She also rather thought Christina's skirts had been rucked up, because an expanse of petticoat was showing.

'They're going to play charades,' she said lamely. Then she turned and scuttled out of the room. Her cheeks were burning and she felt surprisingly shaken. Really, it was no more than she had suspected, but to actually catch them in the act was something of a shock as well as an embarrassment.

Thank goodness she had gone in when she had, before something much worse had happened! But that didn't mean she didn't feel horribly awkward, nor did it do anything to assuage her anxiety about Raymond's intentions towards Christina, or Christina's response. From what she had seen, Christina had certainly been doing nothing to escape his attention, and Edie had the nasty feeling she might even have been encouraging it. She wished fervently that she hadn't been detailed to police the party and that she could now simply slip away to the little room under the eaves that she shared with Nellie. She didn't want to be in the company of the guests, all so confident and sure of themselves, and she certainly didn't want to face Raymond and Christina. But there was nothing for it: she had to rejoin the party.

They'd already begun a round of charades when Edie got back to the drawing room, all shouting at once as Peter Osborne cavorted in front of them. At the best of times Edie wouldn't have had the first idea what he was attempting to act out; her experience outside her own narrow world was vastly inferior to theirs, with their visits to the theatre and opera and ballet, and while the only books she'd ever read, apart from the Bible, were twopenny romances, they had grown up with libraries containing everything from the classics to the Brontës and Mr Dickens. This evening she didn't even try to follow the game.

It was some minutes before Christina and Raymond joined the others, and Edie spent the time worrying about what they might be getting up to. She was relieved when they did slip in, unnoticed by anyone but her in the hubbub. Christina was flushed and primping, Edie saw, but Raymond looked a little miffed, as if he was none too pleased at having his activities interrupted. Hopefully that meant things had not gone any further, but Edie was all too aware that next time – and there would be a next time, she felt sure – it was unlikely she would be on hand to intervene.

The thought was a worrying one, and as the guests partied, she hung back in a corner wondering what she should do. Should she tell Lady Elizabeth of her concerns? But the very thought of it made her prickle with discomfort. She didn't know how she'd find the words to explain what she'd seen, and besides, she remembered all too clearly how Sir Montague had instantly dismissed Sam, the gardener's boy, when he'd been caught kissing Christina. This was worse, much worse, than that fairly innocent incident, even if Raymond was a gentleman and not a common labourer, and Edie was afraid all hell would break loose if Lady Elizabeth got to hear of it.

Should she mention it to Christina herself then, warn her of the dangers of leading Raymond on? But it wasn't really her place to do anything of the sort, and she couldn't imagine Christina would be likely to take the slightest notice of anything she had to say.

But she couldn't just do nothing. She'd never

forgive herself if she simply let it go, only to find Christina had got herself into the sort of trouble that would blight her life.

She was still fretting over the problem when the party broke up. Chauffeurs arrived to collect the guests, and Sir Montague's estate manager came to walk his daughters the short distance home. Rachel Holley, however, had been invited to stay the night, as the rector had no driver to pick her up and no motor car either – he still covered the whole of his parish on foot. She would accompany the Fairley family to Matins in the morning, it had been decided, and then go home with her mother after the service. Since she and Christina were chattering excitedly together as Edie helped them prepare for bed, there was no opportunity for her to speak to Christina about what had happened, even if she had wanted to.

It was only when she was finally in bed herself that a possible solution occurred to her. Perhaps she could confide in Julia. Though she scarcely knew her, Julia struck Edie as being both approachable and down-to-earth. She wouldn't be likely to have a fit of the vapours on hearing what Edie had seen, and she thought telling Julia would be far easier than telling Lady Elizabeth. Besides, Raymond was her brother, so in a way he was her responsibility. With any luck she would have a word with him and warn him off his young and vulnerable cousin.

Satisfied with her decision, Edie was at last able to fall asleep.

Edie's opportunity to speak to Julia came sooner

than she had expected. Next morning – Christmas Day – the family left to attend Matins, but Julia had said that she and Lettice did not intend to go with them.

Sir Montague, typically, had been outraged.

'It's a long family tradition,' he declared. 'There are always Fairleys in church on Christmas Day. The parish expects it of us. It would be considered most odd for you not to be there too, since Raymond is my heir and you are his sister.'

'I'm sorry, but I can't see that anyone would expect me to be there,' Julia said coolly. 'I have no wish to offend, but the fact is I don't have any religious belief, and it would be hypocritical of me to pretend otherwise.'

Sir Montague had huffed and burbled some more, but to no avail. Julia refused to be persuaded otherwise, and when the rest of the family had left, she and Lettice retired to the parlour. It was there that Edie found them, sitting close together on the brocaded love seat, with a pile of torn wrapping paper and ribbon at their feet. They had chosen to exchange their gifts to one another in private rather than with the rest of the family – another determined break with tradition.

In the doorway, Edie hesitated, feeling like an intruder, and nervous suddenly about what she had to say.

'Miss Julia...'

'Oh Edith, I'm afraid we've made the most dreadful muddle.' Julia gesticulated at the discarded wrapping paper.

'I'll clear it up, miss, don't you worry.' Out of

habit, Edie went to pick it up, but Julia stopped her.

'No, it's all right, Edith. I intend to fold it up and save it so it may be used again. Throwing it away would be a wicked waste.'

Edie straightened. 'If you say so, miss.' She hesitated again.

'Was there something else?' Julia asked coolly. She wanted to be rid of her, Edie thought, but she couldn't let this opportunity pass.

'Yes, miss, actually there was. I wondered if I could have a word with you ... in private.'

'Goodness me, that sounds very serious!' Julia laughed lightly. 'But please do feel free to speak in front of Miss Lettice. We have no secrets from each other.'

'It's a very ... delicate matter,' Edie said. The colour was rising in her cheeks and she twisted her hands together in the folds of her skirt.

'Don't worry about me, I can make myself scarce.' Lettice was gathering the paper together. 'I'll take this up to my room to fold, and you can have all the privacy you want, Edith.'

With a smile at Julia, she left the room, taking with her not only the paper but also what looked like a small jewellery box, dark polished wood with an inlay of mother-of-pearl – Julia's Christmas gift to her, Edie guessed. And who knew? There might be some item of jewellery in it too. Whatever it was it had certainly cost a lot of money, and quite put into the shade the embroidered handkerchiefs that had been the family's gifts to the servants, presented to them before they had left for church,

'So what is this all about, Edith?' Julia asked as the door closed after her.

Edie's flush deepened. Now that the moment had come, she felt dreadfully flustered. But it was too late to stop now, and in any case she really felt it was important that someone should know what was going on between Raymond and the innocent Christina.

'I don't rightly know where to start, miss, but somebody has to be told, and I thought you were the best person...'

'Told what?' Julia's eyebrows arched in mystified amusement. 'Really, Edith, anyone would think you were an undercover agent or a spy reporting back on enemy action.'

The word 'spy' stung Edie. Wasn't that just what she was?

'You're not far wrong there, miss,' she said. 'Only it's not the enemy, and I wasn't exactly spying. I just happened to see something I wasn't meant to see.'

Julia straightened her face. Edith obviously didn't see the joke, and she owed it to her to take her seriously, since she had summoned up the courage to come and speak openly about what was concerning her.

'I'm sorry, Edith. It's wrong of me to jest about something that is worrying you. Please tell me what it is and I'll do my best to help.'

Edie took a deep breath. 'It's your brother and Miss Christina. I'm afraid he's taking advantage of her.'

'Good heavens!' Julia said, startled. 'Whatever makes you think that?'

253

'I've noticed a lot of little things. But it was last night that really got me worried. When we were playing Sardines, they went missing, and I found them together in the library. They were...' she hesitated. 'Well, they were in the dark, and ... I didn't like what I saw.'

'They were kissing, you mean?' Julia asked. 'That's not so terrible, is it? It's what young men and women do.'

'I know, but it was more than that. Or would have been if I hadn't interrupted them.' A flush crept up her cheeks. 'Miss Christina's clothing was disturbed, if you get my meaning.'

'Oh, that boy!' Julia exclaimed, exasperated. 'What can he have been thinking of? Christina is scarcely more than a child. It's quite unforgivable that he should molest her and cause her distress.'

Edie twisted her hands together more tightly, not wanting to say what she was about to, but knowing she had no choice.

'That's just it, miss. She didn't seem to be distressed. In fact, I think she was enjoying it. But the thing is that she's too young to know better and she can be a bit silly at times, and I'm worried what might happen if a stop's not put to it. I thought ... well, I thought that if I told you, maybe you'd have a word with him – tell him to leave her alone.'

Julia sighed. 'I'll speak to him, certainly. Whether or not he'll take any notice of me is another matter. It would probably be wise for Elizabeth to talk to Christina too. Warn her of the dangers of leading young men on.'

'I didn't want to tell Lady Elizabeth,' Edie said

miserably. 'I thought she'd go mad. Maybe even have Raymond sent away.'

'Yes.' Julia thought for a moment. It was a distinct possibility, and perhaps for the best, but she had such high hopes that learning how to manage what would be his inheritance would give Raymond some stability and make him grow up.

'I'll see if I can speak to Christina too,' she said at last.

'Oh thank you, miss!' Edie looked ready to cry with relief.

'You did the right thing in coming to me. Off you go, then. And try to enjoy the rest of your Christmas.'

'Yes, miss. And you too.'

Edie hurried out of the room feeling as if a weight had been lifted from her shoulders.

Julia, of course, was feeling the exact opposite. She was not looking forward to either of the conversations she was going to have to have, but she could see no alternative. She was all too aware that her brother was a little too fond of the ladies, and besides being very pretty, Christina had just the sort of winning ways that might very well lead him to believe she was encouraging him. Given his recklessness and her naivety, it could very well end in tears, if not disaster. She had to do her best to ensure that did not happen.

Chapter Sixteen

'This is a treat, and no mistake!' May said, beaming, as she carved slices of moist cockerel and served portions on to the seven plates set out around the kitchen table. 'I can't remember the last time we all sat down together to Christmas dinner.'

'It's not Christmas, Granny!' a small voice piped up. 'Christmas was last week.'

'Maybe so. But this is *our* Christmas, Georgie. Well, mine and your grampy's, anyway. What with your auntie Edie working, and you and your mam and dad at your other grandad's, we were all by ourselves, isn't that right, Wesley?'

'Oh ah, t'were very quiet,' Wesley agreed.

'Didn't Father Christmas come?' Georgie's sister Freda asked incredulously. She was sitting on two cushions so that she could reach the table.

'No he did not.' May hacked a leg off the bird and put it on Wesley's plate. Ted, Edie's brother, would have the other. 'But I reckon he might put in an appearance today if you behave yourselves.'

Two pairs of eyes went round with wonder.

'Today?'

'Father Christmas is going to come today?'

'I said he *might*. Now, do you two want to pull the wishbone?' She tugged it out and passed it to Georgie. 'Just be careful. You don't want to get grease all over your nice clean clothes. Your mam will help you, Freda. But be sure to make a wish before you pull it.'

Edie, who was busy dishing out Brussels sprouts, smiled as her small nephew and niece carefully hooked their fingers round the wishbone. It seemed like only yesterday when it had been her and Ted doing the selfsame thing. Clear as day she could remember wishing for a puppy, and her disappointment when it never materialised, though Wesley had come home one day with a kitten tucked into the front of his coat. And later, when she was older, wishing for Charlie to notice her. She'd given up believing in the power of wishes by then, yet miraculously he had. And look where it had got her...

Edie piled sprouts on to Georgie's plate, determined not to spoil her enjoyment of the day with thoughts of Charlie.

'Don't like them!' Georgie protested, scowling and poking at one with his fork.

'They're lovely! And they'll make you grow big and strong,' Edie said.

'They taste horrible,' Georgie replied flatly.

'No they don't. I love sprouts! When you're as old as me, you will too, and you'll think of all the ones you wasted and wish you'd eaten them when you could.'

'You're a fine one to talk.' Ted gave her a dig in the ribs. 'You wouldn't eat them at his age either. I remember once you hid them under the table when Mam and Dad weren't looking.'

'And you trod on them, accidentally on purpose, and got me into hot water.'

'It *was* an accident!'

257

'Like I believe that.' They were joshing just as they always had, and Edie thought how good it was for the whole family to be together for once. It was at times like this when she realised just how much she missed them all, living in at the Hall.

The minute May had known when Edie was going to have her two days off in lieu of Christmas and Boxing Day, she had organised the occasion every bit as carefully as a military manoeuvre. Luckily, one of the days had fallen on the Sunday, which also happened to be New Year's Day, so neither Wesley nor Ted had to go to work, and as Ted and his family had gone to Sally's parents for Christmas, there was no pressure for them to be elsewhere. She'd ordered the cockerel from Mr Wright the fowl man, saying she was sorry if the poor thing had to be lonely for a whole week when all the others in the coop had met their end in time for Christmas dinner, and Mr Wright had assured her he wouldn't be lonely at all – he'd be making the most of being the only cock among the flock of hens. She'd put the holly and mistletoe that she'd bought from a gypsy at the door into a jug of water and left it in the outhouse to keep cool, so that hopefully it wouldn't lose its berries. She'd made paper chains and cardboard hats for the children – a pirate hat for Georgie and a little crown for Freda – and bought a Christmas tree that had been reduced in price when most folk had had their pick.

Edie had come home on Saturday afternoon, so she had been able to help with preparing the vegetables, though May really wouldn't have minded doing them all herself. A pudding was steaming on the hob and she'd popped a tray of mince pies in the oven to warm through now that the cockerel had come out. To all intents and purposes this was, as she had said, their Christmas Day, and a visit from Father Christmas wasn't an idle promise either – she'd managed to borrow a red outfit trimmed with cotton wool and a bushy white beard on a length of elastic from the local branch of the Royal Antediluvian Order of Buffaloes, who used it every year for their Christmas party. It was a bit on the big side for Wesley, as the man who dressed up annually to distribute presents to the children of the Buffs was a good six inches taller, but she had tacked the hem up roughly and hoped Wesley wouldn't catch his foot in it and fall over. Just as long as the beard didn't fall off, she didn't think there was any chance of the two little ones recognising their grandfather – and they would be far too excited and overawed to notice he was missing.

It was clear to Edie that her mother was thoroughly enjoying herself with all her family around her table. But was there someone missing? She immediately castigated herself for the unbidden thought. Since the night of the Christmas social, when she'd realised fully for the first time just what May must have gone through if Christina really was her baby, she had made up her mind not to do or say anything that would cause her mother any more distress. If her awful suspicion was correct, May must have been to hell and back – in the long months when she was carrying a child who should never have been conceived; on the night she had

259

been forced to give her up to strangers; and throughout the years since. It was no wonder that any mention of the subject upset her so. Quite apart from resurrecting all the pain and despair she must have gone through, she would probably be terrified that the truth might come out. If it did, who knew what the repercussions would be? Her beloved family could very well be torn apart by recriminations and loss of trust.

No, though she still burned with curiosity, the compassion Edie felt now for the mother she loved so dearly was stronger, as was her desire to protect her father. In any case, trying to discover the truth was futile. If one or other of the priests knew anything, they would never tell – the confidentiality of the confessional was sacrosanct – and without asking awkward questions of the friends and neighbours who might have helped May, there was no further avenue to explore. Christina would forget about it in time – in fact Edie thought she already had, for it was some time since she had mentioned it. Her butterfly mind seemed to be focused on Raymond now – much to Edie's concern – and before long it would be some other new interest. If she mentioned the subject again, Edie would remind her that she should just be grateful for what she had. Lady Elizabeth might not be her flesh and blood, but she was everything a loving mother should be, and Christina was lucky to have been adopted into a family who had given her everything she could wish for and more. Hankering after a truth that might cause a great deal of heartache to a lot of people, herself included, was a silly waste of time and energy.

And yet...

Oh Mam, I wish you could bring yourself to tell me the truth, Edie thought. I hate to think of you bearing some shameful secret alone all these years. And I'm really sorry I was so insensitive when I started asking questions. I had no idea there was something you were desperate to hide...

Just now, though, May looked totally happy and content, her face flushed from the heat of the stove, beaming at her family around the table, leaning over to mop a splash of gravy from Freda's chin, whisking the hated Brussels sprouts off Georgie's plate and on to her own when she thought Sal wasn't looking, sharing a satisfied smile with Wesley. This was the mother Edie knew and loved. And she wasn't going to do or say anything else to upset her.

'Oh there you are, Raymond! I've been looking everywhere for you.'

Christina appeared in the doorway of the library, where Raymond was ensconced in one of the more comfortable chairs, a book open on his lap.

'Christina.' He looked up a little warily, then back down at the book.

'What are you reading?'

'Oh, just some boring old thing my cousin said I should.' Still not looking up.

'Why are you reading it if it is boring?'

'Because if I don't put some effort into learning about estate management, I'm going to get it in the neck from Sir Montague. Is that a good enough reason?'

'But it's New Year's Day! Surely you don't need to work on New Year's Day! I thought perhaps we could go out for a drive.'

'Not today.'

'But I'm so fed up being indoors with nothing to do.' Christina pouted.

'Why don't you find a book too? Goodness knows there are enough here to choose from.'

'I don't much like reading.' She approached his chair and perched on the arm, leaning towards him under the pretence of looking at what he was reading, though in reality she was hoping that he might be tempted to pull her on to his lap, but he only shifted away.

'See if you can do some more of the jigsaw puzzle, then. Julia and that friend of hers were having a go at it earlier until they gave up and went off to write some letters.'

Disappointed and frustrated, Christina got up and went over to the round captain's table, where the half-finished puzzle lay – a rural scene with green fields and trees and a huge expanse of blue sky. She didn't much like jigsaws either; she quickly lost patience with them and ended up trying to force pieces into places where they really didn't fit, much to the annoyance of the next person to have a go. But at least it gave her an excuse to remain in the library with Raymond, a far more tempting prospect than wandering off on her own again.

She'd been feeling restless and a little dejected ever since the night of her party. She had enjoyed that so much – the company of young people of her own age and, of course, the interlude with

Raymond here in the library – and the elation she'd felt had carried over for most of Christmas Day. But when the festivities were finished and life had returned to normal, it had been the most enormous let-down, and the brief respite only served to make her even more aware than usual of how tedious her everyday existence was. Just to make matters worse, Raymond seemed to be avoiding her, and now Edie had a couple of days off, so Christina was deprived of her company too.

For a few minutes she fiddled aimlessly with a few pieces of the puzzle that looked as if they might fit, but none did. Frustrated, she gave the half-completed puzzle an impatient push so that a corner of it slid over the edge of the table and broke apart, spilling bits on to the faded Persian carpet.

'Oh, stupid thing!' she exclaimed crossly.

Raymond glanced up. 'You'd better pick up those pieces before they get lost.'

'I don't care if they do,' she retorted, defiant.

'Your mama will care, and so will Julia. There's nothing more annoying than trying to finish a puzzle and finding a piece missing.'

'One of the maids can do it.'

'You're just being petty, Christina. It won't hurt you to do something for yourself for a change.'

'All right. You come and help me then.'

Raymond sighed, closed his book and laid it down on the arm of his chair.

'I suppose I might as well. I can see you're not going to give me any peace. What's wrong with you anyway? You're in a terribly bad mood.'

Christina didn't answer, but a sly smile of satisfaction lifted the corners of her mouth as he dropped on to his haunches and began collecting the fallen pieces. She knelt beside him, leaning across him provocatively to rescue a stray piece and thinking that surely now he'd take the opportunity to make a grab for her and tumble her on to the carpet. She so wanted him to kiss her again as he had on the night of her party – it had been so deliciously exciting! But still he made no move, and she tipped her head to one side, looking at him from beneath the long sweep of her sooty lashes.

'Raymond?'

To her dismay, he actually backed away.

'Stop it, Christina.'

'Stop what?'

'You know very well.'

She pouted. 'Don't you like me any more?'

'Of course I like you. Rather a lot, actually.'

'Then why...?' Thrilled with her own daring, she covered his hand with her own.

He drew it abruptly away. 'Why what?'

Christina felt tears pricking her eyes. 'Why won't you kiss me like you did the other night?'

Raymond sighed. Of course he wanted to kiss her – and more. She was a very pretty girl, and she had a way about her, a combination of innocence and guile, that he found charming. Just remembering what had happened between them the other night in this very room was making him hot with desire. But the little chat his sister had had with him had reminded him all too forcefully that he was playing with fire.

Edith, that prissy little maid, had walked in on

them and reported back to Julia. He'd been lucky she hadn't gone to Elizabeth or Sir Montague with her tales; that really would have set the cat among the pigeons. Next time he might not be so fortunate. And bored though he was with all the dull procedures and facts he was expected to learn, Raymond didn't want to do anything to jeopardise his position here. Fed up he might be, but it could well be a very long time before he inherited and was in a position to employ someone else to run things whilst he did as he liked. Sir Montague was far from an old man, and the Fairleys were known for their longevity. In the meantime, his options were very limited. He didn't want to go to university, even if the results he'd managed in his final exams at school were good enough, which he doubted. There would be even more brainwork to be done there than there was here, under Sir Montague's tuition, and yet more dreaded exams at the end of it. He could go into the army, he supposed; it had been one of the options he and his mother had discussed before Sir Montague had come up with the idea of him moving into Fairley Hall to prepare for his future responsibilities. Several of his peers had done just that, and with a commission he supposed it might be bearable. But the thought of the discipline required was off-putting. He'd probably end up being court-martialled and drummed out in disgrace. No, remaining here at Fairley Hall was by far the most acceptable option, and he didn't want to put it at risk for the sake of a tumble with his admittedly delectable cousin.

But oh, she was delectable and no mistake! The

turquoise eyes bright with unshed tears holding his, the bow-shaped mouth, the little tip-tilt nose, her tiny waist, the curve of her firm young breasts – it was more than flesh and blood could stand.

The hell with it! Raymond thought. And pulled Christina into his arms.

When it was time for Edie to leave, May went with her into the scullery. The others were still in the living room, Freda fast asleep with her thumb tucked into her mouth, Georgie still overexcited from the appearance of Father Christmas, who had given the children presents from his sack – a windmill each, an orange and an apple – and even let them sit on his knee, warning them in a deep gravelly voice that seemed to come from his boots not to pull on his beard. Wesley was dozing now, full of chicken leg and plum pudding and, no doubt, exhausted by his venture into the world of play-acting. Ted and Sal were comfortably ensconced on the sofa playing a game of solitaire, as he and Edie used to do in the days before he had married and she had gone into service.

'It's a shame you've got to go,' May said, 'but it has been lovely all of us being together.'

'Yes, it has been,' Edie agreed.

'Are you sure you don't want your dad or Ted to walk back with you?' May asked as Edie buttoned her coat. She still worried about Edie alone in the dark.

'I'll be fine, Mam.'

'There was something I wanted to say to you, but not in front of the others,' May said, lowering her voice. 'I've been thinking I'd like to go to

266

church again one Sunday.'

Edie was surprised but pleased, and very glad she had made up her mind to say no more about that long-ago Christmas Eve. She'd been right to suspect that Mam had confessed something to Father O'Brien that she was ashamed of, she thought, and now that he was no longer the parish priest, she felt able to return to the services that her awkwardness had kept her away from.

'And I was wondering whether you'd come with me,' May went on.

This surprised Edie even more, though when she came to think about it, she supposed May felt she could do with some moral support, the first time, at any rate.

'Of course I'll come with you, Mam,' she said. 'I'm not sure if it will be next Sunday, but I can always ask. Lady Elizabeth might let me have a couple of hours off even if I can't have the whole day.'

'Do you think she might?'

'I can't make any promises, but I will try.'

'She's good to you, isn't she?' May said. Her eyes had gone far away again. 'Yes, there's no doubt about it, she's a good woman. It's a pity her brother isn't a bit more like her.'

Edie laughed. 'You can say that again. And I'd better get going or I'll be late back, and if he gets to hear of it, he'll have my guts for garters.'

'Off you go then.' May gave her a hug and kissed her on the cheek. 'And just you mind how you go on the way back.'

'I will.'

As Edie went out into the alley, she couldn't

help casting a glance towards the Oglethorpes' house. Had Charlie been home for Christmas, and had he brought his new wife with him? May hadn't mentioned that he had been, but then she probably wouldn't. She wouldn't have wanted to upset Edie today of all days, and spoil the longed-for family gathering.

I wouldn't have let it upset me, Edie said to herself. I've put Charlie Oglethorpe right out of my mind.

But as she walked along the road in the direction of Fairley Hall, she wondered just who she was fooling.

'Yes! A four!' Lettice whooped as the dice wobbled and finally settled. 'Just what I wanted! My game, I think.'

'And here am I chained to the railings!' Julia groaned. 'You have all the luck, Letty!'

They were playing Pank-a-Squith. The board game, named after Emmeline Pankhurst and her nemesis Herbert Asquith, wasn't unlike Snakes and Ladders, but given their obsession with women's suffrage, it was much more fun. Instead of counters, players used little painted lead figures fashioned in the shape of suffragettes, and began the race to the Houses of Parliament, meeting all kinds of obstacles along the way. Instead of sliding down snakes, they were impeded by the police, magistrates or even Asquith himself as they curled around the circular board, where every square depicted a scene showing the obstacles they faced. It had come out last year as the leadership of the WSPU strove to think of new ways to raise funds for the cause, and Lettice had given it to Julia as one of her Christmas presents, but this was the first chance they'd had to play it. Flaunting their passion for the suffrage movement under the noses of their hosts would have been neither polite nor sensible. But this afternoon Elizabeth was out taking small New Year gifts to families on the estate, and Sir Montague had retired to his study – for an afternoon nap, Julia suspected – and the two young women had taken their chance.

'Shall we play another game?' Julia asked.

'If you don't mind getting beaten again.' Lettice smiled at her friend with the smug satisfaction of having already won two games.

'So it has to be my turn. Though I think I'll change my suffragette. I must agree with you, she doesn't seem to have been doing very well.' She replaced the tiny figurine in the box and selected another. 'I'll have the red one. See if she can set things on fire. And it's my start this time, isn't it?'

She retrieved the dice, put it in the eggcup they were using as a shaker, and threw it.

'There we are! A six! I'm off already!' she announced triumphantly.

The dice rattled in the eggcup again as Lettice shook it.

'Oh bother – a two. That's no use to man nor beast,' she groaned as it rolled across the board, then laughed as Julia threw a one. 'But there you are, you see – you've got to go all the way back home. While I ... yes, there we are, I'm off!'

For the next half-hour or so they were engrossed in play, climbing the spiral and slipping back, winning an extra throw of the dice or being forced to miss a turn until, to Julia's frustration, Lettice once again won the race to the Houses of Parliament

'I don't believe it!' she exclaimed. 'Are you sure you're not cheating?'

'As if I would! And how could I anyway? No, I'm just lucky with games of chance. Always have been. Never mind, darling, when we're back in Bristol you can play some of the other girls and I'm sure you'll come out the winner then.' She began packing away the board, the dice and the little lead figurines. 'You are coming back to Bristol with me, aren't you?'

Julia pulled a sad face. 'I want to, of course, but I'm not sure that I can.'

Lettice raised an eyebrow. *Why not?* it asked, without the need to put the question into words.

'It's Raymond,' Julia said. 'Now that Mother is no longer with us, I can't help feeling responsible for him.'

'He's not a child, Julia,' Lettice pointed out. 'He's nineteen years old, for goodness' sake.'

'I know. But he can be so irresponsible. Take this business with Christina. I told you that Edith was concerned that he might be acting inappropriately towards her.'

'I expect she was exaggerating.'

'Perhaps. But I can't be sure. And I'd never forgive myself if...' She broke off, shuddering at the thought of what might happen if Raymond was allowed free rein. He might not be a child any more, but Christina certainly was, and very young in some ways for her fifteen years, though in others she could be quite precocious.

'And what could you do if you do stay here?' Lettice asked. 'You can't be watching him all the time. If he wants to make hay with Christina, he'll find a way to do it whether you're here or not. Do you know, for instance, where either of them is at this moment?'

'That's true, I suppose,' Julia agreed reluctantly.

'Of course it is! Come back to Bristol with me. The cause needs you. *I* need you!'

Julia was silent, thinking. 'If I do, I shall have to return here regularly to satisfy myself that everything is as it should be.'

'It's not a million miles away.'

'No. Perhaps you're right.'

The thought of kicking her heels here with no one but Elizabeth and the very juvenile Christina for company was not a very enticing one, whilst the prospect of being in Bristol with Lettice and the others working for the cause that was so dear to her heart beckoned temptingly.

'I certainly am right,' Lettice said firmly. 'If your house hadn't been destroyed by fire, you'd have gone home with your mother by now leaving Raymond here to learn about the estate, wouldn't you? So where is the difference?'

Julia made up her mind. 'Very well, then, I'll come with you. If you're sure you can put up with me.'

'Oh Julia!' Lettice reached for her hand, squeezing it. 'How can you doubt that for even a moment? I love you, my dear, and you love me, and that's all there is to be said. We'll do great things together, you and I. And next time I make

271

it to the Houses of Parliament, you will be by my side, not languishing in jail, or chained to the blooming railings!'

Chapter Seventeen

As she tidied Lady Elizabeth's toiletries and skimmed loose hairs out of her hairbrush with a long-handled comb, Quilla was wondering how long she should leave it before she made the first move to put her plan for Richard's future into action.

On the one hand, it was galling in the extreme to see that wastrel Raymond being feted as the heir to the Fairley estate; the very sight of him made Quilla's blood boil. But on the other, the more rope he was given with which to hang himself, the more likely it was that Sir Montague would be open to the suggestion that there was another, much better alternative.

Richard was fourteen years old now, and working in the forge with Dick, learning the blacksmith's trade. But he was worth more, much more, than that. He was quick and clever, with a far better head on his shoulders than Raymond Fairley would ever have, and where Raymond was lazy, Richard was hard-working. Quilla had not the slightest doubt that he would find favour with Sir Montague if only he was given the chance. He would learn the ropes in no time, and when he was old enough he would be more than capable of managing the estate and the coal mines. But she had far greater things in mind for him than that.

As things stood, of course, there was no way he could inherit the estate, but that was Quilla's ultimate aim. It was, after all, his right, and she was determined to see that justice be done. She wouldn't stand idly by and watch that nincompoop sleepwalk his way into it all, and perhaps marry Christina into the bargain – she could see which way the wind was blowing.

But not if she had anything to do with it. Her ambition and her determination to look after her own knew no bounds. Already she had gone to lengths she'd never have dreamed of. Beatrice had posed a threat by discovering that she had given birth to an illegitimate baby fourteen years ago, and she had had to be dealt with. Quilla still shrank inwardly as she remembered what she had done, and her conscience did trouble her sometimes in the dead of night, but she knew that if she had to, she'd do it again. Once she'd been as sweetly innocent and gullible as Christina. No more. Fate, and the years, had made her hard, bitter – and determined.

Strangely, her recognition of the terrible thing she had done only served to strengthen her resolve. She couldn't let it be for nothing; she wouldn't. She'd gone this far; now it was time to take that extra step towards her goal. And when she weighed everything up, she could see there was no real advantage in delaying any longer. The household had quietened down now after all the festivities and everything was back to normal. There were no more parties and house guests, and

Julia and that friend of hers had returned to Bristol. Quilla's mouth curved into a sneer as she thought of the two of them and their stupid notions of changing the world. And did they really think she couldn't see what was going on between them? But they weren't her concern.

Nothing mattered except for her child. Nothing ever had. And with the very persuasive arguments in her arsenal, she was going to make sure that justice was done. It might have been a very long time coming, but it would be all the sweeter for that.

The church was dim, lit only by candles standing tall in pewter candlesticks on the high altar and bunched in the wrought-iron sconces dotted along the north and south walls; beneath the effigy of the Blessed Virgin, the tiny votives formed a tree of softly glowing light. The air was heavy with the perfume of incense and resonated with Father Michael's beautiful voice as he recited the hallowed words of the Mass. It was said, of course, in Latin, and Edie couldn't understand a word of it – she hadn't ever been to church with enough regularity for it to become familiar to her – but somehow that didn't matter a jot. The rhythm of the intonations was enough and, sitting in a pew towards the back of the church, Edie was mesmerised by it and by the atmosphere that enveloped her. It was cold enough for her breath to make little clouds in the gloom, and though her hands were so numb that she could scarcely hold the prayer book, she was aware instead of a glow that seemed to warm her from the inside out.

It was, she thought, as if she had come home after a long absence, and the emotion that flooded through her was as unexpected as it was uplifting.

The sole reason she'd come was to keep May company, and when Lady Elizabeth had agreed she could be spared for a couple of hours, her only thought had been that her mother and Father Michael would be pleased. It had never occurred to her for a moment that she would feel like this. As if she had moved from darkness into light, from a cold, unfeeling world to a place of warmth and safety.

May's elbow in her ribs brought her back to full awareness with a jolt. She turned to her mother, who mouthed: 'Are you all right?'

She nodded silently.

There was a shuffling and shifting as the congregation got to their knees, and May indicated with an inclination of her head that Edie should follow suit. Though it was many years since she'd worshipped regularly, all the old rituals came to her as naturally as breathing, whereas Edie was at something of a loss and needed to be prompted as to when she should stand, sit or kneel.

She wasn't sure either what she would do when the time came to take communion. Though she'd been baptised as a baby, she'd never gone through the ritual of religious instruction at eight or nine, never made her first communion. In fact she wondered if that might have been the reason Father O'Brien had come to the house that time when he'd frightened her so – to try to get May to send her to classes so that she could become a full member of the Church, and for some reason

275

May hadn't wanted that and had become upset about it.

Edie knew that not having been confirmed, it would be wrong for her to take communion. May had told her that Father Michael could give her a blessing instead. But now that the moment was approaching, she wasn't sure about that. It would be embarrassing to have him lay his hand on her head as if she were a child instead of a grown woman, and supposing he didn't realise she had never been confirmed and went to place the host on her tongue? That would be even worse. No, she'd remain in her place, she decided.

But as she watched the orderly queue of worshippers shuffling steadily towards the altar rail, where Father Michael stood waiting, a silver salver piled with fragments of wafer held before him, a feeling of regret overcame her, and as she moved aside to let May pass, leaving her alone in the pew, the sense of exclusion was as all-consuming as her former ecstasy.

She couldn't understand it – any of it – how one moment she could be so elated, the next so lonely and lost. She'd never expected such a tumult of emotions, and it threw her into confusion. The rest of the service seemed to pass in a dream, the hymn, the final prayers, and then Father Michael was processing down the aisle towards the porch, passing so close to her that she felt the breeze from the swish of his robes on her cheek and the smell of the incense filled her senses.

Though they were so close to the back of the church that they could have easily been the first to leave, Edie hung back, shy suddenly, so that in fact they were the last.

May gave her a little prod. 'Come on, our Edie. Haven't you got to be getting back?'

As they approached him, Father Michael held out his hands in welcome. 'How very good to see you, Mrs Cooper.'

'I thought it was about time,' May said.

'And you too, Edie.' He turned to her, smiling. 'You didn't take communion, though.'

Edie felt a quick flush burning her cheeks. 'I never have, Father. I'd like to, though. Do you think I could?'

'Well – yes, of course.' Suddenly he looked surprisingly nonplussed. 'You'd need to take some instruction, of course...'

'I realise that.'

'I'm running classes at the moment, but they're all children, and I don't think you'd be very comfortable. And would you be able to get the time off from your employment? It's important that you don't miss anything.'

Edie's face fell. 'Oh, I don't know, Father. I don't suppose I could – not regularly.'

'Hmm.' He thought for a moment. 'Perhaps we could arrange some private classes, at times that suited you.'

'Oh – are you sure? That is so kind...' Edie's flush had deepened.

'When do you next have a day off?'

'Not until a week next Wednesday. But Lady Elizabeth might let me off for a couple of hours if it was at a time when Miss Christina doesn't need me – she's very good like that. In the afternoon, perhaps.'

'What about Thursday at, say, three o'clock?'

Edie nodded. 'I'll ask. If she says no, I'll try to get a message to you.'

'Don't worry, I'm sure I can find plenty of things to do here in the church if you are not able to get away.'

'Thank you, Father,' Edie said. 'I'll do my very best not to let you down.'

Her spirits had lifted again; she could hardly wait.

'Oh dear Lord, why do you make things so hard for me?' Michael wondered as he watched Edie and May walk away down the path between the flower beds, bare now for winter.

But of course he was being tested. And if he could bring another soul into the fold, then what did his personal discomfort matter?

When he had been into the sacristy and removed his vestments, Michael returned to the body of the church, where he sat for a very long while in the pew closest to the altar and prayed for strength and guidance.

Sunday afternoon, and the house was quiet. Sir Montague had retired to the drawing room, Lady Elizabeth was in her sitting room, working on her embroidery, and Raymond and Christina had gone out for a drive with Edie as chaperone – though what pleasure there was to be had from that on such a cold day, Quilla couldn't imagine. But she didn't waste time wondering what on earth could possess them to even consider such a thing. It wasn't her business, and she had other

278

things on her mind.

This was as good a time as any to speak to Sir Montague. She'd rehearsed and rehearsed exactly what she'd say, but now nervousness and suppressed excitement seemed to draw a tight cord between her stomach and her throat, shortening her breath and making her a little dizzy, as if she'd drunk a glass of Sir Montague's good brandy too quickly, and she realised her hands were trembling. She'd just have a cigarette to calm her nerves. Then she'd do it.

She slipped out of the back door, careful to avoid Simon, who would join her, like as not, if he knew she was outside smoking. Usually she was glad of his company; she quite liked Simon – he wasn't stuffy and po-faced, or a foolish flibbertigibbet as too many of the other members of staff were – but today she wanted to be alone to compose herself. The last thing she wanted was to appear nervous. Sir Montague would be a hard nut to crack, and if he spotted any weakness he would be on it in a flash. She needed to be cool and collected, especially if persuasion didn't work and she had to resort to what amounted to blackmail. Thank goodness she had that to fall back on. Without it she wouldn't have rated her chances of success very highly.

In her usual sheltered corner she got her packet of cigarettes and a book of matches out of her pocket, lit a cigarette, cupping it in her hand against the blustery wind, and drew the smoke deep into her lungs. For a moment her head spun and the tremble in her hands seemed to worsen, then she grew a little calmer.

My, but it was cold! She hoped Miss Christina had wrapped up warmly, or she'd catch her death. She spared no thought for Raymond or Edie's welfare, though. Edie was nothing but a jumped-up little madam, whose upbringing in a draughty miner's cottage had probably made her tough as an old boot, and Raymond ... well, if he got pneumonia and died, it would only make the task she had set herself easier.

In the wind, the cigarette was burning down quickly – too quickly. Nervousness twisted again in Quilla's gut. Would it have been better to approach Lady Elizabeth, and let her speak to her brother? Quilla had considered it – if she could get Elizabeth on her side, she would be the ideal one to persuade Sir Montague to go along with her plan.

But for all sorts of reasons she had decided against that. It would have necessitated a lot of explanation and uncomfortable confessions: Lady Elizabeth knew a part of the truth, of course – that Richard was her son and not, as the world believed, her nephew – but there were things Quilla was almost certain she did not know, the things that formed the bedrock of her plan. If she had to resort to the coercion she had up her sleeve, then her relationship with her mistress could never be the same again, and that would be a pity. Quilla liked and respected Lady Elizabeth, even if she did have too soft a heart for her own good, and she knew that Lady Elizabeth thought highly of her. Considering how important it was to her to secure Richard's future, she was strangely reluctant to lose the regard of her mistress. She realised, of course, that Sir Montague might well tell Lady Elizabeth the reason he had been persuaded to take a barely educated lad into the bosom of the family, but somehow she didn't think he would. He would want to keep the secret of his indiscretion, as he had all these years – Quilla rather thought he valued his sister's good opinion just as she did.

The cigarette had burned down; Quilla dropped it on to the paving stone beneath her feet and ground it out with the toe of her boot.

Shivering a little, she let herself back into the house.

Time to do it. No more prevarication. Time to do it, now!

Sir Montague was dozing, his copy of *The Sunday Times* open in his lap, when he was roused by a tapping at the drawing room door. His head came up from his chest with a jerk; he coughed, clearing phlegm from his throat, thinking he must have been dreaming. The servants knew better than to disturb him on a Sunday afternoon. But as he pulled a handkerchief from his pocket to wipe his mouth, the sound came again, soft but insistent.

'What the devil...?' he muttered, and finished wiping his lips before calling: 'Come!'

The door opened; Quilla came in and closed it behind her. That surprised him, on two counts. For one thing, he had little contact with Quilla these days; as Elizabeth's lady's maid, her duties didn't include anything that concerned him. For another, it was unheard of for a servant to close a door behind them when they entered a room;

281

they simply left it open whilst doing whatever it was they had to do, and then left again.

'Yes?' he barked. 'What is it?'

'I'm sorry if I'm disturbing you, Sir Montague, but I need to talk to you.' Her tone was respectful but firm.

'What about?' Sir Montague cleared his throat again; the glob of phlegm was proving stubborn. 'And yes, as a matter of fact, you are disturbing me. So go on, tell me why you want to talk to me, and make it quick.'

Quilla's eyes met his, holding them with a steady gaze.

'Richard,' she said.

The name ran through him like an electric shock. It was years now since he had heard it spoken.

'Richard?' he repeated sharply.

'Your son.' Her voice was hard. 'Have you for-gotten who he is?'

Sir Montague spluttered, not deigning to answer the question.

'What about him? You want more money, is that it? Haven't I paid well enough to provide for him over the years?'

'You've provided something towards keeping a roof over his head.' Quilla's lips twisted into a sneer.

'And handsomely. Though I suspect a good deal of it has gone to provide your brother with whisky and beer. But that's up to him. As far as I'm concerned, I've been a good deal more generous than many would have been in the same situation. You should be grateful for that.'

'It was the least you could do if you wanted to keep things quiet,' Quilla flared. 'It wouldn't have suited you for all and sundry to know you'd fathered a bastard.' Her hands were trembling again; she twisted them together in the folds of her skirt, determined he should not see.

Sir Montague was growing red in the face. 'Nevertheless, he has been provided for. What more do you want?'

She drew a long breath. 'That he should take his rightful place in society.'

There, it was said.

Sir Montague's eyes bulged. 'And what do you mean by that?'

Quilla's mouth hardened; her eyes, small, dark and determined, never left his face. 'You've brought in this cousin of yours,' she said bitterly. 'You're supposedly training him up in readiness to inherit. Don't you think that position is the birthright of your own son?'

'Pssh! I never heard such rot!' Sir Montague spat out the words. 'A bastard inherit one of the great estates of England? Why, it's as ridiculous as suggesting it should pass to a woman. I would have thought that even you would be aware that inheritance must pass through the legitimate male line.'

'Of course I know that,' Quilla snapped. 'I'm not stupid, whatever you might think. But if you were to adopt him, it would be a different matter.'

For a moment, Sir Montague was rendered speechless. His face was redder than ever, and a vein stood out, a dark blue ridge throbbing in his temple. Then:

'Adopt him!' he repeated in a tone of utter

283

disbelief. 'Adopt the son of a servant, a boy who's been raised by a blacksmith? Why in God's name would I do such a thing?'

Quilla took her time in replying. She moved to the chair opposite his and sat down. Whereas until now she had wanted the advantage of standing whilst he sat, now it felt right to place herself on the same level.

'Because he is quick and clever,' she said evenly. 'He's a good boy, honest and hard-working. He's worth ten of that wet dishrag Raymond.'

Sir Montague's eyes flashed. 'How dare you speak like that of your betters? And why are you sitting? Don't you know your place?'

'Flat on my back, you mean?' She saw the pulse throb in Sir Montague's temple, and carried on regardless. 'As for that pathetic specimen, he is not my better. He's a clown who will be the ruination of everything you've worked for. He's lazy and stupid. He'll let things slide – if he doesn't empty the coffers first gambling on anything that moves or indulging himself with every new-fangled contraption that takes his fancy. You must know that. Don't tell me you haven't realised what he's like.'

'He's not what I might have hoped for,' Sir Montague conceded. 'But he'll have managers to help and advise him.'

'Who might well take advantage of his ignorance.' Quilla pressed home what seemed like an advantage. 'Anyone with a sharp enough brain could hoodwink him and line their own pockets. Richard would see through anything like that in an instant. He takes after you in many respects,' she added slyly.

'Hmm,' Sir Montague snorted. 'That's as maybe. But what in God's name would people make of me suddenly deciding to adopt a blacksmith's boy? Tongues would very soon start wagging.'

Quilla smirked slightly. She had the answer to that all ready. 'You wouldn't adopt him straight off, of course. To start with you'd offer him a job, on my recommendation. Then you'd train him up in estate management the way you're training Raymond. When he shows himself more than capable of all the things Raymond makes such a hash of, nobody would be that surprised if you came to the conclusion he was a better bet, and adopted him so he could inherit.'

'Dammit, you have this all worked out, don't you? Well, all credit to you for that, at least. But you must know the very idea is outrageous.'

'Why?' Quilla demanded. 'He is, after all, your son.'

'Good God, woman, how do I know that?' Sir Montague demanded. 'He could be anyone's.'

A tinge of hot colour rose now in Quilla's cheeks. 'Then why have you supported him all these years?'

'For my sister's sake. So that she did not have to lose the services of a maid she held in high regard – still does, though God knows why. Which was also the reason I arranged for you to go to Wiltshire so that no one here would be aware of your disgrace. But this...' he snorted again loudly, 'this is quite beyond the pale. I'm astonished you should even suggest such a thing. It seems I have treated you too well, and you have come to believe you can take advantage of my good nature. This

285

conversation, Quilla, is at an end.'

He rose from his chair, crossing to the table where the whisky and brandy decanters and glasses stood. Though as a rule he tried to avoid alcohol between luncheon and dinner, Sir Montague was more than ready for a drink.

As he turned his back on her, Quilla fumed. How dare he dismiss her as if she were of no more consequence than the lowest of the low, a dog turd to be brushed aside? But it was only what she had expected, and she was glad she was prepared.

'I'm disappointed that you are taking this attitude, sir. I hope you will feel prepared to think again, unless you want certain secrets to be made public.'

Sir Montague half turned, the decanter in his hand.

'You mean you would be happy to admit to having behaved like a whore with your master?' He spluttered scornfully. 'That would hurt you a great deal more than it would hurt me. In fact, there may well be those who would think more highly of me if they believed I had fathered a child with a servant girl. Attitudes may be changing towards these things, but not that much. If you think you can sway me with that threat, you may think again.'

He turned back to the table, pouring brandy into a crystal tumbler.

'That's not what I had in mind, sir.' Quilla's voice was hard and determined, betraying not a trace of the tremble that was afflicting her tightly clasped hands. 'There are other things you have gone to very great lengths to conceal. Perhaps you have forgotten I've been in service here long enough to know your family secrets. I've always been discreet, and I wouldn't like to make certain things public knowledge unless I have to. But make no mistake – deny Richard his heritage, and I will.'

In the moment's silence that followed, Quilla thought she could hear the beating of her own heart. Certainly she could feel it thundering beneath her ribs, reverberating in every pulse point. Then Sir Montague set the glass down on the table with a bang and wheeled round to face her.

'Are you attempting to blackmail me?' he demanded furiously.

Quilla swallowed the knot of nervousness that had tightened in her throat. She had come this far; now there was no turning back.

'Blackmail is an ugly word, sir. I'd rather say that I am due a reward for my loyalty. For keeping what I know to myself all these years. Surely that's not too much to ask? But I'll leave you to think about it. When you have, I'm sure you'll see that it would be much for the best.'

Then, whilst the advantage remained with her, she turned and left the room without a backward glance. Think about it he certainly would, and Quilla was now confident that he would agree to her demand. He would, she felt sure, go to any lengths to ensure that the family secrets should remain just that – secret. It may well be that skeletons rattled in most folk's cupboards, but Sir Montague would certainly not want this one to ever see the light of day.

A tight smile twisted Quilla's mouth. Her son, master of Fairley, with a title and lands. Coal mines and farms and property. The interview had been every bit as difficult as she had known it would be, but it had been worth every excruciating moment.

Oh, but I need a cigarette! she thought, heading for the back door and thinking as she slipped out through it that one day she would have no more need of it – she would be able to go in and out by the front entrance. She would never be recognised as the mother of the baronet, of course. But he would ensure she was treated with the respect she deserved. And even if he didn't... All she had ever wanted for her son was what was rightfully his. If she achieved that, nothing else mattered.

Shaking with impotent fury, Sir Montague drained his glass in one gulp and glowered at the door, which Quilla had left open as a final mark of disrespect.

The sheer brass neck of the woman! How dare she threaten him! How dare she presume for an instant that she could force him to make a bloody bastard his heir? Why, as he had said to her, what proof was there that the boy was even his? For all he knew she could have been granting her favours to every Tom, Dick and Harry. God alone knew she'd been ready enough to open her legs for him.

But outraged as he was, he was in little doubt that she had meant what she'd said. She was as cold as a dead haddock, hard as nails. He'd often wondered over the years what he'd ever seen in her. But she'd been attractive enough in those days, and brazen with it, and he had found that appealing, so different to his wife's gentility. When he had been at his lowest ebb, she'd been there, flaunting herself, and, God help him, he'd succumbed, bloody fool that he was. Now...

Sir Montague reached for the decanter and refilled his glass. His hand was shaking so that some of the brandy splashed on to the highly polished tabletop, and the sharp tinkle of crystal against crystal as the decanter caught the rim of the tumbler set his teeth on edge. His face was burning as if he had stood too close to a blazing fire, and the blood racing hotly through his veins set the pulse in his temple throbbing and roared in his ears. He shouldn't be drinking as much as he did, or indeed at all, according to that young upstart of a doctor. The gout would never improve as long as he did, the doctor had warned, and even hinted at other dire consequences, but Sir Montague wasn't going to be dictated to by him or anyone else, and in any case, he needed it!

What in God's name was he going to do? Though he couldn't imagine that his illegitimate son could make a worse custodian of the estate-than that young fool Raymond, he was determined not to accede to Quilla's request. He'd never be free of the damned woman if she thought she could control him so easily. But he couldn't risk her making his darkest secrets public knowledge either. Even if he denied it, the damage would be done – he and his family would be a laughing stock and the subject of spiteful gossip and conjecture. He wasn't well liked by his workforce or tenants, he knew, and that didn't bother him greatly. But he couldn't countenance the loss of respect, and the thought of the great delight that would be taken in his discomfiture was anathema to him. What was worse, the damned woman must know she could provide evidence to back up her story; she was too wily to have ever broached the matter unless she was sure she would be able to carry out her threats.

Sir Montague downed his second glass of brandy, feeling it burn in his gut and turn in his stomach. He was sweating now as he refilled his glass yet again, his forehead misted in a clammy sheen and beads of moisture rolling down his burning cheeks. God, but he felt ill! Sick, dizzy and weak, the roaring louder than ever in his ears and his head feeling as if it was about to explode.

A sudden panic that had nothing to do with the consequences of Quilla's threat gripped him. He started for the chair, but felt himself swaying. The tumbler fell from his grasp, rolling across the carpet.

Help, he needed help.

Somehow he managed to reach the bell-pull, but when he tried to ring it, his right arm refused to obey him. With an enormous effort he steadied himself against the table, stretched for the bell-pull with his left hand, and gave a sharp tug. Then his legs gave way beneath him and with a heavy thud he collapsed on to the Persian rug, bringing the decanter crashing down with him.

It was Reg who answered the summons; when he saw Sir Montague lying there amidst broken glass and spilled brandy, he rushed headlong back downstairs to fetch help.

Both Percy Stevens and Lilian Parker hurried up to the drawing room, and were horrified by the sight that met their eyes.

'Oh lawks! It looks to me as if he's had a stroke!' Lilian declared when she had got enough breath back to speak. 'I've been afraid something like this was going to happen, the amount he drinks and the way he gets himself so worked up over things!'

'Send for the doctor,' Percy instructed Reg as the lad stood uncertainly in the doorway.

'And let's hope he's in time,' Lilian said softly.

'Amen to that.' Percy straightened up. 'Will you call Lady Elizabeth, or shall I?'

'You do it, Mr Stevens. I'll go and find blankets and pillows to make him comfortable.' Lilian was already on her way, muttering under her breath and shaking her head.

This was a turn-up for the books and no mistake, and although she had indeed been concerned about Sir Montague's health for some time, she couldn't help wondering what it was that had caused this attack to happen just now, on a quiet Sunday afternoon with nothing and nobody to bother him.

Chapter Eighteen

'Whatever is going to happen next, that's what I'd like to know,' Lilian Parker said. The staff were having their evening meal, all seated around the long table in the servants' hall. 'It's been nothing but bad luck in this house ever since you broke that looking glass, Flo. I suppose we can look forward to seven years of this.'

'You don't believe rubbish like that surely, Mrs Parker.' Simon Ford's tone was scornful. 'It's nothing but an old wives' tale. It was Flo broke the glass – she's the one who ought to get the bad luck, and nothing's happened to her.'

'I've got an awful cold,' Flo protested, snivelling loudly to emphasise the point.

'Everybody's got colds at this time of year.' Simon shovelled a forkful of steak and kidney pudding into his mouth.

'You can mock, but you can't deny it,' Lilian said, a little huffily. 'First poor Mrs Fairley's house burns down, then she falls down the stairs and goes and snuffs it, God rest her soul, and now Sir Montague's had a stroke, and goodness only knows whether he'll ever be the same again. It's been one thing after another. Where's it going to end? That's what I'd like to know.'

'I'm sure it's coincidence, Mrs Parker.' Percy Stevens helped himself to more mashed potato. 'Troubles often come all together. You know what they say – it never rains but it pours.'

Lilian pursed her lips and shook her head, saying nothing. She'd been superstitious all her life. She didn't like seeing the new moon for the first time through glass; if a picture fell from the wall, she knew with awful certainty that something terrible was going to happen; and she flatly refused to wear anything brown, which she considered a most unlucky colour. In fact, it had caused quite a rumpus once when her mistress had tried to change the colour of her uniform; in the end Lady Elizabeth had backed down and they'd settled on bottle green, though she'd made it clear she thought it too silly for words. Lilian was quite used to being teased and told it was all rubbish, especially by the men, and she'd given up arguing. They could think what they liked – she knew better, and poor Mrs Fairley was proof of it. She had worn a lot of brown – and look what had happened to her.

'Didn't you say Sir Montague seemed a bit better this morning?' Percy asked Jeremiah Dando, the valet.

'A little, perhaps.' But Jeremiah's doleful tone was not encouraging. 'At least he's holding his own, and the doctor did warn that it would be a long job before we see much improvement.'

'He will get over it, though, won't he?' Edie asked. Though she wasn't overly fond of Sir Montague, it was dreadful to see anyone in the state he was in, his face all twisted down one side, having to be fed sops which dribbled down his chin and unable to string more than a few words together without stumbling, and those difficult to make out so it was often necessary to ask the poor man to repeat himself. Pitiful, that was what it was, especially when you thought of what a forceful personality he had been before the stroke.

Jeremiah shrugged helplessly. 'Who's to say? The danger, as I understand it, is that he might have another one at any time. And that, like as not, would prove fatal.'

Mrs Parker raised her eyebrows as if to say *I told you so*, but said nothing.

'As long as he sticks to doctor's orders, I don't think that's going to happen,' Percy said. 'He's missing his brandy and cigars, no doubt, but he'll give them up for good if he's got any sense. And I'd like to think Mr Raymond would give up those cigarettes of his, too. It would be nice not to have the smell of smoke hanging about the house,' he added.

'I reckon he ought to be sent outside to light up like the rest of us,' Simon joked. 'While we're freezing like brass monkeys, he's puffing away by the fire. What d'you say, Quilla?'

Quilla snorted. 'Chance would be a fine thing,' she said sourly.

Four days had passed now since Sir Montague had been taken ill. Her carefully laid plans had been thrown into disarray, and she could do nothing but fume with silent frustration.

She had no doubt that it was her ultimatum that had been the trigger for the stroke, but she felt not the slightest guilt or remorse. Instead she burned with anger towards the man who lay in his bed helpless as a child. Though she knew she was being irrational, she could not help but feel he'd

294

done it on purpose, out of sheer spite, in order to thwart her. That would be just like him. She had been so confident she'd won the day. She'd seen how horrified he had been at the threat of his family's secrets being made public. He'd have gone along with her demands, even if he had saved face by making out the idea had been his in the first place, she was sure of it. And then, before he could do anything about it, he'd had a stroke. The timing couldn't have been worse if he'd planned it.

She hadn't been able to visit him and see for herself just how bad he was; she had no excuse to go to his room. And what good would it do anyway? She wouldn't be able to say anything about him making Richard his heir – there was a nurse by his bed day and night. And in any case, if what those who had seen him were saying was true, he wasn't in any condition to set things in motion even if he had a mind to. He couldn't string more than a few words together, they said, and he'd lost the use of his right hand, so he wouldn't have been able to put anything in writing either. Quilla was also only too aware that to raise the matter again might trigger another stroke – the doctor had said it was a very real danger – and that would almost certainly be the end of him.

That was Quilla's greatest fear. It hung over her, a black cloud of dread. If Sir Montague died now, all her hopes and plans for Richard would die with him. Raymond would inherit, and that would be that.

Silently she cursed herself for not having pursued her ambition for her son years ago, when Sir Montague had been younger and a good deal fitter. But for some reason it had never occurred to her until that young upstart Raymond had been brought here to be trained up in readiness for his future. It was only then that the unfairness of it had hit her with the force of a thunderbolt. That a cousin who had scarcely ever set foot in the place, and an idle, useless layabout into the bargain, should have all this fall into his lap, while her son – and Sir Montague's – had to toil over a hot furnace from dawn to dusk to scratch a living, and think himself lucky to have a roof over his head and food on the table, was a travesty of justice. It should be Richard behind the wheel of a brand-new motor, driving proudly round the countryside. Richard wearing tailor-made suits and hand-sewn boots of the finest leather. Richard with servants at his beck and call and tenants who tipped their caps to him when he passed. It wasn't such an impossible dream. If only Sir Montague had been in a position to go along with her suggestion to take him on as an apprentice estate manager, he would already be learning how to be a gentleman, and when Sir Montague finally adopted him, he would be all set to take his place as his heir.

Now, with one cruel twist of fate, all that was in jeopardy, and Quilla could think of nothing but that somehow she must find a way to bring her plans a step closer to fruition. Just as long as Sir Montague didn't die in the meantime.

The threat of failure was a bitter taste in her mouth. She set down her knife and fork.

'I'm going outside,' she said, pushing back her chair and getting up.

'All this talk of smoking making you want one, eh, Quilla?' Simon said flippantly. 'I'll be out in a bit, when I've had some more of Cook's lovely steak and kidney pudding.'

'Don't hurry. You'll only give yourself indigestion,' she said, hoping he would take his time in joining her. More than the cigarette – which undoubtedly she was craving – she needed time alone to think. If she couldn't decide on a way to move things forward, she thought she'd go crazy.

But she would find a way. She had to.

There was sleet in the rain that had been falling all day as Edie set out to walk to High Compton for her appointment with Father Michael, and she glanced anxiously at the lowering grey sky. She hoped it wasn't going to come to anything. When there was heavy snow, the drive from the main road to Fairley Hall could become impassable; a few years ago, in a particularly hard winter, they'd been quite cut off for over a week. But even if it did snow, she couldn't imagine that enough would settle in the next couple of hours to make it impossible for her to get back, even if she did have to slip and slither about a bit. Holding the black silk umbrella Mrs Parker had lent her low in front of her face, she stepped out briskly, thinking how lucky she was to work for someone as good as Lady Elizabeth. Given all the trouble with Sir Montague, she'd been half afraid to ask if she could be spared for a couple of hours each week, but when she explained her reasons, Lady Elizabeth had agreed without a moment's hesitation.

'Of course you must go if it's so important to

you,' she had said. 'I'm surprised, though, that you haven't been confirmed before now. I thought Roman Catholics began taking communion at a very young age.'

'Most do, yes, milady, but not me,' Edie said, a little awkwardly. She didn't want to have to explain the niceties of a Catholic first communion to someone used to the practices of the Church of England, nor that her mother had for years been lapsed and she had rarely been to church as a child. But Lady Elizabeth was too preoccupied with her concern for her brother to be overly interested in the situation, and for that Edie could only be grateful.

By the time she reached the church, the sleet had begun to turn to snow, which was falling quite thickly but was still wet enough that the flakes melted almost as soon as they landed. Little ridges of white clung to the bare earth of the flower beds at the front of the church, but it was making no impact on the grass or the path, both of which shone wetly.

Edie put down the umbrella and gave it a good shake before opening the heavy wooden door and stepping into the church porch. She was unaccountably nervous now, and her throat felt dry and tickly. She hoped she wasn't getting Flo's cold.

'Edie!' Father Michael appeared in the doorway leading to the body of the church. 'I thought you might decide against coming, given this dreadful weather.'

'Oh, a little bit of sleet won't do me any harm,' Edie said. 'And I wouldn't let you down if I could

298

help it – not when you've been good enough to give up your time for me.'

Father Michael smiled. 'That's my job.'

Job. As if he were a coal miner or a farmhand, Edie thought. It seemed strange to her that a priest should refer to his calling that way.

'Come inside where it's warmer. And, oh ... you can leave your umbrella there,' he added, indicating a wrought-iron umbrella stand in the corner of the porch.

'It's not mine. Mrs Parker, the housekeeper, lent it to me.' Even as she said it, Edie wondered why she was wittering – because she was nervous, she supposed. She gave the umbrella another little shake and slotted it into one of the compartments in the stand, taking care not to catch the spokes on the iron framework. Mrs Parker would never forgive her if she brought it back damaged. Then she followed Father Michael into the sacristy.

It certainly was much warmer in here, the heat coming from a small three-legged oil stove, the smell of which mingled with the lingering scent of incense. Edie looked around the small room, fascinated by the clutter it contained. Jumbled artefacts of all kinds – goblets, vases, candlesticks, small figurines – filled every available surface; a large framed print of the Blessed Virgin with the baby Jesus in her arms looked down from one wall smiling a beatific smile; other pictures and piles of what looked like hymn and prayer books were stacked against another. Three upright chairs sat on a worn and faded rug in the centre of the room; a shabby armchair piled high with altar cloths occupied a corner. Father Michael indicated that she should take one of the chairs, and Edie picked her way between a faded hassock and a small table strewn with papers and writing materials to reach it. Father Michael sat himself down on one of the other chairs, arranging his soutane around his long legs. As he did so, Edie caught a glimpse of sandalled feet – hardly suitable footwear given the inclement weather, she thought.

'Sorry about the mess,' he said. 'I'm still trying to sort things out. Father O'Brien collected rather a lot of junk during his time here, and until I clear the cupboards, there's really nowhere for things to go.'

'You'll have your work cut out,' Edie said.

'Indeed.' He grinned ruefully. 'If I could only afford to spend a whole day on it, I might get somewhere. But parish matters seem to take up all my time.'

'It's really good of you to spare some for me, then,' Edie said.

'Not at all. Bringing home the lost sheep is one of the things I'm here for.'

Edie wasn't sure she liked being compared to a sheep, lost or otherwise, but even with her limited experience of the faith she knew it was just a biblical metaphor.

'That's me, I suppose,' she said with a little giggle.

'Tell me, Edie,' he cocked his head a little to one side, his eyes on her face, 'what exactly was it that made you decide you wanted to return to the fold?'

More sheep metaphors. She half smiled. What *had* prompted her to take this step? She really didn't know. There was no way she could find the words to explain the emotional turmoil she had experienced when she'd accompanied her mother to church. The feeling of coming home, of being uplifted to a place she'd never been before, a euphoria she could never have imagined. And then the tumble back to earth when she'd been unable to take communion, the sense of loss and exclusion. She could scarcely understand it herself, and in fact, back at Fairley Hall and carrying out her day-to-day duties, it had seemed to her more like a dream than something that had really happened. She'd even wondered if she should put the whole thing behind her, send word to Father Michael that she'd changed her mind. But she hadn't. For all that she had been doubting herself, something still drew her to return to the church. She hadn't expected to feel anything when she came today – there would be no candles sending out their light into the gloom like so many miniature halos, no fresh incense, no mesmeric chanting or uplifting hymns. Perhaps she had thought it would put things into perspective.

And yet the moment she had stepped into this small, cluttered room, she'd felt it again: the same warmth she'd experienced before bubbling inside her. She felt safe, loved, drawn to something undeniably mystical that she did not understand but desperately wanted to be a part of.

'Is it something you've been thinking about for a long time, or was it a sudden decision?' Father Michael prompted her.

'Sudden really,' Edie said, overcome now with embarrassment. 'It was ... well, as if a voice was

301

speaking inside my head.'

He nodded. 'A calling?'

'I suppose... I can't explain it.'

'You have no need to explain a calling to me,' he said.

She looked at him, her eyes brightening. 'Was it like that for you?'

'I suppose it was, yes. It was a very long time ago, of course, when I was quite young. I always knew I wanted to be a priest. But voices have spoken inside my head on several occasions since, showing me the way when I faltered, or felt uncertain.'

'You don't think I'm going funny, then?'

He smiled at the colloquial expression for madness. 'Certainly not. And those voices should always be listened to, Edie. The Holy Spirit moves in mysterious ways.'

Not so long ago Edie would have laughed at such a sentiment. Now it felt as if his words were touching her soul.

They talked on, of things Edie had never so much as thought about before. She was almost unaware of the early January dusk falling until Father Michael rose and lit one of the fat candles that stood on the small writing desk.

'I expect you should be going soon if you're to get back before dark.' He crossed to the lead-paned window and looked out. 'At least it's not snowing now.'

'Is that it?' Edie asked, feeling suddenly bereft.

'For today.'

'But I haven't learned anything,' she protested.

'You'd be surprised.' He smiled. 'Becoming a good Catholic isn't all about memorising prayers and invocations, or even studying the Bible. Though I will give you some literature to take away with you. If you could read through it and familiarise yourself with the catechism and suchlike, that would be helpful.' He slid some sheets of paper, clipped together, into an envelope, then placed a small book on top of it.

'You might like this too. It's the life stories of some of our principal saints. I think you'll find it inspiring.'

'Thank you, Father.'

Edie slipped into her coat, which she had draped over the back of her chair, reluctant to leave this haven of warmth and peace.

'Next time we'll talk about making a confession,' Michael said as he went with her into the porch. 'It's something you'll have to get used to.'

The pleasant muzziness she was experiencing cracked into a million pieces, like Flo Doughty's broken looking glass, and cold reality came rushing in along with the icy draught of sleety air.

Confession.

Edie didn't know what she would confess to when the time came; she couldn't think of anything she'd done that was especially wicked, but there must be something. Lusting after Charlie, perhaps? Wishing Quilla would fall over her own feet and come down in the world so that she was on a level with the rest of them?

Confession. The rite that was supposed to be good for the soul but in fact had been responsible for keeping her mother away from her beloved church for so many years. That had made her ashamed to face the priest to whom she had admitted her guilt for whatever sin she had committed.

'Is this where Christina was found?' she asked before she could stop herself, her gaze skittering around the rough stone walls of the porch.

'I believe so, yes.' His voice was a little diffident now, as if she was broaching a subject he didn't want to discuss. 'Edie...'

'Yes?' She looked at him expectantly.

'You're not still wondering, are you, if it might have been your mother who left her here? You really should put it out of your head. No good can come of unearthing the past. Not for Christina, and not for you.'

Edie didn't answer. He might well be right, but she couldn't let it go so easily. Even if Christina seemed to have forgotten all about it for the time being, the thought that she might in reality be her very own sister still haunted Edie.

'Would Mam have to confess to you too now that she's coming to church again?' she asked.

Father Michael shook his head. 'Whatever her sin, Father O'Brien would have given her absolution. She will have done her penance. The slate has been wiped clean.'

'But it hasn't,' Edie said. 'God may have forgiven her, but she's never forgiven herself. All these years...'

The sound of rain hammering on the tin roof of the porch was loud in the silence that followed. Then Michael said: 'I don't for one moment believe that your mother abandoned her own child. From what I know of her, she would be quite incapable of such a thing.'

'But if she was desperate...'

'Look at it sensibly, Edie.' He touched her arm, and her skin seemed to burn and tingle in the pattern of his fingers through the cloth of her coat. 'The baby was in a drawer. A solid oak drawer, not cheap and flimsy. That would be heavy and awkward. How could she have managed to carry it here? It would be almost impossible for a woman to do that alone, especially one who had not long given birth. Besides that, it was from a dressing table or chest, I'm told. Do you think your mother could have concealed the fact that a drawer was missing? Have you ever seen a piece of furniture missing a drawer in your house?'

'No,' Edie conceded.

'There you are then. You must forget all about this, Edie.' His eyes narrowed. 'That isn't the reason for your interest in the faith, I hope? That you want to pick my brains to satisfy your curiosity?'

'No, Father, it's not!' Edie said, shocked. 'It's like I said, I wanted...' She broke off, suddenly doubting herself. *Was* that what was behind her compulsion to come to church? She couldn't be sure of anything any more.

The priest's face softened. 'That's all right then. But as I said, the Lord moves in mysterious ways... Will I see you at the same time next week?'

She nodded, still very aware of his hand on her arm. 'If I can get away.'

'Good.'

Edie picked up Mrs Parker's umbrella from the stand; water dripped from it on to her boots.

'Thank you, Father.'

'There's no need to thank me. I'm just doing

305

my job.'

That word again. Job. Was that how he thought of it?

'I'm grateful all the same.'

He followed her to the porch door, stood watching as she walked down the path towards the road, but she was unaware of it. The serenity that had enveloped her over the past hour had deserted her now. All the old questions were there again, chasing around and around in her head. She splashed through a puddle, and the rain that was just rain again and not the threatened snow, pattered on the black silk of the raised umbrella, but she didn't notice that either.

I have to know, she thought. Even if I can never tell anyone, I have to know.

'Milady, could I speak to you about something?'

Lady Elizabeth looked up from her embroidery frame, surprised by Quilla's serious tone.

'Of course you may, Quilla. What is it?'

'It's a rather delicate matter, milady.'

Lady Elizabeth slid her needle into the stretched fabric and laid it in her lap, a little frown puckering her smooth forehead. 'Go on.'

'It's about my son.'

'Richard.' Though she had never so much as set eyes on the boy, Lady Elizabeth prided herself on remembering such details. It was important, she always thought, to treat her staff and the tenants too with the same courtesy she extended to her friends. 'He must be quite grown up now.'

'He's fourteen.' Quilla's usual surly expression softened a little with a mother's pride as she

306

spoke of him.

'Good gracious, where do the years go!' Lady Elizabeth gave a small, disbelieving shake of her head. 'He'll be starting work soon, I imagine.'

'He already has, milady. In my brother's forge.'

'Oh yes, of course, your brother is the blacksmith. Are he and his wife well?'

'Very well, thank you, milady.'

'I'm pleased to hear that. I've never met him, but I'm sure he must be a good man. Not everyone would be prepared to take on an extra mouth to feed nor to raise him as his own. But you don't need me to tell you that.'

'No, indeed, milady.'

'He has no sons of his own, I believe?'

'No, milady. Only daughters.'

'So he must be pleased to have someone to carry on his business. It's a steady and respectable trade, Quilla. I'm sure Richard will do well.'

'I don't know about that, milady. What I do know is that it's not right for Richard. He has a good head on his shoulders and he's worth more than that. In fact, that's what I wanted to talk to you about.'

'Really?' Lady Elizabeth's frown deepened and little lines of puzzlement creased the corners of her eyes. 'I'm not sure I follow you, Quilla.'

'It's a bit awkward, milady. The fact is, I talked to Sir Montague not long before he was taken ill, and he agreed to find a position for him here.'

'Here?' Lady Elizabeth was surprised. As far as she was aware, the house was fully staffed; in fact, never one to spend a penny he didn't have to, Montague had been mulling over whether they could manage with fewer servants so as to reduce the not inconsiderable wages bill. He'd actually discussed it with her. What possible reason could he have for taking on an extra footman? But she'd never quite understood the workings of his mind, and if that was what he was suggesting, who was she to argue?

There were other aspects to be considered, though.

'Would you be comfortable with that, Quilla?' she asked. 'Wouldn't it be awkward working alongside Richard without letting anyone know that he's your son?'

'Oh, he wasn't to be a servant, milady,' Quilla said, affronted. 'Sir Montague wanted to train him up for management of the estates and the coal mines.'

'But that's what Raymond is being trained for,' Lady Elizabeth said, puzzled.

'Supposed to be, yes,' Quilla agreed. 'But it seems Sir Montague is not entirely satisfied with his progress. He doubts whether Raymond will ever be up to running things properly.'

'I see.' Montague had mentioned to her that the boy wasn't applying himself in the way he would wish, and expressed doubts about his abilities. Doubts she could not help but agree with. All the same... 'I had no idea my brother was thinking along those lines,' she went on. 'If he wanted to train a manager alongside Mr Raymond, I would have expected...' *That he would have taken on a boy with a good education, public school at the very least, and perhaps university too,* she had been about to say. Realising she was about to break her

308

own golden rule of treating her staff with the same courtesy as she would her friends, she stopped mid-sentence, but even without the words being spoken, Quilla guessed what they would have been, and her face hardened.

'There's something you don't know, milady. The reason why I said this conversation was of a delicate nature.' She paused, then looked Lady Elizabeth directly in the eye. 'Richard is your brother's son.'

Elizabeth's hand flew to her mouth.

'Montague? *Montague* is Richard's father? But I thought...'

'That I'd made a fool of myself with some nobody from High Compton or Hillsbridge, or even one of the other servants, and he'd gone off and left me high and dry? I know what you thought, but you were too discreet to ask. And we never told you. It seemed better that way.'

'Montague!' Elizabeth repeated, still stunned.

She should have guessed, of course she should. Quilla had always been cold and haughty; she'd never have deigned to grant her favours to a miner or a farmhand. And Montague had been going through a dreadful time back then. It had crossed her mind to wonder why he had so readily agreed to her suggestion that they should help Quilla keep her disgrace a secret, even arranging things himself with the help of their cousin, Beatrice's husband, so that she could go to Wiltshire and hide away until it was all over; such altruistic gestures were quite unlike him. But that he should be the father of Quilla's unborn child had never occurred to her for a second. Now it all became clear.

'Anyway, he helped out with Richard's keep,' Quilla said. 'I don't suppose you know that either, but he did. And now he thought the time had come for him to do more. He was even talking of adopting him.'

'Really? He said that?' Elizabeth was at a loss for words.

'Yes, milady. And then ... well, before he could make any proper plans, he had this stroke.'

'I don't know what to say, Quilla. This has all come as a tremendous shock to me, as you must know. And I'm not sure what you are expecting me to do...'

'With Sir Montague unable to speak or even write, there's nothing that can be done about the adoption, of course, milady,' Quilla said. 'But I was hoping that you might be able to help with the other matter. I don't know what is going to happen about Mr Raymond's training while Sir Montague is ill – perhaps his agent is going to take him under his wing? If so, I thought that Richard could share his lessons.' She paused, arranging her features into a suitably respectful expression. 'I'm sure that's what Sir Montague would want.'

Lady Elizabeth stared down at her embroidery frame, thinking.

As she had said, this was all the most dreadful shock, and she really didn't feel that she was qualified to commit to something that could have far-reaching consequences. She wished she could talk to her brother about it; for all that he was physically incapacitated, his mind was as sharp as ever, and he'd at least be able to nod his assent or shake his head to put an end to the suggestion.

But she wasn't at all sure she should mention it to him. He'd kept this from her all these years; might it not distress him to know that she had learned his secret? And distress could lead to another stroke, one that might prove fatal.

Lady Elizabeth was quite used to making her own decisions, and she made one now.

'I'll see what I can do, Quilla,' she promised.

Quilla left the room feeling reasonably satisfied. It wasn't what she wanted, what she'd planned for, but it was better than nothing. And when Sir Montague recovered sufficiently, and could see how well Richard was doing, then perhaps he would be more inclined to do as she'd asked and adopt the boy. Just as long as he did recover. But that was in the hands of a God Quilla did not believe in. For the moment, there was nothing more she could do.

Chapter Nineteen

'Okay, my lad – now you have a go.'

The big swarthy man released the horse's foot, which he had been gripping between his knees, and straightened up, holding out the iron file to the boy who stood beside him. Richard Brimble, who had been watching the blacksmith's every move as he trimmed the hoof, took it apprehensively. He was tall for his fourteen years, and sturdily built, but the horse, which pulled the

311

railway station parcel delivery wagon, looked huge to him, and the thought of lifting that leg and tucking it between his own was a daunting one, never mind holding it there while he filed away at the hoof.

He laid the file down on a low bench that would be within his reach when he was ready for it, and bent over, running his hands down the horse's foreleg and feeling for the knee joint. The horse, sensing his inexperience, shifted restlessly.

'Will you hold her steady?' he asked his uncle.

'If you want me to. But you're going to have to get used to doing it on your own.' Dick Brimble's voice was gruff and a little impatient. Richard wasn't taking to this as he himself had. When he'd been a boy, learning the trade at his father's side, he'd never have dreamed of asking for help. It had all seemed to come naturally to him.

A slow flush crept up Richard's neck at the implied criticism, and he bent his head so that Dick wouldn't see it. Not that it was noticeable: Richard's face was already red from the heat of the furnace as he'd sweated over it hammering the new shoe into shape under Dick's eagle eye. He wiped his damp palms on his leather apron, split down the front so it resembled a cowboy's chaps, and lifted the horse's foot, tucking it between his knees and clamping them together with all his strength as he reached for the file.

'Right. You got her? Now, start at the toe and work round to the heel. And keep your file straight. Just work it up and down... That's it. You got it. Have a feel now. See if it's proud any-where...'

312

Concentrating hard as he was, the sudden roaring noise from the road beyond the open door of the forge startled Richard almost as much as it startled the horse, and her leg slid out from between his own before he could stop it.

'Damn it, boy, look what you're doing!' Richard grunted.

'Sorry, Dad...'

'Bloody motor cars!' Dick had no time for the new-fangled contraptions. As yet, there weren't many of them about, but if they ever caught on, they could be the ruination of his business. 'Come on now, try again. We can't fit the shoe until that hoof's properly trimmed, and they'll be coming to fetch her soon. You've got to hold her tighter. Show her who's boss–'

Dick broke off. A lady had appeared in the open doorway, a fine lady by the look of it, and one he recognised immediately, even though the light was behind her. Her hat was heavy with elaborate trimmings; her coat, nipped in at the waist, then flaring out, looked like quality. Not that Dick knew anything about fabric or fashion, but even he could see it wasn't made of the rough fabric most of the women of his acquaintance wore. And her bearing gave her away too. Almost all the women he knew of that age had a bit of a stoop or even a widow's hump, endless hard work and repeated childbearing taking their toll.

Oh, he knew who she was all right. Lady Elizabeth Fairley, his sister's employer. But that begged the question – what was she doing here? Unless it had something to do with Quilla's plans for Richard...

313

Dick let go of the horse's head, stepping forward and tugging his forelock. It galled him to do it, but he did it all the same.

'Morning, milady. What can I do for you?' he asked, hiding his resentment.

She acknowledged him with a slight tip of her head. 'Good morning, Mr Brimble. But I'm not sure that's quite the right question. The correct one, I think, would be what can *I* do for *you.*'

After Quilla had spoken to her on Sunday, Elizabeth had spent a restless night worrying about how best to deal with the situation she had been presented with. It had been a shock to learn that Montague was the father of Quilla's son, and she was a little hurt, too, that he had not seen fit to confide in her. But she shouldn't be too surprised at that, she supposed – Montague had some peculiar ways, and they had never been close as some brothers and sisters were – and she had no reason to doubt what Quilla had told her. Her maid could be dour and humourless, but she had also proved loyal and discreet over the years, and though Elizabeth had never suspected the truth, now that it had been presented to her, a dalliance between Quilla and Montague was certainly believable. Elizabeth was well aware that her brother's marriage had not been a happy one, and she could remember how handsome Quilla had been as a young woman.

What puzzled her was why Montague should only now be taking an interest in his illegitimate son's future. As far as she was aware, he had never had anything to do with him. But perhaps

314

at long last his conscience was pricking him and he wanted to see the boy settled in a steady career. It could be, she supposed, the fact that Raymond was proving such a disappointment that had made him look elsewhere. To even think of adopting him seemed a step too far, but then sometimes the workings of her brother's mind were quite beyond her, and it was possible that if Richard did well, then adoption was the only way Montague could ensure the estate passed to him when the time came.

There was no point in worrying about that, however. There was nothing she could do about it even if she wanted to; it would have to wait until Montague recovered. If he recovered... Elizabeth had shuddered a little at the thought that he might not. It would be a total disaster if he should die and Raymond inherit whilst he was still so young and foolish. Really, it was no small wonder that Montague was looking elsewhere. But he isn't going to die, she told herself fiercely. Dr Mackay had said the critical period was the first eight or nine days; if he hadn't suffered a second, fatal, stroke within that period, then there was a chance that he would begin to make a recovery. That time had now passed, and certainly Montague seemed to be far more aware of what was going on around him, even if he still couldn't communicate, and the nurse had been pleased to report that today he had finished a whole bowl of broth and even managed to chew a slice of bread and butter. But Elizabeth had a feeling that it would be quite some time before he was capable of doing the first thing about Richard's future, and she certainly wasn't going to try to discuss it with him. He had to be kept quiet, the doctor had said. No excitement, no upsets of any kind, nothing to worry him.

Which left the matter of arranging for Richard to take lessons in the management of the estate and the coal mines entirely in her hands. And used though she was to making her own decisions, she knew that on this occasion she needed help and advice.

The person she had turned to was Clement Firkin, Sir Montague's agent. She liked Firkin and trusted his judgement. He was nearing retirement now, and she sometimes wondered how Montague would manage without him. For the last week, since Montague's stroke, he had taken to working in his employer's study rather than taking the paperwork away with him back to his own office, and when he arrived, she sought him out.

'It would seem that before my brother was taken ill, he had decided to train up another boy in the same way as Mr Raymond is being trained,' she said. 'I don't believe he is very satisfied with Raymond's progress, and thinks he should have someone to help him out with the day-to-day running of the estate and mines when the time comes.'

'Well, it's true Mr Raymond is something of a duffer,' Firkin said bluntly. 'Did Sir Montague have someone in mind? I must say, if he did, he never mentioned it to me.'

'He did, yes. Quilla Brimble, my maid, has a nephew who has recently left school, and my brother was eager to offer him the opportunity.'

'Oh.' Firkin stroked his jaw. 'You can't mean

that young lad who's just started work in the forge, surely? He's no more than a nipper, and he's had no education to speak of.'

'I believe the church school provides a very good grounding in the three Rs,' Elizabeth said, a little affronted, since she was on the school's governing body. 'And as for his age, that can only be a good thing, surely? He could be trained in the proper ways before he has picked up bad habits and practices. The problem is, I'm a little out of my depth when it comes to knowing how to proceed for the best. Whilst I want to go along with my brother's wishes, I hardly feel it is my place to ask you to take on another student, and I don't see how I can discuss it with Sir Montague in his present condition.'

'That's true enough.' Clement Firkin was a man of few words.

'So what do you suggest is the best way forward?'

Firkin's fingers wandered up from his chin to stroke his mutton-chop whiskers. 'What does the lad say about it? Is he keen?'

'I really don't know,' Elizabeth confessed. In fact, she realised, Richard might be quite unaware of the plans being made for him.

'Well in that case, I suggest you find out before we go any further.'

'You're right, of course... I'll go into town this afternoon and talk to him, and Quilla's brother ... the boy's father,' she added, anxious to allay any suspicions the agent might have, given the rather unorthodox suggestion.

'If he seems interested, and if it's what Sir Montague wants, then I'll go along with it,' Firkin said. 'And I'm thinking it might be a good idea to start straight away. Isn't Mr Raymond going away for a week or so to stay with a friend? If I could have the lad on his own for a bit, it would give me a chance to show him the basics and work out what he's capable of.'

'So if both he and his father are agreeable, you'd be happy for me to arrange for him to start more or less at once?'

Clement Firkin nodded. 'Just as soon as Mr Raymond's gone off to his friend's,' he said. 'That would be for the best.'

Lady Elizabeth nodded, hoping very much that she was doing what her brother wanted.

'Well that's it then, my lad,' Dick Brimble said when Lady Elizabeth had left. 'Your aunt Quilla fixed things up just like she promised she would. She always was good at getting what she wanted.'

Richard ran a hand through his thick mop of curly hair, leaving a streak of dirt across his forehead. He didn't know quite what to think of this unexpected development.

It would be a relief not to have to work in the forge any more. Never mind that he was a bit nervous of handling the horses, he'd never really liked the place. When he was a small boy and Dad had brought him here, he'd found it frightening, with the furnace glowing in the darkness like the fires of hell, the ear-splitting clang of the hammer doing its work, and the overpowering smells of molten metal and singed horsehair, sweating beasts and steaming dung. Sometimes other child-

318

ren would gather outside, watching fascinated through the open door, and he could never understand the attraction. But there had never been any question but that he would learn the trade and follow in his father's footsteps, whether he wanted to or not. It would be better than having to go down the mines, he supposed, dragging putts of coal on his hands and knees as most of the boys he knew were doing.

No, the chance of escape from the hellhole that was the blacksmith's shop was tempting, all right, but the thought of having to go to Fairley Hall each day and take lessons from Clement Firkin was a daunting one. Supposing he wasn't up to it? His dad and Aunt Quilla would be really disappointed in him, and he'd feel humiliated too. It shouldn't worry him; he'd always done well at school. Sums and spelling had come easily to him, so much so that he'd sometimes become bored and impatient when the teacher had to go over and over the same things for the benefit of the slower learners. He'd memorised his tables and bits of poetry with equal ease, and his was always the first hand to shoot up when the rector or one of the school governors came in asking questions to test the progress of the pupils. But this was different. He'd either be on his own or competing with Sir Montague's cousin, who was bound to be a clever-clogs and would probably look down on him as an ignorant nobody. Richard didn't like being looked-down on. He was used to being praised and feted as one of the brightest boys in the class, and the thought that he might be considered inferior to anyone was anathema to him.

'I suppose we'll have to see about getting you a good suit, then,' his father said, and that was something else for Richard to worry about. A 'good suit' would be something from the local gents' outfitters, which would look cheap and nasty compared to what this Mr Raymond would wear. *He* had posh clothes, no doubt, made to measure by some swanky tailor.

Still, anything had to be better than a stupid leather apron, thought Richard. And at least he had the rest of the week to get used to the idea that he was going to start on a new chapter of his life.

'Right, I might as well get this horse shod myself,' Dick said. 'No point wasting time learning you how to do it if you aren't going to be working here any more.'

He lifted the horse's front leg, tucking it between his own with practised ease, and gestured to Richard to hand him the file.

As he did so, Richard felt a sudden rush of relief. Whatever lay ahead of him, it had to be better than this.

With Raymond away visiting his old school friend in Wiltshire, Richard started on his new career the very next week. Right away Clement Firkin was mightily impressed with his lightning-quick brain and the way in which he applied himself to the instruction he was given.

'He might only be a nipper, but he's a darned sight easier to teach than Mr Raymond,' he said bluntly when Lady Elizabeth enquired as to how he was getting on.

'And he's not hindered by having only attended the church school?' she said, a little acidly.

'No, I've got to hand it to them, they've taught the basics very well. I must say, I'm impressed with the lad.'

'That's heartening news.'

But she was still fretting that Montague was unaware she had set events in motion.

He was improving now day by day, little by little, and had even been able to come downstairs for a few hours, albeit still wearing his dressing gown. The last thing she wanted was for him to run across Richard with Clement Firkin, or overhear their voices, without any prior knowledge of what was going on, and she decided he was now well enough for her to broach the subject, provided she did it gently.

'Do you remember talking to Quilla before you were ill?' she asked one afternoon when he was installed in his favourite chair in the library. 'I believe you told her you planned to find a position here for her nephew.'

A wary look came into his eyes and the good side of his mouth worked for a moment before he grunted: 'Son.'

'Nephew, dear,' she corrected him, pretending that she thought he had found the wrong word in his confused mind. They were of course both well aware that Quilla was Richard's mother, but most of the rest of the household were not, and although they were alone, no one knew who might be listening – Nellie in particular had a reputation as an eavesdropper.

321

Again Sir Montague appeared to be trying to say something, and she sank to the floor in front of him, taking his hand.

'You've no need to worry about it, Montague. I've taken care of it for you, made all the arrangements. Mr Firkin has taken the boy under his wing, and by all accounts he is doing very well. Outshining poor dear Raymond by a mile. So you see, everything is proceeding as you wished, even if you are not well enough yourself at present to run things. All you have to do is concentrate on getting better.'

'All! Hah!' It came out as a rough bark.

'Yes, dear. I thought you'd be relieved to know, that's all.'

'Damn woman!' The same short guttural growl.

That surprised Elizabeth a little. But then of course frustration at his condition was making him even more bad-tempered than usual.

'I'm sure you don't mean that, Montague.' She patted his hand.

'Women! You're all the same.'

She smiled. 'I can see you're getting back to your old self.'

The good corner of his mouth turned down scornfully. Then: 'Get me some ... oh ... what ... what?' He huffed impatiently as the word he was searching for eluded him.

'Tea?' Elizabeth prompted him. 'A glass of milk?'

'No ... bundy ... bundy!'

Elizabeth regarded him sternly. 'If you are asking for brandy, Montague, that is not a good idea.'

'Soak, then. *Soak!*' His agitation at his inability to find the word he was searching for was obvious. Despairingly he raised his good hand to his mouth, miming the action of sucking on a cigar.

'And nor would smoking help, my dear. In fact, Dr Mackay would be furious with me if I encouraged you to do any such thing. No, I'm sorry, you'll have to get better first. For now I'll have Nellie bring you a nice cup of tea and a scone. Would you like a scone?'

She sighed as she left the room. It was distressing to see her usually dominant and capable brother reduced to this. But he was improving without a doubt. And she had managed to tell him about Richard without upsetting him to the point that he had a relapse, or even – God forbid – another stroke.

She paused for a moment, a hand going to her mouth as a thought struck her. Why, if it was what he wanted, had she been so afraid the news would upset him? Surely she should have presumed that he would only be relieved that his plans had not been delayed? Yet she had felt it. Quite distinctly. An anxiety she couldn't explain.

She gave herself a little shake. All the stress and worry of the past week coming on top of so many other misfortunes, had got her down, that was all. Really, it was quite understandable.

Yet still it remained, an almost unidentifiable niggle. Something was not quite right. Well, whatever it was, no doubt she'd discover the reason for it sooner or later.

She ordered tea and scones for her brother and then went thankfully to her sitting room, her sanctuary, and tried to lose herself in the intricate rosebuds she was working into her tapestry.

Chapter Twenty

The date when Edie would make her first communion was fast approaching. Each week, as winter gave way to an uncertain spring, she had taken instruction from Father Michael, and each week she found herself looking forward more and more to the lessons.

She had come to love the time spent in the sacristy, with its clutter of religious artefacts and the mingled smells of paraffin fumes, incense and a faint mustiness; loved the feeling of peace and holiness that seemed to engulf her like a warm wave the moment she walked through the door. It was as if the very walls were steeped with it, the prayers and exhortations of generations of worshippers caught within the ancient stones. And Father Michael was of course integral to the experience. His mesmerisingly beautiful voice lent reverence to the prayers; his soft nut-brown eyes and chiselled jaw might have come straight out of a religious painting.

Edie marvelled at how much she had changed since she'd gone to church, rather unwillingly, that first time. It was as if she had discovered a whole different way of looking at life, a completely new perspective, and the things that had been so important to her before were now scarcely of any significance at all. She no longer felt any urgency about discovering the identity of the poor woman who had left Christina in the church porch. Though the idea that that woman might have been her own mother still hovered, she had come to accept that she might never know the truth, and perhaps that was for the best. Christina herself seemed to have lost interest in the subject, so she felt no guilt about discontinuing her enquiries.

She had come to accept, too, that Charlie was lost to her for ever. The pain had dulled, and when she did think of him, it seemed as if he belonged in a different lifetime, and that both he and the girl who had loved him so were nothing more than a bittersweet dream. Now it was Michael who was real to her, Michael and the new world he had opened up for her.

At first Edie was too content in her new state of mind to question her feelings for him. To her he was just a part of the whole; a man who, attractive as he might be, was first and foremost the priest who was opening doors for her, introducing her to a new way of life. She had almost forgotten the way he had stirred her senses on those first couple of occasions she had met him, and how the very unavailability of him had added to the attraction. Never once during those private lessons had there been a single inappropriate moment, and she thought that the joy that sang in her when they were together came not from being with him but from her new-found faith.

And then one day everything changed.

It was a bitterly cold day in early April. Although March, too, had been cold, the heavily clouded skies had, for the most part, kept the frost at bay. But they had cleared now, and a little snow that had fallen overnight had failed to melt, so that it still lay in drifts on rough ground and in cracks and crevices, and dusted the rooftops. By four o'clock, when Edie left the church, it was freezing again.

She said goodbye to Father Michael at the porch door, thanked him one last time, and began to walk briskly down the path between the bare, snow-spattered flower beds. Too briskly. In the dusk that was fast becoming darkness, she did not notice the patch of ice that had formed in a dip in the path. As she stepped on it, her booted foot lost purchase, slithering out from under her, and she fell, landing ignominiously on her bottom.

For a shocked moment she remained where she was, sitting on the cold, hard ground.

'Edie! Oh, goodness gracious, are you all right?' Father Michael had seen what had happened and was hurrying towards her.

Feeling incredibly foolish, Edie scrambled hastily to her feet. Her hands were stinging and there was a pain sharp enough to make her gasp at the base of her spine, but it was her pride that was hurt the most.

'I'm fine,' she said, attempting to brush off the back of her coat.

'Come back inside anyway. I'll get you a glass of water. That was an awful fall. How did it happen? Did you slip on the ice?'

'I didn't see it,' Edie said.

'I should have warned you. I noticed it earlier and I was going to put salt on it, but it quite slipped my mind.'

He put an arm around Edie, supporting her

back into the church. At the time, Edie was too shaken up to think anything of it; she was aware only of her acute embarrassment and that her hands were trembling and her legs felt a little unsteady.

But when he had settled her in the worn old armchair and fetched a cup of water, he crouched down beside her, steadying the cup in her shaking hands, and suddenly Edie was very aware of him indeed. His hand on hers – those fingers soft and smooth as a woman's, not hard and calloused as Charlie's were. His face, anxious and caring, just inches from hers. The scent of him, soap and incense, and something undeniably male. An aching desire that was almost new to her, so long was it since she had experienced it, stirred suddenly deep inside her. And something else – a warmth tinged with excitement that seemed to spring from her very soul.

She wanted him. Priest he might be, but he was also a man, a man she wanted with every fibre of her being. Later, when she thought about it, she would realise that it wasn't just a physical need; it was everything that he and the religion he preached had come to mean to her. But in that moment she didn't stop to analyse it. She only felt an all-consuming longing to be with him, completely and for ever.

And he was feeling the same way too – in that moment she was sure of it. It was as if an electric current was flowing between them. Frightened suddenly by the depth of emotion she was feeling, she dipped her head, looking down at the cup of water clasped in her hand, and his hand

327

covering it.

'Edie? Are you all right? You're not feeling faint?'

'No ... no...' She looked up again, and as their eyes met, it was there once more, that connection that sparked and sizzled and burned. For a long moment they looked at one another, then, quite abruptly, he released her hand and stood up, and she could see nothing of him but the black curtain of his soutane.

'If you're sure you feel up to it, perhaps it would be best if you went now,' he said, and there was a strange edge to his voice, hard, aggressive almost, a tone she had never heard him use before. 'You might well begin to stiffen up from jarring yourself like that, and you've quite a way to go, haven't you?'

'Yes.' She was embarrassed again, awkward, and ashamed of the thoughts and feelings that had almost overwhelmed her a moment ago. But she also felt empty and bereft, as if something very precious had slipped through her fingers.

He saw her to the door, even walked with her down the path to be sure she did not slip on the icy patch again, but the feeling of closeness had disappeared as completely as if it had never been. As she walked back to Fairley Hall, Edie still felt a little trembly. Her mind raced in crazy circles, her emotions veered from something like elation to burning shame. But Michael had been right about one thing. The base of her spine throbbed with every painful step, and it was all she could do to keep putting one foot in front of the other. By the time the lights of the Hall came into view at the end of the drive, she could feel nothing but relief.

It didn't end there, of course. Her thoughts kept returning to Michael as she warmed herself beside the kitchen range.

'Seems like that fall shook you up, Edie,' Cook said, noticing that she seemed to be in a dream. 'You want to be careful. You don't want to go breaking an arm or a leg.'

Later, when she had eaten her evening meal with the rest of the staff and attended to Christina's needs, she was glad to be able to escape to her own little room under the eaves. As she tried to get comfortable in bed and forget about the pain that still burned at the base of her spine, she found she couldn't stop thinking about Father Michael and the extraordinary emotions she had experienced in the sacristy. And when at last she fell asleep, her dreams were pervaded by an almost unidentifiable longing and the scent of soap and incense.

Raymond was still away in Wiltshire, and Quilla was more than pleased that he seemed to be taking advantage of Sir Montague's incapacity. The longer he was away, the less well disposed towards him his cousin would feel, and the more chance Richard had to shine. He was doing well, she knew; Lady Elizabeth had told her so. And from the few guarded conversations she'd had with him, it seemed he was enjoying the challenge of his new position.

It was time, she thought, to speak to Sir Montague again about adopting him. Had it not been for the stroke, she would probably have left it a little longer, until Richard had established himself firmly and Raymond disgraced himself, as she was sure he eventually would, so that fewer eyebrows would be raised at the change in their fortunes. But as things stood, she lived in constant fear that Sir Montague might suffer another stroke at any time, and the chance of Richard inheriting the estate would be lost for ever.

Finding the right opportunity was not so easy, however. Although the services of the full-time nurse had been dispensed with, Lady Elizabeth didn't like him to be left alone for too long. Sometimes she sat with him herself, working on her embroidery or writing letters in whatever room he had chosen to occupy; sometimes Clement Firkin visited him to update him on what was happening on the estate or on Richard's progress; sometimes when he was alone Quilla would peep into the room, find him fast asleep and know better than to disturb him.

That morning in early April, however, Lady Elizabeth had gone out to call on one of the tenants whose child was suffering from whooping cough and had been at death's door for the past week, and she had asked Quilla to keep an eye on her brother.

Sir Montague was less than pleased. He was tired of being nannied, and grunted impatiently when Quilla installed herself in the chair facing his.

'Not a baby,' he muttered. 'Nor likely to run off with the parlourmaid.'

'I could fetch you a drink, if you like,' Quilla said slyly.

'Not supposed to have one,' he growled, but a glint had come into his eye.

'I don't suppose one would hurt, and who's to know? I'll have the glass washed up and put away long before her ladyship gets back.'

'Hmm.' His gaze went longingly to the brandy decanter, and he nodded his assent.

Quilla poured a generous measure into a glass and put it in his good hand.

'Sip it slowly now,' she warned, anxious as to what the effects might be if he downed it in one gulp as he was wont to do. But it was a risk she was prepared to take: Sir Montague with a drop of decent brandy inside him was likely to be in a far more receptive mood than when he was denied it.

He took a drink, smacking his lips.

'That's better, isn't it?' she said smugly.

'Hmm.' He grunted again, but this time with satisfaction, and took another, more generous, sip. A little of the brandy trickled down his chin, and she wiped it away with her handkerchief before it could drip on to his collar. She didn't want the smell of it on his clothes, announcing to all and sundry that he had been drinking.

'I've been hoping for the chance to speak to you,' she said, deciding to take the bull by the horns. 'You remember the talk we had before your stroke? When you agreed to adopt Richard?'

I didn't agree to anything of the sort, Sir Montague wanted to say, but the words eluded him.

'Rot,' he managed.

Quilla ignored him.

'He's doing very well at his lessons, I'm told, and works far harder than Mr Raymond ever did. I mean, where is *he* now? Gallivanting all over the country, without a care in the world for his responsibilities. That's how it will be if he inherits. But Richard ... he's still a boy now, I know, but when he's grown, he'll carry things on the way you would wish.'

'Hmm.' Sir Montague emptied his brandy glass and held it out to Quilla with a nod in the direction of the drinks table. She took it from him, refilled it, and stood facing him, the decanter in her other hand.

'You want some more? Say you'll set things in motion, and we can drink to that.'

'Dammit...' He reached for the glass, but Quilla moved so it was just out of his reach.

'Give me your word first, sir. Then you can enjoy your drink knowing your secret is safe. Otherwise...' She tipped her head to one side and levelled her eyes with his meaningfully.

Hot blood coursed up Sir Montague's neck and into his cheeks, a little sunken now from the weeks of illness. Unbeknown to Quilla or anyone else, he had been thinking seriously about her suggestion. He'd asked Clement Firkin to bring the boy in so he could take a look at him, and been impressed by what he saw. Scrubbed clean of the dirt of the blacksmith's shop and buttoned into a suit, Richard was entirely presentable, tall for his age and well built, with a mop of curly hair and a fresh, open face. He answered Sir Montague's questions respectfully but without appearing in any way cowed whilst he hated being contradicted or argued with, Sir Montague had no time for those he referred to scornfully as 'toadies'. And of course Firkin had been quick to sing his praises. Yes, all in all, Sir Montague thought, he was a far better bet than the feckless Raymond, and he had felt a flush of something like pride. Dammit, the boy was his son, albeit that he had been born on the wrong side of the blanket. He might have been brought up in a humble home and not had the benefit of what Sir Montague considered an education, but there was something in his bearing that could come only from breeding. He'd always hoped he would have a son to carry on the line, something Laura had failed to give him, and all the time this lad – his boy – had been growing up just a few miles away on the other side of the valley. No one would ever know, of course, that there was any more of a link between them than the adoption papers, but he would know. His blood ran in Richard's veins and would be passed on to the next generation, and the next. The thought, along with the sly pleasure he knew he would get from telling that idiot Raymond that he had been disinherited, both satisfied him and amused him.

Yes, he was coming around to deciding that adopting Richard would not be such a bad idea, when sufficient time had passed that it would not be obvious that this was the whole reason why he had been brought to Fairley Hall in the first place. What he couldn't stomach was Quilla's clumsy attempts at blackmail. The thought of her crowing over her achievement, believing that her son's advancement was all down to her threats to expose his secrets, stuck in his craw like a lump of undigested meat. And now she was at it again.

'I know you want this drink, sir,' she continued. 'And I know you wouldn't want me to share what

333

I know with the world. Well, I can help you on both counts. Just so long as you promise to have Lady Elizabeth send for the solicitor and tell him to get the papers drawn up. She knows all about it, and she's in agreement that it's for the best.'

'Damn you, Quilla,' he managed through gritted teeth.

'Be sensible, sir. I don't want to have to make the past public knowledge.'

'Think ... about it...'

The colour had heightened in his cheeks. This was as far as she could go today, Quilla decided. She lifted the brandy glass to her lips and emptied it in one gulp, then set the decanter down on the table and turned for the door.

'I'd better get this glass washed up before anybody finds out what you've been up to, don't you think?' she said.

Then, hoping the double-edged remark had found its target, she walked out of the room.

Edie was getting ready to go for her next lesson with Father Michael when she heard footsteps pattering up the bare staircase that led to the servants' quarters. A moment later the door opened and Christina stood there, a little hesitant, as if she were a naughty child. Fond as she was of Christina, Edie wasn't best pleased. She really didn't want to talk to anyone just now. She was horribly nervous at the prospect of seeing Michael again, and though she wasn't usually shy, that was exactly what she was feeling now – shy, and a little foolish. The thoughts she'd been having about him this last week were making her blush even when she was alone; her tummy was trembling and so were her hands, so that she was having difficulty fastening the buttons of her coat, big as they were.

'Miss Christina!' she said. 'What are you doing up here?'

For a moment Christina didn't answer; she was too busy taking in every detail of the room, which she had never seen before – the narrow beds with their rough grey blankets, the plain unvarnished furniture, the little window, bare of curtains, and too high to see out of. It could not have been more different to her own pretty room, and she could scarcely believe two girls shared this tiny space.

'Do you and Nellie really both sleep here?' she asked.

In spite of herself, Edie couldn't help but laugh. 'Where else would we sleep?'

'Oh, I don't think I'd like that! And you have to share a washstand and dressing table too! Don't you get cross if she moves your things?'

'We get along,' Edie said. 'Look, I'm sorry, Miss Christina, but I can't stay chatting just now. I've got to go out.'

'I know. To your religious instruction.'

'That's right. And I don't want to be late.'

'Can I come with you?' Christina asked unexpectedly. 'I'm so bored of my own company.'

So that was the reason she was here. Edie felt a flash of sympathy for the lonely girl who had everything she could wish for but companions of her own age. Oh, the Johnson girls were sometimes invited for tea, it was true, but not very often, and since Lady Elizabeth had taught Christina at home, she hadn't even had the opportunity

335

of making school friends. Remembering her own happy childhood, wandering the fields and woods, playing in the alley along the back of Fairley Terrace until dusk fell with Lucy Day and the others, Edie thought she'd never for a moment swap her cramped little room for Christina's spacious, pretty one if it meant being so lonely. And Christina must be feeling it even more now, with Raymond away and Miss Julia too gone off to London a week and more ago. She was staying with her friend Lettice Winterton, who had taken rooms there, and Edie wouldn't be surprised if she decided to move in with her permanently.

'Please!' Christina begged now, opening her turquoise eyes very wide and fixing them on Edie's. 'I'd really like to come with you so I can see the place where I was found. And you never know, I might even remember something that would tell me who my real mother is.'

So they were back to that subject again now that she no longer had other things – Raymond in particular – on her mind, and it made Edie uncomfortable.

'I think it's very unlikely,' she said. 'You were only hours old from what I've heard of it.'

'But you never know!' Christina persisted. 'I might get a ... a sort of feeling.'

'I'm sorry,' Edie said. 'I'll take you to the church another time if you like. But not when I'm having my instruction. Father Michael wouldn't like it.'

Just saying his name made her tummy tingle again.

'Oh...' Christina pouted, but Edie hardened her heart, picked up her bag and moved to the door.

'I really have to go, miss. But I'll only be out for a couple of hours, and when I get back we could have a game of Pank-a-Squith if you like.'

The board and suffragette counters now lived on the games shelf in the library. Julia had played it with Christina a few times, and as Christina thought it much more fun than Snakes and Ladders or Ludo, Julia had left it where it was easily accessible for anyone who wanted a game.

At the very mention of it, Christina brightened.

'Oh yes, I'd like that.' She hesitated, then added a little slyly 'I don't suppose we could ask that new boy, Richard, if he'd like to play too?'

'Oh I don't know about that.' Like the rest of the staff, Edie had been surprised by Richard's appearance on the scene, and though the general consensus was that he seemed a polite enough lad, he was still the son of a blacksmith and the nephew of a servant. 'I'm not sure your mama would approve,' she said, pulling on her gloves.

'I don't see why she wouldn't,' Christina argued. 'He seems really nice.'

'I'm sure he is,' Edie said, thinking that if Christina was transferring her attentions from Raymond to Richard, it could only be a good thing. He was far closer to her in age, and from the little she knew of him, she thought it was far less likely he would try to take advantage of her than the slimy Raymond. 'But he's here to learn, miss, not to play games. And now I really must go or I shall be late for my lesson.'

And before Christina could delay her further, she hurried out of the room and down the stairs.

Chapter Twenty-One

Left alone, Christina crossed to the dressing table, nosing about amongst the things laid out there. Edie and Nellie must have decided to share the space equally between them, she supposed: a clear central channel divided a jumble of items on one side and a brush, comb and a few little pots neatly grouped together on the other. The muddly side was Nellie's, Christina concluded, as amongst the clutter was a photograph in a wooden frame that Christina was fairly certain was Nellie's long-time fiancé, Teddy. The photograph had been tinted with a wash of colour; Teddy's face was too pink, and his hair too yellow. Christina giggled and turned her attention to Edie's side, picking up a jar labelled Bowyer's Little Round Pot Blush and opening it. The powder inside was a startling rose colour; Christina sniffed it, wrinkling her nose at the scent, which was, she thought, a little like faded rose petals. She dipped her finger into it and smeared some on to her cheeks; the effect was powdery and garish against her pale, creamy skin, though she thought it probably suited Edie's darker complexion. She took out her handkerchief and wiped it off again.

She slid open the dressing table drawers, though she knew she had no business to, poking about amongst the contents. In the little drawer on Edie's side she found a bundle of letters between a pile of handkerchiefs and a heart-shaped lavender bag. They were fastened together with a faded blue ribbon. Feeling guilty yet unable to resist, she undid the ribbon and slid one out of the envelopes. Disappointingly, though, it wasn't the love letter she was salaciously hoping for, but a boring account of everyday life with nothing to spice it up: no flowery phrases, not even a heart or a row of kisses at the bottom, just a simple 'Love, Charlie'. Who was Charlie? Christina had never heard Edie mention anyone of that name. She flicked through a couple more, but they were much the same. She put them back in their envelopes, retied the blue ribbon and replaced them in the drawer, being careful to ensure it looked exactly as it had before she started snooping.

She wandered aimlessly around the room for a minute, then sat down on Edie's bed, trying it out. It wasn't as uncomfortable as she'd expected, though much harder than her own, and she lay back against the pillow with its thin unbleached pillowcase, which had been carefully darned in one place, and wondered what it would be like to be a servant instead of the young lady of the house.

Suppose I was to fall asleep like Goldilocks, what a surprise Edie would have when she came back and found me here, she thought, giggling as she imagined Edie as one of the Three Bears. 'Who's been sleeping in my bed? And she's still here!' she said aloud, trying to imitate Edie's West Country accent. Then, before she knew it, her butterfly mind began hopping from one fairy tale to another, and she was reminded of the old cottage, deep in the woods.

She hadn't thought about it now for years and years, and never went there; in fact, to her knowledge nobody ever did. She'd come upon it as a child when she'd wandered further from the house than she was supposed to. She'd been acting out a fairy tale that day too, pretending she was Red Riding Hood on her way to visit her grandmother, and suddenly there it was, in a clearing, with only an overgrown track leading away from it in the direction of the drive to the main house. She'd stopped short, gazing at it in wonder. She hadn't even known it existed, and now suddenly there it was in front of her, as if she'd stepped into another land where stories came to life. But this little house wasn't at all as she had imagined Red Riding Hood's grandmother's cottage would be; it was more like the gingerbread house in 'Hansel and Gretel'.

It was a curious shape, low and rounded, just like a cake, with a vaulted door and windows set centrally. Ivy covered the rough stone walls and twin turrets on either side rose above the thatched roof, which looked as if it had fallen into disrepair. A low extension, also with a thatched roof and a smaller vaulted window, jutted out to one side. As she stood there gazing at it, it seemed to draw her like a magnet and yet frighten her at the same time. Longing to explore but half convinced a wicked witch would appear in the doorway at any moment, beckoning to her, she took a few tentative steps closer. And then, quite suddenly, there was a rustle in the undergrowth and an unearthly screech, and something came flapping up, almost brushing her face. Startled, terrified, Christina turned and fled, not back into the woods but down the rough mossy track that led to the drive, convinced that she had disturbed something evil and it was chasing after her.

By the time she reached the drive she was sobbing in earnest, tears of fright pouring down her cheeks, which had been scratched by long dangling brambles that had seemed to claw at her like the witch's bony fingers. Her shaking legs gave way beneath her and she sank down on to the grass verge, covering her face with her grubby, blood-flecked hands.

It was there that Mama, on her way home from visiting tenants, had found her. She was driving the little dog cart – this was in the days before Sir Montague had acquired the Rolls. When she saw Christina there, she reined in the pony and was still climbing down when Christina rushed to her, burying her head in her skirts.

'Whatever is wrong?' Mama asked, and between her sobs, Christina blurted it all out.

'Oh my darling, of course there's no witch! And it would have been just a pheasant that flew up in your face. There are lots of them in the woods at this time of year. You frightened it just as much as it frightened you, I expect. But you mustn't go there again. Promise me!'

Still weeping, Christina nodded. 'I promise.'

Nothing on earth would induce her to go back to that place. And she never had been. Whatever Mama said, she couldn't shake the notion that a wicked witch lived in the cottage, and she'd had nightmares for weeks afterwards in which she

341

was being chased through the trees by something or someone she could never see, something or someone who meant her real harm.

Lying on Edie's bed now, Christina smiled to herself. What a baby she had been! But across the years she could still picture the cottage as clearly as if she had seen it just yesterday, and she thought suddenly that she would quite like to go and take a look at it. The weather was fine today, and getting warmer at last, and now that she'd remembered it, the cottage fascinated her now just as it had then. Except that of course she was grown up now and knew there was nothing whatever to be frightened of.

Energised suddenly, she went to her own room, put on her coat and stout boots, found Beauty and clipped on her lead. Then, with the little dog trotting beside her, she set out. At last new growth was springing to life, soft cushions of pussy willow and dangling yellow catkins, and in some clearings, drifts of bluebells beneath the trees. Several times she took the wrong path and came to a dead end; in one place the ground was soggy and her boots sank into the deep mud that surrounded a hidden spring, and she had to retreat and begin again.

And then, just when she thought she would never find it, and was beginning to wonder if it had been a figment of her imagination, she came upon it, and an echo of her childish fear made her heart thud before she reminded herself that there was nothing to be afraid of. It was just a cottage, that was all, a cottage that looked more dilapidated than ever, a cottage that one of Mama's ancestors must have had built long ago, and though it was very peculiar in appearance, there was nothing evil about it.

Thrilled by her own daring, she approached the vaulted front door and tried to peer through the little leaded window panes, but could see nothing but spiders' webs festooned across the filthy glass. It was the same with the window on the low extension. Frustrated, Christina made her way around to the back of the cottage. Here the forest had encroached on what had once been a small garden, so that a tangle of undergrowth grew right up to the walls, and she was about to give up when she noticed to her surprise that one of the windows – not fancy like the ones at the front, but square and plain – appeared not to be properly closed. She fought her way towards it and was able to slip her hand inside, lift the flaking metal handle from its peg and push it fully open.

Too little light filtered through the trees here for her to be able to see inside clearly, but she could make out the shapes of items of furniture – a table and chairs, a dresser. It hadn't been just a folly, then; someone had once lived here. Curiosity overwhelmed her and she wondered if she might be able to climb through the window and get inside. But low as it was, there was nothing she could stand on to reach the sill, and she would almost certainly tear her clothes if she tried to hoist herself up, as well as dirtying them.

Disappointed, she was forced to abandon her adventure. She could always ask Mama if there was a key, she supposed, but she couldn't help remembering how insistent her mother had been all those years ago that she should stay away from the cottage. It could be, of course, that Mama simply didn't want her wandering about in the woods, but she'd never been told to keep away from any other part of the vast and rambling estate, and although she couldn't for a moment imagine why her mother wouldn't want her anywhere near the cottage, she couldn't help feeling that there had been some other reason for her making Christina promise to stay away from the place. No, she didn't think a key would be forthcoming even if anyone knew its whereabouts after all these years.

It would take a man or a boy to climb in through that window, she thought. Should she tell Raymond about it when he returned and ask him to help her? But somehow she couldn't imagine Raymond scrambling through dirty windows. He was too fussy about his appearance, and in any case would probably think it undignified. But Richard, the boy who had been brought in to learn about the management of the estate ... now he might be up for it. He wasn't a gentleman, as Raymond was; he didn't put on airs and graces, and she rather liked him for it. Raymond and his kisses were all very well, but lately it hadn't been just kisses. He'd done other things, things she didn't really understand but didn't like either, and he'd become quite unpleasant when she'd told him to stop. No, she had a feeling Richard would be much more fun and less demanding, and she wished she could get to know him. The trouble was that when he was at the house, Mr Firkin was always with him, and she couldn't see when an opportunity would ever arise.

Christina sighed. She supposed Edie must envy her, with her fine clothes and servants at her beck and call. But really there wasn't much to envy, since she was horribly lonely most of the time and hemmed in by restrictions as to what she could and couldn't do. She'd be kept in this prison until she was of marriageable age, she supposed, and even then she doubted she'd have much say when it came to her choice of husband. The decision would be made by Mama and Uncle Montague. Perhaps they'd decide on Raymond. Once, not so long ago, Christina would have thought that most agreeable. But not now. Somehow, almost overnight, her feelings toward him had changed, and she now found his advances quite repulsive. All because of those things he was trying to do to her that she didn't like at all.

No, she certainly liked Richard a whole lot more, though she'd barely spoken to him.

And when she got the chance, Christina thought, she'd ask him if he would help her get into the cottage.

'It won't be long now until your first communion, Edie, and I think it's time you began getting used to making a confession,' Father Michael said. 'Have you given it any thought?'

'Not really,' Edie said reluctantly.

It had been a strange lesson; for once she felt uncomfortable here in the sacristy she had come to love, all too aware of Father Michael sitting opposite her on an unmatched upright chair. Close enough for her to reach out and touch him, yet a distance that had never been there before seemed to yawn between them. From the moment she had arrived she had felt it. There was a businesslike remoteness in his manner, quite different to the warmth she'd always felt before, and it hurt her more than she would have believed possible. Where had it gone, that spark that had flared between them when he had helped her back into the church after she'd slipped and fallen? Had it existed only in her imagination? She supposed it must have, yet every time she looked at him, her stomach seemed to flutter as if a hundred butterflies were dancing there, and her heartbeat quickened so that it echoed in her throat and drummed in her ears.

'That's a pity. You really should have thought about it.' Father Michael's tone was gently reproving. 'But let's do it anyway. The first time is always difficult, but you'll find it will come more easily with practice.'

'Here?' Edie asked doubtfully.

'No, we'll do it properly, in the confessional.'

The air in the church struck cold after the cosy warmth of the sacristy, and Edie shivered. The faint aroma of incense still hung in the air, but here it was mingled with the hot smell of melted candle wax and the woody aroma of the chrysanthemums in their pewter vases on the altar and on a plinth beside the statue of the Blessed Virgin. Father Michael led the way down the side aisle to the confessional, dark wood decorated with carved fleurs-de-lys, and pulled aside the heavy curtain. A little reluctantly, Edie went inside and sat down on the small carved stool beside the aperture through which she would be expected to confess her sins.

Father Michael closed the curtain behind her, and a moment later she heard the swish of the curtain to the adjoining box, loud in the silent church, and then Father Michael's disembodied voice.

'Are you ready, Edie?'

'Yes,' she whispered, then faltered, uncertain how to begin.

'Father, I have sinned,' Michael prompted her.

'Father, I have sinned,' she repeated, then froze again.

'Just open your heart, Edie,' he encouraged her. 'Remember what I told you when we talked about it before. Just try to acknowledge your faults. None of us is perfect, so you need not be ashamed.'

Her faults. Goodness knows, she had plenty.

'When I get an idea in my head, I'm like a dog with a bone. I just can't seem to let it go, however hard I try. Like wondering if Mam is Christina's real mother. I know you said I should forget about it, but I haven't, not really. And it's not very nice thinking something like that about your mother, is it?'

'Are you having bad thoughts about her? Blaming her?'

'Oh no. If it was her, I feel sorry for her. It must have been awful to have to do such a thing.'

'Then I don't think you need feel guilty about wondering. Curiosity is a very human frailty. Is there anything else you can think of?'

The conversation she'd had with Christina just before she'd left to come to her lesson popped into her head.

'I know I can be impatient, too,' she said

347

hesitantly. 'I have to share a room with Nellie, and I often feel really cross with her. I like things to be tidy, and she ... well, she's really messy. She leaves her stuff all over the place instead of putting it away. Sometimes the clutter on her side of the dressing table spills over on to mine. Everything gets muddled up and I feel like throwing her things in the bin. And I have unkind thoughts about her chap, Teddy, too,' she added as an afterthought. 'She's always going on about him and I think: What's she talking about? He's a big fat lump, and not very bright either. But that's really not very kind. And,' she went on, warming to her theme, 'she's been saying they're going to be married for as long as I've known her, but I don't think they ever will, and sometimes I feel like telling her so and I know that would be wrong but I can't help wishing I could.'

'Why do you think that is?' Father Michael asked.

'Because he's too fond of drink and a flutter on the horses to ever save up enough.'

'No.' There was a tiny suggestion of amusement in Father Michael's tone. 'What I meant was why do you think you feel like telling her what she probably already knows?'

Edie felt a flush creep up her cheeks, partly because she felt foolish at misunderstanding him, and partly because she thought she knew what he was getting at.

'You mean am I jealous of her?'

'Are you?'

'No!'

But perhaps she was. Oh, she wouldn't want

Teddy if he was the last man on earth, but she had to admit she was envious of the fact that Nellie had a chap, even if he never did get around to marrying her. He might have a big round red face and be a bit thick, but at least he hadn't carried on with other girls and then gone off to London, leaving Nellie behind. At least she had someone to go out with on her days off, and hopes and dreams to keep her warm on winter nights when the worn sheets felt cold as a shroud. Edie's own hopes and dreams of a life with Charlie, of marriage and motherhood, had turned to ashes. Perhaps it was jealousy, and bitterness, that made her impatient with Nellie.

'I suppose I might be,' she admitted.

'That's a good start, Edie,' Father Michael said encouragingly. 'It's only when we acknowledge our innermost feelings that we can begin to do something about them and try to live our lives as God would wish. But don't worry, I don't think He will judge you too harshly. I think saying just one rosary will be penance enough – as long as there is not something else that you aren't confessing to.'

Edie caught her breath, her stomach falling away. He knew. He knew that curiosity and impatience and even jealousy were small faults she was willing to admit to because she couldn't tell him the truth – that she was guilty of a far greater sin.

I have feelings for you, Father. The words were so loud and clear in her head, she thought she'd blurted them out aloud.

Panic washed over her in a cold tide. She was no longer even sure why she was here. Was it for

349

the faith? Or was it for Michael?

'I can't do this.' She was on her feet, pushing aside the heavy curtain, running back down the side aisle to the door. On the path outside she stopped, covering her mouth with her hands, her eyes burning with tears.

'Edie! Wait!'

She half turned towards him. He was approaching her, a look of consternation shadowing his face.

'What is it, Edie?'

She shook her head wordlessly.

'Come back inside. Whatever is wrong, we can talk about it.'

'I can't.'

'Come back inside anyway.'

He reached out to touch her arm; she shrank away.

'There's no point. There's something ... I can't confess to. Not to you. And if I can't confess, then I can't take communion. So that's it.'

Not to you... What had she meant by that? wondered Father Michael.

'Oh Edie, Edie...' He spread his hands helplessly as disparate emotions raged within him.

He couldn't let her go like this; he'd be failing in his duty. But at the same time he was agonisingly aware that the dismay he was feeling was not just that of a priest losing one of his parishioners but also of a man losing the woman he had come to care for more deeply than he had any right to. Her distress was tearing at his heart; more than anything he wanted to take her in his arms and comfort her, not with religious platitudes but with words of love, words he had never spoken to any woman but which would come from his heart. He wanted to hold her, stroke her hair, kiss her mouth and those tear-filled eyes. And that could not be more wrong. It contravened the sacred vows he had taken. If he was not careful, he could forget them all in the blink of an eye. Somehow he had to fulfil the task God and the bishop had set him and bring her back into the fold. And at the same time he must find the strength to keep his true feelings hidden.

Dear God, help me, he prayed silently.

Then somehow the words were there, slipping effortlessly from his lips as though some greater being was speaking through him.

'If you have opened your heart to God, and are truly sorry, then there will be forgiveness,' he said, and his voice held no indication of the turmoil he was experiencing. 'Pray to Him, and to Our Lady, His beloved mother, that she may intercede on your behalf. The Lord will not turn His back on a repentant sinner who truly regrets their sin. If your mother had understood that, perhaps she would not have been an outcast from her church all these years. In time you may come to feel that you can unburden yourself to me, or to another priest, and I hope that you will. But don't let guilt drive you away from worship, or from communion.'

'Really?' She couldn't believe it was that simple. How could she worship honestly with this secret burning inside her? How could she bear to sit in church and listen to his voice when she was thinking such wicked thoughts; let him put the host in her mouth when she was experiencing such sacrilegious feelings; make confessions that were not true confessions at all?

'Really. I hope to see you next week at the same time, Edie.'

She nodded, still not daring to look at him. 'Thank you, Father.'

But as he watched her walk away down the path to the road, Michael's heart was heavy, and silently he echoed Edie's words.

Oh dear Lord, I'm not sure that I can do this either.

When Edie arrived back at Fairley Hall, it was to find Christina in a very different mood to when she had left.

'You seem full of the joys of spring, miss,' she said, striving for normality, as the girl came running out to greet her. 'But you shouldn't be out here without a coat. It's still chilly in the wind, and we don't want you catching a cold.'

'Oh, it's only for a minute. And I've something to tell you. Well – quite a lot actually, so I scarcely know where to begin.'

'The beginning is as good a place as any,' Edie said. She was still preoccupied, her mind and emotions twisting this way and that, but she was used to Christina's chatter. As long as she managed a 'well, well' or a 'fancy that' whenever Christina drew breath, she need not really listen.

'To begin with, then, I went for a walk with Beauty to the old cottage in the woods,' Christina said, skipping along beside her. 'It's just like the gingerbread house in "Hansel and Gretel". But you mustn't tell anyone, because a long time ago Mama forbade me to go there. You won't tell her, will you? It's got to be my secret – well, mine and Richard's.'

'Richard?' Edie repeated, a little vacantly. She was already losing the thread of the conversation.

'Richard Brimble. Quilla's nephew. That's the second exciting thing. I've been wanting to get to know him, and would you believe it, as I was coming back up the drive, he caught me up. He was on his way back from a day out on the estate with Mr Johnson. I said hello, of course, and we talked all the way back. He's every bit as nice as I knew he would be. Do you know he was learning to shoe horses before he came to work here? What do you think of that? Isn't it amazing?'

'Amazing.' Oh Christina, thought Edie, you might be a child in many ways, but you certainly have an eye for the boys.

'He liked Beauty too, and she liked him,' Christina went on. 'He tickled her ears and she licked his hand.'

'Good. And you told him about the cottage?'

'Oh no, not yet. After all, I'd only just met him. But I shall. When...' She broke off, clapping her hand over her mouth. 'No – I'm not even going to tell *you* what I have in mind.'

'I hope it's nothing bad, miss.'

'No. Not bad. Just... You're trying to make me tell, aren't you, and I'm not going to. And in any case, it's going to have to wait, because...' She paused, pursing her lips and opening her eyes very wide.

'Because what?' Edie asked, as she knew she

353

was expected to.

'That's the third good thing – and the most exciting of all!' Christina skipped a few paces ahead, then turned, walking backwards.

'There was a telephone call from Julia. You know she's in London? Well, she and Lettice have invited me to stay for a few days. London! Can you believe it? I've never, ever been to London!'

'Well!' Edie said.

'And that's not all.' Christina giggled excitedly. 'Mama said that I can go, but only if you come with me. So we're *both* going to London. Tomorrow!'

Chapter Twenty-Two

It had been Lettice's idea that Julia should invite Christina to visit her in London. As always, she was looking for ways to spread the word of the suffragette movement that was her whole life.

'We need to begin educating the next generation and firing up their ideals. I hope we'll have achieved our objective long before they are old enough to vote, but who knows? It could be years yet, and we'll need young blood to carry on the fight,' she had said one evening as she and Julia prepared for bed in the Kensington house of a well-to-do WSPU sympathiser where they had taken rooms.

'I'm sure you're right,' Julia said. 'But not Christina. She's very ... unworldly, and she can be impetuous too. Aunt Elizabeth would never forgive me if I got her into trouble of some kind.'

'I'm not talking about taking her on any demonstrations.' Lettice tugged her hairbrush through her thick red hair and tossed it down on the dressing table. 'Just letting her see what we are all about and hopefully gaining her interest.'

'If it gained her interest, she'd throw herself in wholeheartedly,' Julia said. 'I'm sorry, Letty, but I really don't think we should try to involve Christina.'

'Her lady's maid, then. I can't imagine your aunt would allow her to come to London without her, and this Edith sounds like quite an independent-minded girl, just the sort we need to broaden our support across the classes.' Lettice swivelled round on the padded ottoman, her very blue eyes sparking with enthusiasm at the idea that had occurred to her. 'We'd be hard put to it to function without fundraisers amongst the wealthy, of course – heaven knows where we would be without the Pethwick-Lawrences – but we need more working-class activists like Annie Kenney. A weaver's assistant in a Yorkshire woollen mill from the age of ten, and now the organiser for the whole of the south-west. You remember meeting her in Bristol, don't you? She's a powerhouse, afraid of nothing, as so many working-class women are. There's a whole strata of society virtually untapped, and if we are to be successful, we need the whole country to rise up with us, not just the well-to-do.'

She might have been making a speech at one of the meetings or rallies, Julia thought.

'This Edith is a miner's daughter, isn't she?'

355

Lettice went on, warming to her theme. 'Miners are known for militancy, and their wives for being strong women, the rock of the household. Can you imagine how they could stir things up in the community if we could only mobilise them? There could be a dozen Annie Kenneys right there in that one small area.' She caught Julia's hand. 'Don't you see? It would open up a whole new world for us.'

'Perhaps,' Julia agreed reluctantly. 'But I wouldn't want to get her into any trouble either, Letty.'

'Don't we all get into trouble if we're caught? Isn't it worth risking prison for the cause?' Her voice was vibrant with passion now, the passion that had inspired Julia from the moment she'd met her. But still Julia hesitated, reluctant to agree to the plan.

'She'd lose her position. Sir Montague would almost certainly dismiss her if he got wind of it, and then where would she be?'

'I thought you said he was incapacitated,' Lettice argued. 'Surely he wouldn't be up to dismissing anyone. And you told me you believe Elizabeth is sympathetic. Why, we might even persuade her to come on board too.'

Julia thought about it. Though Elizabeth had never expressed an opinion one way or the other, she was fairly sure her cousin knew about her activities, and had never condemned her for them. And she sometimes wore the little brooch in the colours of the movement, similar to her own, that Julia had given her for Christmas. Julia couldn't see that she could be ignorant of what it represented. But all the same, she couldn't imagine Elizabeth as a militant suffragette. It just wasn't her way of doing things...

'Telephone her,' Lettice urged. 'She can only say no. Where's the harm in trying?'

Julia sighed. She hated refusing her lover anything, and if Elizabeth was aware of her involvement with the WSPU as she suspected and still agreed to allow Christina to come to London for a visit, then the responsibility for the girl's well-being was shifted from her own shoulders.

'Very well,' she agreed, albeit reluctantly.

'Let's do it then. There's no time like the present.'

They went downstairs, and Lettice asked Mary Dobbie-Ahearn, the lady of the house, if they might use the telephone. It was, she assured her, on WSPU business. Julia picked up the heavy brass instrument and listened to the clicks and clunks as the operator connected her, still fully expecting, and rather hoping, that Elizabeth would refuse the invitation on Christina's behalf. She was astounded, then, when she agreed, on condition that Christina's maid could accompany her.

'They're coming. Tomorrow. Aunt Elizabeth will call back with the time of the arrival of the train, and we're to meet them at Paddington station,' she said as she replaced the receiver on its ornate stand.

'What did I tell you? Well done!' Lettice hugged Julia, who was still a little shell-shocked by the ease with which her mission had been accomplished.

'Promise me you won't involve them in anything that might mean trouble,' she begged.

'Of course I won't!' Lettice returned scornfully. 'I shall just dangle the hook in front of Edith and wait for the fish to bite.'

'That's all right then,' Julia said, and wished she could believe her.

A hundred miles away, in Fairley Hall, Lady Elizabeth also returned the telephone to its stand and stood for a moment, her hand resting on the cool brass, hoping she had done the right thing.

She would never have agreed to such a trip except for the fact that Raymond was due back tomorrow, and she had been growing increasingly concerned about the relationship that had developed between him and Christina. She'd thought in the beginning that it was harmless, but ever mindful that her adopted daughter was still very much a child, in spite of having a body that was fast developing into womanhood, she couldn't fail to notice the looks that passed between them, or the way they often both disappeared at the same time. To make matters worse, Christina also seemed to be taking an interest in Richard Brimble, and Elizabeth had not forgotten the incident with Sam, the gardener's boy. But she couldn't be watching her all the time and she was very afraid that one day Christina would allow one or the other of them liberties that could have disastrous consequences. The same disastrous consequences that had blighted the lives of both Christina's mother and, of course, Quilla. Sometimes it seemed to Elizabeth inevitable that sooner or later history would repeat itself, and now she thought that at least she could relax for a little while if Christina wasn't under the same roof as either of the young men.

She wasn't entirely sure London was the right place for her, though. She herself had only been there once or twice, and had been very glad to get home again, away from the noise and the dirt and the bustle and the perceived dangers around every corner. But Julia was old enough and worldly-wise enough, surely, to ensure Christina's safety, and Edith was a sensible girl too. Between them they would make sure Christina came to no harm, she told herself.

And Christina's reaction, when she told her of the plan, was enough to warm the coldest heart.

'London! Oh Mama, how marvellous!' she'd cried, clapping her hands in excitement. 'And Edith can come with me! Thank you, thank you! It will be the very best thing I've ever done in my whole life!'

'I'm glad you're pleased,' Elizabeth said, and hoped she would not live to regret her decision.

Edie had never been on a train before. She'd seen plenty, of course, rattling along one or other of the two lines that ran through High Compton, the engine belching clouds of smoke and steam. Some were goods trains, with strings of wagons behind them: open ones piled high with coal, or with pieces of farm machinery that had been made in the local foundry; closed ones containing who knew what, and ones with a kind of stable door, over the top of which reddish-brown or black and white cattle poked their heads. These didn't interest her much, but the passenger trains were a different kettle of fish entirely. The windows of the first-class carriages had little curtains fastened with tie-backs at the windows, and Edie had once peered inside one when it had been shunted into a siding for cleaning and seen padded seats with lacy antimacassars and pictures hanging above them. If ever she managed to ride in a train, though, it would have to be in third class, and she didn't suppose those carriages were anywhere near as luxurious. Yet now here she was, going all the way to London with Miss Christina, and no expense would be spared. It wouldn't be a hard wooden seat she'd have to sit on, but one of the plush ones she'd admired so much. She could scarcely believe her luck.

The train they were to catch was due to leave Bath soon after midday. Edie spent the morning packing Christina's things into a large leather suitcase and her own into a smaller one that Lady Elizabeth had said she could borrow. There was also a tapestry carpet bag and Christina's vanity case.

'How am I going to get them all off the train in London?' she asked Simon as he loaded them into the trunk of the Rolls, and Simon laughed at her ignorance.

'You get a porter to help you, of course. And don't forget to tip him. Her ladyship has given you some money, I expect.'

'Yes.' But it was making Edie a bit nervous. She'd never had so much money in her purse, and she was afraid of losing it, or even being robbed. There were pickpockets in London, she'd heard.

Once she and Christina were installed in their seats – of the same kind she'd glimpsed through the window of that carriage in the siding – she began to relax. And though she smiled at the way Christina squealed as the train entered the complete darkness of Box Tunnel, she was startled too, and when they emerged again into the April sunshine, every bit as excited to watch the world rolling by beyond the window.

At last they were pulling into Paddington station, with its vast glass-domed roof, and there, waiting on the platform, were Julia and Lettice. They had already secured the services of a porter, who entered the carriage when Christina waved from the window she had opened, and hoisted the luggage down to the platform and on to a trolley as if it weighed no more than a few feather pillows. Edie was thankfully saved from having to get out her purse by Julia pressing some coins into the porter's hand, for she had no idea how much she should give him as a tip. Then it was into a waiting taxi cab and they were bowling through the busy streets, Julia and Lettice pointing out landmarks as they passed.

'We'll go out and get something to eat as soon as we've got rid of your luggage and you've had a chance to freshen up,' Julia said as they drew up outside a tall, imposing house in a terrace of tall, imposing houses. 'You're famished, I expect.'

'But surely we can't go to a restaurant unaccompanied!' Christina was scandalised. She had been brought up to believe that places of refreshment

361

were not suitable for a respectable woman without a gentleman to escort her.

Lettice laughed, showing her large pearly-white teeth, which put Edie in mind of a horse, though otherwise she was a handsome woman with her strong features, blue eyes and rich red hair scraped into a topknot but with loose curly bangs from a centre parting framing a high forehead.

'This is London, Christina. There are plenty of places women can go to eat and not be bothered by unwanted attention or downright disapproval. Why, we spent all day at the Gardenia on the second of the month, along with a couple of hundred others, didn't we, Julia?'

'What was special about the second of the month, and why did you stay all day?' Christina asked, wide-eyed.

'To escape the census, of course! There was no way we were going to be counted!'

Christina still looked bewildered, but to Julia's relief, as the cab driver had opened the door and was waiting to help them out, there was no chance for her to ask further questions. She didn't want the subject of women's suffrage to come up so soon, and the evasion of the census had been just one of their acts of civil disobedience.

The rooms that Lettice and Julia were renting took up the whole of the second floor of the house – a large drawing room with views out over the square with its gated central garden, a small kitchen and lavatory, and two bedrooms. Julia showed Christina into the smaller of the two, a pretty room, the walls papered in a rose trellis pattern, the curtains and bedspread the exact same shades of pink and cerise.

'Is this your room?' Christina asked. 'Have you moved out on my account?'

'No, this is the guest room. Lettice and I share,' Julia replied easily.

Edie was to sleep in the servants' quarters. When she had unpacked Christina's suitcase and hung her dresses in the heavy oak wardrobe, one of Mrs Dobbie-Ahearn's maids showed her to a little room under the eaves, not unlike the one she shared with Nellie. There was no space for her to hang her things, so she spread the one good dress she had brought with her over the back of an upright chair and left everything else in the suitcase.

It was as she was washing her face in the china basin on a small plain washstand that it suddenly occurred to her. She was in London. Charlie was in London – or had been when he'd last written to her. Just a short while ago her, heart would have thudded at the thought; now she felt almost nothing, except perhaps a pang of nostalgic regret for what might have been. She was over him at last, she told herself. It was Michael now who set her pulses tingling and invaded her dreams.

Out of the frying pan into the fire, she thought wryly. Michael was even further beyond her reach than Charlie had been. And no doubt he would be scandalised if he knew the thoughts she had about him, the feelings he aroused in her. But at least she wouldn't have to face him next week. When she didn't turn up at the sacristy, he would think she'd meant it when she'd said she couldn't go on with her lessons. He'd feel he'd failed as her spiritual teacher, but that was so much better than him knowing the truth.

Determined to put both men out of her mind, Edie brushed the dust of travel from her skirts, dabbed a little rose-coloured Pot Blush into her cheeks, tidied her hair, and went in search of Christina, Julia and Lettice.

The first day or so of their visit was devoted entirely to sightseeing, and Edie gazed in wonder at buildings and monuments she had heard about but never dreamed she'd actually see – Big Ben and the Houses of Parliament, St Paul's Cathedral and the fountains in Trafalgar Square. She was particularly impressed with Buckingham Palace, where she gazed through the railings at the vast building, overawed to think that the King himself might be inside, and admired the guardsmen in their startlingly red tunics and tall bearskin hats as they stood motionless in their sentry boxes, rifles at their sides.

On the second evening they went to the theatre, and Edie wondered if she might get to see her old friend Lucy Day on stage. How truly amazing that would be! But it wasn't a musical theatre, but a serious play that Edie neither understood nor enjoyed, though Christina seemed to find it amusing, giggling along with the audience at what Edie thought were not very funny lines, and clapping so enthusiastically when the cast took their final curtain call that Edie was afraid she'd dislocate a finger.

Every meal they ate out, in restaurants that were not only full of ladies, but staffed by women too – the Tea Cup Inn, Alan's Tea Rooms, and even the grand Gardenia – and it wasn't long before Edie realised that most of the diners were, like Lettice and Julia, suffragettes.

Until now she had given little thought to the movement. She'd seen mentions of demonstrations and arrests in the newspapers, glimpsed as Percy Stevens ironed the morning *Times* for Sir Montague or scanned when the day-old copies were brought downstairs to be disposed of, and of course she'd played Pank-a-Squith with the family. But beyond that her knowledge was sketchy, and she really couldn't understand why women should engage in stone-throwing like ten-year-old tearaways and risk being thrown into prison to gain the vote. Why did they want it anyway? Edie knew very little about politics beyond that her father had always voted Liberal but was very taken with the new party, Labour, and that Sir Montague had been in a filthy mood for days over the failure of the Conservatives to take control of the government. But she couldn't see what difference it made to her which party was in power. She'd still be a maid and Christina gentry, and no silly vote was going to change that.

She was, though, fascinated by the women she was now meeting, and who greeted Julia and Lettice like old friends. There was a sense of purpose about them that was quite unlike anything she'd ever encountered before. Most were ladies who could have been enjoying a life of leisure, which, as Edie had seen at first hand, could be stifling and tedious. Instead they had chosen to fill their days with organising meetings and fundraisers, selling their own newspaper, *Votes for Women*, or planning some outrageous protest to bring their cause to the attention of government ministers and the world at large. They brimmed over with enthusiasm and determination, and there was a solidarity about their support for one another that Edie found enviable. Being a member of the WSPU must be a little like belonging to a large extended family, she thought.

She found herself listening with interest to the conversations about the cause. It hadn't as yet been mentioned by Julia or Lettice, except for the odd remark about the unfairness of being treated as second-class citizens – unbeknown to Edie, the two friends had decided to take an oblique, rather than a direct, approach. But on the third day of their visit, Lettice suggested they might like to attend a lecture and lantern show.

'It won't be nearly as dull as it sounds,' she promised. 'It's to launch a whole new range of things to promote the cause. Lilley and Skinner are going to stock our pretty velvet bedroom slippers, Derry and Toms will be selling underwear in the colours and Selfridges will be the very first department store in the country to stock powder, rouge and red lipstick. As for the lantern show, it will be quite something. It's being presented by Vera Holme, a great friend of ours, so we would really like to go if you can bear it.'

Christina pulled a face. To her, a lecture on any subject, with or without a lantern show, was most unappealing. But Edie's interest was aroused.

'Julia and Lettice have been very kind devoting so much of their time to showing us the sights of

366

London,' she said, quite sternly. 'If they specially want to go, then it would be only right to agree.' *And with good grace*, she added silently.

So it was that that afternoon they set out – by underground train this time – for Covent Garden and the Eustace Miles restaurant.

The Eustace Miles was situated in Chandos Street. It served only vegetarian meals – many suffragettes were also vegetarians – and was the venue for breakfast meetings when the women celebrated the release from prison of one of their number. Edie, already overawed by the ride through the dark subterranean tunnels, was enthralled by the proliferation of shops and cafés, and overawed when Julia told them that the young woman selling copies of *Votes for Women* at a penny a time outside the restaurant was none other than Edith Craig, daughter of the famous actress Ellen Terry.

Today an upstairs room had been hired for the meeting. The equipment for the lantern show had already been set up, and some ladies were arranging the samples of the new merchandise displayed on tables covered with crisp cloths, set on showing it off to its best advantage.

'Letty! Julia!' A woman from whom energy seemed to flow like electricity greeted their arrival. 'I am so glad you could come! And you've brought two new recruits with you, I see!'

'Not exactly,' Lettice said with a smile. 'This is Julia's cousin Christina, and her maid, Edith. They are staying with us for a short holiday.'

'And you haven't talked them into joining us yet? Shame on you, Letty!'

'There's still plenty of time for that. If you put

on a good show tonight, Vera, they may well be persuaded.'

Christina's attention had wandered to the display of powders and paints.

'What a marvellous colour that lipstick is! Do you think I might try it?'

'Only if you buy,' Vera Holme said, her own scarlet lips twitching.

'But I haven't any money! Edith ... Mama gave you some for us to spend, didn't she?'

'Oh, I don't know about that...' Edie didn't think the money Lady Elizabeth had entrusted to her was intended for such fripperies, and she couldn't imagine she would approve of Christina painting her lips, either.

'I'll get one for you,' Lettice said, taking out her purse.

'Oh thank you, thank you!' Christina trilled. She found a little mirror in her handbag and began applying the lipstick. The scarlet was garish against her pale skin, making her look both years older and horribly common, in Edie's opinion, but she was so delighted with the result that Edie bit her tongue.

A large woman in purple silk and wearing a yellow sash and a hat trimmed in green and yellow clapped her hands.

'Sisters! Will you take your seats now, please? We're ready to begin.'

The curtains had already been drawn to shut out the afternoon sunshine; now the lights were dimmed and fuzzy images appeared on a white bedsheet that had been tacked to the wall behind the speaker. Edie gazed at them, fascinated – she

368

had never seen a lantern show before.

The lecture, however, was going right over her head. She still couldn't understand why these women should go to so much trouble to get the right to vote, and she didn't suppose Christina understood it either. But the girl seemed to be quite carried away by the electric atmosphere and by her excitement at wearing lipstick for the very first time. Edie noticed her popping her lips together and even touching them carefully with one gloved finger in between clapping the speaker and joining in the appreciative murmurs of the audience.

When the lecture was over and the lights were turned up again, they all trooped downstairs for refreshments – tea in delicate china cups, all patterned with the WSPU logo, dainty cucumber sandwiches and little fairy cakes on matching china plates. Edie would have thought it surreal if she had known the meaning of the word. Never had she imagined she would one day be taking tea with her betters.

They had almost finished eating when one of the ladies closest to the window gave a cry that cut through the chatter in the room like a knife through a ripe peach.

'No! I don't believe it!'

'They're trying to arrest Edith Craig!' another voice boomed in the sudden hush.

'But they can't! She's not doing anything wrong!'

'That's her pitch!'

'We have to do something!'

'Come on, sisters, let's show them what we're

369

made of!'

As one, the women began surging towards the door, carrying a bewildered Edie along with them. What in the world was going on?

As she reached the door, all became clear. Two burly policemen had hold of a struggling Edith Craig by the arms; she had dropped her stack of *Votes for Women* and they were now blowing about on the pavement and into the road. And the two policemen weren't alone; there was a whole sea of dark blue tunics closing in.

'They must have heard about our meeting and come mob-handed,' someone said indignantly. 'They're trying to provoke us!'

Afterwards, when she tried to recall exactly what had happened next, Edie could never be quite sure. The whole world seemed to have become a seething anthill of bodies and a cacophony of shouts and cries.

'Leave her alone!'

'Stop them!'

'Votes for women!'

One suffragette had fallen to the ground; a man in a top hat who must have seen her predicament was elbowing aside a policeman who stood over her, his baton raised. Others were jostling, hitting out at any officer of the law who tried to restrain them. In the crush, Edie had become separated from Julia and Lettice, but Christina was only a few feet away from her, her face alight as if she was wildly excited by the commotion. Before Edie could reach her, one of the policemen lost his footing, stumbling over the kerb, and as he tried to recover himself, Christina reached out and knocked off his helmet.

'Oh my goodness!' Edie gasped, horrified.

Christina had darted away, but the policeman was on his feet now and charging towards her like an angry bull. Without a moment's hesitation, Edie stuck out her foot and he went down again, sprawling on the pavement. Christina was laughing, actually laughing, her scarlet lips parted, gloved hands pressed to her cheeks. Edie made a grab for her, just as another policeman began to push through the melee towards them.

'Come on! Run!' She took to her heels along the narrow street, dragging Christina with her. She had no idea where she was going; she only knew that if they were caught, they would certainly be arrested and thrown into one of the Black Marias that were pulled up nearby. She ran blindly, with no thought in her head but that somehow she had to get Christina away, and as they neared the end of the street, she thought she had managed it.

Breath coming in uneven gasps, pulses throbbing and a painful stitch starting beneath her ribs, she pulled the girl into a narrow alley between two tall buildings.

'What were you thinking?' she managed.

Footsteps were pounding down the street in their direction, steel toecaps echoing on cobbles. Edie's thudding heart seemed to miss a beat. She pulled Christina further into the alley, flattening herself against the wall as the running footsteps came closer. Would the policeman think they had rounded the corner and run on by? It was her only hope, but she knew it was a vain one. He would almost certainly have seen them turn into the alley. Desperately she looked this way and that but could see no way of escape. The alley ended blindly after just a few yards, and they were hemmed in on all sides by high walls.

'Oh Christina!' she murmured despairingly.

The footsteps slowed and stopped. A tall, broad figure stood at the entrance to the alleyway, silhouetted against the sunlit street, then began to come slowly towards them.

'Edie! Edie, it is you, isn't it?'

She still couldn't make out the face, shadowed as it was by his helmet, but the voice was one she knew. No! Impossible! But there was no mistaking it.

'Charlie?' she said faintly. 'Oh, Charlie!'

Chapter Twenty-Three

'I thought it was you, but I thought my eyes must be deceiving me.' Charlie sounded almost as disbelieving as Edie. 'What the hell do you think you're doing with that rabble, Edie?'

'I'm not one of them!' Edie blurted. 'And nor is Christina. We just–'

'She knocked Maltby's hat off.' Charlie was a little red in the face from the exertion of running in his thick woollen tunic. 'I saw her with my own eyes.'

'She didn't mean to, honestly. She was just–'

'Yes I did!' Christina's eyes were shining with excitement, her painted lips pursed defiantly.

'Are you going to arrest me?'

'Christina, for goodness' sake!' Edie admonished. Then, to Charlie: 'I can't believe you're a policeman! The last time I heard from you, you were cleaning windows.'

'Well I'm not now, as you can see. And by rights I ought to run the two of you in.' Charlie eased his finger between his neck and the high collar of his tunic, where it was chafing.

'Oh Charlie, please...' Edie begged. 'You can't! This is Christina Fairley, Lady Elizabeth's daughter.'

Charlie looked her up and down, his eyes lingering on her scarlet lips.

'She looks like a dollymop to me.'

Christina pouted, puzzled. She had not the slightest idea what the term meant, but she could see from Edie's disapproving expression that it was no compliment.

'I am Christina Fairley,' she said with hauteur. 'I don't know who you are, but I'll thank you to be more respectful or I'll have my uncle, Sir Montague, complain to your superiors.'

Charlie's face darkened. 'Is that right, Miss Fairley? And much good would it do. My superiors, as you call them, haven't got any more time for suffragettes than they have for dollymops.'

Edie's heart sank. Christina had touched a raw nerve, she knew. Sir Montague had owned the mine where the terrible accident that was no accident at all had happened when she was just a little girl, and Charlie had worked there as a carting boy. He'd lost friends when the hudge had gone crashing down into the bowels of the earth – in fact, she thought it had been Charlie who had come running home to Fairley Terrace with the awful news. He'd never talked to her about it; it was something, she'd guessed, that he wanted to forget. But of course he never would. It was a black scar on his soul, and like everyone else he had blamed Sir Montague for being too miserly to replace the hemp rope that lowered the hudge with a steel one.

What she couldn't know was that Charlie also blamed himself – he had been one of the boys who had tormented poor Billy Donovan, and perhaps contributed towards his state of mind when he had hacked through the rope with his mother's carving knife. Billy had been small and skinny, with a mop of ginger hair, always dressed in hand-me-downs and scared of his own shadow. Bullying him was all too easy and they'd never missed a chance to call him names, or worse. On one occasion they'd tripped him up when he passed them and used the pewter jug he was taking to fetch beer for his father as a football. Charlie particularly remembered it because it was not long before Billy did that terrible thing, and also because Billy's big sister Maggie had heard the commotion and come charging in, all guns blazing, and put the fear of God into them. Neither could Edie know that his painful memories had played their part in his wanting to leave High Compton and make a fresh start away from all the things, and the people, that served as a constant reminder.

But for Edie it was enough that Christina was the niece of the hated Sir Montague. Charlie would no doubt take great delight in arresting her and throwing her into a police cell. To him it would be sweet revenge.

'Charlie, please!' she begged again. 'I'm supposed to be looking after her. If you run us in, you'll get me the sack, for sure.'

For a long moment Charlie stared at Christina in open dislike. Then he turned to Edie.

'What are you doing in London anyway?'

'We're staying with Miss Christina's cousin. We've only been here a couple of days.'

'And she's a suffragette?'

'I think so. She must be, mustn't she? Her friend Lettice certainly is. They brought us to a slide show at that café, and it was quite fun, and then all hell broke loose and Christina ... well, Christina did something very silly.'

'She did that.'

'Don't arrest her, Charlie, please! She's only fifteen.'

Charlie looked from one to the other of them, Edie pleading, Christina subdued now. At last, it seemed, she had realised the seriousness of what she had done, and she had become a child again, clinging to Edie's skirts, eyes wide and frightened.

'Say I do let you go, what are you going to do?' he asked.

'Well ... find Julia – that's Miss Christina's cousin – and go home.'

'And how are you going to find her? If you go back there' he jerked his head in the direction of the restaurant – 'somebody else will arrest you even if I don't. And your friends have been carted off to the station already, like as not.'

'Oh!' That possibility hadn't even crossed Edie's mind.

'You'd be best off just going home and hope you find them there.' There was a note of authority in Charlie's voice that Edie had never heard before, but it gave her no comfort. An awful realisation was dawning on her.

'I don't know the address.'

'It's Chelsea,' Christina offered.

Charlie laughed shortly. 'Where in Chelsea though, love? It's a big place. You're not in High Compton now.'

'I don't know!' In vain Edie searched her memory, trying to recall a street sign, or even the name of the lady in whose house they were staying. It was double-barrelled, that much she knew, but more than that... 'I don't know! I can't remember!'

'You're in a bit of a pickle then, aren't you?' Charlie said, straight-faced.

Edie was beginning to panic.

'What are we going to do?'

'We're lost!' Christina cried plaintively. 'I'm frightened, Edith! We're in terrible trouble!'

'You should have thought of that before you got mixed up with that lot and started knocking policemen's helmets off for a lark, shouldn't you?' Charlie said, and again Edie was taken aback by the stern authority he was exhibiting. This wasn't at all the old, devil-may-care Charlie.

'We had no idea something like this was going to happen,' she said.

'This cousin you're staying with should have known better than to involve you too.'

'It's a bit late now to tell us that.'

Charlie sighed, shaking his head. 'Oh, I don't know, Edie. Why did it have to be you?'

A tiny shard of hope sparked in Edie. Quite apart from their relationship, which hadn't really been a proper relationship at all if she was honest with herself, Charlie had known her since she was a little girl, and he had always looked out for her. Surely ... surely he wouldn't leave her now, lost and alone in a big city?

'Help us, Charlie, please!' she begged.

He blew breath over his upper lip. 'Have you got any money?'

'Some...'

'Enough to get home to Somerset?'

'We've got return tickets.'

'Well there you are, then. You can take the underground to Paddington and get a train back to Bath.'

'But I haven't got them with me.'

Afraid she might lose them, or even have them stolen by a pickpocket, Edie had taken the tickets out of her bag and propped them behind the carriage clock on the mantelpiece in her room. Now she realised that by being careful she had only exacerbated their plight.

'That's not a lot of good, is it?' Charlie said, stating the obvious. 'How much money have you got?'

Edie fished out her purse and opened it. 'It's not enough for two train fares, is it?'

'Shouldn't think so, no. Not even if you go cattle class.'

'Then what...?' To her annoyance, she could

feel tears of helplessness pricking her eyes.

Charlie sighed again, thought for a moment, then got out his notebook and a pencil. He turned to the back page, wrote something on it, tore out the sheet and handed it to Edie. 'That's where I live. You've got enough money to pay for a cab, I reckon. Get one and ask the driver to take you there.'

'But...' Edie was almost speechless.

'Tell Gracie – that's my wife – that you're a friend and I sent you. I'm off duty at six...' he checked his pocket watch, 'that's in about half an hour, so long as I don't get held up with this blooming demonstration. When I get home, we'll work out what to do for the best. All right?'

Edie nodded, relief making the tears more insistent.

'Just for Christ's sake don't do anything else silly, or you'll land me in hot water for letting you go.'

'Oh my goodness, I wouldn't want to get you into trouble!'

He grinned wryly, giving her a glimpse of the old Charlie. 'I shall tell them I lost you, but I've got to get back now or they'll be thinking I've been a bloody long time. There's a cab rank just round the corner. Any one of them will be glad to take your money.'

Edie's lip trembled. 'Thank you, Charlie.'

'Go on. I'll see you later.'

'Come on, Christina.' Edie took her charge's arm, still not totally trusting her not to do something foolish.

At the end of the street, she turned, looking over

her shoulder. All she could see of Charlie was a dark blue figure disappearing into the distance.

'How do you know that policeman?' Christina asked as the cab wound its way through the unfamiliar streets.

'He used to live next door but one to me in Fairley Terrace.'

'He's very handsome, isn't he?'

'Yes, I suppose he is,' Edie said. She was still all a-tremble, not just from their narrow escape, but also as to what they would do if they couldn't find Julia or the house where they were staying, as well as at the thought of turning up unannounced on Charlie's doorstep. And, she admitted to herself, from actually seeing Charlie himself so unexpectedly after all this time.

Christina was right. He was handsome. Especially in his uniform... She could still scarcely believe that he was now an officer of the law, much less that he should actually have been amongst the posse sent to harass the suffragettes. But there it was. 'It's a small world,' her mother sometimes said, but May's world *was* small. That Edie should meet Charlie in the sprawling city that was London, and under such bizarre circumstances, was beyond belief.

But thank goodness it had been him who had set off in pursuit of her and Christina. She went cold at the thought of what might have happened had it been some other keen, conscientious young copper, who had followed them. And what would have become of her and Christina, lost in London, had he not offered his help?

For the moment she was too upside down to feel anything but anxiety, and gratitude to the fates that had sent Charlie, of all people, in her hour of need. But other, deeply entrenched, emotions were there too, bubbling beneath the surface, even if, for the moment, she was choosing to ignore them.

As the cab carried them through the unfamiliar streets, it seemed that Christina had quite recovered from her fright. Now she was the eager, excited child once more.

'What an adventure!' she exclaimed, taking Edie's hand. 'I can't wait to tell Raymond! And Richard! They'll never believe it!'

'I think it's as well you don't tell anyone,' Edie said. 'If your mama gets to hear of it, she'll never let you out of her sight again, and I'll be dismissed for sure.'

She was feeling increasingly nervous. The cab driver had looked very surprised when she'd handed him the scrap of paper on which Charlie had written the address, as if he'd never before been hired to take anyone to such a place, and that was borne out by the look of the neighbourhood through which they were passing. Row after row of soot-blackened houses and ugly tenement buildings faced one another across narrow streets, and there were what seemed like dozens of public houses. Outside one a group of men squatted against the wall, mugs of beer in one hand, cigarettes in the other. The women pushing broken-down perambulators or carrying shopping bags looked shabby and worn out; the children, playing in the gutters or kicking what Edie thought might be a pig's bladder for a football, were ragged and dirty, and they stared in astonishment at the cab as if they had never seen a motor before. If it had been anyone but Charlie who had given her the address, Edie would have thought they were the victims of a cruel jape, and even though she was sure he would never play a trick like that, she wondered if there was some mistake. She just couldn't imagine how Charlie could bear to live in a place like this after growing up amidst the green fields of Somerset.

Eventually the mean-looking streets and alleys gave way to a wider road where the buildings, although soot-blackened, at least looked to be well maintained, and the cab came to a halt outside yet another public house. 'The Frederick Arms' was emblazoned in flaking gold paint over a double frontage.

'This can't be right,' Edie said, puzzled and even more anxious. 'It's a house we want – number one, Frederick Court.'

'Must be through there.' The cabby pointed to an archway to one side of the building. 'Now, if you'd like to pay me, that'll be–'

'I need to know this is the place I want first.' Edie had no intention of parting with her precious money until she was sure she hadn't been brought on a wild goose chase. 'Stay in the cab, Miss Christina, while I go and see.'

'Don't be long,' the driver said in a tone she didn't at all care for. 'Time is money, remember.'

He made no attempt to get out and open the door for Edie. She climbed down on to the pavement, walked back to the archway and ventured through it, feeling awkward and apprehensive. She'd never been on licensed premises in her life – public houses were no place for girls or women – and to her this alley looked like part of the business. Empty beer crates were stacked against one wall alongside a couple of barrels. The end of the passage, however, gave on to a broad yard with ramshackle buildings that might once have been stabling on two sides; on the third she could see that yet another old building had been converted into a dwelling house. Though it was scarcely imposing, the windows were clean and the door had been freshly painted a cheery red. Beside it stood an earthenware pot filled with purple and yellow pansies.

Still anxious to be sure they had been brought to the right address before paying the cabby and letting him go, Edie took her courage in both hands and pulled on the bell beside the door. In the seemingly endless moments before it was answered, she looked around and saw a little wooden truck with a string attached abandoned in the middle of the courtyard. Perhaps this was the right place then; she remembered her mother saying that the woman Charlie had brought home with him, and who was now presumably his wife, had a little boy.

'Yes?'

Her back to the door, Edie wasn't aware it had been opened until the woman spoke. She swung round.

'Mrs Oglethorpe?'

It sounded strange to her ears. Mrs Oglethorpe

was Charlie's mother, plump, cheerful Dolly, not this tiny birdlike girl.

'Yes.' Her eyes were puzzled in her pale face, huge blue eyes made even larger by the dark circles beneath.

'I'm Edie Cooper, a friend of Charlie's. He gave me your address and said it would be all right for us to come here...' She broke off, uncertain how to go on. 'If I could just pay off the cab and fetch my friend, I'll explain.'

Without waiting for a reply, she hurried back to the main road, where she paid the driver and helped Christina out of the cab.

'We can't go into a public house!' Christina said, half scandalised, half excited.

'It's not.' Edie took her arm, helping her over the uneven cobbles.

The woman was still standing in the doorway, but a small boy had joined her, peeping round-eyed from behind her skirts.

'I'm sorry, but who did you say you are?' she asked, looking from Edie to Christina and back again.

'Edie Cooper. Charlie and I were neighbours back in High Compton. Miss Christina and I are lost and in a good deal of trouble. It's a really long story, but Charlie said he'd help us when he gets off duty.'

'Oh ... well...' The girl – Edie really couldn't think of her as a woman – looked completely nonplussed. 'In that case, I suppose you'd better come in.'

The room into which Gracie Oglethorpe led them was small, but immaculately clean and tidy, apart from a pile of coloured building blocks and another wooden pull-along toy.

'Don't fall over them,' Gracie warned. 'I have to let Alfie play in here unless I can watch him outside. He's prone to wandering off, and the main road is too close for comfort. He's been building a house and knocking it down most of the afternoon.' She smiled indulgently at the little boy, who had returned to sit amidst the jumble of bricks and was now laboriously balancing one on another.

'Can I help?' Christina asked, dropping to the floor beside him. For a moment a pair of dark eyes regarded her with suspicion, then he pushed a yellow block towards her and watched as she placed it carefully on top of his edifice.

'I think we should build a castle, not a house,' she said. 'Wouldn't you like that better?'

Edie was amazed. To her knowledge, Christina had no experience of children. But it was clear that she had an empathy with them. And there was no doubt that Alfie was a very winning child, with his mop of curly hair, big dark eyes fringed with long lashes, and dimples that puckered his cheeks when he smiled. He was sturdy, too, with plump limbs that would be strong and muscled when he grew. She wished she could scoop him up and cuddle him.

'Would you like a cup of tea?' Gracie asked, and Edie nodded.

'That would be lovely.'

Half an hour and several cups of tea later, Edie had not only explained their predicament, but had also learned a little of how Charlie had joined the police force and how he, Gracie and the children – besides Alfie, there was a baby – came to be living in a converted stable behind the Frederick Arms.

'When we got married, Charlie wanted a steady job with prospects, and he was lucky enough to get into the police,' Gracie explained. 'It's how we came to get this place too – the pub landlord liked the idea of having a policeman on the spot, a deterrent to troublemakers, he said. But I do worry about Charlie, knowing the sort of thing he has to deal with. Silly, I suppose. He could just as easily have fallen off his ladder when he was cleaning windows and broken his neck. But London can be a dangerous place. There's violent crime of all sorts.'

'Charlie can take care of himself,' Edie said with confidence.

'I suppose, but ... oh, I really don't want to think about it.' Gracie shivered, wrapping her arms around herself as if to ward off the dreadful possibility, and not for the first time Edie noticed just how thin she was. There was scarcely any flesh on her at all, and her cheap cotton dress hung from her skinny frame as if it were several sizes too large, apart from where it pulled over one full breast – she was still feeding the baby, presumably.

As if on cue, a wail from a perambulator parked in the corner announced that the little one had woken up and was hungry.

'Do you mind?' Gracie asked.

'Of course not.'

But as Gracie lifted the small, tightly wrapped

bundle from the perambulator, cradling her tenderly, a tide of emotion washed over Edie. Charlie's baby. Once, all she had wanted in the world was to marry him and have his babies. She felt her throat thicken and averted her eyes.

Christina, however, quickly lost all interest in building castles and jumped up, leaving a disgruntled Alfie to knock down the edifice, scattering bricks all over the floor.

'Oh, what a beautiful baby! Is it a boy or a girl? What's his name? How old is he?'

'She's a little girl,' Gracie said. 'She's three months old and we call her Vicky, though her real name is Victoria.'

Victoria. Her friend Lucy Day had once had a doll called Victoria, given to her by Lady Elizabeth after her father had been killed so tragically, Edie remembered. Again the sweet yet painful sensations stirred in her; echoes of long-gone days when she had been a little girl and Charlie had been her idol.

Gracie was unbuttoning her dress, freeing a breast and putting the small, eager mouth to it; again Edie averted her eyes, but when she heard a sharp intake of breath, she looked back and saw that Gracie was wincing, her eyes half shut, biting down hard on her lower lip.

'Is she hurting you?' Christina asked disingenuously.

'A bit.' With an effort, Gracie gave her what was intended to be a reassuring smile. 'The trouble is, I can only feed her on the one side. The other...' she patted the curiously flat area over her heart, 'well, it's no good, I'm afraid.'

Edie frowned. She'd never heard of a woman having only one working breast when the milk came in, but then what did she know? And she didn't think it was a suitable topic of conversation for Christina anyway.

'Charlie should be home by now.' Gracie's eyes flicked anxiously towards the door.

'He said he might be delayed,' Edie tried to reassure her, but she couldn't help hoping he wouldn't be much longer. Being here with his wife and children, pleasant and surprisingly welcoming though Gracie might be, was hardly the most comfortable situation. Besides which, she was still anxious about what was going to happen to her and Christina. All very well for Charlie to say they'd work something out, but Edie was at a loss to know what that might be.

Gracie had finished feeding baby Vicky, changed her nappy, and put her back down in the perambulator before they heard the front door opening and Charlie's voice calling: 'I'm home!'

'Oh, thank goodness.' Gracie moved toward the door to greet him, but stopped short, head bent, wincing again, this time pressing a hand to her stomach as if she had been caught by a sudden pain. What in the world is wrong with her? Edie wondered, but before she could give it any more thought, Charlie was in the doorway, unbuttoning his tunic.

'You found it then, Edie,' he said.

She nodded, overcome suddenly by a rush of emotion.

'Right,' Charlie said. 'Just let me get changed, and we'll talk about what we're going to do to

387

'sort you out.'

Since neither Edie nor Christina had the faintest idea where in Chelsea they had been staying, or the name of the lady whose house it was, and since in any case Charlie rather thought Julia and Lettice had been taken into custody, he suggested that their only option was to call Fairley House and let Lady Elizabeth know of their predicament. There was a telephone in the Frederick Arms; he'd ask the landlord if he might use it.

Edie was reluctant to enter licensed premises, nervous about using a telephone, something she'd never done before, and even more nervous about confessing to her employer what had happened, so Charlie left her outside and went in through a back door to make the call himself. Whilst she was waiting, Edie rescued Alfie's toy truck and put it on the doorstep where it wouldn't be forgotten. It wasn't long before Charlie was back. He leaned on an empty beer barrel and she perched on another one while he filled her in on the conversation.

'I've told Lady Elizabeth I'll lend you enough money for the two of you to get back to Bath,' he said, taking out his cigarettes and a book of matches. 'It's too late for you to go tonight, though, so I've said you'd best stay the night here and I'll see you to Paddington myself in the morning before I go in for my shift. She seemed satisfied with that.'

'Was she very angry?' Edie asked apprehensively.

'She's very worried,' Charlie said bluntly. 'But

she's more cross with this cousin of Christina's than she is with you, and I must say, so am I. She should never have taken you to that meeting. She ought to have known the sort of thing that might happen.'

'It was awful.'

'That was nothing compared to what it might have been. I've seen a lot worse.' He lit his cigarette and blew a stream of smoke into the early-evening air.

'I'm so sorry to inconvenience you like this,' Edie said. 'But where will we sleep? Have you got room for us?'

He squinted at her through the smoke. 'We haven't got room, no. It's a nice little place, and it's ours, but we don't run to guest rooms, I'm afraid.'

'Then where...?'

He nodded in the direction of the Frederick Arms.

'Jack Purvey, the landlord, says they've got a room you can have.' He grinned at her dismayed expression. 'It's all right, you can go in the back way. There's a staircase that's all shut off from the bars, so madam won't have to see the hoi polloi. I'm sorry, Edie, but it's that or our sofa, and I think the two of you would find that a bit of a squash.'

'Oh Charlie...' Edie pressed a hand to her mouth. This whole experience seemed to have drained her of her usual resilience.

'Glad I was able to help.'

'I honestly don't know what we'd have done if... You've been so kind. You and Gracie. She's...' she hesitated, 'she's lovely, isn't she?'

'She's a good girl, yes.' There was something in his tone that Edie could not read. She waited, and after a moment, Charlie went on: 'Truth to tell, I'm a bit worried about her. She's not been at all well since she had Vicky.'

'The birth is bound to have taken it out of her,' Edie said, trying not to think about the dark circles under Gracie's eyes, the apparent sudden pain that had made her gasp, the strange flat breast and the girl's extreme thinness – as if a puff of wind would blow her away, as Mam would say.

'It's been longer than that if I'm honest.' Charlie dropped his cigarette and ground it out with the toe of his boot. 'Hardly surprising. She's had a tough time of it. I'm afraid I didn't treat her very well.' He hesitated. 'You know it isn't just the baby that's mine? Alfie is too. But I wasn't there when she needed me. I was off doing my own selfish thing and it was left to Victor to take care of her. That's why we named Vicky after him. He was a top bloke. There's not many that would take on a woman who's expecting somebody else's baby.'

Edie didn't want to hear any of this. It was just too painful. But it explained where Alfie's dark eyes and curls had come from. She wouldn't be surprised if he didn't grow up to be the spitting image of Charlie. She slid down from the beer barrel and pushed herself away.

'I must go and tell Miss Christina what's been arranged.'

'I didn't treat you very well either, Edie,' Charlie said unexpectedly.

Edie glanced round at him and he went on.

'I'm sorry. I was a fool. And worse. What we had was good, wasn't it? I never appreciated it – or you, come to that – and I'm sorry.'

'Well, it's all water under the bridge now, Charlie. You're married with a wife and children.' She was making a huge effort to sound nonchalant.

'I'm doing my damnedest to make sure I don't hurt them any more. And to make up for all the harm I've caused.'

'You're certainly doing that,' she said. 'A policeman! When I think of all the times Sergeant Love was after you... He'd never believe it if he could see you now.'

'He knows.' Charlie leaned back against the barrel, hands in trouser pockets. 'He gave me a good reference, too. I don't suppose I'd have got in without it. Well...' He grinned, the old mischievous grin that seemed to light up not just his face but the whole world around him, and something sweet and painful twisted in Edie's gut. 'He must have seen some good in me, I suppose.'

'There *is* good in you, Charlie. A whole lot of good. Why else would I...' She broke off, embarrassed. *Why else would I have fallen for you and stayed in love with you all these years?* wasn't something to be said out loud.

'If there is, I kept it pretty well hidden for a damn sight too long,' Charlie said. 'It was like I had to make the most of my life, do all the living my mates couldn't – you know, Frank Rogers, Jack Withers, even poor young Billy Donovan. They were always there; I could never get them out of my head. I spent years trying to get away from them, but I never could.'

'Oh Charlie...'

She'd never for a moment realised the terrible effect the tragedy had had on him. She'd seen how it had affected the families of those who had lost loved ones, the grief, the hardship, but not once had she given a thought to the boy, younger than Christina was now, who had gone off to work one morning with his mates and not only witnessed the terrible event and its aftermath, but had to run home to break the news of the tragedy. No wonder he'd tried to find escape, no wonder he'd been unable to commit, no wonder he'd wanted to leave Somerset and start afresh.

She reached out to touch his arm in sympathy, then drew back, shy suddenly, and all too aware that it was not her place to comfort him. He had a wife now to do that. But he caught her hand, holding it for a moment and squeezing it hard.

'You understand, don't you, Edie?' he said, and the torment he had long experienced was there in his eyes and in every line of his face, making him look every year of his age.

'I understand,' she said softly.

'And can you forgive me?'

'Charlie,' she said, 'there is nothing to forgive.'

Sleep was impossible. Edie slid out of the double bed, careful not to disturb Christina, who, exhausted by the events of the day, was fast asleep, and crossed to the window. From here she was looking directly down on to the courtyard of the Frederick Arms and the frontage of the house where Charlie and his family now lived.

I love him, she thought. I always have and I

392

always will.

It was a love that came from the very heart of her, warm and deep and eternal, as much a part of her as every breath she breathed.

She thought of Father Michael, and wondered how she could have imagined even for a moment that she was falling in love with him. Because he was part of a spiritual experience that had taken her by surprise? Perhaps. Because he was the only man, apart from Charlie, whom she had ever felt an attraction for? Because he was unobtainable? Perhaps. And perhaps a combination of all those things.

She could see now that it was nothing but a pale shadow compared to the love she felt for Charlie. A mirage in a desert, glimpsed from afar. Edie knew she would never again mistake lust for love. But there was not a single thing she could do about it.

In the event, it was not Charlie who took Edie and Christina to Paddington the next morning, but Julia.

She and Lettice had indeed been arrested, but they had eventually been released without charge since there was no evidence that they had actually committed any offence. Frantic with worry as to what had become of Christina and Edie, they had returned home to Chelsea to learn that Lady Elizabeth had been trying to contact them.

Julia had returned the call and been told by a furious Lady Elizabeth that the two girls were safe and spending the night at Frederick Court, but that they were to return home first thing the next day.

'Perhaps you would be so good as to reunite them with their belongings and see them safely on to the train so as not to put this PC Oglethorpe to any more trouble,' she had said, frosty as an iceberg. 'I assume I can trust you to do that without leading them into more trouble or losing them again.'

It was by now too late for Julia to go to Frederick Court that evening. She packed up Christina and Edie's things and ordered a cab for very early the next morning so as to be sure to get to them before they left for Paddington.

Later, she and Lettice had their first serious row, as she blamed her friend for them having taken the girls to the meeting whilst Lettice protested that Julia had been every bit as responsible.

As a result, she went alone to collect a surprised Christina and Edie, and took them and their luggage to Paddington station.

Christina, disappointed at having the holiday cut short, sulked for most of the short journey, but Edie was only relieved not to have to spend more time in Charlie's company. It was just too painful for her.

As for Julia, she thought it would be a very long time before she dared venture to Somerset again. She watched the train steam out of the station, then returned to Chelsea to try to mend her bridges with the woman who was now the whole world to her.

Chapter Twenty-Four

Edie had made up her mind. In reality she thought she had known from the moment she had fled from that last lesson with Father Michael, the confession she had so nearly made trembling on her lips and her cheeks burning with embarrassment and shame.

She couldn't face him again. The fantasies she had concocted about him made her stomach contract so it felt as if it was curling in on itself. How could she have allowed herself to be so foolish? How could she have imagined for even a moment that there was something unspoken between them? Father Michael was a priest. He had committed his life to God. For her to have thought of him in such a way for even a moment was a sin.

A sin she could never bring herself to confess, at least not to Michael himself. But to continue with her lessons and go on to take communion without absolution would be terribly wrong, and for the first time she had come to understand completely the dilemma her mother had faced.

Edie knew now that her feelings for Michael had been nothing but a fleeting fancy, a stupid dream she had conjured up to fill the empty place in her heart. Charlie was the only man she had ever truly loved, and probably always would be. Meeting him again in London had left her in no doubt about that. But that didn't alter the fact that she couldn't continue with her lessons without confessing, and she'd die before she could bring herself to do that.

No, the only thing for it was to give up the idea of becoming a full member of the Church. The realisation made Edie feel curiously empty. She had been uplifted by the age-old rituals and the atmosphere of peace, comfort and adoration that seemed to have impregnated the very walls of the former tithe barn that was now St Christopher's. But perhaps things would change in times to come. Perhaps Michael would move on to another parish. Perhaps she could find the courage to confess to another priest so that at least her conscience was clear. Perhaps she would be able to put the guilt and shame behind her and begin again.

For now, though, there was nothing for it but to see Michael one last time and tell him of her decision. She dreaded it, but she knew she owed him that much.

'Do you think I could be spared for an hour on Sunday so I can go to church?' she asked Lady Elizabeth. 'I won't be asking for time off to go to my lesson next week; I've decided to give them up. But I need to see Father Michael to tell him.'

'Of course you can be spared, Edith,' Lady Elizabeth said, rather surprised, since the maid had seemed so committed until now. Could her change of heart have something to do with her visit to London? But she couldn't imagine why; Edith didn't seem to have been converted to the suffragette movement, heaven be praised. Although Lady Elizabeth had a great deal of sympathy with their objectives, she wholeheartedly disapproved of the methods they employed in order to achieve them.

And so when Sunday came, a nervous Edie arrived at the church and slipped into a pew beside her mother, who was already there. To her surprise, however, it was not Father Michael who emerged from the sacristy to take the service, but a young priest she had never seen before and, tripping along behind him, Father O'Brien.

Edie raised her eyebrows at her mother in a questioning look, but May only shrugged and pulled a face that said, *I have no idea.*

Well at least she would be spared from having to tell Father Michael her decision face to face, Edie thought, still puzzled, but relieved, as the inexperienced young priest and the ageing Father O'Brien bumbled through the Mass. She'd ask Father O'Brien to give him a message and that would be an end to it.

When the service was over and they left the church, Edie couldn't help but notice how uncomfortable her mother looked as she shook the old priest's hand and moved hurriedly on. That long-ago confession, whatever it might have been, still cast a long shadow over May's relationship with Father O'Brien, and Edie felt more sure than ever that it would be the same for her if she ever revealed the shameful feelings she had entertained towards Father Michael.

As he took her hand in his own gnarled ones, Father O'Brien smiled at her.

'It's good to see you, Edie. You are going to

make your first communion soon, I understand.'

Edie swallowed the lump of nervousness in her throat.

'Actually, Father, I wanted to speak to Father Michael about that. It's why I came to church today ... but he's not here.'

'No, he has accompanied a group of sick parishioners on a pilgrimage to Lourdes,' the old priest said. 'Father Benjamin, who was to go with them, has been taken poorly and Father Michael agreed at the last minute to take his place... Ah! Of course! I almost forgot! I was to tell you Michael won't be able to see you this week, but he'll expect you next week as usual.'

'Oh...' For a moment Edie's resolve almost wavered. Then she took her courage in both hands.

'Actually, Father, I've decided not to go on with my lessons. Would you tell Father Michael that for me, please?'

'Oh my dear...'

A look of distress shadowed Father O'Brien's eyes and she hurried on, 'I'm really sorry, but there it is, I've changed my mind. If you could pass the message on I'd be really grateful.'

'Are you quite sure about this, Edie?' Father O'Brien asked.

'Quite sure.' Edie couldn't meet his eyes. 'You won't forget, will you, Father?'

'I'll tell him as soon as he gets back, Edie.' He smiled wryly. 'I'm not quite senile yet, though I know some think I am.'

Truth to tell, he wasn't entirely surprised, nor indeed sorry, though failing to bring another soul into the fold was always a cause for regret. But he had become uneasy about the private lessons Father Michael was giving Edie. There was something different about the young priest these days, especially when he returned to the abbey after those lessons, a sort of remoteness that was quite unlike him, and Father O'Brien had noticed that he was spending a good deal of time in prayer. Besides which, he had agreed to take Father Benjamin's place on the pilgrimage with alacrity. All in all, Father O'Brien couldn't help thinking that maybe it was not such a bad thing that he would not be seeing Edie again.

'What was all that about?' May asked as Edie joined her outside the porch.

'I've decided not to continue with my lessons.'

May looked shocked. 'Why ever not?'

'Oh Mam, I really don't want to talk about it.' Unexpectedly, Edie found she was close to tears. 'I can see you're disappointed, and I'm sorry, but there it is,' she said wretchedly.

'I don't know about me, but Father Michael will certainly be disappointed,' May said shortly. 'He's a good priest, that one. A real breath of fresh air.'

When Edie didn't reply, she went on: 'I suppose I'm not one to talk, staying away from church all these years. But I'm back now, and that's all thanks to Father Michael. But if your mind's made up...'

'It is.'

'Ah well, there it is. Now, are you coming home for a bit of dinner?'

'No, I've got to get back.' Edie hugged her

mother. 'But I've got an afternoon off next Friday and I'll see you then.'

With that, she set out on the long walk back to the Hall, feeling as if a load had been lifted from her shoulders.

For Father Michael, the visit to Lourdes had been an uplifting experience. When he had volunteered to take the place of the ailing Father Benjamin, it had been partly in order that the sick and lame parishioners who had saved so long and hard for their pilgrimage would not be disappointed, though had he not made the trip he felt sure some other priest would have stepped in. But his overwhelming motive, he admitted to himself, was a selfish one. The torment of his meetings with Edie and their aftermath was draining his resolve and making him question his calling, and for all his efforts to deny his feelings for her, he was not succeeding. The battle between his duty as a priest and his longings as a man was a constant one now, and the guilt was tearing him apart.

That last conversation he had had with her had only served to intensify the guilt.

There was something Edie was unable to confess, and whatever it was she had felt it precluded her from making her first communion, though he had, he hoped, persuaded her otherwise. Her reluctance was, it seemed to him, both honest and honourable, whilst he, who was supposed to be an example to his parishioners, was concealing his darkest secrets under a cloak of piety. He, who had sworn chastity, was aching with forbidden desire. He, who had committed his life to God, wanted only to be free to commit to a woman – not just any woman, but this one. He should be on his knees confessing to one of his fellow priests, but he was no more able to do that than she had been. And he was much less honest and honourable than she. He still gave and received communion. Every time he did so, he was practising a dreadful deceit that might not be known to another human soul but would certainly be known to God.

Had he made a terrible mistake? Should he leave the priesthood? Renege on the solemn vows he had made? He didn't know. He was being tossed this way and that on a stormy sea of indecision, and he hoped that some time away from the abbey, away from Edie, would help to make things clearer.

And it had worked. Pushing a wheelchair, lending his arm to the frail and infirm, standing before the effigy of the Blessed Virgin in the grotto, meditating quietly when his day's duties were done, Michael had found a sense of peace. This was his life, dedicated to the service of God and his fellow man. He had witnessed no miracles – no cripple had leapt to his feet and walked, no blind person had miraculously regained their sight. But he had felt the power and the holiness that had inspired him so long ago, and which had deserted him lately, and a sense of rightness of the way he had chosen.

When the pilgrimage was over, however, as they travelled back across France and the Channel, the feeling of oppression had begun to grip him once more. When he got back to High Compton,

401

nothing would have changed. He would see Edie, and the Devil would once more sit on his shoulder, offering him the glory of the love of a woman, tempting him to commit what would be, for him, a mortal sin.

For all his assurances to Edie, it was several days before Father O'Brien remembered what it was that had been lost in the murk of his increasingly clouded mind. Each time he passed Father Michael in the cloisters, he felt vaguely that there was something he was supposed to do, but before he could grasp what it was, it had slipped away again. Then, quite suddenly, seeing him on his knees in the Lady Chapel, it came to him.

He approached the young priest, afraid that if he did not speak now he would forget again what it was he had to say.

'I'm sorry to disturb you, Michael, but...'

For a fleeting moment as he passed on the message, he saw raw pain in Father Michael's eyes, but it was quickly replaced by an expression that looked very much to Father O'Brien like relief.

'Thank you,' was all he said, and Father O'Brien wondered whether it was him Father Michael was thanking, or a higher power.

Father Michael couldn't have answered that, even if he'd been asked. He only knew that the cross he had been bearing seemed to have been lifted from him. He was sorry Edie had turned her back on the Church, just as her mother had done so many years before, and he hoped that one day she would feel able to return. But to another priest, not to him. He would miss her; he would even miss the all-too-human emotions that had warmed as well as tormented him. But life would be much simpler. He need no longer wonder if he should renounce his vows. He could concentrate on becoming a good parish priest.

Or perhaps an opening could be found for him working with the sick. The visit to Lourdes had opened up whole new vistas, and he wondered if perhaps he might be called in that direction. He thought he would find that wonderfully fulfilling.

But whichever way the path led him, at least he would be free of the temptations of the flesh. Michael folded his hands and uttered a prayer of heartfelt thanks that was certainly not this time meant for Father O'Brien.

At last summer was coming. The chilly April had given way to a warm May, and June came in hot and sunny. In the rose garden, the roses were in full bloom, clusters of pink and yellow and white, and the air was full of their fragrance. Bees buzzed around the buddleia and lavender in the flower beds and the nettles and wild flowers in the meadows beyond; birds sang from morning till nightfall, and the hayfields were almost ready for the first mowing.

The whole country was getting ready to celebrate the coronation of King George and Queen Mary. Union Jacks fluttered from flagpoles, townsfolk made bunting and planned street parties, and at Fairley Hall, Flo cut out every picture of the royal couple from the previous day's newspapers before they were thrown away and pasted them into a scrapbook, while Cook was experimenting with special celebration recipes for

403

a reception Lady Elizabeth was planning for the tenants.

Other than that, life continued as it always had, except that Richard Brimble had now moved into the quarters that had in the old days been home to several stable lads, and took his meals in the servants' hall with the rest of the staff. To see him there, treated no differently to the other menials, irked Quilla, but she had come to the conclusion that patience now was her best strategy. Sir Montague was gradually improving, and the risk of another stroke had receded. She would wait until he was fit to send for the solicitor and set things in motion before mentioning adoption again. There was no hurry now, and it was important that the enormous step, when it came, appeared to be part of a natural progression, which she felt sure it would. Richard was doing extremely well; Clement Firkin and the colliery managers too were most impressed with his progress, and it was only Percy Stevens who had his doubts about the wisdom of the step Sir Montague had taken in deciding to train him up for overall management of the estate and coal mines.

'I can't say as how I'd trust him,' he said to Lilian Parker during one of their chats in the butler's pantry.

Lilian raised an eyebrow. 'He seems a nice enough lad to me.'

'That's as maybe, but have you forgotten it was him and his father that I caught poaching? Or would have if I'd stuck my foot out and tripped them up like I meant to until I recognised Dick Brimble.'

'You don't know they were poaching,' Lilian pointed out. 'You said at the time they didn't have sacks or guns, and there was never any traps found, or not that I heard of.'

'Whatever they were doing, they were up to no good. I don't like it, Mrs Parker. I should have gone to Sir Montague and told him, and I would have done if we didn't have to work with Quilla.'

'Well it's too late for that now,' Lilian said. 'And just because Richard was there doesn't make him a bad 'un. His father's a bully, as well you know. If he said Richard was to go with him, the boy wouldn't have had any say in the matter.'

'I just hope you're right, Mrs Parker.' But Percy was still a little worried that his failure to report what he had seen in the woods that night might somehow impact on the future of the estate that meant almost as much to him as it did to Sir Montague himself.

Raymond, meanwhile, was as indolent and un-interested as ever.

During his visit to Wiltshire, he had met a young lady who had taken his fancy; when he wasn't writing letters to her and planning his next visit, he was thinking about her and the pleasures she had afforded him and hopefully would in the future, so his mind was on his studies even less than it had been before. But for the moment at least it meant he had lost interest in Christina, and he got along surprisingly well with Richard. Had he known of Quilla's plan for Richard to usurp him it would have been a different matter, of course, but as things stood, it seemed to him that Richard's arrival was to his advantage, both now and in the future. With their tutors thinking so highly of Sir Montague's protégé, they paid far more attention to him than they did to Raymond, and were less concerned with his inattentiveness. And in any case, what did it matter? When the time came for him to inherit, he would have a ready-made manager to make things easy for him. Just as long as he kept him on side. And charming everyone from his peers to the servants was something Raymond was very adept at.

Whenever the opportunity arose, Christina too was making every effort to strike up a friendship with Richard and, it seemed, succeeding. The two were quite often to be found together when Richard had been excused his studies. For all her initial doubts about such a relationship, Lady Elizabeth did nothing to discourage it. She had come to like Richard, and it was good for Christina to have a friend close to her own age – and one with noble blood in his veins too, though she prayed that no one besides herself, Montague and Quilla would ever know it.

As for the unfortunate London episode, she had tried to put it out of her mind, though never again would Julia be truly welcome at Fairley Hall. If she wished to come here, Elizabeth could hardly refuse her, but she would treat her with the utmost caution. Putting Christina in the way of such danger had been completely irresponsible, and Elizabeth could only thank the Lord that the level-headed Edie had been with her. No, she would never be able to forgive Julia, or trust her. But at least it seemed that the repairs to their family home in Wiltshire were now nearing completion, so it was to be hoped that if she wanted to return from London, which at present seemed unlikely, she would be able to go there.

Back in Fairley Terrace, Dolly was fretting over Charlie's latest letter. It seemed he was worried about Gracie's health, and Dolly wondered how he was going to manage with two small children if she got really ill. She wished she could talk it over with May, who was one of her best friends as well as being a neighbour, but it didn't seem tactful to mention it, given that Charlie's marriage seemed to be something of a sore spot with May.

For her own part, she had come to accept it, though she still regretted that Charlie hadn't made a go of it with Edie. But Gracie seemed a nice girl, Alfie and the new baby, Vicky, were adorable – she only wished she could get to see more of them – and Charlie appeared to be happy and more settled than he had ever been. She was very proud of him joining the police force. Whoever would have thought it? But she didn't talk to May about that either, except when May brought up the subject by telling her how Charlie had saved Edie's bacon when she'd been in London with Miss Christina. It just didn't seem right somehow to draw attention to the fact that he was happy and doing well when Dolly rather thought he had broken Edie's heart.

Father Michael, meanwhile, had spoken to the abbot about his interest in working with the sick, and the abbot had been cautiously encouraging. There was no such opening at present, but he would give it some serious thought. Father

Michael felt energised and optimistic. He still thought fondly of Edie, but with the possibility of new horizons opening up for him, he was beginning to believe he had been able to put the torment of longing for her behind him, just as he had with the red-headed girl all those years ago.

And so began the long, hot summer of 1911, when the days dreamed by and no one at Fairley Hall or in High Compton had the slightest idea of the dramatic events that lay ahead

Chapter Twenty-Five

'Let's go for a walk, Edith,' Christina said.

'Isn't it a bit hot for that at this time of day, miss?' Edie said doubtfully. 'Wouldn't it be better to wait until it's cooler?'

Temperatures had been soaring for days now, and Edie, who had just finished cleaning Christina's silk ribbons, was already feeling uncomfortably warm. Once washed, the ribbons had to be pressed while still wet with a very hot iron, and the heat from the fire had made her perspire so much that her skin felt sticky and her hair, where it touched her forehead and the nape of her neck, was damp.

Christina, however, was not to be deterred.

'It'll be cool in the woods, and there's something I can't wait to show you.' Her face was bright and eager, her eyes sparkling. 'You mustn't tell a soul, though. Especially Mama.'

'Is it the cottage?' Edie asked.

'Oh! You know!' Christina pouted. 'I thought it was my secret. Well – mine and Richard's.'

'You told me about it, don't you remember?'

'Oh yes, so I did. And that I was going to share it with Richard when I got to know him better. Well, I did, and the funny thing was, he already knew about it. It seems his father set out to take him there once, but someone saw their lights in the woods and raised the alarm, thinking they were poachers.'

'Good gracious!' Edie remembered the commotion that night in December. 'That was Richard and his father?'

'Yes. They weren't poaching, though. Richard said they were going to try and get into the cottage, though he had no idea why and his father wouldn't tell him. He never did find out what it was all about.'

'How peculiar!' Edie said, puzzled.

'Anyway, never mind about that now,' Christina continued. 'We went there, Richard and I, and he managed to get in through a window that wasn't properly closed and opened the door so that I could go in too.'

'I thought your mama expressly told you not to go there,' Edie admonished.

'Oh pooh! That was years ago, when I was little.'

'But since you're so anxious she doesn't find out you are going there now, you must know she'd still disapprove,' Edie said sternly.

'No, that's not it at all,' Christina objected. 'I just want to have some secrets of my own.

Something Mama doesn't know about. It's only fair. After all, there are plenty of things she keeps secret from me. Who my real mother is, for one thing.'

'She probably doesn't know that any more than you do,' Edie pointed out.

'I think she does.' The pout was back, dimpling the corners of her mouth. 'Do you really think she'd have adopted me if she didn't know where I came from? I doubt it very much. But she won't tell me because she thinks if I knew, I might want to go and live with my real family.'

Edie bit her lip, remembering how her own mother had refused to discuss the subject, and the awful suspicions she had tried to put to the back of her mind.

'I thought you'd forgotten about all that,' she said.

'Of course I haven't. I still think about it almost every day. But there's no point, is there? I'm never going to know the truth, so why go on about it?'

'That's very sensible,' Edie said, thinking there was no way either that she herself was ever going to know whether her suspicions had been correct and Christina was really her sister. 'There are some things that will always be a mystery.'

'So are you going to come with me or not?'

'I suppose so, if that's what you want.'

Christina picked up one of the freshly ironed ribbons – a turquoise one that matched her eyes – running it carefully between her fingers. 'I think I'd like to wear this ribbon. It's my favourite. Will you do it for me?'

'I think it would be sensible to wear the one

410

you've got in now if we're going into the woods,' Edie suggested. 'You don't want to catch that one on a bramble.'

'Oh, very well. I don't suppose anyone will see me today. Richard and Raymond are both out with the pit manager, aren't they?'

'I believe so, miss.'

As always, Edie felt a little anxious at Christina's constant preoccupation with how she would look to the opposite sex. Coupled with her childlike naivety, it was dangerous, especially given how very pretty she was, with or without a ribbon that matched her eyes. But it really wasn't her place to mention it.

'Shall we go, then?' Christina asked eagerly.

As Christina had predicted, it was cool in the woods. She let Beauty off the lead, and apart from stopping for the occasional sniff, the little dog trotted ahead of them as if she already knew which way they were going.

Christina, too, seemed perfectly familiar with the myriad of paths that criss-crossed through the trees at peculiar angles. Many of them had become overgrown with the onset of spring and summer, and Edie had to several times pull her skirts free of the undergrowth that narrowed the path to less than an arm's width in places, and hold aside brambles and branches to enable them to pass. And then, quite suddenly, the trees and bushes opened out and she had her first sight of the cottage.

'Well?' Christina had stopped, both to catch her breath and to relish the view that had become the centre of so many of her fantasies. 'Isn't it amazing? Doesn't it look exactly like the gingerbread house in "Hansel and Gretel"?'

'I suppose it does,' Edie said. Likening it to the witch's house in the fairy tale was something of a stretch of the imagination, but it was certainly true that the cottage was quaint, with its strange leaded windows and its thatched roof, and there was something about it that felt oddly threatening, though she had no idea why.

'Come on then!' Christina took her hand and led her around the low extension that jutted from the main part of the house. Roses, long since gone wild, straggled over the rear wall, defiantly struggling for life amid the proliferation of nettles and weeds, and amidst the jungle of undergrowth in what must have once been a garden, a plum tree already bore small unripe fruit. Christina picked up Beauty, who was now hanging back, and pointed to a small square window that stood ajar.

'That's the way Richard got in, but we couldn't get it to close again.'

'You don't expect me to climb in through it, I hope!' Edie said.

'No, of course not. Richard managed to get the front door open. It was locked on the inside, and he found a spare key hanging on a nail beside it.' Christina smiled triumphantly. 'We left it open. It's not as if anyone is likely to want to break in and steal anything, is it?'

Edie was too busy freeing her skirts from the brambles that were snagging at them to point out that apparently Dick Brimble had wanted to do just that.

412

At the back door, Christina turned to her.

'Will you open it? I don't want to put Beauty down. Her fur will catch all the burrs.'

Reluctant for no reason she could explain, Edie turned the heavy iron handle and gave the door a shove. She felt it give a little before it jammed again.

'You have to push really hard,' Christina told her. 'Richard said the wood has warped.'

Edie renewed her efforts, but the door remained stubbornly shut.

'I don't think I can do it,' she said, inexplicably relieved. 'I don't suppose I'm as strong as he is.'

'Oh, let me help.' Christina clipped Beauty's lead on to her collar and put her down. 'Now – try again.'

Resigned, Edie put her shoulder to the door, and beneath their combined strength it seemed to give a little.

'And again. We're doing it!' Christina urged.

Little by little the door scraped back over a flagged stone floor until it was partially open.

'There we are!' Christina squeezed through the gap, motioning Edie to follow. 'It wouldn't be much fun if it was easy, would it?'

Edie was thinking it wasn't much fun either way. They were in a small, musty room that she imagined had once been a kitchen; a stone sink was let into the wall beneath a window, an old range surrounded an open fireplace opposite it, and various pans and cooking pots, all festooned with spiders' webs, hung from beams that bridged the ceiling.

'I don't know why you want to come here,

413

'miss,' she said.

'Because it's exciting! Don't be such a spoil-sport, Edith. You haven't seen anything yet.' Christina danced down a step to the right of the kitchen. 'Come and see the parlour!'

Reluctantly Edie followed her through a door-way and into another, slightly larger, room.

'This is the one I looked into when I first came here,' Christina said. 'Look – all the furniture is still here! Anyone would think the witch had just popped out and will be back any minute and find us here. That's what makes it such an adventure!'

'She's been gone a very long time by the looks of it,' Edie said.

But she could see why Christina found it easy to imagine such a thing. Although a thick covering of dust lay everywhere, and gossamer webs were draped around the windows, from lampshades and from every jutting angle, the room was indeed fully furnished, with a table and upright chairs, an ornate chiffonier and a chaise longue. A patterned carpet set centrally on bare varnished boards covered most of the floor, curtains hung at the windows, and faded silk cushions were stacked on the chaise. There were even ornaments on the top shelves of the chiffonier – a porcelain shepherd and shepherdess, an array of photo-graphs in wood and silver frames and a horrid stuffed bird in a glass dome. A tarnished silver cruet sat in the centre of the table and an ornately carved clock on the mantel above the fireplace. A musty smell pervaded the air, and when Edie gingerly touched a muslin shawl that was draped over the back of one of the dining chairs, it disintegrated in her fingers.

'I thought at first it hadn't been lived in for hundreds of years,' Christina was saying. 'But these things aren't that old, are they? I mean – they're *old*, but not hundreds of years old. And look – there's salt in the cellar, though it's gone gloopy, and mustard in the mustard pot.'

'Perhaps it was a dower house and your grandmama – your mama's mother – lived here. Or one of the estate workers,' Edie suggested.

'Perhaps. Oh, isn't it exciting?'

'I think it's horrid,' Edie said bluntly.

'It's not! It's amazing! Come on, Edith, you have to see the rest.'

Christina skipped off towards a doorway on the far side of the room, dragging Beauty behind her, and unwillingly Edie followed. It led into a room furnished with a brocaded sofa and easy chairs, occasional tables and bookshelves. From one corner a stairway led upwards. Christina picked up Beauty again and called to Edie to follow her.

'I'm not sure those stairs are safe!' Edie cautioned. 'They could have rotted.'

'Oh, they're perfectly fine!' Christina, already halfway up, called over her shoulder. 'Come on!'

Shaking her head, Edie followed, making sure she tested each tread before putting her weight on it.

They were obviously in the main body of the house now. At the top of the staircase, Edie found herself in a strange domed room where the ceiling curved to an arc above a bare board floor dotted with rugs. In the centre was a bed with tarnished brass knobs at its head and foot, and covered with

415

a faded brocade quilt. There was a double wardrobe with intricately carved doors, a marble-topped washstand with a jug, bowl and soap dish and a discoloured towel hanging from a rail on one side, a dressing table on which crystal glass pots were arranged, and even a tortoiseshell-backed mirror and a hairbrush and comb.

'You see – the witch definitely lives here!' Christina announced triumphantly.

'You may be right,' Edie said. 'Now, can we please go?'

She turned abruptly and suddenly froze. Behind the door, and out of immediate view, was another item of furniture. A wooden chest, with two double drawers, and two single ones above. Except that there weren't. There was only one. Where the other should have been was nothing but a gaping hole. Edie took a step towards it on legs that seemed to no longer belong to her.

Why on earth would anyone remove a drawer from a chest? Unless...

Oh, it wasn't possible, surely?

But she could see no good reason for such a thing except for the one that had flashed instantly into her head.

Christina had been found in a drawer. Could it be that this was the chest it had come from?

'What's wrong with you, Edith?' Christina was standing at the head of the stairs, Beauty in her arms. 'You look as if you've seen a ghost!'

'It's nothing...' With an effort, Edie pulled herself together. If Christina had not noticed the missing drawer herself and put two and two together, Edie was not going to draw her attention to it. She

416

needed time to think, to work out what this might mean. 'Just be careful on those stairs, miss. And then I think we ought to be getting home.'

Sleep was impossible. As the grandfather clock in the hall struck midnight, Edie slipped out of her narrow bed and pulled on a cotton wrap. Since returning from the walk, she had not had a single moment to think through the implications of what she had seen. If it wasn't Christina making some demand or other, it was the chatter in the servants' hall, and though what she had discovered was never far from her mind, giving it serious thought had had to wait until bedtime. But it was stuffy and hot in the tiny attic room, and with Nellie snoring and snuffling in the other bed, Edie found it hard to arrange the fuzzy thoughts that were chasing one another around inside her head.

Quietly, so as not to disturb Nellie, she opened the little window as far as it would go to let out some of the accumulated heat of the day, but there was not so much as the slightest breeze to stir the curtains, and Edie crept from the room and down the servants' staircase, letting herself out of the back door. As she slipped around the corner of the house, she saw the glow of a cigarette in the darkness on the other side of the courtyard. Someone else who couldn't sleep, she thought – either Quilla or Simon, and most likely Quilla. The last thing she wanted was to bump into her. Keeping close to the wall where the shadow was deepest, she made her way around the side of the house and into the rose garden. There was a seat, she knew, at its very heart, and she followed the paved path between the bushes, heavy with blooms, until she found it. Then she sat down and began to try to unpick her tangled thoughts.

If she was right and the drawer Christina had been found in was indeed the one missing from the chest in the cottage, it could mean only one thing. Christina had been born there and the drawer used to transport her to High Compton. It also followed that whoever had given birth to her was most likely the same person who had last been in the cottage, who had perhaps lived there for the duration of her confinement, hidden away from the world, with no one to see her shame. The person who had reclined on the chaise with its silk cushions, kept the cellar filled with salt so as to season her lonely meals, slept in the bed, combed her hair in front of the dressing table mirror. But who?

The one person it could not have been was her own mother. Though she had only been a small child when Christina had been found, Edie felt certain that May had not been missing for so much as a day. Such a thing would have been something she wasn't likely to forget. In any case, as far as she knew, May had no connection whatsoever to the Fairleys, so why would they let her have the use of a cottage on their land? And even if for some reason they had, there was nothing about the accoutrements she had seen this afternoon that would lead her to believe they had belonged to her mother. Silks and crystal and porcelain and tortoiseshell-backed mirrors and brushes weren't May's style, even if she could have afforded them. They looked like the belongings of a lady.

Coming to that conclusion was like having a weight lifted off Edie's heart. It wasn't you, Mam, she thought. Whatever it was you confessed that you were so ashamed of, it wasn't that you had given birth to a baby secretly and abandoned her in the church porch.

For a moment she castigated herself: how could she ever have believed such a thing? The whole idea was preposterous. But even so, it was the most enormous relief to know that her imaginings had been unfounded.

But if not Mam, then who?'

Around and around ran Edie's thoughts; again and again they reached the same conclusion.

Lady Elizabeth.

If Lady Elizabeth had been the mysterious inhabitant of that isolated cottage, it would explain so much, not least why she had been so ready to adopt Christina. What better solution to her problems than that she should conceal her pregnancy from an unforgiving world, arrange to have the child taken to a place where she knew she would be found before any harm could come to her, then agree to give her a home and the sort of upbringing she would wish for for her child? She could have care of her, watch her grow, build the closest of relationships with her and not be the subject of malicious gossip; not have to bear the shame of being a fallen woman but instead be held in high regard for her seemingly altruistic action. Through careful planning she would have attained the best of both worlds.

419

If Edie was right, it also went some way to explaining why Lady Elizabeth had never married. Was it possible she thought a husband would know she was no virgin and had actually gone through childbirth? Edie didn't know. But whether or not that was a factor, she had committed her life to raising her child. It could be that she had still been in love with Christina's father – a man who was already married, perhaps. Edie thought of her own situation and felt the familiar pang. She knew only too well how that felt.

But Lady Elizabeth! Who would have thought it? How dreadful it must have been for her, forced to see out her confinement in that horrid cottage. It was bad enough now, in the summer; in the winter months of November and December it must have been almost beyond endurance. Isolated, cold and dark, with the trees that surrounded it keeping out what little light there was during the short days, and nights when they would have creaked and groaned like some creature in distress. Had she been frightened on those long and lonely nights? Edie imagined branches knocking on the windows and the wind whistling in the chimneys and rattling the window frames. And supposing she had gone into labour with no one to assist her? It didn't bear thinking about.

She must have had help, though. Someone must have brought her provisions and checked on her welfare. And someone had been there when the baby was born, or soon afterwards.

Someone who had put her in a drawer and taken her all the way to High Compton.

Her lover, perhaps? Or one of the trusted servants? The one thing Edie was certain about was that it wouldn't have been Sir Montague, though the whole thing had probably been his idea. He would never have countenanced allowing his sister's shame to become public knowledge. But it was quite likely that Mr Stevens and Mrs Parker had been in the know. And they would have been loyal enough to keep the whole sorry business secret. No wonder talk of Christina's true origins was frowned upon in the servants' hall as well as upstairs. No wonder the subject was brought to an abrupt close if anyone dared mention it.

I suppose I'll never know the truth, Edie thought, and if I did, I'd never be able to share it with Miss Christina. But she couldn't help being more curious than ever. For her own satisfaction she longed to discover what had happened.

Now, though, she really must go back to bed and try to get some sleep, or she'd be good for nothing in the morning. At least now she felt cooler, her skin less sticky, even if her mind was as busy as ever.

As she made her way back around the house, she was taken by surprise to see a dark form approaching the back door from the stable quarters. Quilla. Edie had thought she would long since have finished her cigarette and gone to bed. She drew hastily back into the shadows, then, when she heard a man's cough, dared to peek around again.

Heading away towards the drive was a bulky figure. Not Simon, certainly, and not Richard, and suddenly Edie was remembering that other time, back in the autumn, when she'd seen Quilla sharing a smoke in the darkness with an un-

421

known man.

Did she have a lover who visited her when the rest of the household was asleep? Just one more puzzle, but not one that bothered Edie unduly. Quilla's liaisons were of scant interest to her compared with the enormity of the enigma that surrounded Christina's birth.

She waited a little while longer to be sure Quilla had gone back inside before emerging once more from the shadows. She only hoped the older woman hadn't locked the door behind her; if she had, Edie would have to spend the night out here in the garden, and answer questions next morning as to how on earth she had come to be locked out.

Fortunately, the door was still unlocked. Edie crept back up the stairs. Nellie was still snoring contentedly. She closed the bedroom door, checked that the window was open wide enough to let in what little air there was going, took off her wrap and slipped back into bed.

Amazingly, she fell asleep almost as soon as her head touched the pillow. But her dreams were dark ones. A feeling of being trapped pervaded them, trees creaked and branches tapped against the window. Throughout the night she tossed and turned, and when she rose at cock's crow the next morning, the feeling was still with her, a dark veil shadowing the brightness of what was sure to be yet another fine, hot day, and the unanswered questions were still buzzing around inside her brain.

Chapter Twenty-Six

The constant sweltering heat was beginning to take its toll on everyone but Quilla; there was Mediterranean blood in her veins, and she relished it. But tempers were frayed below stairs, where Mrs Davey sweated over a hot stove and yelled more frequently than ever at a frazzled Flo; Mrs Parker took off her shoes at every opportunity to ease her throbbing bunion and took out her discomfort on Nellie and Alice; and Jeremiah Dando got into a fierce argument with Simon Ford, though afterwards neither of them could remember how it had started or what it had really been about.

Upstairs, things were not much better. Sir Montague was uncomfortably hot and fractious, frustrated by his continuing limitations and his craving for the spirits and cigars he was being denied. Lady Elizabeth was suffering from a summer cold – why did a cold seem so much worse in this heat than in the winter? – and Christina was bored and restless. Richard, by whose friendship she had set such store, was out all day with either Clement Firkin or Edward Johnson, the estate manager, and Raymond seemed to have lost all interest in her. Though she'd come to find his attentions repugnant, still it irked her that he no longer made advances towards her. He had plenty of time on his hands, after all; Clement and Ed-

423

ward had both more or less given up on him and were concentrating all their efforts on educating Richard.

On that hot June afternoon, not even Edith was around to relieve the tedium; she'd gone into town to buy a set of new buttons for one of Christina's jackets – one had come off and been lost, and there hadn't been a matching one in the button tin in Edie's sewing box.

Though it was now getting on for four o'clock, the heat was still as unbearable as it had been in the middle of the day. Christina had wandered into the woods, where it was cooler. She'd considered going to the cottage – her secret place, as she thought of it – but she wasn't sure she would be able to open the door without help, and in any case, it wouldn't be such fun without Richard or even Edith. In fact, truth be told, it had somehow lost some of its magic for her. Edith had been so scathing about it, and some of her distaste had rubbed off on the ever-impressionable Christina. So instead she wended her way towards the little river that ran through the valley beneath the woods. On the Fairley Hall side the trees extended as far as the water's edge, whilst on the far bank the ground sloped steeply up again in broad steps, an open expanse of rough grassland occupied in summer by a herd of cows.

Christina was a little nervous of the cows, though Richard had assured her they wouldn't harm her. They'd back away if she stared them straight in the eye, he'd said, but she wasn't convinced. This afternoon, however, they were nowhere to be seen, and she guessed they must have wandered further upstream in search of a shadier spot, which made her bold enough to cross the rickety wooden bridge that spanned the river. In winter, the water here became a raging torrent after heavy rain, but today it was reduced to scarcely more than a trickle as it meandered over the clean-washed stones, and hot as she was, it looked inviting. She scrambled down the bank, sat down on a boulder and took off her shoes and stockings so that she could dabble her feet, the water tickling deliciously as it trickled over her toes.

A little further downstream the river broadened into a pool, dammed on the far side by a large fallen branch. Christina hitched up her skirts and made her way carefully towards it, squealing each time she trod on a sharp stone but enjoying the refreshing feel of the water too much to give up. Soon it was up to her knees and the hem of her dress was getting wet despite her best efforts to hold it up, and it occurred to her that if she took it off, no one would be any the wiser. She waded to the bank and undid the buttons with some difficulty – she wasn't used to managing them by herself – but at last she had unfastened enough of them to get the dress over her head and slip her arms free of the sleeves. Feeling flushed with daring, she laid it out on the bank, along with her petticoat, and waded back into the water wearing nothing but her chemise and drawers.

The cool water, lapping gently round her calves, was exhilarating; she stood there, arms outstretched, facing the open fields so that if the cows came back, she would see them before they reached her.

'Hey, Christina!'

She jumped as a man's voice called her name, and swung round to see Raymond standing on the bank on the wooded side of the river. In her surprise, she lost her balance, tottering and wobbling, and before she knew it, she had toppled over, landing on her bottom in the water. For a moment, the shock of it, and of Raymond's unexpected appearance, rendered her both speechless and unable to move, but as she began to struggle to her feet, she became horribly aware that Raymond had a grandstand view of her clad in nothing but her underwear.

'Stop staring at me, you beast! Go away!' she cried, hot colour flooding her cheeks. 'I thought I was all alone!'

Raymond-laughed. 'Tell me another!'

'You followed me!' she accused.

He only laughed again. 'I'm surprised you didn't hear me.'

'You had no business!' she retorted, furious in her embarrassment.

'But oh I say, I'm glad I did!'

Raymond continued to stare at her with open appreciation. The thin cambric of her chemise and drawers, now soaking wet, had become almost transparent, and clung to her every curve and hollow so that she might just as well have been naked. As he gazed at her, Raymond forgot all about the girl in Wiltshire who had taken his fancy. It was some weeks now since he had seen her, and in any case, compared to the fresh, innocent deliciousness of Christina, she seemed old and blowsy.

'Stay where you are!' he called as Christina edged cautiously towards the far bank. 'I'm coming in to join you!'

He bent to remove his boots and roll up his trousers to the knee, and Christina took advantage of the moment to wade a little closer to her abandoned clothes before a loose stone underfoot caused her to lose her balance again. The water was shallower here, and she was able to struggle to her feet and reach the bank, but by the time she had scrambled up it, Raymond was right behind her.

'Don't be shy, little mermaid!' he taunted her.

Christina grabbed up her petticoat, holding it in front of her, a wholly inadequate curtain.

'Go away! Leave me alone!' she squealed. But Raymond, on fire with desire, was in no mood to do that. He scaled the bank easily and reached out for her, one hand gripping her arm, the other tugging at the petticoat. His eyes were glittering, his lips curled away from his teeth in a grimace that was almost feral. In a state of panic now, Christina let go of the petticoat and began beating at his chest with both hands, but to no avail. Laughing, he pulled her close, trapping her arms between them as he clutched her buttocks and pressed her against him, then lifted her bodily, tipping her on to the sun-baked bank.

The thud of her head against the hard turf stunned her momentarily, but through a haze of stars she was aware of Raymond throwing himself down on top of her, his weight knocking what little breath she had left out of her. Sobbing with pain and fear, she struggled weakly, but his hands were

427

everywhere, his body pinning her to the ground, and no matter how she kicked or wriggled, she couldn't escape him.

And then, unbelievably, quite suddenly she was free, Raymond's weight no longer pressing her into the hard ground, and she was aware of someone else towering above her, someone who was hauling Raymond to his feet, then punching him full in the face. She heard Raymond's grunt of pain, followed almost at once by a loud cracking sound as a sharp uppercut caught him beneath the chin. Raymond staggered a few unsteady steps backwards, toppled over the edge of the bank, and went sprawling into the shallows beneath. For a moment his assailant stood looking down at him, hands still balled to fists, then he dropped to his knees beside Christina.

'Are you all right? Has that bastard hurt you?'

It was Richard.

Christina struggled to a sitting position, wrapping her arms around herself. She tried to speak, but no words came. Instead she burst into tears.

'I'll kill him!' Richard was on his feet again, making for the water's edge, where Raymond had struggled to his feet, half senseless, blood pouring from his nose.

Somehow Christina found her voice, frightened now for quite a different reason.

'Richard – no!' she squealed. He stopped, looking back at her. 'Don't ... please don't... I'm all right. He scared me, that's all.'

Richard looked uncertainly from one to the other. Though anger still boiled in his veins, the rush of adrenalin that had propelled him down the hillside when he had spotted Christina and Raymond was subsiding now, and he could hardly believe what he had done.

He'd been making his way back to Fairley Hall across the fields when he had seen them there together on the riverbank, and his initial reaction had been dismay and fierce jealousy – he'd thought they were enjoying a lovers' tryst well away from the house. In his awkward adolescent way, Richard had fallen in love with Christina, though he would have died rather than admit it to her – or even to himself. He was the black-smith's son; she was gentry, and far beyond his reach even in his wildest dreams. When she began courting, it would be someone from her own class who would be her lover. He'd thought he'd accepted that, but when he had seen her in Raymond's arms, the sharpness of the pain in his chest and the way his stomach had fallen away had told him he hadn't accepted it at all.

In that first confused moment, his instinct had been to retrace his steps and take the long way back to Fairley Hall so as to avoid them; then his stubborn streak had surfaced and he'd thought: Why should I? And as he drew nearer, he had realised that what was going on was far from consensual. The resentment he had been feeling about the unfairness of the world had turned to blind fury. With the red mist before his eyes, he'd certainly meant what he'd later said – he *had* wanted to kill Raymond, or at least smash his sneering face to a bloody pulp. He still wanted to, and he could do it, too. That milksop would be no match for him. Richard might still be a boy

429

while Raymond was a man, but he was strong as a young ox, with muscles honed and hardened from swinging the heavy hammer in the blacksmith's shop. Now, however, caution was beginning to creep in, along with the realisation that beating up Sir Montague's cousin was not likely to go down well with his employer, no matter how much he deserved it.

'Damn you!' Raymond was fishing in his trouser pocket for a handkerchief to mop the blood that was pouring from his nose and splattering scarlet on the front of his white shirt. 'Damn you to hell! I'll have your job for this!'

'Stop it, both of you!' Christina was pulling on her petticoat, crying again as she did so. The violence that had erupted had frightened her almost as much as Raymond's assault. All she wanted now was to run away and hide.

'Christina!' Richard took a step towards her, and she backed away, all too aware that he had seen her in a state of undress, and afraid that he might grab her as Raymond had done.

'Go away! Leave me alone!'

For a moment Richard gazed at her, turbulent emotions seething within him like lava bubbling in a volcano about to erupt. She was so beautiful – her hair falling in wet tendrils about her face, her shoulders smooth and creamy, her breasts small and rounded beneath the sodden fabric of her chemise and her legs long and slender under the thin skirts of her petticoat. He had never seen a woman's body before and it took his breath away. But at the same time he was shamed by the effect it was having on his own body; that thing that he had thought only happened at night when he was in bed and dreaming was happening now.

Abruptly he turned away, picking up her dress from where it still lay on the bank and holding it out to her.

'You better put this on.'

She did as he said, pulling it over her head and flicking her wet hair out over the collar, where the drips of water quickly bled into the fabric. She was struggling to fasten the buttons, arms raised behind her so that her breasts thrust against the pink and white gingham.

'Help me, please!' She was beginning to regain some of her inbred imperiousness, so at odds with her childish innocence. 'Come on, quickly now!'

Richard glanced towards where Raymond was sitting now on a grassy mound, still attempting to stem the bleeding from his nose, which he thought might be broken. The fight had gone out of him; he looked like a beaten lion, slunk away to lick his wounds. But that wouldn't last for long. Back in his element, he would soon become the master again, and Richard dreaded to think how he would exact his revenge.

'Richard, will you help me, please!' Christina demanded again.

His thick fingers fumbled with the tiny buttons. Already he was dreading the repercussions of all this, but still he did not regret what he had done. Perhaps it would cost him the job he so enjoyed and the future he had begun to look forward to. But at least Christina was safe, and he was going to make sure she stayed that way.

'Come on, I'll see you home,' he said when the

last button was done up.

He took her hand, which was trembling, and led her across the ramshackle little bridge and into the woods. Neither of them spoke, and neither looked back to where Raymond still sat, shamed and hurting, on the riverbank. And something that might have been pride and satisfaction swelled in Richard's chest. In the space of a few short minutes, it seemed, he had left his boyhood behind. Now, he thought, he had become a man.

Back at Fairley Hall, Richard left Christina at the front door and went around to his own quarters above the stables, but it wasn't long before Nellie came running up the stairs to tell him that Lady Elizabeth wanted to see him now, this minute, in her sitting room. She had caught the dripping-wet Christina on the stairs, it seemed, and while she was questioning her as to how she had got into such a state, Raymond had returned, also wet through and covered in blood.

He and Christina were both in Lady Elizabeth's sitting room when a nervous Richard knocked and entered, Raymond, still looking groggy, perched on a spindle-legged chair, a tearful Christina standing dejectedly beside her mother.

'Richard. I understand that you were involved in all this,' Lady Elizabeth said in a tone far sterner than he had ever heard her use before.

'Yes, milady,' he muttered.

'May I have your side of what occurred?'

Richard hesitated. He had no idea what either of the others had said by way of explanation, and disgusted as he was with Raymond, he was no

432

tittle-tattle.

'I told you – we were fighting,' Raymond said into the silence. His voice sounded nasal, as if he was suffering from a heavy cold, and he was still dabbing at his nose with a bloodstained handkerchief.

'Yes, Raymond, that much is clear,' Lady Elizabeth said impatiently. 'It does not, however, explain why you and Christina are both soaked to the skin, while Richard appears to be not only dry, but also unscathed.'

'I lost my balance and fell in the river,' Raymond said sullenly. 'I told you that.'

'And Christina? Did she lose her balance too?'

'I thought he was hurt. I went in after him to see if I could help.'

Lady Elizabeth shook her head. 'The whole story sounds highly implausible to me. I'd like your version of events, Richard.'

At least he knew now the line they were taking. Neither of them was prepared to admit to what had really happened, and he couldn't say he blamed them.

'It's like they say,' he mumbled.

'So what were you fighting about?'

Raymond shrugged; Richard stared at his boots. Lady Elizabeth looked from one to the other.

'Well? Have you both been struck dumb?'

'Raymond called Richard a rude name,' Christina said, evidently struck by inspiration. 'Mr Johnson had taken Richard out for the day and Raymond was jealous. Richard came back across the fields, and Raymond started saying things to him. So Richard hit him.'

433

'Is this true, Richard?' Lady Elizabeth demanded.

Richard hated lying, but he couldn't admit to the truth either, so he merely nodded, still avoiding her eyes.

Lady Elizabeth sighed. 'I have to say I am far from convinced, but it seems I am not going to get a satisfactory explanation from any of you, so I dare say I have no option but to let the matter rest. Raymond – you were quite wrong to say whatever it was you said to make Richard angry enough to strike you. In future, you will treat him politely, and with respect. And you, Richard, should know better than to resort to violence, no matter what the provocation. If it comes to my notice that you have been using your fists again rather than your very able brain, then I can assure you I shall take the matter very seriously. This time I'm prepared to let you off with a warning. Next time the consequences will be a great deal more severe. Do I make myself clear?'

'Yes, milady.'

'Very well, you may go. And on your way please ask Mr Dando to come and attend to Mr Raymond. He needs to get out of these wet clothes, and possibly requires some attention to his nose, too.'

'Yes, milady.'

Richard found Jeremiah Dando in the kitchen, sitting at the long bare board table with a couple of the others, drinking tea and eating the off-cuts from a Swiss roll Mrs Davey had just taken out of the oven. He delivered the message and hurried out, refusing Mrs Davey's offer of a cup

434

of tea himself. He didn't want to be around when Jeremiah got back from attending to Raymond. When he told the others the state Raymond was in, they would be agog, and Richard had had enough of questions for now, though he knew he wouldn't be able to escape them later.

He dreaded going down to the servants' hall for his evening meal, and would have given it a miss had he not been so hungry. But when he braved it, he found to his surprise that they regarded him as something of a hero. Raymond was not popular below stairs, and there was a good deal of satisfaction – and amusement – that he had been put in his place at last.

'He's a sight too big for his boots, that one,' Mrs Davey said, and Simon agreed.

'There's been plenty of times I've felt like giving the big-headed sod a good smack.'

Percy Stevens and Mrs Parker were a little more restrained; both of them were of the opinion that, trying as Raymond might be, violence was not the answer.

Nellie kept asking Jeremiah to repeat his account of the state Mr Raymond had been in, delighting in the gory details, which she couldn't wait to relay to Teddy the next time she saw him, and Flo simply gazed adoringly at Richard. He might be a bit young for her, but he was big and strong and obviously afraid of nothing.

Only Quilla sat stony-faced and silent, barely picking at the boiled cod and parsley sauce on her plate, and when the meal was over and Richard left to go to his own quarters, she followed him out into the courtyard and motioned him towards her

435

favourite corner, a place she felt afforded them some privacy. There she turned on him with cold fury.

'What in God's name were you thinking of? How could you be so stupid as to attack Mr Raymond like that?'

Richard kicked a loose stone and sent it skittering across the courtyard. He had a healthy respect for his aunt's authority, but he didn't want to go into the details of what had happened with her any more than he had with Lady Elizabeth.

'He was asking for it,' he muttered.

'That's no excuse. You don't go hitting gentry if you know what's good for you. Didn't you stop to think it might mean the end for you here at Fairley Hall? You're lucky Sir Montague is in no fit state to deal with it. If he had been, he'd have sent you packing, I shouldn't wonder, and you'd have thrown everything away.'

'I'm sorry.'

'Sorry's not good enough. You don't know what's at stake here, but I think it's time you did. It's not just an estate manager's job. If we play our cards right, you'll inherit everything.'

Richard stared at her, uncomprehending.

'Sir Montague wants to adopt you.' It was a distortion of the truth, but Quilla didn't let that stop her. 'He'd have set things in motion by now if he hadn't had that dratted stroke. But he's so much better now I think he'll see to it soon. I, for one, don't want it going on any longer, just in case he should be taken bad again. Once the legal formalities are dealt with you'll be his heir, and when he dies, the house, the estate, everything will go to you.'

'That's crazy!' Richard said, thinking his aunt had taken leave of her senses. 'Why would he do something like that?'

Quilla's lips tightened into a smirk.

'Oh, he has his reasons. Believe me, he'll see you set up for life.'

Richard still couldn't make head nor tail of what she was saying, but the very suggestion horrified him.

'What if I don't want him to adopt me? Don't I have any say in it?'

'You wouldn't be such a fool as to turn down an opportunity like this.' Quilla's voice was hard. 'At least, I hope not!'

'You're serious, aren't you?' he said, incredulous.

'Never more. I want this for you, Richard, more than I've ever wanted anything.'

'Well I don't want it, and you can tell him so,' he retorted. 'What would my mother and father think if I turned my back on them?'

'Dick already knows,' Quilla said bluntly.

Richard's jaw dropped. 'My father *knows?*'

'Yes, and he's all for it. He knows you'll see him right when you inherit.'

'He wouldn't do that! It would be like ... well, like selling me. He'd never go along with it,' Richard protested.

'You're wrong there, my lad. He's been good to you, I know, but it's not what you think. There are reasons why you'll be getting no more than your birthright when you inherit.' Quilla felt in her pocket for her cigarettes, got one out and lit it. This wasn't the way she'd planned to tell Richard the truth, but she could see now there was no more avoiding it.

'Dick took you in fourteen years ago and raised you for my sake, but he's not your father,' she said bluntly. 'Sir Montague is. That's why he wants to adopt you. So that you'll come into what's rightfully yours.'

'What are you saying?' Richard's mind was boggling. 'That my mother and Sir Montague...?'

'Dick is not your father,' she repeated. 'And I am not your aunt, as we've always made out. I am your mother.'

Richard gazed at her, shocked to the core.

'I don't believe you! You're making all this up. Why are you telling me these lies?'

'It's not lies. It's the truth.' Quilla took a long puff on her cigarette. Her hand was shaking. Though she had known Richard would be shocked by the revelation, she hadn't anticipated this outright denial, and it was a knife thrust in her heart.

'Don't look like that,' she said harshly. 'We shouldn't have kept it from you, I suppose, but what we did was for the best, and now you'll reap the benefits. Don't you breathe a word of this to anybody, though. Not about Sir Montague, nor about me. As far as the outside world is concerned, Sir Montague will have just seen the best chance for the future of the estate by leaving it to a boy who'll take good care of it. And you'll be made for life.'

'I don't want it!' Richard shouted. 'I don't want to be his son! Or yours! I don't want lands and money. I just want things to go back to the way they were!'

'Oh don't be so stupid!' Quilla exploded. 'You're not thinking straight. I didn't mean for you to find out like this, but it's done now, and all I want is for you to have what's rightfully yours.'

'I don't want it, I tell you! Why are you doing this to me?'

'It's what mothers do – look after their own.' Quilla was almost pleading now. 'I'd do anything for you, Richard – and I have. Things... Well, you don't want to know what I've done. Let's just say I'd swing for it if anybody knew the truth about what happened to Mrs Fairley. So don't you dare throw it all back in my face...'

A sudden rustle made her break off in mid-sentence, and she swung round to see Edie standing there in the shadows.

'What...?'

'Quilla, I'm sorry to interrupt, but Lady Elizabeth is asking for you.'

As always when she felt threatened, Quilla went on the offensive. 'Can't she leave me in peace for five minutes?'

'I'm just passing on the message,' Edie said coolly, then turned and walked away across the courtyard.

Quilla stood staring after her, her mind in turmoil. How long had she been standing there? How much had she heard?

With a quick, nervous movement, she dropped her cigarette butt and ground it out.

'I have to go,' she said to Richard. 'But we'll talk again. Perhaps one day your mother will be

439

the lady of the manor, not the one being ordered about like that. Just think about it before you throw this chance away.'

But as she hurried towards the house, the awful fear that somehow all her plans were going awry weighed so heavily that she found she was shaking again.

She could bully Richard into doing what she wanted, she told herself. He'd change his mind when he got over the shock of her revelations and had a chance to get used to the idea of the future that could be his. But she couldn't dismiss so easily the anxiety she was feeling as to what Edie might have overheard. She was a sharp girl, and if she was to put two and two together...

In spite of the warmth of the evening, Quilla shivered, and the chill seemed to come from deep inside her, from her very bones. But her resolve was as strong as ever.

If Edie became a threat, she'd just have to find a way to deal with her. She'd done it before, and she'd do it again. Nothing and no one could be allowed to jeopardise her son's future.

In his room over the stables, Richard sank down on his bed and buried his face in his hands. The muscles in his neck felt tight and knotted, his knuckles still stung from the heavy blow he'd landed on Raymond's nose, and his stomach was churning. But at the same time he felt numb and empty. In the space of a few minutes down there in the courtyard, the bottom had fallen out of his world and he couldn't make sense of any of it. If what Quilla said was true, he was no longer who he thought he was. His whole life had been a lie. His mother and father weren't his mother and father at all, and his sisters weren't his sisters. Quilla his real mother? Sir Montague his father? He didn't much like either of them. No! It couldn't be true!

But why would she make up something like that? To persuade him to agree to Sir Montague adopting him? Never! He hadn't wanted to follow his father – no, not his father: his uncle! – into the blacksmith's trade, but he wanted to be a gentleman even less. He wouldn't know where to begin! Being an estate manager was one thing. He'd been enjoying learning the ropes, been excited at the opportunity to better himself, looked forward to being out in the country he loved and even to managing the accounts and all the other clerical tasks that went with running what was in effect a successful business. But to be lord of the manor was a different matter entirely.

He wouldn't do it. He couldn't. But neither could he go back to his old life. Never again could he sit around the family table for a Sunday roast knowing they'd lied to him, deceived him, and he wasn't a part of their family at all. That his so-called father had plotted all this behind his back with Quilla. He never wanted to see either of them again.

He massaged his aching neck with hands that shook slightly. He'd run away. Right away, where no one knew him and he could start afresh. Be anyone he wanted to be. But who? What? Where?

He got up and prowled the room, his thoughts spinning, anger boiling up from the hollow place inside him. As it came to a head, he punched the wall as he had punched. Raymond's sneering face, once, twice, so hard that a hole appeared in the daub and wattle and his knuckles bled.

He stuffed them into his mouth, biting down hard on the bruised and bleeding skin. And for a brief moments the physical pain eclipsed the pain in his heart.

Chapter Twenty-Seven

May was suffering from sciatica – at least that was what Dr Mackay said it was. She only knew that she could hardly walk for the sharp pain that started in her hip and ran in a line of fire all the way down her left leg, and she wasn't sleeping properly as it was impossible to get comfortable in bed at night. She'd called the doctor out because she didn't feel able to walk all the way to his surgery in High Compton and she had got to the point where the expense of it had ceased to matter. She hoped that the club Wesley paid into would cover at least part of the bill, but Wesley had said she wasn't to worry about that. She couldn't go on the way, she was; it would drive him mad as well as her, with her tossing and turning and disturbing him all night.

'There's times when there's more important things than money, m'dear,' he'd said, pragmatic as ever.

But really Dr Mackay hadn't been much use at

all. He'd prescribed a painkiller, which helped somewhat, but beyond that, he had said, there was nothing more he could do. The best thing would be for her to try and move about as normally as possible and it would go when it was good and ready.

'You've put something out in your back, I expect,' he'd said in his lilting Scottish accent. 'Have you done anything to strain it lately?'

May had huffed impatiently. She was always doing things that made her back ache, things she used to be able to do without a second thought, but which were a great deal more effort these days and left her tired out.

'The house had to be spring-cleaned from top to bottom after we had the chimney sweep,' she said. 'I couldn't leave it all black with soot, could I? And then there's the garden.'

'Doesn't your husband take care of that?'

'He's got his work cut out with the vegetables,' May said. 'Potatoes, beans, cabbages, parsnips – he grows them all. And jibbles.' 'Jibbles' was a local term for spring onions. 'Wesley does like a nice jibble. But the flower garden – that's down to me. And you know what the weeds are like at this time of year.'

'Well I'm afraid you're just going to have to let them grow if you want your back to get better,' Dr Mackay said bluntly. 'Don't do anything to aggravate it. But do try to keep moving, as I said.'

May had tried, but still she didn't feel up to going to church, walking – or hobbling – all the way into town and having to sit in a hard wooden pew. After all the years she had stayed away, she

443

thought it strange that she should mind so much about missing it now, but she did. In the last six months or so it had become part of her routine, and she looked forward to both the service and the chat afterwards with people she rarely saw otherwise. Father Michael had introduced light refreshments for those who wanted a cup of tea and a biscuit, and May had joined the rota of the ladies who crept out quietly during the last hymn to bring the simmering urn to the boil and set out cups and saucers.

But she had to be sensible, she told herself. Dr Mackay had said the sciatica wasn't likely to last for more than a few weeks. And until it was better, the good Lord would just have to forgive her absence.

The first Sunday that May didn't go to church, Father Michael didn't think anything of it. Hers wasn't the only familiar face missing: some, the better-off, away on a week's holiday at Weston-super-Mare or Weymouth – one family had even gone across the Bristol Channel to Barry Island – and others, mostly the elderly and frail, who were suffering in the blistering heat. But when she missed a second Sunday, he began to be concerned, especially since it was her week to help with the refreshments; he'd never before known her to miss her turn. Duty told him he really should call on her and make sure she wasn't ill, but he was oddly reluctant in case he should come face to face with Edie and set off the relentless cycle of emotions he had fought so hard to subdue. Nevertheless, the welfare of his parishioners was all part of his pastoral duties, and wanting to avoid Edie for his own selfish reasons was no excuse for shirking them. In any case, what were the chances of her being in her old home on a weekday morning? When he'd first met her – how long ago now it seemed! – she'd only been there because of her sprained ankle. It was highly unlikely he'd find her there this time.

When he turned into the track that ran along the back of the Ten Houses and saw May sitting on a stool outside number 1 podding broad beans into a colander, his relief was tinged with treacherous disappointment. Perhaps he had not been as successful as he liked to think in putting Edie out of his mind.

'Good morning, May,' he said as he reached her. 'My, but those beans look good.'

'Morning, Father. It's Sally and the children's day to come for their dinner. Sal loves broad beans, though getting the children to eat them is another matter.' She dropped an empty pod into the basket by her side. 'But this is a surprise. We don't usually see you out here in the middle of the morning.'

'I suppose not. But I've noticed you haven't been in church the last couple of weeks and I was a little concerned and thought I'd come and make sure you are all right. It's not like you to miss your turn for helping out with the teas.'

'I'm sorry about that, Father. I should have let you know, but I thought they'd be able to manage without me this once.' May was flustered now, and guilty.

'They did, don't worry. It's just that I was afraid

you might be ill.'

'Not ill, Father, but I've got this blessed sciatica and it's giving me gyp.'

'Oh dear. That can be painful, I know. Father Augustine suffers from it.'

'It's not much fun, but I dare say there's a lot worse off than me.' May set down the colander and winced as she got to her feet. 'It's very good of you to take the trouble to come and see me, though. Can I get you a cup of tea?'

'A glass of water would be fine,' Father Michael said. He didn't want to put May to the trouble of making tea, but he was hot and thirsty. A soutane was not the coolest of garments.

'I always find a cup of tea is the best thing in this heat,' May said, reading his mind. 'I'm making one anyway, so it's up to you.'

'Very well then, I'll join you. A cup of tea would be nice, I must admit.'

Once they were seated round the kitchen table sipping May's strong brew, he asked after Edie. Just mentioning her made him uncomfortable, but May would think it odd if he didn't, and the Devil was sitting on his shoulder once more, making him ache for news of her in spite of himself.

'She's the same as usual, as far as I know. It's been a week since I saw her,' May said. 'I'm so sorry she gave up her religious instruction after you were good enough to spend all that time with her. I don't know what got into her, I'm sure. She seemed so keen.'

'I think there were elements of our practices she was uncomfortable with.' Father Michael played with the handle of his cup, wondering

446

whether it was wise to go down this road.

'You mean confession,' May said, making it easy for him.

'That was part of it, I believe. And confession is a very important part of preparing for the Mass. But of course you know that, and how difficult it can sometimes be.'

Dim as it was in the kitchen after the unrelenting brightness of the sun outside, he saw her cheeks flame scarlet. He'd touched a nerve, of course. Father O'Brien had been right when he'd said it was the shame of something she'd confessed that lay behind May's long absence from church. And whatever it was, it was haunting her still.

'It is good for the soul, though,' he said, and cursed himself for a hypocrite who couldn't bring himself to practise what he preached.

'I can't for the life of me think what it could be our Edie wouldn't want to confess,' May said, neatly turning the subject away from her own shame. 'She's a good girl – always has been. Never given me a moment's worry. Unless of course it has to do with Charlie.'

'Charlie?' Edie had never mentioned a Charlie.

'Charlie Oglethorpe. Used to live next door but one. She's been sweet on him all her life, and they went out for a couple of years before he took off for London and picked up with somebody else. But she still carries a candle for him, that I do know, and I wouldn't be surprised if he doesn't feel the same way. She met up with him when she went to London back in the spring, and he got her out of a bit of a hole. He's married now,

447

though, I understand. Perhaps something went on there that shouldn't have. It was when she came back that she said she'd decided not to go ahead with her confirmation.'

'Oh dear, I do hope that's not the case,' Father Michael said. His heart had plummeted in a way it had no business to, and not from fear for Edie's immortal soul. He was jealous, he realised. The thought of Edie with another man, married or not, was more than he could stomach.

'You and me both, Father,' May said fervently. The worry of it had been niggling at her ever since Edie had told her how she'd spent the night in a room over a pub just across the courtyard from where Charlie lived. But she wasn't going to say that to Father Michael. She'd had enough of sharing secrets and living to regret it.

'Another cup of tea, Father?' she asked.

'Thank you, no. I must be on my way.' He got up. 'I do hope your sciatica will be better soon, May, and it won't be too long before we see you in church again.'

'I hope so too, Father.'

Raymond lolled on his elbows on the colliery office desk, idly doodling on the blotter and feeling sorry for himself. Clement Firkin had decided he should get some in-depth experience of the day-to-day running of a coal mine – in truth, he was glad to be rid of his infuriating pupil for a week or two. Raymond had spent the last three days at Marston Colliery under the critical eye of its irascible manager, Taffy Jones, and hated every minute of it. The heat in the office was insufferable, since the windows and doors were mostly kept closed against the ever-present coal dust, though even so it managed to blow in, covering everything with a thin sooty layer, and Raymond hated that too. His clean white shirts quickly became grimy, especially the collar and cuffs, and the shine of his boots turned dull and matt. That same dust seemed to find its way into every orifice, so that when he wiped his nose, still sore from Richard's punch, his handkerchief was covered in black splodges. He even thought he could taste it, bitter and metallic.

Today he had been set the task of collating the end-of-month returns on the quantity of coal hewed and, never good with figures, he was struggling with the conversion of hundredweights into tons. But half an hour ago Taffy had been called away to deal with some problem on the screens, where the coal was sorted, and Raymond had taken the opportunity to slack off.

It wasn't a pleasant daydream he'd drifted into, though. Since the episode on the riverbank, he couldn't seem to stop brooding about what had happened, and the humiliation of it burned away like a slow fever under his skin. The ease with which Richard had got the better of him was hard to take; at school, he'd been feted for his sporting prowess, and even been considered a reasonable boxer. But he'd discovered to his cost that there was a world of difference between dancing nimbly away from an evenly matched opponent and being taken by surprise by a much bigger, much stronger adversary. And to have ended up in the river, especially in front of Christina, had been a terrible blow to his pride.

Just as hurtful was the way she'd reacted when he'd come on to her. Time was when they'd had fun flirting and kissing – and a bit more. And goodness only knew she'd been asking for it that day, brazenly cavorting in her underwear. He couldn't believe she hadn't known he was following her; the twigs and dry leaves crackling beneath his feet must have surely given him away. No, she'd known all right, and chosen to lead him on. A tease, that was what she was, and she'd have got her comeuppance if Richard hadn't arrived on the scene and poked his nose in.

Raymond supposed he should be grateful neither of them had snitched to Lady Elizabeth about the cause of the fracas. If they had, he'd have been in deep trouble, maybe even asked to leave Fairley Hall. The repairs were completed now on the house in Wiltshire, and Lady Elizabeth might well have decided he should go home. Much as he disliked the lessons that came as part and parcel of living here in Somerset, he wouldn't have wanted to be sent home either. Or not at the moment, at least. Julia and Lettice were there at present – Julia had brought her friend to the country to recuperate from a spell in prison for stone-throwing. She'd refused food, apparently, and been force-fed, and when she'd been released she was very weak and ill. Raymond hadn't asked the details; the very thought of it made him feel physically sick. But in any case, he really didn't fancy sharing a house with the two of them. They were so obsessed with their mission to get rights for women – something he couldn't understand

and didn't sympathise with – and there was something about their relationship that made him uncomfortable, though he couldn't quite put his finger on what it was.

Later, when they'd gone back to London, perhaps. If he had the house to himself, he'd be able to do as he pleased, and for a moment he felt more cheery as he envisaged the parties he'd throw and the ladies he'd be able to entertain.

But it wasn't long before he was thinking of Richard and Christina again, and how much he hated them and wanted his revenge.

It had become almost an obsession with him, but as yet he hadn't been able to come up with a plan as to how he could achieve it. He had toyed with the idea of doing something to discredit Richard, but it wouldn't be easy; the young toad was held in such high regard by both Clement Firkin and Edward Johnson. In any case, Raymond didn't think it would be in his own interests to have Richard accused of something serious enough to warrant his dismissal. Having him around to divert attention away from himself was useful, and in years to come, when he inherited, it would be good to have an estate manager who knew his place rather than some college-educated upstart. Besides, oddly enough, it was Christina he most wanted to punish, and he hadn't been able to think of a way to do that.

Now, however, an idea occurred to him, triggered, perhaps, by thinking about the fire that had almost destroyed his old home.

The cottage.

Christina thought he didn't know about it, but

there wasn't much that escaped Raymond's notice. He knew she went there often, sometimes alone, sometimes with Richard, and he'd over-heard her talking to Edith about it. From what she had been saying, the place was very special to her – some nonsense about it belonging in a fairy tale.

Supposing it was to burn down? She'd be in a terrible state about it. And it might impinge on Richard, too, if they went there to get up to mis-chief. The thought fuelled Raymond's anger. He wouldn't be surprised if she behaved with Rich-ard the way she used to behave with him. Well, if the cottage burned down, they'd have to find somewhere else for their carrying-on, and it would serve them right.

He was really warming to the idea now. The place would go up like a tinderbox, with its thatched roof that had collapsed in places and all the old timbers nicely dried out by this long spell of hot weather. Especially if he could get in and douse it with petrol. He'd long suspected that was the reason their house in Wiltshire had burned so fiercely: some village louts had started a fire deliberately while the family were away on holiday. He even had a good idea who they were. He'd reported a couple of them for throwing stones at his car only a few weeks earlier, and they'd had a clip round the ear and a good telling-off from the local bobby, and hidings from their fathers. They'd set the house on fire out of spite, he was certain of it, but no one had ever been brought to book for it, and no cause had ever been established.

Well, if they could do it, so could he! And he had

an even better chance of totally destroying the place than those louts had when they'd set fire to his home. That was in the middle of a village, with neighbours around to raise the alarm. The cottage was deep in the woods; no one would know it was on fire until it was well alight, if then, and even if they did, it would be far too late to save it. The fire engine would have to come all the way from Hillsbridge and then battle its way along the overgrown drive. And there would be no water – there was little in the river after the prolonged dry spell, and he doubted the hoses would stretch that far anyway.

Raymond chuckled as he thought of it. Just as long as he didn't get caught with a can of petrol, it would be fine, and sweet revenge indeed.

Through the little window in front of the desk he saw Taffy heading back across the pit yard, and pulled the ledger and pile of chitties towards him once more. When Taffy came into the office, he was surprised to see Raymond apparently working diligently.

'How are you doing then, my boy?' he asked, looking over Raymond's shoulder.

'Making progress, Mr Jones,' he replied.

And only he knew it wasn't the production returns he was talking about.

It was another day that promised to be as hot as the ones that had gone before. May's sciatica was a little better today, but even if it hadn't been, there were things she needed from the shops, and she decided to go into town early so as to be back again before the sun was at its zenith. Sally, thoughtful as always, had brought a few basic provisions with her when she came for dinner the previous day, but they were right out of cheese, and Wesley did like a nice bit of bread and cheese at bedtime, and the biscuit tin was nearly empty too.

As she emerged from her back door, she heard a loud 'Cooee!' and Hester Dallimore came hurrying down the rank – she had been washing her doorstep and cleaning her windows so as to be able to intercept any of her neighbours and be the first to pass on the news.

'Have you heard the latest?'

'What's that then?' May asked, a little impatiently. She had little time for Hester and her gossip.

'Dolly Oglethorpe has had to go up to London all of a rush. The taxi cab picked her up first thing this morning before most folk were up and about. I wouldn't have known myself but I haven't been sleeping in this heat and I heard the car. Well, I couldn't help but come down and ask her if anything was wrong, and it seems Charlie's wife has been taken into hospital and Dolly has had to go and help look after the children. Just a baby, the one is. Awful, isn't it?'

'Oh dear,' May said.

Dolly had mentioned that she was worried about Charlie's wife, her anxiety overcoming her reluctance to mention Gracie to Dolly, and Dolly had tried to console her by saying that plenty of women were poorly after giving birth, especially if they happened to be a little bit of a thing like Gracie. But she didn't like the sound of this.

'Let's hope it's nothing serious.'

'Whatever would they do if anything happened to her?' Hester was glorying in the ghoulish drama of it. 'I suppose Dolly would have to have the children here, but that would be no picnic. She's not getting any younger, and neither is Ollie.'

'Don't be such a Job's comforter, Hester,' May said. 'It may be nothing at all.'

'I'm just saying...' Hester huffed.

'I know you are, but that's all it takes for rumours to start, and before you know it they're being passed on as gospel.' May was past caring if she offended Hester, whom she disliked intensely. 'Let's wait until Dolly gets home and tells us what's up before we start jumping to conclusions.'

She hitched her shopping bag up on her arm and walked away, prickling with irritation at the woman's persistent gossip and busybodying. But she couldn't help wondering all the same what would come of it if Hester was proved right and there was something seriously wrong with Charlie's wife. Bad enough when old folk took ill and died, but a young mother of two little children... It didn't bear thinking about.

May shuddered. She might be suffering with this blooming sciatica, but that was nothing but a fleabite in the great scheme of things. At least her health had held up while she'd had children to raise, and she thanked the good Lord that they had grown up fit and well, and her grandchildren too.

A sudden thought struck her. If Dolly was in London, who was getting meals for Ollie and that lodger of theirs, young Clarence? Men were useless when it came to cooking, and if Ollie was anything like Wesley, he'd be too tired to bother much anyway. She'd have a word with him and offer to cook a bit extra while Dolly was away. Taking it just next door but one would be no trouble at all. And perhaps she'd shop for a few things that they might need while she was in town.

Gritting her teeth against the sharp nagging pain that ran from her hip to her knee, May reached the main road and set out on the long walk to High Compton.

Chapter Twenty-Eight

Afterwards, Edie could never be quite sure why she went to the cottage that night. Goodness knows she had found it creepy enough on a sunny afternoon, let alone after dark. She supposed that curiosity had finally got the better of her. 'Curiosity killed the cat,' her mother used to say when she was a little girl and forever poking her nose into things she shouldn't. She'd burned her fingers on the hot iron once (once was enough to teach her that wasn't a good idea) and had been violently ill after eating what had looked like a pretty flower – 'I wanted to know what it tasted like!' she'd said plaintively when she'd stopped being sick. When Christmas was approaching she would creep into 'Mam's corner' between the dressing table and the wardrobe and try to pick open the corners of the mysterious brown paper packages hidden there, and after she learned to read, she couldn't resist peeking into the letters May got from her sister Winnie, though there was never anything interesting in them, just the everyday doings of 'dear Wilfred' and 'dear Louie', her cousins who were just a bit older than she was.

But the curiosity she'd felt then was as nothing to what was eating away at her now. Could Lady Elizabeth really be Christina's mother? Had she hidden away in the cottage for the duration of her confinement, given birth there and taken the drawer from the dressing table to use as a crib? Who had taken the newborn baby into town that Christmas Eve and left her where she would be discovered? Had Lady Elizabeth always intended to came forward and offer to take the child in, or had she in the end been unable to let her go to strangers? And who was Christina's father? Was he someone Edie knew, or a stranger, long gone?

Around and around in her head went the questions, and Edie thought she might find some clue to the answers in the cottage. She had no business going there, of course, no excuse for investigating any further. Even if she found proof that her mistress was Christina's mother, it wasn't her place to tell the girl what Lady Elizabeth had chosen to keep from her. But she was sorely tempted, all the same, to learn what she could to satisfy her own curiosity, and that night in early July she decided to pay a visit to the cottage.

'I'm going for a walk to get some fresh air,' she said when she returned to the servants' hall after

457

getting Christina ready for bed.

For an awkward moment she thought Nellie was going to offer to accompany her, but in the end she said she thought she was too tired, and would take a stool and sit outside in the courtyard instead. She still hadn't made a move, though, when Edie left, and there was no one to see her go but Quilla, smoking a cigarette in her usual corner.

'Where are you going, then?' she called as Edie passed.

'Oh, I don't know ... just down to the road and back,' Edie lied.

'Funny time of night to go for a walk.'

Edie didn't bother to reply. Quilla had been in an even worse temper than usual these last few days, and Edie thought it might have something to do with the altercation she'd overheard between her and Richard. But she didn't know what it had been about, and cared less. She had other things on her mind.

She set off down the drive. She didn't fancy going through the woods tonight; now that the sun had set, it would be almost pitch dark under the trees and she didn't want to risk tripping over a root or perhaps even getting lost. Though overgrown, the track that ran from the drive to the cottage was much less hazardous.

As she reached the cutting, an arrow of lightning split the night sky somewhere out over the valley beyond, and she almost turned back. It could well be that a storm was brewing; that was often the way a hot dry spell ended. But she decided to take a chance on it. Now that she'd come this far, it seemed a shame to abort her mission.

When she reached the cottage, she was relieved to see the door standing slightly ajar; remembering the difficulty she and Christina had had opening it, she had wondered if she'd be able to manage it alone. Now, however, by putting her weight against it, she was able to open it sufficiently to be able to slip inside.

Remembering that there had been candle stubs in the candelabra in the drawing room, she had brought a book of matches. Now that her eyes were getting accustomed to the dark, she was able to make her way through, and was aided still further as another flash of lightning – sheet this time – illuminated the room.

Again she wondered if it would be sensible to go back to Fairley Hall before the storm broke; again she decided to have a good look around first.' She lit the candles, waited for the flames to steady, then, heart thumping uncomfortably, she climbed the stairs.

As Edie disappeared down the drive, Quilla dropped the remains of her cigarette, stubbed it out with the toe of her boot and set off after her.

Ever since the day she had been arguing with Richard about his inheritance and turned to see Edie standing there, she had been worried as to how much she might have overheard, as well as fuming over Richard's refusal to go along with her carefully laid plans. That in itself was bad enough, but she was fairly confident that when the shock of what she'd told him had worn off and he'd had the chance to think about it, she could persuade him round to her way of thinking.

Edie, and what she might have overheard, was another matter entirely. Quilla didn't think she'd been there long enough to hear her telling Richard who he really was. But she must, surely, have overheard her referring to Mrs Fairley. Thank God she had not actually put it into words! But Edie was a sharp girl. It had been common talk below stairs that Beatrice had claimed that someone had pushed her down the stairs, and everyone knew that Quilla had been with her when she unexpectedly took a turn for the worse and died. Perhaps it was only her bad conscience that made her fear that Edie would put two and two together, but until she knew for sure, she didn't dare proceed with her plan. She couldn't risk anyone making the connection. And if Edie did suspect, something would have to be done about it.

As she rounded a bend in the drive, she was surprised to see Edie turn off on to the track leading to the cottage. Why would she do that? Was it just a whim? Or was she meeting someone there? If so, it would scupper any hope Quilla had of talking to Edie in private and pumping her as to what she had overheard. But when the cottage came into view, it was in total darkness. Edie disappeared through the front door, and a few moments later a faint guttering light showed through one of the windows. Quilla waited, watching and listening for someone else to approach along the track, but no one did.

The faint light now showed through the upstairs window, and Quilla wondered whether she should go back to the drive and wait there until Edie returned – common sense told her she could hardly

460

claim that it was pure chance that had taken her to the cottage just when Edie happened to be there. But given the caustic comment she'd made about it being a funny time of night to go for a walk, it was hardly likely to ring true that she'd then decided to take one herself. She'd follow Edie into the cottage and go on the offensive, she decided. Edie was used to her trying to exert her authority, and with any luck she would be too worried at being caught somewhere she shouldn't be to question Quilla's explanation for having followed her.

Her mind made up, Quilla strode purposefully towards the cottage.

A flash of sheet lightning lit the drawing room where Sir Montague and Raymond had retired after dinner. Raymond hated having to spend time with the old man, but it was required of him, part of the price he had to pay for being his heir. In the weeks following his stroke, when he had been too ill to come downstairs, Raymond had enjoyed a respite from the tedious ritual, and now that Sir Montague had recovered enough to take his evening meal with the rest of the family, he was more resentful than ever of the expectation that he would sit with his cousin until he was ready for bed.

The old man had taken to defying doctor's orders and begun enjoying a glass or two of brandy after dinner, but though he had recovered a good deal of his speech and could walk, albeit uncertainly, with the aid of a stick, his right arm still refused to obey him. If he tried to pour his own brandy left-handed, more ended up spilled on the table than in the glass, and Raymond had become indispensable to him. He might find the boy irritating, but he was the only one willing to pour him a drink – even the servants were under strict instructions from Lady Elizabeth to refuse to do so, and this annoyed him even more than Raymond's foppish appearance and empty-headedness. Incapacitated he might be, but he was still master in this house, and it was his opinion that Elizabeth was getting above herself.

'Storm brewing,' he said now, lifting his glass to his mouth with his good hand. 'Is it raining?'

'I don't think so.' Raymond went to the window and looked out. 'No, it's not.'

'Bad sign. Don't like dry storms. Never have. Can do a lot of damage, especially when we've had no rain to speak of for weeks.'

Raymond's eyes narrowed thoughtfully. His uncle was right. A lightning strike when everything was tinder dry could well start a fire. He'd been mulling over the best way to cover his tracks; perhaps fate was offering him a helping hand. If he was to set fire to the cottage during an electric storm, everyone would assume that had been the cause and not look any further.

A little imp of nervous excitement twisted in his gut. It was the best cover he could ever hope for – if only he could get away unnoticed.

'You're looking tired, sir,' he ventured.

Sir Montague snorted. 'Always tired these days. Tired of being an invalid. Tired of growing old. Tired of life. Pour me another brandy, will you?'

Cursing inwardly, Raymond did as he was

asked, resisting the temptation to refill his own glass. If he got the chance to slip away and carry out his plan, he would need to be in full possession of his faculties, not half cut on Sir Montague's best brandy. As his cousin sipped his drink with infuriating slowness, however, Raymond succumbed, pouring himself another small measure. He was sober enough to do what he had to, and goodness only knew he could do with a little Dutch courage.

At last Sir Montague drained his glass, set it down on the small occasional table beside him, and reached for his stick.

'Think I'll be calling it a day, my boy. Ring for Dando for me, would you?'

Raymond breathed a sigh of relief and did as he was asked. He waited with contrived assiduity until the valet arrived, then, without further ado, slipped out of the front door and around the house to where his car was garaged. He always kept a can filled with petrol in case of emergency; now, with a last look round to ensure he had not been seen, he picked it up and set off for the cottage.

Another bolt of lightning, forked this time, split the sky. With adrenalin pumping and the anticipation of sweet revenge bubbling, it was all Raymond could do to keep from laughing aloud.

In the bedroom of the cottage, Edie held the candelabra aloft and gazed at the vacant space in the chest where a drawer should be. She felt more certain than ever that she had reached the right conclusion; there was no other feasible explanation for the missing drawer. The appearance of

463

what had been a fine piece of furniture was utterly spoiled by the gaping hole; no one in their right mind would remove a single drawer without good reason. It could, she supposed, have become infected with woodworm, but she could see no evidence of that in what remained of the chest, despite its age.

Cautiously she pulled open the other drawers one by one and was surprised to find they still contained items of clothing – underwear, two or three nightgowns, petticoats and blouses, neatly folded, but damp now and mouldering. There were dresses, too, hanging in the wardrobe, and several pairs of boots and shoes laid out in pairs beneath. Why on earth had Lady Elizabeth left them all here when she vacated the cottage after Christina's birth? Had she been unable to face wearing, or even seeing, them again? That, Edie thought, must be it. But what a dreadful waste! Though the fabrics were spotted now with mildew, it was obvious they had been beautiful in their day, and of the very best quality. It offended Edie's frugal nature that they should have been left here to rot, and she was surprised that Lady Elizabeth should be guilty of such extravagance. She always seemed so down to earth.

There was a hat, too – on a shelf above one half of the wardrobe – that didn't seem the kind the Lady Elizabeth she knew would ever choose. Fashions had changed, of course, and flower-garden hats were rarely seen these days, but even so, this confection of blue velvet trimmed with pink roses, blue ribbons and a full lace veil looked far too frivolous for her, especially if she was confined in an isolated cottage. The thought of a heavily pregnant lady stepping out into the woods wearing it would have been almost amusing if Edie had stopped to picture it, but she was set now on finding out all she could of the secrets this abandoned cottage held while she had the chance.

She closed the wardrobe door and turned her attention to the dressing table. On the main surface were the tortoiseshell-backed brush, comb and hand mirror she'd seen when she'd visited the cottage with Christina, all covered with a thick layer of dust, and above it, on an ornately carved shelf raised on little legs and supporting a much larger mirror, porcelain trinket boxes and several small photographs in silver frames that she hadn't noticed before.

Curious, she held the candelabra high in order to get a better look at them. One in particular caught her attention, and she picked it up, holding it closer to the light. It showed a woman, and the hat she was wearing was unmistakably the same one Edie had just discovered in the wardrobe. But it was certainly not Lady Elizabeth. The picture had been tinted, and beneath the broad mesh of the veil the hair showed a garish auburn, the cheeks blushed pink. Even if the colouring had been all wrong, so were the features. A tip-tilted nose, a heart-shaped chin, and the eyes... A chill whispered over Edie's skin. The eyes were a brilliant turquoise.

A tip-tilted nose. Christina's nose. Turquoise eyes. Christina's eyes. The portrait could have been of Christina herself. Except that it must

465

date from the middle 1890s, before Christina had even been born.

This woman was Christina's mother; there could be no other explanation for the striking resemblance. It hadn't been Lady Elizabeth who had given birth to Christina here in the cottage after all. It had been this incredibly beautiful woman. But who was she?

Edie put the photograph down on the dressing table alongside the tortoiseshell toiletry set and picked up another. It was of the same woman, but this time with a man beside her – a man who was instantly recognisable, though perhaps twenty years younger than he was now.

Sir Montague.

Edie gasped, hardly able to believe the evidence of her own eyes. The woman in the photograph must be his wife, who had, she understood, died many years ago. She had no idea what had been the cause of her death, but now she wondered – did she die in childbirth? That would explain why all her clothes were still here; the poor woman had no more need of them and no one had ever taken the trouble to dispose of them. But why had she been living here in the cottage? Why had she given birth here?

And why had Christina been taken to the church and abandoned, only to be adopted by Lady Elizabeth? It made no sense at all.

Edie set down the second photograph and picked up the first one again, mesmerised by the beautiful face that was almost a mirror image of Christina's, her thoughts tumbling around in a whirling kaleidoscope that refused to settle into any recognisable pattern.

What had happened here? And why ... why?

So lost was she in her imaginings that she scarcely noticed the creaking of the stair treads, and even if she had, she would have thought it was just the old timbers shifting and settling. It was only when a board immediately outside the door of the strange circular room creaked that she looked round, startled and alarmed.

'Who's there?'

No one answered her. But as lightning flashed again, illuminating the room as clear as day, she saw the woman standing in the doorway.

In that first startled moment, Edie felt nothing but relief that it was not some tramp or poacher who might well do her harm standing there.

'Quilla! You frightened me half to death!' Her voice was shaking with the shock of it.

'What in the world do you think you are doing here?' Quilla demanded.

Edie experienced a flash of guilt and reacted by going on the offensive.

'I might well ask you the same thing.'

'I decided to take a walk myself and saw you turn up the track, so I followed you.' Quilla's tone was accusatory. 'You could be in deep trouble if Sir Montague or Lady Elizabeth knew you were disobeying orders. You know very well that this place is out of bounds.'

Only a short time ago Edie would have argued that she could see no reason why that should be. Now, however, she understood. There were secrets here within the crumbling walls that had been kept for a generation, and were meant to be kept for ever.

'Yes, and I'm beginning to see why,' she said. 'Did you know Lady Fairley, Quilla? Was she still alive when you first came to work here?'

It was too dark in the room now, between lightning flashes, for her to be able to see Quilla's face, but the older woman's tone, when she spoke, was short and almost alarmed.

'What are you talking about?'

'Lady Fairley. Did you know her?'

For a moment Quilla didn't answer. Edie had never known her to be lost for words before. Then she said in the same sharply impatient tone, 'Yes, I knew her. But she was off her head. It was nothing but a blessed relief for all concerned when she went to meet her maker.'

'Off her head?' Edie repeated. 'You mean...'

'You know very well what I mean. Surely I don't have to spell it out? And why are you asking about Lady Laura? She's been dead and gone for years.'

Edie took a deep breath. Quilla did know something, she was sure of it. Everything about her was defensive somehow.

'Fifteen years,' she ventured.

Quilla huffed impatiently. 'Oh, I don't know. I haven't been keeping count.' Lightning flashed again; in the momentary light of it she noticed that Edie was holding something in her hand. 'What have you got there?'

Edie took a step towards her, holding out the photograph.

'Is that her?'

She knew at once that she was right. There was no mistaking the look of horror on Quilla's face, illuminated by the light of the candelabra. Then Quilla's hand shot out.

'Give that to me!'

Startled, Edie took a step backwards, still clutching the photograph.

'Give it to me, I said!' Quilla's voice was cold with fury.

Again she made a grab for the photograph, again Edie backed away, and as she did so, she cannoned into the vanity stool that stood in front of the well of the dressing table. For a fleeting second she staggered helplessly, then crashed backwards. As she fell, the back of her head connected with the carved top of the dressing table, snapping it sharply forwards. The candelabra fell from her hand, the flames from the stubs flaring briefly as it hit the floor, and brighter lights by far flashed before Edie's eyes as she went down, chin on chest, collapsing into an untidy heap.

For a long moment Quilla stood over her, then she wrested the photograph out of her unprotesting hand, grabbed the other picture that lay on the dressing table and turned towards the stairs. She hurried from the house, stopping only to pull the door closed behind her, and was perhaps fifty yards down the overgrown track when her legs almost gave way beneath her. She blundered into the trees that lined it on either side, leaning against the trunk of one briefly before sinking down on to the stump of another.

Damn photographs! If Dick had been able to get into the cottage and remove them as she'd asked him to, she would have had all the evidence she needed to back up her threats to Sir Montague, and there would have been no risk of anyone else coming across them and learning the truth. Why the hell hadn't she asked him to try again? But she'd been too afraid he might be seen, and that too would have been disastrous. Well, it was too late now. The damage had been done. But at least the evidence was in her possession. She'd have to decide what to do about Edie later, when she was able to think straight.

Quilla felt for her cigarettes and matches in the pocket of her dress and lit one with hands that refused to stop shaking.

Fuelled by anticipation and nervous excitement, Raymond carefully picked his way through the woods to the cottage.

As he had expected, the doors were closed, and though he tried them, they refused to budge. But yet another flash of lightning had shown him that one of the windows in the one-storey annexe that jutted from the main building was partially open. That would do nicely, he thought. If he could set a fire in the annexe, it would burn through to the rest of the house but it would take much longer for the thatched roof of the main building to catch light, which was all to the good. Being the tallest point, it was the one most likely to be spotted by anyone still abroad at this time of night, which meant he would have more time to make a clean getaway. Besides which, the fire would already have rampaged through the ground floor.

He opened the window as wide as it would go

and hoisted himself up so that he was hanging over the sill. He wasn't going to go right inside; he didn't want to risk finding himself trapped when the fire ignited. He had already unscrewed the cap on the can; now he sloshed petrol over as wide an area as he could reach. As he stretched over in an effort to empty out the very last drops, he almost dropped the can but managed to hold on. Whew! That had been a close one! He doubted anyone would bother to pick through the ashes and debris when the fire at last burned itself out, but if they should, he didn't want his petrol can to be found. Not that it would immediately point to him – it was scarcely unique – but there weren't that many owners of motor cars hereabouts, and he didn't want to have to purchase another one, which would draw attention to him.

He slid back down, placed the can on the ground beneath the window and felt in his pockets for his matches and a taper. His hands were shaking so much it took him two or three attempts before the taper was alight, then he leaned in through the window and dropped it into the room.

The speed with which the petrol flared up startled him; he jerked back and almost fell. A sheet of flame had shot up like a molten waterfall in reverse, a sudden roaring sound echoed in his ears, and he could feel the heat on his face.

Time to beat a hasty retreat. Raymond grabbed the empty petrol can and disappeared like a shadow into the woods, whilst behind him the flames flickered and spread and grew.

Perched on a tree stump at the edge of the track,

Quilla drew deeply on her cigarette. She was still shaking violently and one of the framed photographs she had dumped in her lap fell off and landed in the undergrowth beside her. She reached for it, scrabbling in the grass and nettles, wincing as they stung her hand, but only wanting to know she had it safely in her possession.

Would it be enough? Threatening to tell the world the truth about Lady Laura's sad fate and Christina's lineage had been her trump card. Now she was dreadfully afraid that Edie must have seen enough to put two and two together. Christina was the living image of her mother, and it was only surprising that no one had noticed it before.

Then again, perhaps not so surprising. Even before her fragile state of mind had tipped over into madness, Laura had never been one to visit the families who lived on the estate as Lady Elizabeth did, host social events or even attend church. The friends she and Sir Montague had entertained in the early days of their marriage had long since been dropped, and apart from Lilian Parker, Martha Davey, Percy Stevens and Quilla herself, none of the present staff had been at Fairley Hall when Lady Laura was mistress. Percy and Lilian both knew her fate, of course, and had probably connived in it, but their loyalty was unquestionable, and Martha Davey's eyesight, never good, had worsened over recent years. Christina's face was probably no more than a blur to her these days on the rare occasions when she saw the girl, and if she had ever had her suspicions as to where extra portions of food from her kitchen had gone, she would have been too anxious to keep

472

her job to question it.

Quilla herself, of course, had been only a lowly parlourmaid at the time, and certainly not privy to any confidences. Like everyone else, she had been told that Lady Laura was visiting relatives, and later that she had sadly passed away. But not much escaped Quilla. She was ten times sharper than any of the other servants and good at piecing together things that were seemingly unconnected.

From the outset she'd noticed that Lady Laura was rather too friendly with James, the handsome young groom who occupied the accommodation over the stables. She had always loved to ride, but that year she seemed more eager than ever to be out on horseback, and since Sir Montague feared she might take a tumble and lie undiscovered for hours in the countryside if she went alone, the groom went with her. On one occasion Quilla had gone to the stables with a message for Laura and found the two of them there together, supposedly stabling the steaming horses, though she knew instantly that something more had been going on – it was written all over them. Afterwards she had taken note of the looks that passed between them, the secret smiles and the seemingly accidental touches as James tightened the stirrups on Lady Laura's mare or helped her mount or dismount. On another occasion she'd seen them emerging from the doorway that led to James's quarters and surmised that things had gone much further than a mere flirtation – it wasn't only her looks Christina got from her mother; she'd inherited her flightiness too. Then, not so long afterwards, James had been suddenly dismissed and Lady Laura left for her so-called 'extended visit to relatives'. Quilla was not fooled, though – she guessed that the affair had had unfortunate consequences and Lady Laura was in the family way. She had watched and listened, revelling in the situation, and it was then that she had made a startling discovery. She had noticed that there were more sheets and towels to wash than came from the bedrooms in the Hall, and undergarments that looked suspiciously like Lady Laura's, and one day she surreptitiously followed Lilian Parker when she left the house with a basket covered with a clean white cloth. To her amazement, she learned that far from being away visiting relatives, Lady Laura was in fact hiding in the old cottage in the woods.

Smugly satisfied with her discovery, Quilla had said nothing about it to anyone, but she had become more vigilant than ever. When one cold December day Mrs Parker kept going missing in spite of the fact that the whole household was busy with preparations for Christmas, Quilla had guessed Lady Laura must have gone into labour, and wondered what in the world they were going to do with a baby born in secret. But she did not have to wonder for long. When it was reported that a baby had been found abandoned in the porch of the Catholic church, she knew her question had been answered, and it explained too why Percy Stevens had been absent from the house that evening – it must have been him who had transported her there.

She was, though, as surprised as anyone when Lady Elizabeth announced her intention of adopting the poor little soul, though of course that was Lady Elizabeth all over, too kind-hearted for her own good. And she was even more surprised that Lady Laura didn't return to the Hall.

Christmas came and went, and New Year, and still the story was that she had stayed on with her relatives to be with an old aunt who was sick and of whom she was very fond. There was speculation amongst the servants that she and Sir Montague had fallen out and were considering divorce, or that Lady Laura was attending the bedside of the elderly aunt in the hope of being left a goodly sum of money in her will when she eventually died. Quilla, of course, knew this was all fabrication, and was puzzled by Lady Laura's continued absence. Surely now that the baby had been born she wasn't still living in the cottage?

One night, overcome with curiosity, she had crept out there, looked through the window and seen her sitting at the table, head in hands. Her hair was wild, as though it hadn't been brushed properly for days, and Quilla could see that she was crying. Perhaps Sir Montague had refused to have her back. Perhaps rather than go through with a scandalous divorce, he was keeping her a prisoner there.

It wasn't so long after that that she realised Lilian and Percy were no longer leaving the house with baskets of supplies, and on another occasion when she managed to get away and creep through the woods in order to satisfy her curiosity, she found the cottage in darkness.

Lady Laura had left, it seemed, and for all her sly ways, Quilla was unable to discover what had become of her.

It was only later, when she became Sir Montague's mistress, that she had learned the truth – it was surprising what you could get out of a man when he had drunk too much brandy, however intent he might be on keeping his secrets when he was sober.

Always emotionally fragile, Laura had become completely unhinged by the whole sorry business. She couldn't be trusted not to blurt out the story. And determined that no one outside their tight-knit little circle should ever know that he had been cuckolded by his groom, and that his wife had given birth to the groom's child, Sir Montague had kept her incarcerated in the cottage until she had, unsurprisingly, sickened and died.

The terrible story had shocked Quilla, and she could feel nothing but revulsion for a man who could treat any woman so, and especially his poor defenceless wife. From that moment on she did her best to resist his advances, but it wasn't easy; as master of the house, the power was all his.

When she discovered she was pregnant, the thought of bearing his child was almost as dreadful as the shame and disgrace that would be heaped upon her. And when Sir Montague told her he had arranged for her to go to a friend in Wiltshire for the duration of her confinement, she was terrified that she might suffer the same fate as Lady Laura and be locked away somewhere or even murdered in her bed.

In the end, lonely, lost and frightened, she had run away, back to High Compton. She had arrived at her brother Dick's cottage in the middle of the night, and to their credit Dick and his wife Addie had agreed to let her stay, hidden from sight, until the baby was born. It was ironic, really, Quilla sometimes thought, that in the end she had been just as much a prisoner for that time as poor Lady Laura had been. But in other ways she had been much more fortunate.

Dick and Addie had agreed to raise the child as their own – they had daughters, but not the son they longed for. Addie was a plump woman; it wasn't difficult for her to pretend she hadn't realised she was pregnant until she went into labour, and given her rolls of fat, she was believed, though the story had caused some amusement in the town. Leaving her son with them, Quilla had returned to her former position, though Sir Montague had never bothered her again for her favours.

The moment her son was born, however, Quilla had experienced the fiercest maternal emotions. She couldn't nurse and nurture him, she had to be content to be known as his aunt, but she knew she would lie, cheat, steal and kill for his wellbeing. And so she had.

But now, with Edith having seen the pictures in the cottage, her threat to make Sir Montague's secret public was no longer the powerful tool it had been and her plans had all been thrown into disarray.

Quilla fished out another cigarette and lit it from the glowing butt of the first as she wondered frantically what she could do to avert the disastrous scuppering of all the hopes and dreams she had for her beloved son.

As he hurried back to the house, Raymond glanced over his shoulder several times, looking for any sign that the fire had taken hold, but the cottage was hidden from view by the thick trees and as yet there was no telltale plume of smoke. It wouldn't be long before there was, though. The flames would illuminate it, picking it out as a dark cloud against the night sky, shot through, perhaps, with showers of sparks. He didn't think there would be anybody out and about tonight to see it, but he was taking no chances.

He returned the fuel can to the boot of his car, let himself in by the front door and hurried upstairs to his room to wash the smell of petrol from his hands. Then he undressed and put on his silk dressing gown. He thought about going back downstairs to help himself to another glass of his uncle's brandy, but decided against it. As far as he knew, no one had seen him leave the house or return. But he didn't think he should take the chance that he might be caught sneaking downstairs. Better that no one should think he had ever left his room.

Instead he went to the window and stood there looking out over the lawns to the woods beyond, relishing the thrill of what he had done as well as the satisfaction of knowing he had revenged himself on Christina and Richard.

Just what had alerted Quilla to the fact that the cottage was on fire she was never entirely sure. Had it been the smell of burning in the clear night air, the distant crackle and roar in the silence, no more than the buzzing of a swarm of bees at this distance but audible just the same, or simply some sixth sense that all was not as it should be? Puzzled and vaguely uneasy, she got up from the tree stump and made her way back to the track. There she stopped short, gazing in horrified disbelief at the sight that met her eyes.

The single-storey extension was no longer in darkness but bathed in flickering vermilion and scarlet that danced behind the windows like a vision of hell painted in glowing oils. As she stood there frozen by the shock of it, part of the roof collapsed with a loud crash and flames shot up into the night sky along with a cloud of dense black smoke.

Quilla's first thought was that the fire had been started by the candelabra that had crashed to the floor when Edith had stumbled and fallen. But that made no sense. They had been upstairs in the main part of the house, while the seat of the blaze appeared to be in the single-storey extension. Was it possible that the girl had picked the candelabra up again, staggered downstairs, still groggy, and somehow managed to set light to the old drapes? All these thoughts flashed through Quilla's mind in the space of those first startled seconds, and then...

Edith!

She'd been lying motionless against the heavy old dressing table when Quilla had hurried from the room with the incriminating photographs. Might she still be there, senseless and unaware of the fire raging below? The breath caught in Quilla's throat and her knees went weak at the thought. Edie might die there, trapped and help-less – she almost certainly would unless she had already regained consciousness and left the cot-tage. It was too horrific to contemplate. And yet...

If Edie died, Quilla's problems would be over. No one would ever know the truth she had stumbled upon. There would no longer be a threat to Quilla's hopes, dreams and plans. Richard, master of Fairley Hall. Richard – Sir Richard – set up for life, enjoying everything that was his birthright. And Quilla herself – his mother, though she could never publicly admit to it – comfortably installed as mistress of the house, with servants to wait on her instead of the other way round. If Edie died, it was still all hers for the taking. She'd killed already in the pursuit of her relentless ambition for Richard. If there was one more death, what was the difference?

But it *was* different. Beatrice Fairley had been a miserable old woman whom Quilla had despised. Edie had her whole life before her, a young woman who had never knowingly done harm to anyone. If she died trapped inside the blazing cottage, it would be because Quilla had struggled with her so that she had fallen and hit her head. With a sudden rush of conscience such as had not troubled her for years, Quilla knew she couldn't abandon the girl to such a horrific fate. She had to know if she was safe, or if she was still inside, senseless and helpless.

Stopping only to conceal the two framed photographs in the thick undergrowth at the edge of the track, she began to run towards the cottage. As she neared it, another section of the roof of the annexe collapsed; yet more flames and thick acrid smoke shot up into the night sky and a shower of sparks flew towards the thatch of the main house. Now she could feel the heat of the blaze on her face and clearly hear the spit and crackle of burning timbers. As she drew nearer, the flickering light of the flames was bright enough for her to see that the front door was still firmly closed. Surely if Edie had come out that way, she would have left it open? Hard as Quilla had slammed it when she left, it had resisted, and she was twice as strong as the slightly built Edie – nor had she been running for dear life.

Edie must still be inside. Panic was tightening Quilla's chest now, but she ran to the door, pushing at it with all her might until it gave, scraping over the flagstones.

The room inside was already thick with smoke, and little rivers of flame were creeping outwards from the annexe and licking at the door frame.

Covering her face with her hands, Quilla ran to the staircase.

Edie surfaced through layers of muzziness. Where was she? In those first confused moments, she didn't know. But her head was hurting, and when she tried to lift it from her chest, a sharp pain shot up her neck. And what was that awful smell of burning? Had Mrs Davey left a fatty pan on the stove, or the potatoes to burn? But that wasn't right. It wasn't that sort of smell. It was more like the fires had smelled when she was lighting the kindling in the grates in the days when she had been a housemaid at Fairley Hall...

In a sudden blinding flash, Edie remembered. The bedroom of the cottage, that was where she was. And Quilla had been here too, angry, accusing, snatching the photograph from her. But she wasn't here now, and something was horribly wrong. The smell of smoke was stronger than ever; her eyes and throat were burning with it. She covered her mouth with a weak hand and blinked hard against the stinging that was making her eyes water and close involuntarily. Then, as she opened them again, she caught a glimpse of a glow in the ceiling above the wardrobe, and the first flicker of flame.

The cottage was on fire! Terror galvanised her. She tried to get up, but her legs buckled beneath her and she went down again in an untidy heap. A bit of burning thatch fell down between the rafters and landed on the bed. Again Edie tried to rise; again her legs gave way beneath her. Sobbing, coughing, panic-stricken, she began to crawl towards the door, but all her strength seemed to have deserted her. And then...

'Edith!'

Quilla was there in the doorway, coming towards her. For a moment Edie shrank away, half expecting to be attacked again. But Quilla's strong arms were around her, hoisting her to her feet.

'You've got to get out of here!' Her voice seemed to be coming from a long way off. 'Come on, help yourself, for God's sake.'

She half dragged Edie to the head of the stairs. The room below was thick with smoke now, flames licking at the curtains and furnishings. Again Edie shrank away. She couldn't think straight, was aware only of the terror overwhelming her. Quilla pushed her towards the stairs, supporting her until she was able to cling on to the wooden banister, then holding her round the waist.

'Go on! Go on! I've got you!'

Somehow, falteringly, Edie started down the stairs. To head into the smoke and flame below was contrary to all her instincts, but at the same time she knew she must. To go back upstairs would be to be trapped, and already the thatched roof above was alight. Besides, Quilla was blocking the way back as she urged her on down the stairs.

What felt like a sharp push in the centre of her back accompanied by a sudden loud crack and the sound of splintering wood made Edie jerk around. The torn muscles in her neck and shoulder screamed in protest, but she scarcely noticed. Quilla was no longer standing tall behind her but sprawled backwards against the stairs. One leg was buried shin deep in a gaping hole in the tread.

For a fleeting moment Edie couldn't make sense of it, then realisation came flooding in. She'd warned Christina to be careful of the rotten stairs the first time they'd come here, but in her panic she'd forgotten all about that, and Quilla hadn't thought of it at all. Her foot had gone clean through the old wood.

'Quilla!' Edie screamed as the older woman struggled vainly to free herself. She descended a couple of stairs, then turned and knelt in an attempt to help, clawing frantically at the splintered wood. Her eyes, streaming from the smoke, kept squeezing shut in painful spasms, and she had begun to choke and cough, but somehow she managed to break off chunks of rotten wood with her bare hands, and at last – at last! – Quilla was able to pull her leg free, hauling herself up on to the stair above. Blood spurted scarlet from a jagged gash, spraying Edie's face and the front of her dress.

'Get out! Go!' Quilla yelled at her.

Dazed, choking, Edie stumbled down the remaining stairs and through the open door into the blessedly fresh air. As she coughed and struggled for breath, a loud crash from within the burning house made her jump in fright, and smoke and sparks billowed through the open doorway.

'Quilla?' she gasped.

There was no reply.

The world was swimming around her, the dancing flames seemed etched in darkness, terrifyingly close but at the same time strangely far away, and she barely registered that rain had begun to fall, heavy drops that would soon become a downpour. Her legs once more buckled beneath her and she collapsed into the thick undergrowth. Though her last conscious thought was for the woman trapped inside the burning cottage, Edie was no longer capable of doing anything at all to help her.

It was Richard who raised the alarm. Woken by a loud crack of thunder, a blindingly bright flash of lightning and the sound of rain beating against the window, he had got up to watch the storm. At first when he saw the glow on the horizon he thought it was just a trick of the light, but it didn't disappear with the electric flashes, only became more obvious.

Fire. Had one of the forks of lightning struck a tree and set light to it? But Richard had an unerring sense of direction, and he guessed correctly that it was Christina's cottage that was blazing in the thick darkness. He pulled on a shirt and trousers and a pair of shoes, then raced downstairs and across the courtyard. The back door of the house was unlocked; he ran in, shouting for help. While Mrs Davey phoned for the fire brigade, he and the other men set out for the cottage. None of them noticed that Raymond seemed highly amused – excited, even. None of them noticed that Quilla and Edie were missing. It was only when they came across Edie collapsed in the undergrowth and she gasped out that Quilla was in the cottage did they begin to realise the full horror of the situation.

It was a night none of them would ever forget.

Chapter Twenty-Nine

Everyone at Fairley Hall was in a state of shock. Quilla dead! Though she was far from popular amongst the staff, none of them would have wished such a terrible end for her, and Richard, of course, was dreadfully upset. He hadn't much liked her either, and learning that she was his mother rather than his aunt as he had always believed was something he had yet to come to terms with. But whatever, she was family, his blood, someone who had always been a part of his life, and he was numbed by the thought that he would never see her again. When Christina had come to him weeping about the destruction of her 'fairy-tale cottage', he had reacted angrily. 'Never mind the cottage. That was just wattle and daub and mouldy thatch. Quilla is dead, Christina. Dead! Don't you understand that?'

The events of that terrible night were still, days later, a nightmare that played itself out over and over every time he closed his eyes, a film reel that would not stop

By the time they had reached the cottage, it was nothing more than a shell from which flames still shot up and clouds of black smoke billowed into the sky. And then they'd heard coughing coming from the nearby undergrowth and found Edie lying there, struggling for breath.

'Quilla!' she wheezed. 'Quilla is in there! Do something! You have to do something!'

There was, of course, nothing to be done. It was plain that if Quilla was still inside the cottage, she was beyond help. Percy Stevens, who had come panting up a good hundred yards behind the others, took care of Edie while Simon ran back to the house to get the Rolls and drive her to the cottage hospital.

Never in all his short life had Richard felt so totally helpless, so utterly terrified. The whole world was painted in shades of scarlet and black, and what was happening was an enormity he could scarcely comprehend. But the horror of it was all too real, and it would haunt him for the rest of his days. Quilla, his mother, had perished in that inferno, and the last words he had spoken to her had been in anger. There was no way he could ever change that now, and the guilt was a terrible weight on his heart.

At least it seemed that Edie would make a full recovery – she had been discharged from hospital and was at home in Fairley Terrace recuperating, which was a great relief to everyone.

'Thank the Lord!' Mrs Davey said, raising her eyes to heaven when the news reached the servants' hall, and was quick to give Flo a sharp clip round the ear when she said: 'I hope she's back to work soon so we can find out what she and Quilla were doing out there in the middle of the night.'

'Show some respect, my girl!' Mrs Davey snapped, but the truth was that every one of them was wondering the same thing.

What *had* they been doing there? It made no sense at all. They weren't friends, or even allies. What could have taken the two of them to the derelict cottage in the middle of the night, and how had the fire started?

'Knowing Quilla, it wouldn't surprise me if she was up to no good,' Percy Stevens said to Lilian Parker when they were having one of their little chats in the butler's pantry.

'You shouldn't speak ill of the dead,' Lilian chided. But she couldn't help but agree with Percy all the same. The two of them knew all too well the secrets the cottage had kept for so many years, and Quilla was nothing if not a scheming mischief-maker. But Edie? It defied all that Lilian knew of Edie that she should have somehow become embroiled in one of Quilla's plots.

Upstairs, the mood was no less sombre.

Raymond was in total shock that his attempt at revenge on Christina and Richard had ended in death, though he told himself it was not his fault. How was he to know that Quilla and Edie were there? They had no business to be! They had no one but themselves to blame for what had happened. But typically his greatest concern was that it might yet come out that he had been responsible for the fire. So far it seemed he had got away with it, but there was no escaping the possibility that something or someone might give him away, and the dread of that happening hung over him at every waking moment. Supposing he had been seen creeping into the woods that night? It was not beyond the realms of possibility that whoever might have seen him was keeping quiet about it for the moment for some reason. Or what if Simon went to borrow some petrol from the can in the boot of his car? Unlikely, but if he did and found it empty, suspicion was bound to be aroused. He didn't even dare to go to the garage and get the can refilled in case someone started asking questions.

The unacknowledged guilt lay heavily on him, making him anxious and nervy, and when he could stand it no longer, he begged a few days off from his studies to go home to Wiltshire on the pretext of inspecting the repairs to the house, which were now completed. He didn't relish the thought of Julia and Lettice's company, but anything was preferable to remaining here, where it was impossible to avoid being reminded of the consequences of his actions.

Lady Elizabeth, of course, was as puzzled as everyone else as to the reason why Quilla and Edith had been at the cottage, but she was also dreadfully upset at the loss of the lady's maid who had been her companion for so many years. Though she was aware of what she thought of as Quilla's funny ways, they had always got along very well, since Quilla always took care to be respectful, discreet and indispensable.

Sir Montague's reaction, however, was predictably very different.

'Good riddance!' he grunted when Lady Elizabeth told him what had happened. 'Good riddance to her, and to that bally cottage too.'

'Oh Montague, don't say such things!' Lady Elizabeth said, distressed. 'The cottage ... well, I can't say I'm sorry that it's gone. It was never a happy place. But poor Quilla... She could be contrary, I know, but she had a good heart, and I for one shall miss her.'

'Ha! A good heart? I don't think so. What if I told you she was trying to blackmail me?'

'Over your indiscretion with her? Oh surely not!'

'Not that, no.' Sir Montague struggled for a moment to locate the right words, which still sometimes evaded him if he became stressed or lost his temper. 'Laura. She knew about Laura.'

Lady Elizabeth's eyes widened. 'But how?'

'Don't ask me. Poked her nose in where she

had no business to, I imagine. But she knew all right, and threatened to speak out if I didn't do as she asked and adopt Richard and make him my heir.'

'What!' Lady Elizabeth was astounded.

'That was Quilla for you. Little did she know, if she'd behaved decently I might have decided to do just that. He's my son, when all's said and done, and worth a dozen of that useless layabout Raymond. Now she's out of the picture I might consider it, but I wasn't going to let her think she had the better of me.'

For a moment Lady Elizabeth was silent, then she smiled faintly. 'Do you know, Montague, I think that is rather a good idea,' she said. 'I agree that Raymond has proved to be something of a disappointment, while Richard seems a very nice young man. And as you say, he is your son. It would be good to know that the estate will remain in the direct line, even a somewhat unorthodox one.'

And it would be a fitting memorial to Quilla, she was on the point of adding, but thought better of it.

'Let me think about it.'

His eyes went longingly towards the brandy decanter. If Raymond had one use, it was to pour a drink for him. But he was getting stronger every day and he thought he'd soon be able to manage it for himself without spilling good brandy on the table or carpet, a terrible waste and a telling give-away. Yes, all in all it would be a great deal more satisfactory to know that the title and the estate would pass down the direct line, even if Richard had been born on the wrong side of the blanket. He might take a little persuading, but that was the sort of thing Lady Elizabeth was good at, and since it seemed she approved of the idea, she would be the ideal one to talk to the boy.

'What the devil were Quilla and Edith doing at the cottage is what I'd like to know,' he said, changing the subject back to the fire.

'I've no idea why Edith was there, but Quilla... Do you think it's possible she was gathering evidence to back up this blackmail attempt?' Lady Elizabeth asked.

'I wouldn't put it past her,' Sir Montague retorted. 'God alone knows, we should have got rid of it all years ago.'

'We should, I know. But we didn't, for one reason or another. I think it made us uncomfortable to think about it, let alone destroy it. At least it did me. Poor dear Laura. What she must have suffered. I wish with all my heart I hadn't gone along with it, Montague. We should have looked after her here, in the house, or had her committed to an asylum where she could be properly cared for.'

'And have her blurt out the whole shameful business to anyone who would listen? You know very well we had no choice.'

'It was your decision, Montague. For my part, I shall never forgive myself.'

'You've nothing to reproach yourself with, Elizabeth. You have raised Christina as your own daughter, devoted your life to her.'

'It was the least I could do. And I love her dearly.'

491

'Hmm,' Sir Montague huffed. 'It worries me that she is the image of her mother, and too like her in many ways. If she loses her mind too, it will break your heart, Elizabeth.'

'She won't,' Lady Elizabeth said, with more confidence than she felt when she lay awake worrying over Christina's mercurial temperament and the ease with which she could be manipulated. But then she felt sure it had been Montague's harsh and uncompromising nature that had pushed Laura over the edge. Just as long as Christina found a husband who loved, supported and understood her, she would be fine. Someone strong and sensible and kind. Someone like Richard... With an impatient shake of her head, she sought to push the thought away. Richard was still scarcely more than a child himself. But he and Christina did seem to have formed a very close friendship, and it wouldn't be so long before he was a young man.

'What I really don't understand is what Edith was doing at the cottage with Quilla,' she said, returning to their previous discussion.

'Quilla was no doubt showing her the evidence. Or preparing to,' Sir Montague spluttered.

'Do you really think so?'

'What other reason could there be? We could yet find the whole disgraceful affair in the public domain. Damn the woman! I hope she rots in hell.'

'I think we can trust Edith,' Lady Elizabeth soothed – she was worried her brother was working himself up to a state where he might well suffer another stroke.

'You can't trust anybody.'

'You've trusted Mr Stevens and Mrs Parker all these years,' Elizabeth pointed out. 'Edith is cut from the same cloth. I was planning to go and visit her and see how she is. I can question her gently while I'm there and if necessary explain to her the importance of discretion. It won't fall on deaf ears, I can assure you.'

'It had better not.'

'Just one other thing.' Lady Elizabeth turned in the doorway as she made to leave. 'I intend to offer to pay for Quilla's funeral. Her family are far from wealthy and I think it is the least I can do. I presume you will be agreeable to that?'

'Oh, do what you like,' Sir Montague huffed.

As soon as Elizabeth had left the room, he shuffled over to the occasional table and managed to pick up the brandy decanter. If he spilled some and got caught out, so be it. Dammit, if ever he had needed a drink, it was now.

'Oh my word ... whoever...?'

May was washing up at the scullery sink when the Rolls came chuntering around the corner and stopped outside number 1. As she recognised the elegant lady in the rear seat, she gazed for a moment in shock, her hands suspended over the soapy water, then made a grab for the drying-up cloth, mopping at them roughly as she hurried, all a-flutter, into the living room, where Edie lay propped up against a pile of cushions on the sofa.

'It's Lady Elizabeth! Oh my Lord! Whatever next?'

'Go and let her in then, Mam.' Edie pulled herself up into a sitting position and May hurried back to the scullery, untying the strings of her apron as she went.

'Mrs Cooper.' Lady Elizabeth was standing at the door, which was open. 'I'm sorry to call unannounced, but I am so anxious about Edith. Is she well enough for visitors?'

'Oh milady!' May bobbed a curtsey. 'She's much better, thank you, but oh ... you must excuse the mess... We've not long had our dinner...'

'Please don't worry on my account. May I come in?'

'Yes ... yes, of course, milady... She's in there...' May gestured towards the living room, then hung back nervously.

'Edith.' Lady Elizabeth crossed to the sofa. 'No, please don't try to get up. How are you, my dear?'

'I'm fine, thank you, milady.' Her voice was still a little hoarse and raspy.

'You plainly are not! But you are recovering?'

'I am, milady.'

'Thank heavens for that! And thank heavens you were found so quickly. If you had not been ... but we won't dwell on that. The whole business is tragedy enough.'

'Quilla?' Edie was almost reluctant to speak the name, her eyes fixed imploringly on Lady Elizabeth's face.

'I'm afraid poor Quilla perished.' Lady Elizabeth was equally reluctant to tell Edie that her almost unrecognisable remains had been found beneath the charred timbers.

'Oh no!' It was no more than Edie had expected, but to have it confirmed was devastating. 'Oh poor Quilla! She saved my life. If she hadn't come back...'

She broke off, tears filling her eyes. She hadn't liked the woman, still couldn't understand why she had followed her to the cottage and attacked her so viciously when she'd seen her with the pictures, then gone off leaving her senseless on the bedroom floor. But for all that, when she'd realised the cottage was on fire, she had come back and helped her to safety. For that she had paid with her life.

'Can I get you a cup of tea, milady?' May was hovering in the doorway, still flustered at having gentry in her house, and unsure of the proper way to entertain her.

Lady Elizabeth nodded and smiled. 'That would be very nice, Mrs Cooper. But I really would like to speak to Edith alone, if you won't be offended.'

'Oh no, of course I won't...' May retreated into the scullery, pulling the door closed behind her, though she was wondering what in the world her ladyship had to say that was not for her ears, and determined to try and overhear if she could.

Lady Elizabeth perched carefully on the edge of one of the armchairs so that she was on a level with Edie.

'I'm sorry to be harking back to something I am sure you are anxious to forget,' she said gently, 'but the cause of the fire is a complete mystery, unless of course it was caused by a lightning strike. And Montague and I are very puzzled as to why you and Quilla should have been in the cottage at all. Now please don't think I am accusing you of being responsible, my dear, but Montague is most anxious to get to the bottom of the business.'

She sat back, looking at Edie expectantly.

Edie's heart sank. That she should be called upon to explain her presence in the cottage in the middle of the night was something she had been expecting, and dreading, and though she had been desperately trying to think of an excuse, nothing had suggested itself to her. Now, faced with the direct question, she could see no way out but to admit to the truth.

'I know I had no business being there, and I shall quite understand if you want to dismiss me,' she said, shamefaced. 'But I think there is something you should know. Some time ago Miss Christina asked me if I could help her find out who she really is – she thought that since it was my mother who found her, I might know something. I told her it should be you she was talking to, but she said you wouldn't discuss it with her. It really matters to her, milady, so I agreed to do what I could by asking a few questions...'

'I see.' Lady Elizabeth's voice was hard suddenly. In the light of the conversation she'd had with her brother, the whole business was beginning to make sense to her now. 'Quilla provided you with the answers, I imagine. That's the reason she took you to the cottage.'

Edie looked startled.

'Quilla didn't take me there. I went because when I was there one day with Miss Christina, I saw–'

'Christina has been going to the cottage?' Lady

496

Elizabeth asked sharply.

Edie nodded uncomfortably, and a guilty flush rose in her cheeks.

'She thought of it as her special secret place, like something out of a fairy tale. I know it was supposed to be out of bounds, but there didn't seem any harm in it. You know what she's like, making up stories and pretending things...'

'Yes, I'm afraid I do.'

'I'm sorry, milady. I expect you think I should have told you.'

Lady Elizabeth gave a small shake of her head.

'Never mind that now. You were telling me why you went to the cottage.'

'Yes, milady. When I was there with Miss Christina, I saw a chest with one of the drawers missing, and I remembered that when she was found in the church porch she was in a drawer. And I thought maybe...' She swallowed hard. 'I thought maybe she had been born in the cottage. I wanted to go back for another look, but I couldn't do it when Miss Christina was about – that's why I went at night, when she was in bed.'

'I see. And Quilla?'

'I think Quilla must have followed me, but I don't know why. She never said. She was acting very peculiar. I asked her some questions, but she wouldn't answer, and then she saw I was looking at the pictures and she went mad.'

'The pictures? What pictures?' Lady Elizabeth demanded. Her eyes were narrowed now, her expression steely.

'Of Miss Christina's mother. As soon as I saw them, I knew it had to be. Miss Christina is the image of her. There's no mistaking it. I am right, aren't I? And...'

She broke off. She had been going to say that she'd also worked out that Sir Montague was Christina's father, but somehow that seemed a step too far.

'She tried to snatch them away from me,' she went on instead. 'That's how I came to fall and hit my head. And I don't really remember anything else until I came to and the cottage was on fire.'

For a moment the memory of her terror then threatened to overwhelm her. She covered her face with her hands, blinking at the tears that started to her eyes.

'Oh my dear...' Lady Elizabeth reached out a gloved hand and patted her shoulder.

Edie gulped, brushing away the tears impatiently and composing herself with an enormous effort.

'I'm sorry, milady.'

'*I'm* sorry, Edith, that you have become caught up in all this.' She was silent for a moment, then she went on: 'You realised, I imagine, that it was Lady Laura who was Christina's mother. But you are wondering, I expect, why she was living in the cottage, and why she wasn't able to take care of Christina herself. The fact is, Edith, she was a very sick woman. Not physically – though that inevitably followed – but in her mind. It would have been for the best if she had been committed to an asylum, but Montague wouldn't hear of it. He didn't want it to be public knowledge that his dear wife was mad. But I'm afraid that is the long and short of it.'

'Oh, I'm so sorry...' Edie was shocked at the revelation, and though later she would wonder why the whole charade that followed Christina's birth had been embarked upon, for the moment it didn't occur to her.

'I adopted Christina because Lady Laura was in no fit state to care for her,' Lady Elizabeth went on. 'It seemed the best possible solution to a most terrible dilemma. And I have to say that she has brought me a good deal of happiness.' She paused, levelling her eyes with Edie's. 'I do hope, Edith, my dear, that I can rely upon you not to repeat what I've told you. Sir Montague would be as upset today as he ever would have been if such a thing got out. I'm sure you can well imagine what a furore it would cause. So I am asking you very humbly if you would please treat it as strictly confidential.'

'Of course I will, milady,' Edie said at once. 'But what about Miss Christina? Like I said, it really matters to her that she should know who she is...'

Again Lady Elizabeth was silent for a long moment. Then she nodded. 'I think it is time that I spoke to Christina myself. Perhaps I should have done so long ago. I thought it was enough that she knew she was loved – and believe me, she is.'

'I never doubted that, milady. But I know it's been troubling her all the same.'

'I am so sorry about that.' Lady Elizabeth's expression was concerned. 'But I must also thank you, Edith, for performing your duties toward her with such diligence, and for being such a good friend to her. She's missing you, I know. I hope it won't be long before the doctor says you are recovered enough to return to the Hall.'

'I hope so too, milady. I'll be seeing him tomorrow and I expect he'll sign me off.'

'Good.' Lady Elizabeth rose. 'Don't try to get up, Edith. I'll see myself out.'

In the doorway she turned back, as another thought struck her. 'You said you fell and hit your head...'

'That's right, milady.'

'It isn't possible you knocked over a candle, I suppose? Could that have been the cause of the fire?'

'No, milady. It didn't start in the room where we were, but downstairs.'

'Ah well. I suppose then it will remain one of life's mysteries.'

With that she left, and a few minutes later the Rolls drove away.

'What was all that about?' May asked, tying the strings of her apron, which she had put back on the moment Lady Elizabeth was out of the door.

'Oh Mam, I'm sorry, I can't tell you,' Edie said. 'It's Lady Elizabeth's private business. And I hope you weren't listening on the other side of the door.'

'As if I would!' May retorted, though a faint flush had risen in her cheeks. Truth to tell, she had tried to listen, but Lady Elizabeth had been speaking quite quietly, and just as things had begun to get interesting, her chauffeur had started up the engine of the motor car right outside the back door and begun fiddling about under the bonnet, and the noise had drowned out most of the conversation.

The fragments she had overheard before the racket began, though, had fired up her curiosity. And why not? she thought. After all, she had been the one to find the baby.

'It was something about Miss Christina, if I'm not mistaken,' she said, contradicting her denial of a few moments earlier. Edie didn't reply, and she went on: 'And I reckon Lady Elizabeth is her real mother. Made her out to be a foundling and then adopted her to cover things up.'

'No, Mam, that's not it at all,' Edie said. 'Though I have to admit I thought she might be at one time. But then I even wondered if *you* were her real mother.'

'Me?' May exclaimed. 'Why ever would you think that?'

'Because I knew there was something you confessed to Father O'Brien that you were so ashamed of that you couldn't face him afterwards. And Christina was found in the porch of your church, and you were there. It all seemed to add up.'

'Well!' May exclaimed, indignant. 'A fine opinion you have of your mother, I must say.'

'It was stupid of me, I know. But you refused to talk about that night, ever. And that seemed to tie in too. It looked to me as if there was something you were ashamed of, and it had to do with Christina.'

May was getting flustered. 'I wish I'd never asked you what Lady Elizabeth was on about

501

now,' she said crossly. 'I'm going down the garden to pick some beans, and when I get back, I hope we can forget all this nonsense.'

She bustled out, collecting a bowl for the runner beans as she went, and Edie shook her head despairingly. She simply could not understand what it was that upset her mother so whenever that Christmas Eve was mentioned. And, she supposed, she would never know.

Out of sight of the house, shielded by the tall row of runner beans, May set her bowl down and pressed her hands to her flaming cheeks. All very well to tell Edie she hoped 'all this nonsense' could be forgotten. With any luck she wouldn't mention it again, today, at least, but May would never forget.

How could she have been so stupid? It was a question she'd asked herself many times over the years, and although she had no doubt as to what had motivated her, she still couldn't understand how she could have given in to the temptation. How could she have sunk so low as to steal from a poor defenceless newborn?

The purse had been in the dresser drawer, tucked beneath the shawl that covered her. May had stuck it in the pocket of her coat for safekeeping when she'd lifted the baby out and carried her into the sacristy. In the to-do that followed, she'd forgotten all about it; it was only the following week, when she'd put on her good coat to go to church, that she'd found it there, and been horrified at having failed to hand it over along with the baby. Now, a little curious, she opened it and was startled to find it contained a wad of notes and a handful of silver sovereigns, florins and half-crowns. She had imagined the baby must belong to some poor woman who was in no position to keep her, but this was surely much more than any working-class woman or desperate young girl could afford. To May, it represented wealth beyond her wildest dreams.

Times were hard and money was short. Though Wesley was earning a better wage in Wales than he had here in Somerset, his board and lodging had to come out of it. All too often, by the time she'd set aside what would be needed to pay for coal and gas and Wesley's contribution to the Friendly Society, she was left with barely enough to feed herself and the children, let alone buy them new clothes and shoes. And they were growing so fast! Ted had been complaining for days now that his boots were hurting him because they'd become too small, and Edie's smock was almost up to her backside.

What I could do with all that money! May thought. New boots for Ted, a dress for Edie, and no need to have to count the pennies at the end of the week to see if she had enough left over to buy a half-pound of sausages, or whether it would have to be tripe and onions again, or a stew of onions and carrots without any meat.

But it still hadn't occurred to her to keep the money for herself. May was by nature as honest as the day was long. She fully intended to hand it over to Father O'Brien so that it could go to whoever had taken the baby and help pay for her needs. The little mite had no mother to take care of her, unless of course the poor girl had come forward in the meantime, but at least this would ensure she didn't start out in life destitute as well.

It was when she got to church and learned what had happened to the child that she'd been tempted.

'You'll never guess who's taken in our baby,' Hetty Jones had said when they met on the way in. 'Only Lady Elizabeth Fairley! She's landed on her feet all right, that little one. A life of luxury, that's what she'll have. And there was us thinking she was going to end up in the workhouse.'

'Good Lord!' May was staggered. 'Lady Elizabeth! Well I never!'

'Goodness only knows why she would do such a thing.'

Hetty shook her head in disbelief. 'Must have been the Christmas spirit got into her, I suppose.'

'She was always a good woman,' May said. 'A different kettle of fish to that brother of hers. She's been very kind to the families who lost their menfolk at Shepton Fields back in the summer. She gave the two little Day girls a beautiful doll each – their father was one of them killed – and she used to look in on poor Queenie Rogers who lost her son, that I do know.'

'But taking in a baby that's come from goodness knows where! She could be lonely, I suppose, with no children of her own. And I don't suppose the expense will worry her. She can certainly afford it.'

'That's true enough.'

The imp of temptation was sitting on May's shoulder now, and her fingers tightened over the purse in her pocket. All through the service she kept thinking about it. Of course she should hand over the money to Father O'Brien as she'd intended. By rights it belonged to the baby, even if with Lady Elizabeth taking her in she would want for nothing. But oh, what May could do with it! There'd be no need for Ted's toes to be squashed into too-tight boots, or for the wind to whistle up Edie's skirt. No need to worry about raiding the coal or gas money jars to put food on the table at the end of the week. If she was careful, she could make it last for ages.

No! It's wrong! her conscience warned her. But at the end of the service, when Father O'Brien spoke to her in the porch, telling her what she already knew – that the baby was now in the care of the Fairleys – she said nothing. All the way home she trembled with guilt, and it hung over her, a dark cloud, as she took Ted to the shoe shop next day for new boots, bought a length of material in the drapery shop to make a dress for Edie, and a nice piece of mutton at the butcher's for their dinner.

Too late now to hand the money over as she knew she should have done. She'd spent it, and she'd just have to live with the consequences.

The trouble was she didn't find that easy. It played on her mind dreadfully, and she could take no pleasure either in the things the money had bought, nor comfort in attending Mass. Eventually, tormented by guilt, she had haltingly made her confession to Father O'Brien.

Though he refrained from saying as much, he was disappointed in her, she knew. He had given her a penance of ten rosaries before absolving her, but he had urged her to hand over the money to its rightful owner, which shamed May further. It was spent now, or a good deal of it, and there was no way she could afford to replace it. Guilty as she felt, she could no longer bear to face Father O'Brien, and she swore to herself that she would never tell another living soul what she had done.

'Mam? Mam – where are you?' Edie's anxious voice was coming closer down the garden path.

'Mam? Are you all right? You've been gone such a long time!' She came into view. 'Oh Mam, whatever is the matter?'

May straightened up, brushing a strand of hair off her hot face and wondering what good it had done her, this secrecy. None at all. Her beloved daughter had actually thought that she might have been the one who had given birth in secret and then abandoned her baby. What must she be thinking now? What would she come up with next to explain whatever it was her mother was hiding? Suddenly May was tired of it all, tired of keeping to herself what she had done. Perhaps it was time to tell Edie the truth.

'I'm all right, Edie,' she said. 'But there's something I want to tell you. Something that's been preying on my mind for years...' Her throat closed for a moment at the thought of the enormity of confessing once again, and to Edie of all people, but it was too late now to change her mind.

'Let's go indoors,' she said.

'Oh Mam, fancy tormenting yourself like that.' Edie took her mother's hand in hers, squeezing it, and her voice was soft with compassion.

'Honestly, anyone would think you'd done something really terrible.'

'It was terrible. Wicked.'

'Mam, you haven't got a wicked bone in your body. It was wrong, of course, but quite understandable. Plenty of others would have done the same.'

'That's no excuse. I've always brought you up to know right from wrong, and I'm a fine example to you, aren't I? Stealing from a poor innocent little baby.'

'You would never have kept the money if you'd thought Christina needed it,' Edie assured her. 'I know you, Mam. You'd have found a way to replace it somehow.'

'I would have. I really would. And you honestly don't think too badly of me, Edie?'

'Oh Mam, of course I don't. I just wish you'd told me years ago and perhaps I could have persuaded you to stop punishing yourself over it. You've got to put it behind you. Promise me you'll try.'

May nodded wordlessly. Love for Edie was filling her, bringing her close to tears. How lucky she was to have such a wonderful daughter.

'Oh Mam, come here.'

Unbeknown to May, Edie was feeling just the same. That she loved her mother more than words could ever tell.

She put her arms round her, holding her close and thinking she had the most special mother in the world.

Chapter Thirty

'I think it's time we had a talk, my boy.'

Sir Montague had sent for Richard, who stood awkwardly in front of the man he now knew was his father.

'What would you say if I told you I mean to adopt you officially and make you my heir?'

Richard shuffled from one foot to the other. His boots felt too tight – his feet were growing again, as was he. At least if he agreed to Sir Montague's proposal he wouldn't have to worry about where the next pair were coming from, he thought. But he was still no more enthusiastic about the plan than he had ever been.

'Speak up, lad. I'm waiting!'

'I don't want it, sir. I'm happy as I am.'

'Hmm!' Sir Montague grunted. 'You've got your mother's stubborn streak.'

Richard lifted his chin, his eyes meeting Sir Montague's with a direct challenge.

'Maybe I got it from you, sir.'

For a moment Sir Montague looked to be on the point of apoplexy, then, unexpectedly, he laughed.

'Maybe you did. And I'm glad to see you've got some spunk about you too, unlike that toady Raymond. But you can protest all you like. My mind's made up. I want you to inherit the estate and the title, and that's an end of it. If you're half the man I think you are, you'll step up to the mark and make a fine job of it. But for the moment you are a minor and you'll do as you're told.'

'And what have my mother and father got to say about it?'

Sir Montague's expression became grim again. 'If you are referring to Dick Brimble, he is not your father. I am. And his wife is not your mother.'

'They brought me up.'

'And were well recompensed for it. If you talk to them I think you will find they are very much in favour.'

Richard shuffled awkwardly, remembering what Quilla had said about Dick's acquiescence that night when she had told him things that had brought his world crashing down around him. Dick had known what his sister was planning and had gone along with it, plotted with her, even taken Richard with him to the cottage that night when they were almost caught for poachers. Richard had never known what all that had been about, only that they'd had to make a run for it. But realising the man he had always called Dad had been willing to let him go so readily still had the power to hurt him. A cuckoo in the nest, that was what he had been all his life and never known it.

'That's decided then. I shall set things in motion immediately.' Sir Montague paused, thinking. Then:

'Richard Fairley,' he said, rolling it on his tongue. 'Yes, that's quite acceptable. I don't think we will need to change your given name.'

'Well thank you, sir, for that,' Richard said, his tone heavily sarcastic, and Sir Montague laughed again.

'I think we shall get along together very well, you and I. Now, before you go, perhaps you could pour me a large brandy.'

'I think it's time we had a talk, my boy.'

It was Raymond's turn to be summoned to the library, where Sir Montague was seated in his usual armchair. He had slunk back from Wiltshire after a week or so, still worried that his part in the fire would be exposed, and now his uncle's stern face made him fear the worst.

'Sir?' he mumbled.

'It need not take long. I'm sure you are eager to get back to whatever it is you waste your time on. You will be pleased to learn that you will soon be able to return to Wiltshire and not have to endure any more of the lessons you have found so tedious.'

'Sir?'

'I have decided to adopt Richard as my son and heir. I'm sorry if you are disappointed, but if you had knuckled down and proved yourself worthy, then it would have been a different matter. That's all. You may go now.'

Raymond was staring at his cousin in disbelief.

'You're joking! I am your heir! The only male in the Fairley line!'

'And totally unworthy. Close the door on your way out.'

'But...'

'Just pour me a brandy as you pass the table, if

510

you please.'

Raymond's face was red, the colour extending down his neck and disappearing into the pristine white starched collar of his shirt. His face puckered, his lip trembled. 'Pour it your bloody self!' he said.

'Christina, there is something I have to tell you.'

Christina dimpled. 'You are going to rebuild the cottage.'

'Oh, Christina, no! It's beyond repair, and I wouldn't think you would want to go there any more after what happened. No, it's about me. Sir Montague is going to adopt me and make me his heir.'

She stopped pirouetting and gazed at him wide-eyed.

'What? But Raymond is...'

'Not any more. Don't blame me. I don't have any say in it. Sir Montague has arranged it all with my mother and father, and he's sent for the solicitor to do whatever it is that has to be done. I'm sorry. I expect Raymond will be in a bit of a way about it, and so will you...'

'No!' Christina exclaimed. 'I won't be upset at all! It's wonderful news!'

'Really?'

'Yes, really! I like you so much more than Raymond!'

'Oh!' Colour rose in Richard's cheeks above the downy hair that had begun to sprout around his jawline. He liked Christina too, liked her a lot. He often thought about her when he was alone in his quarters over the stables. She might sometimes behave in a foolish way, but she was gay and pretty and quite unlike any other girl he had ever known. Yet friendly as they had become, it had never occurred to him that she might like him too. Even though he had rescued her that day by the river, he still imagined that he ranked lower than Raymond the gentleman in her estimation. For all he knew she might have been playing a game, pretending to resist while all the time leading Raymond on. There were girls who did that, he'd heard, though he had no experience of them. The thought had tormented him. And now he could hardly believe it when she took his hands in hers and gazed at him with a rapt expression.

'If Uncle is going to adopt you, you will come and live in the house!' she exclaimed. 'How marvellous will that be! Oh, I can't wait! We shall have such wonderful times!'

'I shall have to work harder than ever at my studies,' he warned her. 'The estate and the mines will all be my responsibility one day.'

'But you'll also be able to do whatever you like. You could build a folly in the woods to take the place of the cottage. Oh, I can see it now! It will be circular, with a sort of porch where we can sit in the sun...'

'There wouldn't be much sun under the trees,' Richard pointed out.

'Overlooking the river, then! Let's go and look for the perfect spot right now. Beauty needs a walk. Oh Richard, come with me, please!'

She let go his hands, picked up Beauty and danced to the door, where she stopped and turned to him, her face alight.

'Come on!'

'All right, you win,' he said, smiling.

As far as he was concerned, Christina could have whatever she wanted so long as it made her happy.

'Well at least you'll have the house to yourself,' Julia said when a disgruntled Raymond arrived back in Wiltshire. 'Letty and I are going back to London. We can be of far more use to the cause there.'

'Is that all you've got to say about it?' Raymond snapped. 'I've been disinherited, just like that! I should've thought you'd be as indignant as I am.'

'I'm sorry if I sound unsympathetic, Raymond, but I can't help but think you are the author of your own misfortune,' Julia said steadily. 'What are you planning to do now?'

'How should I know?'

'You'll have to give it some thought, and rather quickly. I suggest you look up some of Papa's old friends and do a spot of grovelling. Failing that, you could always become a vicar.'

Raymond was outraged. 'A vicar! You can't be serious!'

Julia suppressed the desire to chuckle. 'No, perhaps you wouldn't be best suited to the cloth. I think finding a young lady from a wealthy family to marry might be more your style. What about Harriet Dempsey? Her father owns several carpet factories. He might even find a job for you.'

'Harriet Dempsey looks like the back end of a pantomime horse!'

'That's a very cruel thing to say, Raymond. And you would do well to recognise that outward appearance is not everything. What's inside is much more important. Harriet Dempsey is a very nice young lady.'

'Very nice isn't good enough. Good God, how could a fellow marry a woman who'd need a sack put over her head before he could so much as bring himself to kiss her, eh? And as for working in a carpet factory, under the thumb of that stuffed shirt of a father of hers ... I don't fancy that at all.'

Julia shook her head impatiently. 'It's high time you grew up, Raymond, and stopped thinking the world owes you a living. Honestly, sometimes I despair of you. You had the most wonderful opportunity at Fairley Hall and you've thrown it all away because of your stupidity, and laziness and arrogance.'

'Oh not you too!' Raymond turned away angrily. But for the first time he wondered if he *had* brought all this on himself, and felt the first stirrings of guilt over starting the fire. He'd been lucky to get away with it, but because of him a woman had died. It was something he thought might come back to haunt him over and over again during the years to come.

Perhaps losing his inheritance was no more than he deserved.

Dr Mackay hadn't signed Edie off the club on the day she'd expected him to; instead he had insisted that she needed a further week to recuperate properly.

514

'It's not just the smoke you inhaled,' he explained, 'though the effects of that can be bad enough. But you also took a severe blow to your head, which knocked you unconscious, from what you tell me. You should be resting, not doing heavy work.'

'My work's not heavy,' Edie protested, but the doctor remained adamant.

'If you go back before I think you're ready, I won't be responsible for the consequences,' he had said, and May had backed him up.

'The doctor's right, Edie.'

And so Edie was still at home when yet another motor car came chuntering along the alleyway at the back of the houses; not the Fairley Rolls this time, but Cyril Short's taxi. Though there were more on the roads these days, a motor car was still uncommon enough to cause a stir; it was usually only delivery wagons drawn by horses that turned into Fairley Terrace.

May went to the door and looked out. The taxi had stopped outside the Oglethorpes' house. Perhaps it was Dolly coming home from London – she'd been there for some weeks now, looking after Charlie's two children while his wife was in hospital. May hoped that was the case; besides being a little concerned as to what could be wrong with Gracie that would entail Dolly staying so long, she missed her friend. It was good having Edie at home, of course, but there was nothing like sharing a cup of tea and a good old chinwag with Dolly.

To May's surprise, however, when the door of the taxi opened it was not Dolly who emerged but a small boy she recognised as Alfie. He stood on the path looking lost and on the verge of tears. Then a pair of black button boots appeared, followed by Dolly's not inconsiderable bulk heaving herself out of the motor. And in her arms was a bundle wrapped in a shawl.

May's heart leapt into her mouth. 'Dolly?'

'Oh May. I can't stop to talk now. I've got to get these two inside and fed.' Dolly looked as if she had all the cares of the world on her shoulders.

'Is there anything I can do?' May asked, worried.

'Not really. Just give me a chance to sort myself out and then pop round if you like.'

'Is it Gracie?' May asked before she could stop herself.

Dolly nodded. 'She's gone,' she said heavily. 'A growth, it was. She was riddled with it. I honestly don't know what we're going to do, May.' She shifted the baby into the crook of her arm and unlocked her door. 'I'll see you later.'

She went inside, little Alfie clinging to her skirts, and there was nothing May could do but go home herself and share the news with a shocked Edie.

The details, when Dolly filled May in, were grim. Gracie had never come out of the hospital; she'd just wasted away. Dolly had been caring for the children while Charlie was on duty. One evening he'd left to work a night shift but was home again within the hour – a message had come through from the hospital that the end was close. He'd woken Alfie and taken him across London to see his mother one last time. 'That poor little mite,'

Dolly said, her eyes filling with tears. 'He's not old enough to understand, of course, but he knows something's going on all right. He's usually full of it, but right now he's timid as a mouse. I just hope he'll perk up a bit when Charlie gets here.'

'He's coming home then?'

'He's got compassionate leave, but he's had to stay in London to make the funeral arrangements. After that he's coming here for a few days to settle the children in.'

'You mean you're having them here?' May asked anxiously.

'It's a case of having to. Our Charlie's got to go to work, somebody has to look after the children and I can't stop in London any longer. I've said I'll have them here with me for the time being until we can work out what's best.'

'Oh dear, oh dear.' May shook her head. 'What a cruel world it is we live in. Those two poor little ones losing their mother, and with their father miles away too...'

'We're doing the best we can,' Dolly said, a little huffily. Then: 'I just wish he'd never gone off to London, May, and that's the truth. But what can you do?'

'When's he coming?' May asked.

'The day after tomorrow, all being well.'

'Just let me know if there's anything I can do. You know I'm not far away if you need me.'

'Thanks, May. And thanks for being such a good neighbour. I haven't thanked you properly for keeping the menfolk fed while I was away. But I really am grateful.'

'What's the world coming to if we can't help

one another out?' May said.

Dolly nodded, and the two women smiled at one another, smiles that spoke of a lifetime of friendship.

Charlie arrived as expected, swinging along the rank with a rucksack on his back. Edie was sitting on the bench outside the back door, and her heart missed a beat when she saw him. It was almost as if the years had rolled back and he'd never been away. Except that now he was not only a police officer but also a widower with two young children to support.

'Oh Charlie, I'm so sorry,' she said as he drew closer.

'Me and all. But that isn't going to change anything.' Although he was as prosaic as ever, the strain showed in every line of Charlie's face. In the last months he'd been to hell and back, and things were not getting any better.

'She was so lovely,' Edie said 'So kind when me and Miss Christina landed up on the doorstep that day we were in a pickle.'

'She was a good girl, yes.'

'Whatever are you going to do?' Edie asked. 'I know your mam's got the children here for the time being, but...'

'I'm going to try and get back here myself,' Charlie said.

'What? You don't mean go back in the pits?'

'Not if I can help it! No, I'm going to try to get a transfer to Somerset – here in High Compton, when there's a vacancy. My station sergeant thinks I stand a good chance, seeing as how Sergeant

Love gave me such a good report when I applied to the Met.' A ghost of a grin crossed his face so that for a moment he looked like the old Charlie. 'Bit of a turn-up for the books, wouldn't you say? Me hassling the rowdies of the town instead of the other way round.'

'It would be lovely if you could,' Edie said. 'You'd live with your mam, I suppose?'

'I suppose. Look, Edie, I must get on. Mam and the children...'

'Of course you must.'

'I expect I'll see you again before I go back to London.'

'I expect so.'

Edie watched him walk up the rank. The sun was hot on her face and the warmth seemed to have crept right inside her. She was terribly sorry for Charlie, of course, and for Gracie, whose life had been cut so cruelly short, and for the children, left without a mother. But she couldn't help the tiny whisper of hope that was stirring deep inside her.

I'll be here, Charlie, she told him silently. If there's anything I can do to help. If you ever want me. I'll be here.

Chapter Thirty-One

There was great excitement below stairs at Fairley Hall. A blushing Nellie Saunders had just announced that she and Teddy had at last set the date and were to be married at the end of September.

'Well, well!' Mrs Davey, dishing up vegetables for the servants' dinners, stopped what she was doing to cast a sly glance over her shoulder, trying to catch a glimpse of Nellie's stomach. After such a lengthy engagement, she could think of only one reason that would have pushed Teddy into taking the plunge, and that was a baby on the way. But Nellie had pulled her chair well into the table and Mrs Davey could not see enough of her to satisfy her curiosity.

'Oh Nellie, that's lovely!' Flo Doughty said, covering her mouth with her hand and looking as if she might burst into emotional tears.

'And about time too!' Simon Ford clapped Nellie on the back.

'Congratulations,' Percy Stevens said, nodding approvingly. 'I should think perhaps a little celebration is in order. There's a bottle of claret that wasn't to Sir Montague's taste in the pantry. There'll never be a more fitting occasion for us to share it.'

'I suppose this means we'll be having to look for a new maid,' Lilian Parker said as he departed to fetch it. She sounded less than pleased with the development, as well she might. Nellie had been in the position so long, she needed little supervision. A new maid would mean training someone else up in her duties.

'I'm so pleased for you, Nellie,' Edie said. But she couldn't help feeling envious. Lucky, lucky Nellie, looking forward to a future with the man she loved and who loved her.

Seeing Charlie again had reignited all Edie's feelings for him. She knew now that he was the only one for her and always would be, and sometimes in the quiet of the night she dared to imagine that now he was a single man again, there might be a chance for her. But the thought only made her feel guilty. Could it somehow be her fault that Gracie was dead? Oh, she'd never consciously wished for such a thing, of course, and her heart bled for Charlie and the children. But she wanted Charlie so much – had wanted him so much for so long, and with every fibre of her being – that she couldn't quite rid herself of the awful feeling that somehow, without ever meaning to, she had brought the tragedy about. Be careful what you wish for; she'd heard that saying. Suppose the strength of her feelings had somehow summoned some dark force? No matter how often she told herself she was being ridiculous, that such a thing was impossible, she couldn't quite dispel the notion.

Not that Gracie's death was likely to make her dream of becoming Charlie's wife any more of a reality – and neither should it, she scolded herself. Charlie was in mourning; it would be a long time, if ever, before he would even think of marrying again, and when – if – he did, why should she imagine for a moment it might be her? She'd never been more than a friend, someone to have fun with. If he'd had real feelings for her, something would have come of it long ago. Fond of her he might be, but there it ended.

For now, his life revolved around his children and his job. He'd been successful in obtaining a transfer from London to the Somerset constabulary, with the help of good references from his superior officers and from Sergeant Love. But there were no vacancies at present in High Compton or Hillsbridge, and he had been stationed in Shepton Mallet, almost ten miles to the south, and lodgings found for him there.

'At least he can get over to see the children on his days off,' Dolly had said to May. 'But I'm in hopes it won't be too long before he can work close enough to be able to travel from here.'

'Do you think that's likely?' May had asked.

Dolly had shaken her head non-committally. She looked very tired these days, May thought.

'Your guess is as good as mine. But I've told Clarence to look around for somewhere else to live. I want to have the room empty and ready for Charlie just in case.'

Edie had only seen Charlie a few times since that day when he had come marching along the rank, his rucksack on his back. Her days off seldom coincided with his, and when she had seen him he'd been understandably quiet and preoccupied, stopping only for a brief word.

She'd seen plenty of his children, though. Dolly

522

had got hold of a second-hand pram, and baby Vicky spent much of the time in it, sleeping peacefully outside the back door. 'I only wish she'd sleep as well at night,' Dolly said to May. 'Seems to me the minute I drop off, she's ready to wake up.'

Little Alfie was often outside too, pushing his wooden engine back and forth along the rank or sitting on the doorstep sorting bits of broken china he'd found by digging in the garden with the small trowel Dolly used for tending her flower beds. He quickly became a favourite with the older children who lived in the rank, and sometimes they would take him for rides in their trucks or throw a ball for him to kick back, tottering on his sturdy little legs.

Edie played with him too when she was at home. She'd fallen in love with the little boy who looked, she imagined, exactly as Charlie must have looked at his age, and her heart warmed as he came running eagerly to greet her whenever he saw her, calling her name: 'E-die! E-die!'

She'd acquired a second-hand bicycle, which Wesley had taught her to ride in the track that led from the terrace to the main road, running along beside her holding on to the saddle and picking her up and dusting her down when she wobbled and fell off into the soft grassy banks that lined the track. Now she'd got the hang of it, it made the journey home from Fairley Hall much easier and quicker, giving her longer to spend at home, something that was coming to mean more and more to her. And it was something else to enter-tain Alfie with too – he loved it when she perched him on the saddle, holding on to him with one hand and the handlebars with the other and scooting up and down the rank.

Charlie had gone one better. When he found that getting back and forth to Shepton Mallet on foot ate into his days off, he had bought himself a motorbike. Dolly was horribly suspicious of the contraption – 'You just go careful, my son!' she said when he first came roaring along the rank in a cloud of blue smoke. 'Whatever would become of these little ones if anything happened to you?' – but Ollie was fascinated by it and stood staring at it, shaking his head and saying, 'Well, well, whatever next!' and wishing, no doubt, that he could tinker with the workings, or even go for a ride.

Others in the rank were not so keen, Hester Dallimore in particular complaining long and loud about the noise and the smoke, but they all felt sorry for Charlie, his loss and his predicament, and for the most part kept their reservations to themselves.

At last – at last – as August drew to a close, the heatwaves that had characterised the summer began to lose some of their intensity and the weather turned cooler and more changeable. Most folk were relieved – much as everyone loved the sun, it was possible to have too much of a good thing – but the organisers of the Miners' Gala, which was to take place on the last Saturday of the month, looked anxiously at the sky. A wet day would spoil everything, and how ironic that would be after the days of unbroken sunshine and soaring temperatures!

The Miners' Gala, like the Foresters' Fete earlier in the summer, always began with a procession of decorated carts through Hillsbridge, led by the town band, and weaving its way up the long hill to the recreation ground. Stalls and attractions, including some fairground rides, would be set out around the perimeter, while the field itself would be the scene of sack, egg-and-spoon, and three-legged races for the children, a tug-of-war and knockout five-a-side football between the various collieries and, later, dancing.

It was traditional for the local mine-owners to take turns putting in an appearance at the gala and presenting the prizes to the winning teams, and this year it should have been Sir Montague. Since he was still somewhat incapacitated, Sir William Osborne, who owned half a dozen mines in and around High Compton, had offered to do the honours, but Sir Montague had decreed that Richard should take his place. Arrangements for his adoption had been set in motion, and Sir Montague was keen for him to be introduced to the pit workers and the district at large as his heir.

Richard was less than enthusiastic – the very idea of standing on a platform in front of a large crowd who knew him as the blacksmith's son frankly terrified him, even though Sir Montague assured him he need do no more than murmur a few words of congratulation to the winning captains and hand over the trophies. Eventually Sir Montague had come up with a compromise – that Christina should go with him and make the presentations while he stood beside her. He knew the men of his workforce appreciated a pretty face.

Lady Elizabeth, however, had some reservations about the wisdom of the plan.

'These things can become a little rowdy,' she said doubtfully. 'There's fierce competition between the collieries, as well you know, and if the men have been spending their money in the beer tent, their inhibitions can desert them.'

'By four in the afternoon? I should hope not!' Sir Montague huffed. 'And in any event, I would hope the organisers can be trusted to ensure Christina is safe from any trouble.'

'I can only agree to it if Edith goes with her,' Lady Elizabeth insisted; besides her worries about the sobriety of the crowd, she wasn't at all sure it would be proper for Christina to make a public appearance at such an event without a chaperone.

And so it was settled. Richard, Christina and Edie would go to the gala. Simon would drive them, and Lady Elizabeth gave him strict instructions that he should remain with them the whole time they were there. Simon was big and strong enough to be a sort of bodyguard for Christina, she reasoned, though when she remembered the altercation between Richard and Raymond, she rather thought Richard would be more than capable of the same thing. But two hefty young men could only be better than one.

Although the skies were a little overcast on the morning of the gala, it was still pleasantly warm, and by the afternoon the clouds had cleared and the sun was shining once more.

The little party set out in the Rolls soon after luncheon, Richard sitting in the front seat next to Simon, Edie and an overexcited Christina behind them. Edie couldn't help feeling a little uncomfortable that folk would think she was getting above herself, but Richard appeared to be enjoying the occasion. Already he was beginning to slot comfortably into his new station in life, and as they passed the forge at the bottom of the steep hill, he felt nothing but pleasure in knowing he would never again have to swing a heavy hammer with sweat pouring in rivers down his neck, nor try to fit a shoe to a restless horse.

Edie had not been to a gala since the day she had met up with Charlie at the Foresters' Fete when she was just seventeen, and the memories came flooding back as the Rolls swung in through the main entrance to the recreation ground. Charlie rescuing her from the louts who had harassed her, Charlie propelling the swing boat so high that her stomach had turned somersaults and she had squealed at him to stop even though she had felt she was touching the sky and loving every terrifying moment. Charlie giving her her first dancing lesson, one arm about her waist, one hand holding hers. For a brief moment she relived the excitement of it, the pure happiness that had lifted her heart, the feeling of standing on the brink of a great adventure, a dream in which anything could become a wonderful reality.

Christina had seen the swing boats too, and was typically enthusiastic.

'Oh Richard, look! Swing boats!' she trilled. 'Will you take me on them? Oh please say you will!'

Edie swallowed at a lump that had risen in her throat. Christina was probably feeling exactly as she had felt that day, eager and excited. Edie only hoped that her dreams didn't turn to dust as her own had.

But the swing boats would have to wait, and in any case, Edie wasn't sure it would be quite proper for Christina to be seen climbing into one and sailing up into the sky.

'Later, perhaps, miss,' she said. 'I think you should attend to your official duties first.'

'But there's plenty of time!' Christina protested. 'They're still playing the football matches and then there's the tug-of-war and the children's races to be run.'

'There are people you need to talk to,' Edie said firmly. 'You're here to represent Sir Montague and your mama, remember.'

'Oh fiddlesticks!' Christina pouted. But even as she said it, Clement Firkin was beside the Rolls, opening the door and extending a hand to help her down.

'Miss Christina! This is a pleasure indeed.' He turned to shoo off some small boys who had come running over to take a closer look at the impressive motor, the like of which they had never seen before.

'Mr Firkin.' To Edie's relief, Christina adopted the demeanour of a young lady. 'You are most kind.'

'If you would care to come with me, there are some people I'd like to introduce you to. Our colliery officials and their wives...'

He led her off towards a small marquee, Edie, Richard and Simon following.

Suddenly a small figure erupted from a crowd that had gathered around one of the stalls – a magician performing conjuring tricks.

'E-die! E-die!'

Startled, Edie stopped and turned to see Alfie, brandishing a half-eaten toffee apple, racing towards her as fast as his sturdy little legs would carry him.

'Alfie! Good gracious!'

'Alfie!' Charlie's voice, sharp. Edie looked up, the familiar emotion twisting deep in her stomach.

'No, Alfie!' Charlie caught him just in time as he reached out for Edie's skirts.

'It's all right,' Edie said.

'No, it's not. He's all sticky fingers.' Charlie picked him up, swinging him easily into his arms, and Edie's heart turned over. There was something incredibly moving in the picture they made, the big man and the little boy who was so like him, the man's tenderness and the way the boy's arms fastened trustingly around his neck. A little boy who had lost his mother, to whom his father was his whole world.

'Fancy seeing you here,' Charlie said.

'And fancy seeing you.' Edie's voice was not quite steady.

'Small world, isn't it?'

'You've got a day off.'

'Weekend, actually. I only get one in four, but seeing it's this one, I thought I'd bring Alfie to the gala.'

'Have you brought Vicky too?' Edie's eyes skittered round, looking for the pram.

'No, I've left her at home with Mam. She's a bit young for this sort of thing.'

'Yes, I suppose she is.'

Edie felt a stab of embarrassment. She seemed to be incapable of anything but the most banal

529

remarks. How stupid was that? She and Charlie had always been so at ease with one another. But too much water had flowed under the bridge since those days, and the tragedy of Charlie's situation, together with the strength of her own unrequited feelings for him, rendered her tongue-tied.

Alfie was wriggling now, reaching out again for her with those sticky little fingers.

'Stay still, Alfie, there's a good boy.' Charlie hoisted him back up, restraining him. 'He's certainly taken a shine to you, Edie.'

'I'm very fond of him too. He's a great little lad. We have fun when I'm at home, don't we, Alfie?'

'Bike,' Alfie said.

'Yes, you shall have a ride on it again soon,' Edie promised. 'But we can't today. I don't have it with me.'

'There are plenty of other things to do, son. Plenty to see.' Charlie looked at Edie. 'I don't suppose you'd like to come with us?'

'Oh, I can't. I've got to look after Miss Christina,' Edie said regretfully. There was nothing she would have liked more.

As if on cue, Christina emerged from the tent accompanied by Clement Firkin and another man Edie recognised as Taffy Jones, manager at Marston Colliery.

'Edith!' She beckoned quite imperiously – perhaps at last she was beginning to grow up and into her role in society, Edie thought. 'Mr Firkin, Mr Jones, may I introduce Edith, my lady's maid? I'm sure she would like to join our tour of the attractions.'

Faint colour rose in Edie's cheeks. With one last

glance at Charlie, she stepped forward and Christina took her arm.

'Isn't it wonderful, Edith? Have you ever seen anything like it?'

Edie smiled to see her mistress revert to type so swiftly.

'Yes, miss, it's fun, isn't it?'

Suddenly Christina seemed to notice Charlie, still standing there with Alfie in his arms, and a faintly puzzled expression crossed her face.

'Oh, good afternoon! Am I mistaken, or do I know you from somewhere?'

Edie wished the ground would open up and swallow her, so embarrassed was she at Christina's failure to recognise her rescuer on that disastrous visit to London.

'It's Charlie Oglethorpe, miss. The policeman who helped us out...'

'Oh yes, of course. Goodness, you look quite different when you are not in uniform. How very nice to see you again, and your little boy too.'

'You look different as well – not as if you'd been pulled through a bush backwards.'

Edie's hand flew to her mouth, horrified that Charlie should be so impertinent. He might have saved their bacon that day, but even so ... to speak to gentry like that in public... But of course it was Charlie all over. He hadn't changed; he never would.

Clement Firkin treated him to a long, hard stare of warning, then turned his attention to Christina, purposefully drawing her away.

'Now where shall we begin, Miss Christina? With the flower stand, perhaps? The dahlias are quite something to behold...'

Edie could do nothing but follow, but inwardly she was seething with mixed emotions. Annoyance at Christina that she could so easily forget the man who had rescued her from a desperate situation, burning anger at Clement Firkin for snubbing him so effectively, admiration for Charlie's proud stance.

And, of course, a fresh wellspring of love for him.

As the little party moved away, she cast a glance over her shoulder. Charlie was still standing there, watching them go. Edie felt as if she was leaving a part of her with him.

The afternoon was racing by.

The five-a-side football competition had finished with Shepton Fields the eventual winners, and Marston had managed to beat all opposition in the tug-of-war. 'A good day for the Fairley pits,' Clement Firkin commented, though Taffy Jones took a slightly less rosy view. 'There'll be trouble later on, mark my words, especially if they overdo the celebrations in the beer tent.'

The children's events were hardly less competitive, with four small boys getting into fisticuffs at the finish of the three-legged race, a little girl wailing inconsolably because she kept dropping her egg in the egg-and-spoon race and finished last, and quite a few casualties in the sack race, although the boys took their wounds of war more stoically.

Christina, with Richard at her side, handed out the prizes which were passed to her from a small card table' at the side of the platform by an attentive Clement Firkin, and Edie, watching from immediately below with Simon Ford, thought that she was handling her duties beautifully.

Charlie, standing on the edge of the crowd that had gathered to watch the presentations, with Alfie sitting on his shoulders, was in contemplative mood. Like Edie earlier, he was remembering that other gala, the Foresters' Fete. It seemed now to have been a lifetime ago, yet the memory of it was as clear as if it had been just yesterday, and stirred feelings he'd thought he'd forgotten.

That day, three years ago now, had been the first time he'd noticed Edie as anything other than a little girl, a skinny child in pinafores and white hair ribbons, of whom he'd always been fond but never for one moment imagined he would one day walk out with. That day he'd seen her through different eyes entirely and realised with a shock that she had become a young woman who, though not beautiful exactly, was stunningly attractive, and he had fancied her like crazy.

But even then he hadn't realised she was as lovely inside as she was out. He'd been too intent on living his life as he wanted to, having a good time, escaping from the shadow of the disaster that had taken the lives of so many of his workmates and friends. Now, though, he had become aware of the inner Edie. He'd seen the way she took care of her mistress, that spoilt little Fairley girl, concerned only for her welfare; he couldn't fail to notice her sweetness with Alfie, who had obviously come to love her. If a toddler had been able to see it, how could he have been so blind as not to? How could he have treated her so badly?

But then she wasn't the only one. Look at the way he'd treated Gracie. His past behaviour made him cringe with shame every time he thought about it. In the end he'd been able to make it up at least in part to Gracie, and she'd never known – or at least he hoped she hadn't – that for him there was something missing in his feelings for her, that he'd probably never have married her but for duty. He had loved her in his own way, he thought, but he'd never experienced the over-whelming tide of emotion that was consuming him now as he watched Edie standing there proudly beside the platform, her head tilted a little one side as she looked up at her mistress. She wasn't vulnerable as Gracie had been, yet he wanted to protect her from anything that might threaten or hurt her. She wasn't openly salacious as some girls were, yet he wanted her with every fibre of his being. She wasn't especially beautiful or clever or so very different from any of the other women he'd known – except that she was. She was Edie, his Edie, and he loved her.

The realisation came as something of a shock to him. When he'd gone to London, he'd walked away from her with scarcely, a backward glance, probably hurt her badly, and never stopped to think what he was leaving behind. Was it too late now to try and begin again? There had been something still there between them that night when they'd talked in the courtyard of the Frederick Arms. He'd felt it then, the first pangs of regret, the first acknowledgement that what they had shared had been special, but he had been too worried about Gracie's failing health to give much thought to it. Now, quite suddenly, he could think of nothing else.

The world might think it was far too soon for him to be so much as looking at another woman, but there was an urgency now in Charlie that would not be denied. He had to at least find out if he still stood a chance with the woman he had loved for so long without ever realising it. He'd speak to her at the first opportunity, ask her if they could see one another again. It wouldn't be easy – how often would their days off coincide? But he'd find a way. And perhaps soon there would be a vacancy back in High Compton – surely one of the old constables there must be coming up to retirement?

All these thoughts and more were chasing one another round and round in Charlie's head as the last of the children waddled proudly on to the platform to collect their prizes. And as if echoing his own sentiments, Alfie suddenly caught sight of Edie, and began calling her name.

'E-die! Want E-die! E-die, look at me!'

It was, Charlie thought, an omen – and perhaps a blessing.

'Now can we go on the swing boats?' Christina begged Edie.

The formalities over, Christina had reverted to being a child again, impatient, eager, excited.

'I should think so, yes,' Edie said, feeling more like a parent than a lady's maid. She was still doubtful about how seemly it was, but Christina had behaved impeccably and deserved a reward.

535

'Come on, Richard!' Christina grabbed hold of Richard's hand and together they ran ahead of Edie and Simon, who followed at a more sedate pace.

'Shall we have a ride too?' Simon suggested.

It was the last thing Edie wanted; her memories of that day when she and Charlie had soared into the sky were too a precious – and too painful. But she couldn't really see how she could refuse, and in any case, perhaps it was time to move on, to exchange old memories for new ones.

'Why not?' she said recklessly.

'Time to go home, Alfie,' Charlie said.

'Sweeties!' Alfie lisped, pointing towards the stall selling fairings.

'No, you've had quite enough treats for one day. You won't eat the tea Granny will have made for you, and then I shall be for it.'

He hoisted Alfie, who was pouting and dragging his feet, up on to his shoulders and was making for the gate when he suddenly caught sight of Edie and a young man in the queue for the swing boats. They were standing quite close together and Edie was laughing at something her companion had said. Charlie's stomach gave an uncomfortable lurch, and his brow furrowed. He didn't recognise the man, but he was a sight too good-looking for Charlie's liking, and whoever he was, he was taking her on the swing boats!

So much for her having to look after Christina Fairley! he thought, a flash of the old fierce temper that he had more under control these days, but which still lurked beneath the surface, darkening his eyes. He couldn't know, of course, that the man running the ride had given the next available swing boat to Christina as soon as he'd seen her joining the queue, and at this moment she was swooping up and down with Richard tugging on the rope. All he knew was that Edie was there waiting her turn with a young man, and that jealousy was making him see red.

Only an hour or so ago, he'd finally accepted what Edie meant to him; only an hour or so ago, he'd made up his mind to see if she would give him a second chance. Now it looked to him as if it was too late. She'd found somebody else.

And who could blame her? The only wonder of it was that she hadn't done so long ago. It was no more than he deserved to be the one who lost out, the one who was hurt. How could he have been so stupid, so selfish?

Setting his jaw so tightly it made his teeth ache, Charlie turned towards the gate once more, but after he'd gone only a short distance he stopped again, his anger both at himself and at the un-known man with Edie suddenly replaced by a steely determination.

He couldn't let her go so easily. If he did, he'd regret it for the rest of his life. He might be about to make a complete fool of himself, but he wasn't going to give up on Edie without a fight. What-ever the outcome, he had to at least try.

He turned back towards the swing boat ride; Edie and the chap were at the head of the queue now. Charlie broke into a trot, holding fast to Alfie's legs to ensure he didn't slip off his shoul-ders. One of the boats was slowing, the arc of motion becoming smaller, and Edie's chap had an arm around her waist, ready to help her up on to the wooden platform. Charlie made straight for them, jostling his way through a small group of onlookers who were watching the ride.

'Excuse me!' he said roughly, taking Edie's hand and pulling her away from the man. 'I think this girl's mine, pal.'

Edie turned, startled, and the man took a step towards him, looking puzzled and annoyed.

'Hey, what d'you think–'

'Cut it out! I don't want no trouble here!' The swing boat proprietor headed purposefully towards them.

Charlie raised both hands in a gesture of surrender. 'Me neither. I just want to take my girl on the ride.' He glanced at Edie's companion. 'You got any objection to that?'

A bemused Simon looked at Edie. 'Edie?' he said, seeking her reaction to this unexpected turn of events.

'It's all right, Simon. Charlie's an old friend.'

Simon spread his arms in a gesture of confusion and helplessness. 'Makes no odds to me. If that's what you want...'

The swing boat had come to a stop now; the occupants had climbed out and were going down the steps, looking curiously at the unusual goings-on.

'Make up your blooming minds!' the swing boat proprietor snapped. 'There's other people waiting besides you.'

A flush had risen in Edie's cheeks, partly from embarrassment at the scene they were making, partly from incredulity, and a glow of joy was spreading through her veins.

'Oh yes, Charlie.' She put her hand on his arm so there could be no doubt of her meaning.

Charlie nodded abruptly at Simon, lifted Alfie into the swing boat, then turned to help Edie climb in.

'Can you have him?'

She nodded, and lifted Alfie on to her lap. He clutched at her skirts with still-sticky fingers, chuckling with delight.

'Sit tight now, Alfie.' She wound her arms around his solid little frame, holding him fast.

'Remember the last time we did this?' Charlie grasped the tasselled rope and the gondola began to swing gently.

'Don't you dare go so high as you did then!' Edie cautioned.

'Don't worry, I won't. And this time I'm not going to mess up, either.'

It was hardly the most eloquent of apologies or advances, but Charlie had never been one for fine words. Actions spoke much louder, and what he had just done said everything Edie could have wished for.

She cradled Alfie on her lap as Charlie pulled on the rope and the swing boat arced gracefully, bathed in a rosy glow of joy. No, this time, with Alfie on board, there was no way he was going to take them recklessly high over the watching crowd. But to Edie it felt as if they were touching the sky.

Chapter Thirty-Two

'I'm sorry, m'lady, but I'm afraid I'm going to have to give notice,' Edie said.

A tiny frown creased Lady Elizabeth's smooth forehead.

'Oh Edith! Surely not! But why?'

'Because I'm going to be married, m'lady.'

Just saying the words out loud sent a thrill of warmth through Edie, though she had dreaded facing Lady Elizabeth with the news, and was even more concerned as to what Christina's reaction would be. Since Quilla's death she had been acting as lady's maid to Lady Elizabeth as well as Christina. Her ladyship would have no difficulty in securing the services of another suitable maid, probably one who had already seen enough service to fit seamlessly into the role, but Christina was a different matter entirely. Edie's only consolation was that at least the girl had a close friend now in Richard, and she had the feeling that it wouldn't be long before the relationship developed into more than that. And fond as she was of Christina, she had other priorities now.

Since that day at the Miners' Gala, everything had moved so quickly that Edie's head spun just thinking of it. It was as if in some ways the years they had been apart had never been, and yet everything was immeasurably better. The unsettling doubts that had dogged their early courtship had disappeared; Charlie no longer left her feeling anxious and insecure. He had changed so much – grown up at last, she supposed. Instead of champing restlessly at the bit, he knew what he wanted, had set out to get it, and had not the slightest intention of ever letting it go again. Much of their courtship had, of course, been dictated by circumstances. But a few weeks ago the news had come through that a vacancy had arisen at the Hillsbridge police station. The position had been offered to Charlie on compassionate grounds, and he had, of course, accepted it gratefully. He had moved back into Fairley Terrace, into his old room, now vacated by Dolly's lodger, and although his shift patterns meant that he wasn't at home every evening to put the children to bed or even to see them up in the morning, he was able to do his fair share of caring for them, and spend time with them too.

And then, quite out of the blue, had come the proposal that was hardly a proper proposal at all, but very typical of Charlie all the same.

It was a chilly October afternoon, when the leaves on the trees were turning to red and gold and russet, with some drifts already piling up beneath them, brought down by the blustery wind. Charlie was working a night shift; it was Edie's day off. He had got up at about noon, and after dinner Edie had gone around and spent the afternoon with him and the children. It was too cold for them to be outside, so they'd amused Alfie with some toy soldiers Charlie had got for him, and Edie had jiggled little Vicky on her knee when she woke and wanted attention. She'd even given her a feed of milk from her bottle while May went for a nap to make up for the broken nights she was still having.

When it was time for Edie to go back to Fairley Hall, Charlie had walked with her. The nights were drawing in, and he was as concerned for her safety as May had always been. Edie didn't protest that she would be perfectly safe, as she had used to with May; she looked forward to the time alone with Charlie.

They'd reached the drive leading down to the Hall, and Charlie stopped, leaning against a gate in the hedge and pulling Edie into his arms. He'd kissed her, and she was snuggling into his overcoat, when he suddenly held her a little away and asked, 'How would you feel about marrying me?'

Edie tipped her head back a little, looking up at him. Her heart had missed a beat, but she kept her tone light. 'What sort of a question is that?'

'Well I don't know really...' Charlie sounded embarrassed. 'I was just thinking ... but it's a lot to ask. Taking on two children...'

Edie could scarcely believe what she was hearing; was afraid, almost, to believe it.

'Charlie, you know how much I love them,' she said.

'I know, but still...'

She could bear the suspense no longer. 'Are you asking me to marry you?'

'I suppose I am. Yes. If you think you wouldn't mind being a policeman's wife.'

'I'd be so proud.'

'Well then ... shall we do it?'

Edie smiled, joy giving her confidence, making

her mischievous. 'Only if you ask me properly.'

Charlie's face was in deep shadow; she couldn't see it properly. But his voice told her he was smiling back.

'All right. Will you marry me, Edie?'

Sudden tears stung her eyes. 'Oh Charlie, of course I'll marry you!'

'When d'you think, then? Would Christmas be too soon?'

'Tomorrow wouldn't be too soon for me! Just as long as...' A sudden thought struck her, undermining the soaring happiness. 'Charlie, you're not asking just because you need a mother for Alfie and Vicky, are you? I mean ... I'd marry you anyway. What does that say for my pride? But I really need to know...'

'Oh, you silly girl!' Charlie pulled her close again, kissing her hair. 'Of course that's not it, though I can't deny they do need a mother, and you'll be a wonderful one. But that isn't the reason. I know now I was a fool to ever let you go. I don't want that to happen again.'

'You mean...?'

'I love you,' he said, the words that he'd never before spoken to anyone awkward on his tongue. 'I think I've always loved you.'

'And I love you, so much...'

'Christmas, then?'

Edie nodded. 'Just as long as Lady Elizabeth can find a replacement for me by then. I can't leave her in the lurch, Charlie – she's been so good to me. First she lost Quilla, then Nellie...'

Charlie nodded. He thought the Fairleys would manage perfectly well, but he respected Edie's sense of duty. And just as long as he knew she would be his when the time came, he could afford to be patient for a little while.

'But you'll give notice? Tell them to start looking for someone to take your place?'

'Of course I will,' Edie said. 'I'll talk to Lady Elizabeth tomorrow.'

Satisfied, Charlie pulled her into his arms once more, and it was a long time before they set off again.

Ever since Sir Montague had sent Raymond away, Julia had been worrying and wondering what to do about him. Reluctantly she had returned from London to their old home so as to be able to keep an eye on him and try to work out a future for him now that he had been disinherited. Lettice had come down to join her, and the two of them held a council of war and eventually came up with a solution.

Now they sat in the parlour with Raymond while Julia explained what they had decided was best.

'I think we should sell the house, Raymond, and you can use the proceeds to go abroad and start a new life. I've heard there are many opportunities in America for young men like you, and if we manage it carefully, the money should be enough to keep you until you can find gainful employment.'

'And if I can't?' Raymond said belligerently. 'What then? You'd have me starve?'

'I don't think it's likely to come to that. And I am quite sure Sir Montague would supplement your income if necessary. He is, after all, your father's cousin.'

'You mean I'd be a remittance man?' Raymond was secretly excited by the idea, which seemed to him impossibly romantic. He was getting a little tired of being stuck in the wilds of Wiltshire with nothing much to do but drink, gamble and chase young ladies whose mamas were becoming more and more intent on keeping their daughters well away from him. But he wasn't going to let Julia know she'd won so easily.

'America is all very well,' he said, 'but it's a long voyage, and you know I get seasick. Think of that time you, me and Mama went to France. I was dreadfully ill, and that was only across the Channel.'

Julia was prepared for this objection.

'There's a new ship being built in Ireland – the biggest and most luxurious to ever put to sea. Her maiden voyage will be to New York in the spring – and the sale of the house should be completed by then. I'm sure you wouldn't be seasick on a ship that big. And just imagine how exciting it would be! They say no expense has been spared. There will be fine dining, dancing to a wonderful orchestra, and I'm told excellent sports facilities – a gymnasium, a salt-water swimming pool and a squash court. There are even electric and Turkish baths for relaxing afterwards. I think you would be far too well occupied to even think of being unwell.'

After a moment, Raymond nodded. This certainly sounded like a great adventure.

'Very well. I'll do as you suggest. I must say, I

rather like the idea of seeking my fortune in America.'

'Oh good.' Julia sighed with relief and reached for Letty's hand. 'Shall we book you a passage, then?'

'Might as well,' Raymond said laconically. 'What's this ship called, by the way?'

Julia gave a slight shake of her head and caught Letty's eye, signalling her disbelief at how little interest her brother took in newspapers or current affairs in general.

'It's called the *Titanic*,' she said.

There was no question but that the wedding should take place in the Catholic church, though Edie was a little anxious about facing Michael for the pre-marital advice that was a part of the preparation. However, to her immense relief, May was able to tell her that he was no longer the parish priest.

'Really? Why ever not?' Edie asked.

'He's got a different job,' May said. 'Don't ask me the details – I can't tell you – but I do know it's something to do with looking after the sick, both in mind and in body, at least that's what Father O'Brien said. There's a new young priest taken over – Father Dowdeswell, his name is. I think you'll like him.'

'But what he knows about married life I don't know,' Wesley had muttered from the depths of his armchair.

'Oh, take no notice of your father,' May said. 'He doesn't understand, and never will.'

'I could tell them more than he can,' Wesley

retorted. 'Not that our Edie and Charlie need much telling if you ask me.'

They were, he thought, one of the best-suited couples he'd ever come across, and he was delighted by the match. He'd always liked Charlie, even when he'd had a bit of a wild streak, and now that he'd turned respectable – an officer of the law, no less – Wesley couldn't think of anyone he'd rather see Edie settle down with, even if it did mean her taking on two children.

When they visited the church, they discovered that Father Dowdeswell was indeed a very pleasant man, a little older than Michael but a good deal younger than Father O'Brien. As he took them into the sacristy, the familiar scent of incense wafted Edie back to the times she had spent with Michael and, more importantly, to the wonderful comfort and sense of belonging she had experienced here in the church before her misguided feelings for him had driven her away.

Perhaps now that he was no longer here, she would be able to attend services when she could. It would not be every week, for Charlie's shift patterns would mean that he was not always at home on a Sunday, and the police house that went with his new position was a good three miles away from Fairley Terrace and Dolly and May, either of whom might look after Alfie and little Vicky. But perhaps she could take them with her, she thought, if Charlie was agreeable. He wasn't Catholic, and wouldn't expect his children to be brought up in the faith, but she'd like them to experience the wonderful peace and joy that filled the church during Mass all the same.

That, though, was something for the future. For the moment, it must be one step at a time.

And what wonderful steps! As she and Charlie emerged from the church into a cold, clear afternoon, she felt as if she was walking on air.

'I hope the weather is just like this for our wedding,' she said.

Charlie took her hand in his. 'Doesn't matter what the weather is like,' he replied. 'Even if it's pouring with rain, it will be the best day of my life.'

'Mine too,' Edie said simply.

And knew that it was the truth.

Introducing the Families
of Fairley Terrace...

The Withers at No. 10

Gilby and Florrie Withers are devastated to lose their beloved son Jack in the mining disaster. Luckily their other son Josh wasn't working at Shepton Fields. But will they be able to keep him close by when his feelings for his late brother's fiancée become too strong to ignore?

The Donovans at No. 6

When the hudge goes down, the Donovans lose their patriarch Paddy. With her elder brothers Ewart and Walter working away, it's up to daughter Maggie to help her mother Rose keep the roof over their heads and look after younger son Billy, whilst dealing with the loss of her fiancé Jack Withers too.

The Days at No. 4

Twenty-eight-year-old Annie Day loses her loving husband John, leaving her two little girls,

Kitty and Lucy, without their beloved father. Surely it's only a matter of time before they are turned out of Fairley Terrace – how will they survive?

The Oglethorpes at No. 3

Dolly and Ollie Oglethorpe are well known in the community, with Dolly serving as midwife for the Ten Houses. They are one of the lucky families as both Ollie and their son Charlie escape the disaster.

The Rogers at No. 2

Queenie and Harry are not so fortunate – they lose their young son Frank in the accident and things are never the same for them again.

The Coopers at No. 1

Edie Cooper and her family are blessed not to lose anyone in the mining disaster, but the repercussions of that day are to have a greater impact on Edie's future than she can imagine. A whole new world opens up to her when she takes a job at Fairley Hall, where she discovers both friends and foes amongst the staff and the Fairley family.

The publishers hope that this book has given you enjoyable reading. Large Print Books are especially designed to be as easy to see and hold as possible. If you wish a complete list of our books please ask at your local library or write directly to:

Magna Large Print Books
Magna House, Long Preston,
Skipton, North Yorkshire.
BD23 4ND

This Large Print Book for the partially sighted, who cannot read normal print, is published under the auspices of

THE ULVERSCROFT FOUNDATION

THE ULVERSCROFT FOUNDATION

... we hope that you have enjoyed this Large Print Book. Please think for a moment about those people who have worse eyesight problems than you ... and are unable to even read or enjoy Large Print, without great difficulty.

You can help them by sending a donation, large or small to:

**The Ulverscroft Foundation,
1, The Green, Bradgate Road,
Anstey, Leicestershire, LE7 7FU,
England.**
or request a copy of our brochure for more details.

The Foundation will use all your help to assist those people who are handicapped by various sight problems and need special attention.

Thank you very much for your help.